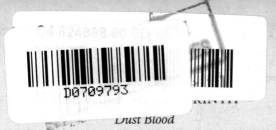

Dust Blood

G. P. Taylor is the author of several best-selling novels, including *Shadowmancer*, *Shadowmancer: The Curse of Salamander Street*, *Wormwood* and *Tersias*, as well as the *Mariah Mundi* trilogy. A former vicar of Cloughton in Yorkshire, he has enjoyed a varied career, moving from rock music to social work to ten years in the police force before his ordination. He now lives with his family in Scarborough.

Praise for *Mariah Mundi*

'When Harry Potter hangs up his wizard's cloak, booksellers will be looking to G. P. Taylor's *Mariah Mundi: The Midas Box* to keep the cashtills ringing.' BBC News

'It really is wonderful, wonderful stuff . . . Mariah Mundi surpasses Potter on just about every level there is. Highly recommended.'
The Bookbag

'The book that combines the big story of C. S. Lewis and the plot of an Indiana Jones movie. We could genuinely be looking at the book series that will replace Harry Potter at the top of every child's wish list.' *BuddyHollywood Review*

by the same author

SHADOWMANCER
WORMWOOD
TERSIAS
SHADOWMANCER: THE CURSE OF SALAMANDER STREET

MARIAH MUNDI: THE MIDAS BOX
MARIAH MUNDI: THE GHOST DIAMONDS
MARIAH MUNDI: THE SHIP OF FOOLS

THE VAMPYRE LABYRINTH: REDEYE

Praise for *Shadowmancer*

'The biggest event in children's fiction since Harry Potter.'
The Times

'The adventure unfolds at a vivid and breathless pace.' *Observer*

'*Shadowmancer* is flying off the bookshelves as if a wizard had
incanted a charm on it.' *Herald*

'A magical tale of vicars and witches.' *Daily Telegraph*

'A compelling and dark-edged fantasy . . . highly recommended.'
Independent

Praise for *Wormwood*

'*Wormwood* is breathtaking in scope . . . an extraordinary
achievement told by a master storyteller. The book is, quite simply,
marvellous.' *Guardian*

Praise for *Tersias*

'It is, in a word, brilliant. Colourful, dramatic, relentless, accessible
to children – and more frightening for their parents.' *Scotsman*

'The plot hurtles along carrying the reader from one cliff-hanger
to the next.' *Daily Telegraph*

THE VAMPYRE LABYRINTH

Dust Blood

G. P. Taylor

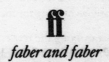

faber and faber

First published in 2011
Faber and Faber Ltd
Bloomsbury House
74–77 Great Russell Street
London WC1B 3DA

Typeset by Faber and Faber Ltd
Printed in England by CPI Bookmarque, Croydon

The right of G. P. Taylor to be identified as author
of this work has been asserted in accordance with Section 77
of the Copyright, Designs and Patents Act 1988

A CIP record for this book
is available from the British Library

ISBN 978–0–571–22696–2

DUST BLOOD

DUSTING

[1]

The Lutyen Hagg

THE ROWING BOAT slid silently through the still water. The blades of the oars cut against the black tide and scattered ripples in the light of the full moon. Neither man spoke. Each had pulled his collar high and his cap tight against the night. As he heaved the long poles with paddle ends, the small fat man grimaced. His face was flushed red; a single lock of hair fell across his brow. With every drag of the oar he groaned to himself as the blisters swelled in the palms of his hands.

Chain by chain, the boat glided towards the shore. The black, glassy water hardly moved as the full moon was eased from the tranquil sea. No seabird called or rock-dog cried; all was silent but for the gentle sloshing of the paddles as they beat against the water.

Far ahead, the island loomed from the sea. The stone-banked shore gave way to thick twists of hemp-grass. There, rising up like the arched, scaled back of a colossal dragon, was the crag. At the pinnacle of the rock were the dark shadows of the castle, which stood half-ruined by long years of battle. The bleak stone clung to bleak stone, held fast by nothing more than tufts of heather and the will to stand.

3

High on the ramparts at the smallest window was a light. It was the only thing that burnt in the darkness. It stared, shadowed by the moon, and glinted on the sea like the eye of a beast.

'Three shillings . . . three shillings is not a price for a secret trip across to the island,' the boatman said belligerently, hoping the man who sat in the back of the boat would hear his words. 'Could cost me my job. Not right to be doing this – there is a war on.'

'I am sure the war will not pay as well,' the man answered in a soft Irish voice as he rubbed the chin of his thin face and scowled from under the brim of his black hat. 'We are all lucky to have work.'

'Work?' the man asked. 'Gudruns have been doing this since the time of the Ulrich. I am the fifty-third son of a Gudrun to row these waters. This isn't work, it is life.'

'Then Gudrun, you will get me safely to the island?' the man asked.

'What do you want at this time of night? Couldn't it wait until the morning?' the boatman asked in a voice that resembled the growl of a large cat.

'The causeway has been mined against an invasion and what I need has to be done tonight,' the man answered, not caring how much he gave away.

'Wouldn't step foot on that island, too many ghosts,' the fat man answered. Beads of sweat dripped from under the brim of his hat and trickled along the strand of hair.

'That is what I love about the North. You are all believers in superstition.'

'Lutyen Hagg isn't a superstition. I saw her myself. Stands

4

on the rocks under the castle and howls. Many a ship has gone down at her call. We all keep away.'

The passenger sat back in the rowing boat and smiled to himself. 'I would love to meet such a woman,' he laughed as the boat slipped slowly into the shadow of Castle Lutyen. 'Tell me, have you ever been in the castle?'

Gudrun stopped his rowing and panted as he looked at the man from the tip of his polished boots to the top of his crooked black hat.

'You're not from these parts,' he answered, staring at the fingers of the hand-stitched leather gloves that the man wore. 'If you were, you would have never asked such a question. No one goes to the castle, tide or no tide. Day or night, it is not a place for humans.'

'And the one who lives there, do you see much of him?' the man asked.

'His food is left by the harbour and no one waits until he collects it. Leaves the money in an empty barrel,' the boat-man answered as he took up the oars and began to row again. 'If you ask me, he doesn't like people. Been on that island for twenty-seven years and never left. How can a man live like that?'

'Does he have visitors?' the man asked.

'You are the first, and if you get from that place you will be the last.'

The boatman shrugged his shoulders and sighed. The castle loomed, blotting out the night with its dark shadow. All around them the water was still and unbroken. It was as if they crossed from land to island on a darkened looking-glass.

In the silver light of the moon the castle brooded in dimly tarnished languor. The man looked up. There in the spire where the lamp shone was the shadow he wanted to see. A face looked out, as if all they had said had been overheard.

'I think I am expected,' he said. 'The news of my arrival has gone before me.'

'Don't know how,' answered the boatman as he steered the craft towards the shore and skulled in and out of the jagged rocks. 'Treacherous place, like the teeth of a dragon. So many men have been ripped to pieces on these rocks.'

'Guided by the voice of the Lutyen Hagg?' the man asked.

'You will not jest when you see her. I stop here. Won't let my boat touch the shore,' he said. He shipped the oars and tied the boat to a large rock that appeared to be the first of a number of stepping stones.

'How do I get ashore?' the man asked.

'You can fly if you want – or hop or even swim – but I go no further.'

Crawling from the boat, the man stepped on to the rock. Gudrun looked up. In all his life he thought he had never seen anyone as tall or dressed as strange. A long black coat trailed on the rock, hiding the pointed shoes that stuck out of the narrow trousers. Underneath the coat, the boatman had seen that his passenger wore an old naval tunic with brass buttons.

'You English?' the boatman asked.

'No,' the man answered curtly. 'Do I look English?'

'Never seen anyone so strange. You look as if you are in fancy dress, this being 1940 and all that.'

'We all dress this way in Dingle,' the man answered as he looked down and made his way from stone to stone until he stepped to the beach. 'I will be back within the hour and you will wait.'

'If I must and only because I want my money – don't be late back or I won't be here.'

His words went unheard. The man had crossed the shingle beach and picked his way over the broken rocks that through the ages had fallen from the high crag. Soon he was out of sight of the boat. Looking back to the land, he could see the far hills and the outline of a harbour.

'Just another mile,' the man said as he pulled himself through the barbed grass and on to the track that led from the landing on the far side of the island. Below the crag were the broken, derelict houses of the old village. All were made of upturned sailing boats that had come to grief on the rocks. Their tarred hulks were now open to the sky. Rowan branches burst through the doors, and windows hung on broken catches. For a moment the man wondered why so many people had left the island. When he turned to the castle and looked up and saw the battered ramparts, he could understand why.

By the time the moon had broken over the battlements, he had walked the mile of twisting pathways in and out of the strewn rocks. Before him was the door to the castle, its bleached oak frame glowing in the moonlight. Four iron teeth jutted from the bottom of the small portcullis that slid into the stone roof.

The man took hold of the metal rapper and beat it three times against the wood.

The door trembled and shuddered. Footsteps scurried across dry stone steps.

'Who is it?' enquired the voice. 'I have invited no one to my island.'

'Toran – Toran Blaine,' the man said.

There was a sudden whirring noise above his head and the portcullis dropped suddenly. As it smashed into the stone Toran Blaine pressed himself against the door.

'You have no business here, no business at all,' the voice said from inside the castle.

'I am here to find Vincenzo Verzenzi,' Blaine shouted.

'There is no one here of that name,' the man answered.

'I know it is you. I have heard your voice before,' Blaine said.

'I am an old man. A writer and a recluse. I do not know anyone called Vincenzo Verzenzi,' the man argued, hoping that Toran Blaine would leave. 'Don't you understand, I wish no harm. Go away.'

Blaine pressed himself against the door and listened. The bars of the portcullis pushed into his back. He could hear the man breathing. They were slow, deliberate gasps of breath.

'I need to talk to you. Vinnie, it is important.'

'You have the wrong man and the wrong place. Go back to your boat and leave this castle,' the man answered.

'I will, if you answer me truthfully one thing,' Blaine said as his hand gripped the iron handle.

'And you will go?' the man asked.

'I promise,' Blaine replied.

'And all I have to do is answer truthfully?' the man said as he stepped closer to the door. 'Very well, ask what you wish. You stand on the outside of an impregnable castle. Many people have tried to smash down that door and all have failed.'

'Then you have nothing to fear,' Blaine answered. Slowly he began to climb the door, his fingers gripping each iron stud, his feet pressed against the wall. 'Are you Vincenzo Verzenzi?'

'Is my name so important?'

'Do you know that man?' Blaine asked.

'Yes,' he answered.

'And . . . Sibilia Trevellas?' Blaine asked. 'Is the name familiar to you?'

The man did not answer. There was silence. Blaine listened as he climbed higher into the chamber above the door. The metal chains of the portcullis hung from the high ceiling. The winding handle was locked so the gate could not be lifted. From the small balcony he looked down into the hallway of the castle. The room was lit with oil lamps that cast long shadows on the vaulted stone roof. A raging fire burnt in the grate of the large stone fireplace that looked as though it was made from a myriad of beach stones washed in by the tide. There he could see the man. He looked much younger than Blaine had expected. The man held a sword in his hand, a cutlass with wrist guard, the metal as bright as the day it was forged. He wore riding breeches and a thick tweed jacket. His long black hair was tied back with a gold clasp. This was not the old man that Blaine had been told lived in the castle.

Blaine took from his pocket an old portrait painted on a wooden block of white holly. He looked at the face painted upon it. The hair, the eyes, everything was just as it should be. He read the words painted beneath in a fine gold script in a woman's hand:

Vincenzo Verzenzi, Rome 1658

'So you are still alive?' Blaine asked as he looked down.

Without any sign of surprise, the man looked up and stared at him.

'You are the first one ever to get inside this castle,' he said as he gripped the sword tightly. 'Before I kill you, please tell me why you are here?'

'I have tracked you across a continent,' Blaine answered.

'To a castle in the North of England by the German Ocean?' Verzenzi answered as he stepped back towards the fireplace. 'A good place for you to die.'

'For one of us to die,' Blaine answered.

'So, Irishman, am I just another Vampyre to add to the list of my friends you have murdered?' Verzenzi asked.

At that moment Blaine leapt from the balcony of the portcullis to the floor below.

'Who said anything about murder?' Blaine asked as he pulled a small silver-capped bottle from the pocket of his long coat.

'Baron Muller, Vienna 1934 – François Dupec, Paris 1936 – Lord Lawrence, Glastonbury 1937 . . .' Verzenzi listed the names ceremoniously as if he read them from an epitaph. 'Some of the friends I have lost, and in each case the name of Toran Blaine was mentioned as the murderer.'

'Murderer?' Blaine asked as he took the cap from the bottle and dripped two drops of green liquid on to his finger. 'It is impossible to kill that which is already dead.'

'A Vampyre is very much alive, Mr Blaine. It is only people like you who live in a world of pain and drudgery who are dead. I am surprised that you have never been tempted.'

Blaine caught a fleeting glimpse of himself in the large gilt mirror that filled one wall of the hallway. His face was gaunt and lined beyond his years. Several sleepless nights had darkened the eyes. A growth of beard covered his chin.

'I did once,' he answered. 'Then I realised that you are outside the created order, you are creatures of death and could not be said to be living.'

'I heard François Dupec nearly killed you – is that right? Didn't he try to cut off your ear?' Verzenzi asked.

Blaine threw his hat to the floor and pushed back the long strands of red hair that covered a scar. 'It was a lucky blow. Dupec was resistant to the poison,' he answered.

'Myrrh balm?' Verzenzi said as he eyed Blaine to see when he might strike. 'In all my years I have never seen it before.'

Blaine screwed the silver cap back on the bottle and then dipped the flask back into his coat. From another pocket he pulled a long knife with a curved blade. He smeared the blade across his palm.

'There is always the option that you could just allow me to kill you,' Blaine said. 'How long have you been alive?'

'I was born in November 1177 on the day Saladin was defeated,' he said proudly as he watched Blaine inch closer.

'Isn't that long enough?' Blaine asked, his eyes flicking from the door to the window, wondering how the Vampyre would try to escape. He knew Vampyres well and could see the battle in his mind. Verzenzi would attack half-heartedly and then run. He would hope that Blaine would give chase.

11

There would be a room somewhere in the castle where Verzenzi would strike. The plan would have been rehearsed many times. It was what Vampyres always did.

'Life can never be long enough. I am thankful that I became a Vampyre so young. I have never had the moribund thoughts of death that plague humankind,' Verzenzi said as he stepped towards a spiral stone staircase at the side of the room.

It was as if Verzenzi were trying to look into Blaine's mind. He eyed him warily, his eyes flickering across his face, wanting to hear his inner thoughts. Blaine realised what he was trying to do.

'Can't you understand my thoughts?' he asked.

'They are somewhat blurred. I knew you were coming to the island. Gudrun told me. He has been my assistant for many years, as were his father and grandfather. His mind is an open book. The wild and barren lands of Lindis blow through his thoughts like bread flour. Everything can be heard, even the thoughts he knows little about.'

'And me, my dear Verzenzi. What do my thoughts tell you?' Blaine asked.

'I cannot hear a thing, it is as if you are a –' Verzenzi stopped. A sudden and frightening thought rushed through his mind. 'Impossible! No, never . . .'

'A Vampyre? Is that what you are trying to say?' Blaine asked as he stepped forward.

Verzenzi didn't stop to cast a blow. He ran for the spiral staircase. Up and up, faster and faster, as Blaine followed. The Vampyre dived into a recess in the stone wall and pulled a curtain as he opened a secret door.

Blaine tore down the drape just as the stone slab was sliding back into place. He stabbed the wall with the knife. The stone crunched against the blade and he heard Verzenzi screaming in the passageway.

'Leave me – what have I done to you?' he shouted.

Calmly, Blaine pushed at the stone. It opened slowly to reveal a torch-lit passage within.

'It is no use running,' Blaine shouted as the shadowy figure of Verzenzi disappeared into the darkness.

In ten long strides, Blaine was at the end of the passageway. It opened out into a large room that looked like the captain's cabin on a grand old sailing ship. Blaine stepped into the room. An iron sceptre hit him square in the chest and he fell to the floor, the wind gone from his body.

'I thought you would have known?' Verzenzi asked, as he stood over him ready to strike again.

Blaine kicked his legs from him. As Verzenzi staggered back towards the open fire Blaine was already on his feet.

'Do you remember Sara Giardina?' Blaine asked as Verzenzi stood before the flames, clutching the sceptre in both hands.

'Should her name mean anything to me?' he asked as he made ready to strike.

Blaine could see the blow. Every muscle twitched as Verzenzi struck out. The sceptre missed by inches. Blaine lashed out with the knife, the steel cutting through the tweed jacket and white shirt as if they were paper.

As he fell back into the fire, Verzenzi screamed. The fire took hold instantly.

'Madrid, 1939 – Sara Giardina, aged twenty-seven . . .' Blaine answered.

The blazing body of Vincenzo Verzenzi fell from the fireplace on to an ornate Persian rug, which began to smoulder.

In the small bay beneath Lutyen Castle, the boatman waited. The dark figure stepped from the shadows of the crag and tiptoed across the stones.

'I thought you would have gone?' Toran Blaine asked as he placed a tightly tied canvas bag into the boat and stepped in, taking his seat quickly.

'I never expected –' the boatman answered.

'Vincenzo said you were a faithful servant and that you would never leave anyone in distress,' Blaine answered eagerly, the arm of his long black coat still smouldering from the fire.

'You know the master?' Gudrun asked as he pushed the boat from the rocks and began to paddle.

'An old friend,' Blaine answered.

'But I thought you didn't know him?' the boatman said.

'Didn't know if *you* knew our secret. Vincenzo assured me you do,' Blaine replied as he sat back in the boat.

'So you and the master are . . .?'

'Certainly one would think so,' Blaine said.

'And the bag?' Gudrun asked. 'A gift?'

'Proof,' Blaine replied as if he didn't care any longer. 'You may look if you so desire.'

Eager to see, the boatman stowed the oars neatly and began to untie the canvas bag. It was smoking, and had the smell of herrings on an oak rack. He rolled back the fabric of the bag so the moonlight would reach the inner depths. Then he froze as the eyes of Vincenzo Verzenzi stared back at him – locks of burnt black hair tight to the scorched skin, the mouth open, the teeth like a dog's fangs in the severed head.

'The master?' Gudrun asked. 'You killed him?'

Blaine kicked the paddle across the boat. Gudrun suddenly fell back into the sea.

'Never lie to a man like me,' Blaine said, and he watched Gudrun reach out in vain as he slipped beneath the water.

[2]

Hawks Moor

JAGO HARKER stared out across the sea. He could not sleep. Night had become a time of terror. As soon as he lay down his head, the dreams would come. Within his mind he would see the meteor as it plunged towards the earth, and Sibilia Trevellas standing over him with sword outstretched. The nightmare left him breathless, his chest pounding, his mind dazed. It had been seven days since the Lyrid of Saturn, the night when the stars had fallen to earth and the sea had washed away the labyrinth at Hawks Moor.

Each night, just before sleep he had heard the same voice. It whispered in the land between waking and slumber as if it were waiting for him. Throughout the dark hours, it called to him. Jago knew it was a voice of warning, but could not tell if it came from the life beyond or from his own heart.

In the moonlight Hawks Moor looked as it always had for hundreds of years. The stone gargoyle still sat on the roof and stared its frozen stare. The wisteria clung to the high baronial walls like a witch's hands clambering to dig deep within. Arched stone windows faced the sea and the light from his bedroom burnt brightly. Jago looked up and counted the windows as the breeze blew the leaves from the salt-washed trees. He smiled, remembering how Jack Henson had found codfish stuck in the high oak, washed in by the gigantic wave that had broke against the cliff. It had threatened destruction and yet the house of Hawks Moor stood firm. To the north, the town of Whitby had escaped the rage of the sea. It was as if the wave had come upon the house alone.

There had been no sign of the Gladling boys. Lawrence and his brothers were missing. It was believed by Hugh Morgan that they had drowned in the deluge, with no hope of survival. That was also the fate of Sibilia and Ezra Morgan. Since the night of the Lyrid, they had not been seen. A sense of disturbed tranquillity hung over the house. Hugh Morgan smiled more than ever. His father, Ezra Morgan, was gone and he cared not.

'Having a Vampyre for a father was not always easy,' Hugh had said that morning at breakfast. 'You could never tell friends and I could certainly not tell Martha,' he added as he served the scrambled eggs.

'But she found out in a way that cost her her life,' Jago had answered, in a way that ended the conversation for the whole day.

Jago was too tired to care. He craved sleep, but was too fearful to close his eyes during the dark hours. Like every night, he would wait for morning. He would damn the equinox for dividing the light and wished for summer. Jack Henson had said that the time of oak was over and holly would rule until spring. Jago didn't understand what he meant. All he knew was that as winter approached the dark hours would grow longer and he would have to wait until he knew it was safe to sleep.

'Still here?' Jack Henson said as he strode through the arched doorway and across the shingle left by the great wave. 'Thought you would be tucked up in your room. Safe inside, better than out here.'

'Somehow, the dark isn't as frightening when you stand under the moon,' Jago answered.

'They won't be back,' Henson said as he laid a consolatory hand on his shoulder. 'If there's one thing that will kill a Vampyre it is drowning. There were at least a hundred here that night and not a body was found. All of them washed out to sea and if you ask me, that is the best place for them.'

'But I know that Strackan is not dead,' Jago answered as he took the steaming cup of Ovaltine from Henson and cupped it warmly in his hands. 'I can hear his voice.'

Just the mention of the name made Jago shudder. Strackan had come so close to killing him, taking his blood and transforming Jago into a Vampyre. He could still smell the beast as he drew close and that voice would never be forgotten.

'He's dead,' Henson insisted, 'and the Lyrid of Saturn is no more. That night you were supposed to die. He would have drunk your blood and been transformed.'

'But he still can,' Jago answered. 'I am still here and Strackan is still alive.'

As he spoke a solitary wishing-star sped overhead. It crossed the heavens from east to west and vanished far over the high moor.

'Take it,' Henson said. 'Pray on the star and keep that promise.'

'Superstition,' Jago muttered as he sipped the hot drink and felt the malted chocolate trickle down his throat.

18

'It was knowing superstition that kept us all safe,' Henson answered.

'And now it stops?' Jago asked. 'Every time I talk to Hugh it is as if he wants to get on with our new life. *Happy families*.'

'What can you expect? He has found you, his son, after many long years of knowing you were alive but not being able to be with you. Don't you expect him to feel that way?'

'But it's the voice and the dream. Every time I close my eyes at night I can hear the voice of Strackan and see Sibilia Trevellas with the sword.' Jago looked out across the bay and watched as the waves broke on the shore. 'It is as if I am being told something.'

'Dreams can be made of cheese. They are our minds telling us what troubles them,' Henson said as he put his arm around Jago. 'I remember a night when I saw a boy who looked so frightened by all this. Dreams – whisperers – ghosts . . . You had trouble believing, Jago.'

'Now I know they are true. I have seen them with my own eyes.'

'Then go to sleep. Rest and take comfort – all will be well.'

Together they looked out to sea. Far to the south, they could hear the drone of enemy bombers. The horizon began to glow red with the flames of the town. The low rumble of exploding bombs came nearer like distant thunder.

'Hull is getting it tonight,' Jago said, and he remembered the bombing raid that killed his mother.'

'It will all soon end, Jago,' Henson said. 'Come inside, Biatra has been asking for you.'

Jago was not sure if he wanted to see Biatra. He followed Henson across the driveway and back to the house. The large oak door stood proudly open and there by the fireplace was Biatra. On her wrists were the holly bands that kept the venom from the Vampyre bite in control. Jago knew that without them she would become a monster just like Sibilia Trevellas.

In the time since she had been attacked, Henson had studied every book in Hawks Moor to see if there was a cure. They had even taken her to Mallyan Spout and held her beneath the waterfall. It was what the hermit had told them to do. Sagacious had said it would cure her of the venom. Jago remembered his words. 'There is a place. A spring of water that falls over holy rocks. It is spoken of in the Book of Krakanu. Take her there, it is not far,' the hermit had said as the magic took the life from him and dried his bones until he turned to dust. 'Push her deep within the pool and hold her down until she cannot breathe.'

All Biatra felt was cold and wet. Whatever magic there was, whatever incantation they made, it had not the power to break the spell. That night, as the moon rose from the sea, she wanted blood. Now she paced the hallway of Hawks Moor restless and ill at ease.

'Where have you been?' she asked edgily as Jago stepped down into the hallway and walked towards her.

'Couldn't sleep. I was outside watching the stars,' Jago answered.

'Next time I'll come with you. We could go into the woods or to Whitby,' she said quickly, her eyes flashing around the room. 'Is that chocolate?' she asked as she took the cup from him and sipped the dregs. 'So thirsty, can't get enough to drink.'

'You should try to rest, Biatra,' Henson answered as he tried to comfort her. 'Better stay inside and not go out at night, not like this.'

'Like what?' she snapped. 'Like a Vampyre?'

'That's –' Henson tried to reply.

'That's what I am. I can feel it. There's no lying. You know it and I know it. I'm changing to be like *her*,' Bia argued.

'There will be a cure,' Jago interrupted, having heard her talk like this for the last seven nights. 'I will stay awake with you and in the morning we will sleep.'

Biatra appeared to calm down. She crossed the stone floor and sat on the high hearth of the fire. She picked a log from the basket, then placed it into the flames.

'Feel so cold,' she said as she pulled her coat tighter to her chest. 'Can't get warm.'

Jago noticed a thin blue haze edging her lips. It was as if she was starved of blood and that nothing filled her veins. He had mentioned it to Henson, who had assured him that it was temporary and she would be well.

'Then I will bring more Ovaltine and some food,' Henson said, nodding to Jago.

Jago had seen that look before. He knew it meant to keep an eye on Biatra and not to let her from the house. Hugh Morgan had said that she could stay with them for ever. Hawks Moor would be her home until her mother was found or her father came back from the war.

Biatra thought they were both dead. She had tried not to believe it but in her mind the evidence was overwhelming.

Yet there was something about Hawks Moor that made her feel welcome.

Jago sat with her and held her hand. It was icy cold and sent a shiver down his spine. The fire raged in the grate, the logs burning brightly. As he slipped his arm around her, Biatra felt chilled to the bone.

'I keep seeing her,' Biatra whispered, 'Sibilia . . . every time I close my eyes. I know she is somewhere very close.'

'Hugh has searched the caves beneath the house and blocked off the entrance to the sea. There is no one hiding,' he said.

'I checked the painting. Her face has not appeared on the canvas. Come and see.'

Biatra got up from the fireplace and pressed the panel on the wall that made the secret door open. Jago stepped aside as she opened it further to reveal a small room set into the wall next to the large stone fireplace. As it had done for eight hundred years, a candle burnt brightly on a table by the far wall. A cladding of dripped wax covered the holder until it could not be seen. On the wall high above everything else was the old painting of the Vampyre Quartet. It was set in a gilt frame that looked as new as the day it had been made.

Two of the faces were unfinished, as if the artist had been called away and never returned – and they would remain unfinished until those members of the Quartet were dead, at which time their features would appear. Everything else about the image was perfect. Staring down at them was the smiling face of Crispin Draigorian. Jago remembered the eyes clearly. They were the same as on the night when Draigorian had begged Jago to kill him. There too was Julius Cresco, scowling as if his life had been taken from him without his consent. Each figure had the stain of blood across the back of a hand. It ran from the wrist and followed the course of the veins to the longest finger.

'I can't believe they were Vampyres,' Jago said. 'I knew Cresco so well. He cared for me since I was a baby.'

'It was for a reason,' Henson said as he stepped inside the small room and closed the door. 'The Vampyre Quartet wanted you for their own purpose. They were not to be trusted.'

'I am amazed that when they die their faces appear in the painting,' Jago answered.

'Soon we will see the face of Ezra Morgan and Sibilia Trevellas. They have to be dead,' Henson said as he handed Biatra a steaming cup of chocolate.

'She isn't dead,' Biatra replied as she sipped the drink very slowly. 'Her face would have appeared in the picture by now.'

Henson looked at the painting as if he were willing the image of Trevellas to appear.

'Then we have to believe she will leave us alone,' he said.

'Is that likely?' Jago asked.

'We shall know tonight. I couldn't tell you before, but now seems a good time.' Henson pulled a chair from the wall and sat down. 'Hugh went away this afternoon to find out what has happened to his father. He thinks . . . he thinks his father may still be alive.'

'How?' asked Biatra, and she shuddered at the thought of Ezra Morgan being alive.

'Last night, just before dawn, Hugh heard someone in the library. At first he thought it was one of you walking the house, unable to sleep. Then he realised it was not.' Henson paused momentarily and looked at them. 'The sounds were coming from Ezra's old room. When Hugh opened the door he saw what he thought was Ezra Morgan disappearing into the passageway.'

'He had come back – that is what the voice kept saying,' Jago answered as he held Biatra by the hand.

'But how will he know for sure?' Biatra asked.

Jack Henson looked more than slightly uncomfortable. He fidgeted in the chair and ran his long fingers through his fine strands of white hair.

'He has gone to see a Vampyre – slightly aged and very benign. What happened at Hawks Moor has attracted the attention of the Lodge Maleficarum.'

'What?' Jago asked.

'There are more Vampyres in this land than just the ones you know of,' Henson said with a ruffled brow. 'I thought even from your brief encounter that you would have realised that.'

'But how do they go undetected?' Biatra asked.

'By keeping quiet and living lives away from the world,' he answered. 'The Lodge Maleficarum keeps them from harm's way and maintains the status quo.'

'To let them murder and kill when they want?' Jago said standing to his feet.

'Kings, prime ministers, writers, famous men and women have all had the taste of blood. If you live for ever and always look young, imagine what you can do in several lifetimes. Just like old Crispin Draigorian, there are Vampyres who are kept well and live long with the help of their living companions.'

24

'Blood-bottles like Clinas Macarty?' Bia asked.

'Just like Clinas and Bartholomew Bradick. Clinas helped old Draigorian for many years,' Henson answered.

'Then what is the Lodge Maleficarum?' Jago asked Henson. The eyes of the face of Draigorian in the painting appeared to follow him around the room.

Jack Henson swallowed hard, as if what he was about to say was impossible to believe.

'The Lodge Maleficarum is a gathering of Vampyres. They have summoned Hugh Morgan to explain all that has happened. In return they have promised to try and protect you both from Strackan and Trevellas.'

'Vampyres are protecting us?' Biatra asked.

'It would seem that they have a sense of conscience,' he said suspiciously. 'I more suspect that they are frightened. Their fear is that *what* and *who* they are will seep into the world of men and they will be exposed, hunted and killed.'

'It seems ridiculous. I thought it was just Strackan we had to deal with.'

'Jago,' Jack Henson said, and then paused. 'In this land there are millions of people. Hugh Morgan told me that out of those millions there are no more than two thousand Vampyres. They have been added to year in and year out by the likes of Strackan. For three centuries the Vampyres have had the Lodge Maleficarum. I heard of it some years ago but didn't believe it to be true.'

'Where has he gone?' Biatra asked.

'To Whitby, the White Horse and Griffin Hotel in Church Street,' Henson answered.

'By the Town Hall?' Bia said.

'That is where they gather,' Henson answered. 'He had to meet the afternoon train from London. A Miss Vibica de Zoete.'

The room fell silent. Jago opened the door and stepped back into the hall. The fire burnt brightly and yet the room was chilled. It was as if a window was open somewhere in the house. Far away in the dark high tower a door slammed. Biatra stood in the doorway of the secret room and listened. She pulled the long overcoat around her to keep in the warmth and her eyes scanned the high ceiling, as if she traced the path of a star across the sky.

'What can you see?' Jago asked, knowing her eyes were following some hidden thing.

'I can't see them. But I know they are there,' she answered.

'Listen,' Henson said as a sound of whirring blades settled on the galleried landing above them. In the shadows of the oak staircase, high on an upper landing just out of sight, a creature drew breath and sighed. Through the narrow banisters it stared down at Jago and it picked its teeth with a long claw.

'Can you see anything, Biatra?' Henson asked.

'I can hear it breathing. It has travelled far, that is all I know.'

Henson snatched a sword from the wall and then gathered two more. He gave them to Jago and Biatra.

'I have a bad feeling,' he said as the whirring started again.

Without warning, the creature fell towards them. Down and down it plunged, arms outstretched, claws forward and wings folded. Then like a primeval beast it swooped and turned.

'Look!' Biatra shouted as it plummeted towards her.

Jago lashed out with the sword. It struck the creature a glancing blow.

'Quickly,' Henson said. 'Back in the room!'

He pulled Biatra towards the open door in the oak panels as Jago watched the creature get to its feet and cower in the corner by the kitchen door.

'It is a poltergeist,' he shouted to Henson. 'Just like Sagacious the Hermit.'

'Get inside, quickly,' Henson ordered as Jago stepped towards the middle of the hallway.

'It's too late,' Jago replied, knowing he would never make it.

The creature paced slowly towards him, half man, half beast. Its feet slipped on the stone floor as it drew closer. Like an old gargoyle, it stared at Jago with one eye while the other gazed back and forth across the room.

Jago could not believe what he saw. In the shadows of the fire the creature gathered itself, breathing slowly as a trickle of blood oozed from its side.

'Jago Harker?' it croaked as it rose up and shook its dragon-like wings.

'That is who I am,' Jago answered.

'I bring you these,' it answered, and it rolled two gold coins across the floor towards him.

'Leave them,' shouted Henson from the doorway. 'It has to pay you luck-money before it takes your life.'

It was too late. The coins rolled to his feet. Jago stooped

and picked one from the cold stone. It burnt, hot to the touch, as he rolled it in his fingers.

'Time to die,' the poltergeist screamed as it leapt towards him.

Jago fell back, dropping the sword. Biatra ran from the room, pulling the holly bands from her wrists.

'NO!' he screamed as Bia pounced upon the creature.

Jago cowered by the fireplace as Biatra pulled back the neck of the creature and bit deep within its fish-like skin, then plunged her sword through its heart. The rapier burst through its chest as she twisted the blade.

There was a sudden shrill scream that rattled the rafters as the poltergeist shuddered, squirmed and breathed its last.

Biatra let the limp body fall to the floor as she wiped the blood from her mouth.

'Tastes like cabbage.' Biatra laughed, the hunger gone from her belly. 'But beggars are never choosers.'

'Burn the beast – can never trust them to be dead unless they have been burnt,' Henson shouted as he pulled the sword from it and dragged the poltergeist towards the fire. 'Take it by the hand and help me. Come on, Jago.'

Jago hesitated as he looked at Bia taste the blood on her fingers. He got to his feet and hauled the beast to the fire and watched it burn.

'Why?' he asked as the flames of the fire grew brighter. 'Why should it want to kill me?'

'Because *you* are the one,' said a soft Irish voice from the steps at the front door. 'The one that has been chosen to put an end to all this.'

[3]

Vibica de Zoete

STANDING IN THE DOORWAY of Hawks Moor was a young woman. She was as tall as Jago and immaculately dressed, every inch pronouncing she had taken great care in her appearance. A large silver brooch clasped the scarf around her neck. She smiled as she looked around the room, her eyes stopping for a moment at Biatra as she wiped away the blood from her face.

'Have I missed supper?' she asked, her voice soft and warm.

'Vibica de Zoete,' Henson whispered so only Jago would hear.

'Quite correct,' the woman replied, clearly having heard what he said.

'She's staying the night,' Hugh Morgan added as he stepped in from behind the long curtain carrying a small leather case. 'There is not a train until the morning and I thought it would be better if she was with us.'

Henson shrugged his shoulders.

'I see you are not convinced?' Vibica asked. She pulled off her leather gloves and folded them neatly and placed them in her leather bag. 'I take it you do not like Vampyres?'

'Jack Henson is a good friend, Vibica. He won't mind – will you, Jack?' Hugh Morgan asked in a way that Henson could not refuse.

'We live in strange days,' he answered.

'I promise I won't bite,' Vibica quipped. 'And this must be Jago Harker – you look just like your father.'

Jago didn't know what to say. He looked at Hugh and then Biatra.

'I have a painting of me when I was a lad and the resemblance with Jago is amazing,' Hugh answered, breaking the silence.

Vibica stared at the burning remains of the creature in the fire and the bloodstained sword in Henson's hand. She turned to Hugh and whispered something to him.

'What happened?' Hugh asked as he took her long leather coat and stepped towards the fire where the creature burned.

'We were attacked,' Biatra said casually. 'It *died* . . .'

'So I can see,' Vibica answered as she glanced at the burning bones. It looked as though Henson had been cooking a dragon. 'Did you kill it?'

Biatra didn't reply. She looked away as she checked her fingers for blood.

'Did the creature make itself known?' Hugh asked Jack Henson as Vibica picked the gold coins from the floor and examined them closely.

'It would never have told you where it was from or who had sent it, Hugh,' Vibica said. She looked at the coins and held them towards the light of the fire. 'I have seen something similar when I visited Reykjavik. Once you touch the coins then the creature has the right to kill you. There, they call it *Soul Money*.'

'Why should it come here?' Hugh asked.

'Why here?' Vibica replied as she handed the coins to Jago with a smile. 'What has happened recently is of interest to many people.'

'Vampyres,' Henson muttered.

'We are still people,' she chided. 'I never asked to be this way. It was something that was thrust upon me. I was little more than the age of Biatra when I was taken. I have regretted that moment every day for the last two hundred years.'

Her voice trailed off into a whisper. She looked at Hugh Morgan, hoping he would intervene.

Jack Henson shrugged his shoulders. 'You want sympathy?' he muttered.

'I can assure you, Mr Henson, I do not need sympathy. I have done well with my life as a Vampyre and try to harm no one. My companion sees to all my needs.'

Hugh looked uncomfortable; he glared at Henson, his eyes pleading for him to say no more.

'I am sorry, Miss Vibica. I should never have spoken that way. You are welcome here.' Henson tried to smile as he bowed his head.

'My visit is reluctant but I hope it will be worthwhile. We have much to talk about.'

Jago noticed her eyes narrow as she smiled at Henson. She was beautiful, but there was something about her that he found threatening. It was as if she could see everything he thought and read his mind like an open book.

'I promised Vibica some supper. She would like to talk

with you, Jack, about all you know. She has information that may be of help to us,' Hugh said as he walked towards the drawing-room door. 'I am sure she will want to talk to you as well,' he added as he looked at Biatra and Jago, 'in the morning.'

'But –' Jago protested.

'You have trouble sleeping? Conversations in your mind that keep you awake?' Vibica said.

'Yes,' he answered.

'Try this,' she said, and she reached in to her leather bag and produced a bag of what looked like boiled sweets. She held them towards him. 'There is one for Biatra as well. I know how hard the transformation really is.'

Biatra and Jago hesitated.

'It will be fine,' Hugh said. 'I trust her implicitly.'

Henson shrugged as he stacked the fire with even more wood and poked the embers with a sword. 'This thing won't burn as well as it should,' he scolded.

'Take one,' Vibica said, offering them both the bag.

Jago reached out and took a sweet from the brown paper. He held it to his lips and touched it with the tip of his tongue. 'Lemon?' he asked.

'More than that,' she answered. 'One will be enough.'

Jago rolled the sweet in the palm of his hand as Biatra reached in, took a candy and ate it. She crunched against the toffee coating and smiled.

'I promised some time with Vibica,' Hugh said. 'We will see you in the morning.'

Parents were always the same, Jago thought, knowing that Hugh's look meant they both had to go upstairs.

'But what if there is another one of *those*?' Biatra asked. 'I heard a door slam in the tower.'

'I will go,' Henson offered as Hugh Morgan opened the door of the drawing room.

'In the morning, then,' Jago said as he followed on.

Instinctively he took hold of Biatra by the hand. She felt strangely warm. He smiled at her as they looked briefly at each other. She knew what he was thinking.

'I feel well. It's the blood – well, that and the boiled sweet.' Biatra laughed. It was the first time he had heard her sound so happy. She squeezed his hand tighter. 'All will be well,' she said.

'What?' Jago asked as they followed Henson up the wooden stairs to the landing above.

'All will be well,' she said again. 'I don't know what it means but I know it is true.'

The staircase turned on the landing. Jago looked at all the paintings of the Morgan family throughout the ages. Many were of Ezra Morgan in his various lives throughout time. In each he had tried to disguise himself in some way. Yet in them all, the same eyes shone through. Eyes like a wolf, steel blue and cold. Eyes like the man on the train that had brought Jago from London to Whitby on the day he was evacuated.

'Do you trust her?' Jago asked Henson as he opened the door to the tower room.

'I never trust a Vampyre,' he answered.

'You trust Hugh Morgan,' Biatra said dreamily. 'He's a Vampyre.'

'Born of a woman. Makes him different in so many ways,' Henson answered. 'And he has never been bitten.'

'Do Vampyres ever fall in love?' Biatra asked as Henson crossed the room and pulled the window shut.

'Why do you ask?'

'Nothing . . .' she said as she slumped on her bed and looked up at the ceiling.

'Well, you'll be safe. Nothing will get in here now,' Henson said as he walked to the door. 'Keep this locked. I'll bring you some supper before I turn in.'

'Are you staying here?' Jago asked him, wondering why he hadn't gone back to his home in Whitby.

'Hugh has asked me to live here for a while. Doesn't want to be on his own,' Henson answered as he tapped the door with his fingers. 'Keep this locked,' he insisted.

They didn't speak until they knew he had gone. Jago counted his footsteps along the landing until they could hear them no more. Henson had the most annoying habit of listening at doors when least expected.

'She's going to fall in love with him,' Biatra said.

'With Henson?' he asked.

'With Hugh . . . I could see it in the way she looked at him.' Bia seemed to be dreaming with her eyes wide open.

Jago didn't like the thought. It made his stomach churn.

'She's a Vampyre,' he said.

'So am I,' Bia answered. 'I don't think I will be cured and I will be just like her. One day I will fall in love and what then?'

She looked at Jago as he stood before the fireplace and she smiled. His face was hidden from her but the memory of it was forever in her mind.

'There will be a cure. I made you that promise,' he said

34

as he pushed a log deeper into the flames with the tip of his boot. The fire sparked and smouldered, sending smoke into the room.

'I've been thinking. Perhaps it is better if you leave me this way.' Biatra yawned.

'It's not right. I couldn't,' Jago said as he turned to her.

Biatra was asleep and snoring gently. It was the first time he had seen her that way since Sibilia Trevellas had attacked her. There had always been a look of torment in her eyes. But now she was peaceful.

'It is sometimes . . .' she whispered, her words carried in her dream.

'Boiled sweets,' Jago said as he took the candy from his pocket and again tasted it with the tip of his tongue.

He was unsure if he should eat the candy. Something made him wary, told him he would do better to sit and guard Biatra as she slept. Taking a handkerchief from his pocket he wrapped the candy as tightly as he could and held it in the palm of his hand. Then, hearing voices downstairs, he unlocked the door and walked on to the landing. Words were broken by laughter. Hugh Morgan spoke loudly as he recounted the night of the Lyrid of Saturn. He was excited and he stammered his words. Every now and then, Jack Henson would speak. Jago crept down the stairs and observed what took place through a crack in one of the panels of the drawing-room door.

'He did well. It was a fearful night for us all, but the boy did well.'

'And you have found your son,' Vibica answered. 'What is it like to be half Vampyre?'

'That is a curse within itself,' Hugh answered truthfully, his voice quieter than before.

Vibica looked about the room. She was surprised by its grandeur. It was filled with objects of great beauty.

'We are like magpies,' she said. 'Vampyres tend to surround themselves with shiny objects and things of beauty. Don't you find?'

'Are you familiar with the story of my ancestor Tristan Morgan?' Henson asked Vibica as she sipped on a small glass of sherry that she held precisely between her china-white fingers.

Vibica de Zoete nodded her head to say she did. Henson went on regardless to explain the history of the Morgan family. Hugh spoke every now and then to fill in the details of the history of the house. He found it hard not to sob when Henson spoke of the murder of his mother at the hands of Sibilia Trevellas. Then, when he told her of how the same woman had murdered his wife and child, Vibica's face changed.

'I can understand your contempt for Vampyres. Sometimes I forget how those who breathe think of us,' she answered.

'Do you breathe?' Henson enquired. 'I often thought that true Vampyres were not in need of air, water or food, and yet you enjoy the sherry as do I.'

'That is the misconception. We are not monsters, as some would have the world believe. Sadly, there are those of us who out of their own desire will take a life. At the Lodge Maleficarum we try to ask those who seek our help to live a silent life.'

'But what of your need for blood?' Henson pressed her to answer as he stood up.

Vibica tried to remain calm. She could see the next sentence formulate in his mind and she wanted to answer it before he spoke.

'You are right in thinking that there have been murders and yes, I do pay for the blood I drink. I know a doctor in London who supplies my companion with whatever I need. In Lyme Regis, life is still quite sedate.'

'And no one suspects?' Hugh Morgan asked.

'Not in two hundred years,' she said with a half-hearted smile. 'Companions come and go. Every fifty or sixty years I move on and start again. I have a collection of wigs and make-up so I can change my age.' She was about to continue when she saw what Henson was thinking. 'I would never starve myself, Mr Henson. I have heard that was the fate of Pippen Draigorian. I could never do that.'

'So what of Strackan and Ezra Morgan? Are we to be in fear of them?' Henson asked.

'You should fear them in every waking moment. As Regent of the Lodge I have heard much in this last week. Many were killed by the wave at the Lyrid of Saturn and some would say the world is well rid of them. But Strackan has been seen. He fled to the north with Ezra Morgan and Sibilia Trevellas. A loyal companion has told us that Sibilia wants the girl. She has developed an *attraction* for her.'

'But what of Jago?' Hugh Morgan asked about his son.

'Jago is to be killed. They have realised that he is the one who has been sent to put an end to the Vampyre Quartet,' she said as Jago listened in his hiding place. 'They will wait until they can strike and then take their chance.'

'And Jago – what chance does he have?' Hugh asked. 'He

is a boy of little more than fifteen. How can he be protected from Strackan?'

'The rumour is that it is your father who has been tasked with his death. That is why the poltergeist was sent,' Vibica said as she pulled the coins from her bag and held them out for Hugh to take.

'My father?' he asked.

'It was thought quite fitting as it would test your loyalty.'

'Strackan toys with you, Hugh,' Henson interrupted.

'I wish that was the only concern of the Lodge Maleficarum.' Vibica de Zoete sighed as Henson poured her another glass. 'There is an assassin on the loose, a henchman paid good money to take the life of a Vampyre.'

Henson smiled. 'Perhaps he could do our job for us?' he asked Hugh Morgan.

'This man cannot be trusted. He kills because he enjoys it. He has destroyed several of our Lodge. He knows much about our ways and some suspect that he may even be a Vampyre himself.'

Vibica looked down as she spoke. She didn't want them to see that she was crying.

'Why should a Vampyre kill a Vampyre?' Hugh asked Vibica as she moved uncomfortably in her chair.

'Why do humans kill humans?' she asked as she held back the tears and swallowed hard. 'We have the same desires and vices as everyone else who shares this world. We are no different in that.'

'Do you know this man?' Henson asked.

'He will not help you. I know what you are thinking. What you desire is a cure for Biatra. You only have one hope.'

She stopped and put the glass on the small table next to her.

'What is that hope?' Henson asked.

'Dust Blood . . .' she said slowly.

'A riddle for mortals?' Henson replied warily.

'The blood of the Vampyre that first bit you. It has to be bled on the full moon whilst the Vampyre is still alive. Then it is dried, powdered and mixed with milk. Taken the next night on a silver spoon it will stop the venom.'

'So to save Biatra we have to find Sibilia Trevellas?' Hugh asked.

'I think it will be more likely that Sibilia will want to find you,' Vibica said heedlessly as she brushed the dust from her jacket. Taking a gold vial from her purse, she painted her lips. 'Whatever you do, for the sake of the Lodge Maleficarum, I request you do it quietly.'

'Quietly?' Henson asked, incensed by her words. 'It is the life of two people at stake – possibly more.'

'There are hundreds of innocent Vampyres and their companions who could die because of this. I know from your heart that you have no concern for any of us. But I ask you, Jack Henson, do *not* start a war.'

Vibica bristled with anger. Her voice was sharp as glass. She stared at him after she had stopped speaking.

'Jack is right, Vibica,' Hugh said as he held her hand to stop it from shaking. 'Our concern is for Jago and Bia. We wish it could all end now. If you could get a message to Strackan and Sibilia – a truce –'

Vibica de Zoete laughed loudly as she touched his face with her fingers and traced the line of his jaw to his neck.

'Strackan is a monster. He will not listen. I heard the wound to his neck nearly killed him. It took the blood of three young children to keep him alive,' she said coldly.

'You know much of Strackan,' Henson said as he warmed himself by the fire. 'Are you sure *you* can be trusted?'

'You are the last person in the world who would ever trust a Vampyre. Should I ask the same of you? When I sleep here, could I not be pinned to the bed with a holly wand through my heart and a stone put in my mouth? I can sense that you have thought about it more than once as we have spoken, Jack Henson.'

'Old habits die hard,' Henson said. 'You remind me of Sibilia Trevellas. There is something of her in your ways.'

'Hardly surprising,' Vibica de Zoete answered. 'We are bloodline. It was Sibilia who killed my parents. That was in Dublin, in the Bread Riots, 1740. She kept me imprisoned as a companion for two years and then needed my blood.'

Dust Blood

MORNING CAME quickly; the shadows of the night were soon long gone. Hawks Moor was silent as Jago walked from his room and down the oak staircase. The door to the drawing room was open. He could see that the thick velvet drapes were still closed. Chinks of sunlight burnt in through the moth holes. They cast rods of light across the darkened room like the bars of a prison.

Pushing open the door he stepped inside. The remnants of the fire smouldered in the iron grate. Empty glasses cluttered the table next to a neatly folded newspaper. Jago pulled back the drapes and looked out of the leaded window. For a moment, the sun burnt brightly. He closed his eyes as he winced with the light.

'Did you hear everything you needed to?' the voice behind him said.

Jago turned quickly. Close behind him was Vibica de Zoete. She was smiling and still dressed as she had been the night before. Her perfect features were like those of a china doll. He could see a fluttering of powder on her cheeks; her red lipstick was glistening in the light, and her teeth were bright white. In the corner of her mouth the teeth like those of a dog, the only way he could tell she was a Vampyre, were hardly visible.

'Needed to?' he answered without thinking.

'Last night. You were listening. I could sense you were close by,' she said as she smoothed a finger across his cheek.

'Do you know everything?' Jago asked.

'I am a Vampyre. It cannot be helped. We sense when humans are near to us. Like a lion hunting its prey.'

'Is that what we are – dinner?' Jago answered as he tried to step away from her.

Vibica stepped forward, following him, keeping close.

'I am here to help, Jago. As you heard, you will need protection from Strackan and Sibilia. That is what I can give to you.'

Vibica placed her hand on his shoulder. Jago felt uncomfortable; she was too close. He watched her eyes as they flickered across his face.

'It might be you who needs protection,' he said quickly. 'If what you said is true then a Vampyre hunter could be after you.'

'I am well guarded and not many people have seen my face. My life is quiet . . . sometimes too quiet for my own good.' Vibica stepped towards the window and looked out. 'Tell me, Jago. Did you ever think that it might have been better for you to have become like us?'

He thought for a moment. There had been an instant just before Biatra had pressed the dagger into his hand on the night of the Lyrid of Saturn when he could have given in. Just as Strackan had leant forward and Jago had felt the breath on his neck, just for that brief second he had wondered. Then the thought had gone. He knew he would have to kill the creature.

'Perhaps,' Jago said, knowing that Vibica had seen every thought that had just passed through his mind.

'You would make a good Vampyre,' she said. She reached out and held his hand. 'There is still time – if you change your mind.'

Jago sensed something. It was a ripple of fear, the covering of a sudden thought. He listened, hoping to hear it again.

'Better a friend than an enemy – is that what you just thought?' he asked Vibica.

She laughed, her face exploding in a beautiful bright smile.

'You are closer than I could have imagined. I shall have to be careful of what I am thinking. If you were one with us, Strackan would have no need to kill you.'

'So, Dust Blood – does it really work?' Jago asked her as he held her hand in his own.

'I only know of one such case.'

'And?'

'The woman died. It turned out that she took the blood of the wrong Vampyre and it killed her,' Vibica answered as she tried to take her hand from him.

Jago held her hand softly but would not let go. There was an energy that came from her that excited him. All he could do was hold her hand and look into her eyes. They were mesmerising and tender, the deepest green imaginable. Her lips moved as if to speak again.

'I would rather Biatra stay a Vampyre than risk her dying,' he whispered.

'It is a painful friendship when one is eternal and the other

43

is subject to decay. I have experienced this many times. For the Vampyre to watch those whom they love walk towards death is part of our curse,' Vibica said as she slipped her hand from his.

'What else is there?' he asked, already knowing the answer.

'I think you already know,' Vibica said, and she stepped even closer to him so he could feel her breath on his neck. 'Don't worry about Hugh Morgan, he would understand. I am sure of it.'

Her head came closer. Jago stood in silence as his mind raced. Jago knew that what she was suggesting made sense. He could always be with Biatra. Strackan would have no cause to kill them. They could live their lives together at Hawks Moor.

'Family,' Jago said, as if he repeated her thought.

'That's right, Jago,' she said in a dull groan-like whisper. 'Family . . .'

She moved even closer, her lips touching his neck.

'Breakfast?' Biatra said as she stood in the doorway. 'Jack said that he had cooked breakfast in the kitchen.'

She looked warily at Vibica, who slowly moved from Jago.

'I didn't hear you coming – have you been there for long?' Vibica asked. She had been aware of Jago's presence when he had listened at the door the previous evening, but Biatra was different.

'Not long,' Biatra answered as she turned and walked from the room. 'I will tell Jack you are ready.'

'Jago,' Vibica said urgently. 'You could end all this quite quickly.'

He looked away from her as his heart raced. She looked

not much older than him and yet he knew she had lived for two hundred years.

'Better get to breakfast,' he said as he walked ahead of her into the hallway.

'Jago, just let me know,' she whispered, as if what was to come was inevitable. 'I promise all will be well.' She used the same words that Biatra had spoken the night before. 'I will know when you are ready.'

Jago looked back as the woman followed him through the hallway. The house was still; the remnants of the hall fire smoked in the grate. He could see the badly burnt body of the creature. The beast's ribs had split apart and all that was left were the charred bones.

'You should have this,' Vibica said. She stopped Jago and handed him a gold coin. 'They are very rare.'

'Henson said it was a poltergeist. Where did the creature come from?' Jago asked.

Vibica sighed, as if she wasn't sure of the answer.

'I don't think that is what it should be called. Poltergeists are creatures of spirit. That is a creature of earth. I would prefer to call it a Gohlem.'

'A what?' Jago asked.

'A Gohlem – something brought to life through the desire of another – a creature transformed,' Vibica answered. 'It was sent to kill you – quite simple.'

'Was it a man?' he asked.

'It would take a long time for a man to be transformed into a creature like that,' she mused.

'I have seen such a creature before. When I met Sagacious the Hermit,' Jago said.

45

'And he is now dead?' she asked, seeing the vision in his mind. 'How many people have you killed, Jago?'

He bowed his head as he looked at the remains of the beast in the fireplace. They were covered in dust and wood ash and looked as though they had been there for a thousand years.

'Just a Vampyre,' he answered as he turned to walk away.

'I knew Pippen Draigorian,' she said as she kept pace with him. 'He was a close friend and would often come to visit me in Lyme Regis.'

'He didn't like his life any more and begged me to kill him,' Jago answered, wanting her to know he was not a murderer.

'Was it easy?'

'Yes,' he said plainly as he pushed open the kitchen door.

The others were already eating. The large room echoed with subdued conversation. Brass pots hung from the racks on the ceiling surrounded by bundles of dried herbs. The fire crackled in the large iron stove in the corner of the room. Jago looked at the salt mark around the walls where the wave had swept through the house on the night the star had fallen into the sea. The stone floor had traces of sand across it. They gathered in the corners of the room in miniature dunes that waited to be swept away.

Hugh Morgan stood as Vibica came in.

'Did you sleep well?' he asked, smiling.

'I stayed in the drawing room. It felt safer there,' she said as she looked at Jack Henson, who was stabbing a particularly fat sausage with his knife.

'A good place,' Hugh answered. 'Your train leaves at midday. There is plenty of time. Thirty minutes to the station, that's all.'

'I was expecting to see Bartholomew Bradick. I was told he had met with a tragic accident,' Vibica said slowly as she smiled at Biatra.

'Tragic,' Henson muttered. 'Should have chosen his friends wisely.'

'Indeed,' she said as she sat at the table and pulled the plate towards her.

Jago chose the chair next to her. He watched as she took a thin piece of toasted bread from the rack and spread a meagre slice of butter upon it.

'You seem to know a lot about Whitby, Vibica,' Henson said as Jago watched her sip from the teacup.

'It is a town that has always attracted many of my kind. There was a time when we would gather at the Griffin Hotel every year. Pippen Draigorian always liked to take a party of us to see what new name had been placed on the grave in the church. He would spend hours inventing who he would be next. I came up with the name of Crispin. It suited him, don't you think?' Vibica asked.

'Death suited him better,' Henson chuntered.

'I can see I will never win you over, Mr Henson. But Vampyres are a part of the world and always will be.'

'Do you ever get bored living for ever? Are you not scared someone will find you out and kill you?' asked Biatra as she sat back in her chair, not wanting to eat.

'Just think of what you could do,' Jago answered for her. 'In many lifetimes, always young, never growing old.'

'You are beginning to sound like my father,' Hugh said,

his voice concerned. 'Eternal life came at a price. Death was never a fate my father wanted to face.'

'That's the trouble with Vampyres,' Henson added as he chewed on the gristle of the sausage and let the juices dribble down his chin. 'They all think they will live for ever, but death waits for them.'

'You are right, Mr Henson. A Vampyre never dies a natural death, but it still comes, at the intervention of someone else.' Vibica placed her cup in the centre of the saucer and pushed the handle away from her.

'So the war is a very convenient cover for all that you do,' Henson said.

'I am not sure what you mean,' Vibica answered.

'You can kill as many people as you like and blame it on the bombings.'

'I don't think that is fair, Jack,' Hugh butted in before he could say any more.

'It is true,' Vibica answered. 'Some of my kind have used the war to their advantage. The Lodge Maleficarum has tried to stop all that. It is not in our interests to be revealed. Could you imagine what it would do to the world if it were discovered we were real?'

'My father told me about the great persecution when hundreds of his friends were hunted down and killed,' Hugh said as he looked at Vibica.

'Hunted and burnt as witches,' Vibica replied in agreement, smiling at him.

'Didn't catch enough of them, if you ask me,' Henson muttered.

'We can all trace our fate to the night when your father

set out with his companions to rid the world of Strackan,' Vibica said.

'But Sibilia had set a trap for them – she was a sorceress in love with him,' Henson said, reminding them of the story.

'Have you ever thought of Dust Blood?' Jago asked her. 'You could track down the Vampyre that bit you and be free.'

'I have, but decided against it and I will save you your breath, Mr Henson. I decided against it because I am happy with who I am. Isn't that what you were going to say?'

Henson shrugged, annoyed that all his thoughts were so visible, and then smiled with a single raised brow. 'You and Biatra have something in common, being bitten by the same fiend. Perhaps we can spare you some Dust Blood when we track her down.'

'Sibilia Trevellas may not be that easy to catch,' she insisted. She was watching the pendulum of the kitchen clock swing back and forth.

'It was Sibilia who made you a Vampyre?' Biatra asked.

'It was a long time ago in another land,' Vibica answered.

An awkward silence fell on the room. It was as if no one wanted to ask the forbidden question. Jago finished his food and yawned. The night had been slow to pass and sleep was a stranger. He had listened to hour after hour of Biatra snoring – he had never known her sleep so well. She had not spoken or called out. He had watched her through the last of the dark hours and as the sun rose over the bay had known hope for the first time.

'Thought you could help me get the car ready, Jago,' Henson said, as the plates were stacked. 'Have to fill it with fuel. Hugh said there was some in the barn.'

Jago nodded and looked at Biatra.

'You coming?' he asked.

'I thought I would ask her to take me for a walk in the gardens,' Vibica said as she looked at Biatra. 'Hugh has told me that there are still fish hanging from the branches of the trees.' Vibica stood and held out her hand towards Biatra. 'I think the morning air will do us good.'

Hugh walked with them to the door of Hawks Moor and watched them as they crossed the driveway and took the steep cliff path. By the time he had returned to the kitchen, Jago and Henson were in deep exchange.

'We have no other option but to trust her,' Hugh said, breaking into the conversation. 'I know what you feel, Jack, but we have to give her a chance.'

'She is a Vampyre and they all want the same thing in the end. How do we know she isn't working for Strackan or your father? You heard her say that it was Sibilia Trevellas who took first blood.'

'I trust her,' Jago said. 'At first I wasn't sure, but now I do.'

'Beguiled, Hugh. The lad is beguiled,' Henson protested. 'It is the duty of a Vampyre to kill. Blood is what sustains them. They cannot be left to carry on. We should go after them and destroy them one by one. That is what Jago has to do.'

'I don't know if I can,' Jago said.

'You have to. You have to try,' Henson said.

'We could reason with them. I could find my father and tell him that we will leave them alone,' Hugh said as he stood by Jago. 'We could agree to peace.'

'You heard her say that there was a Vampyre hunter.'

'What of it? There have always been hunters,' Hugh said.

'Appeasement will never work. They could come looking for Biatra. She is of the line of Trevellas now and therefore is linked to Strackan himself. And if not Strackan or Sibilia then the Vampyre hunter.'

'How would he know of her?' Jago asked.

'The Maleficarum, the scroll on which the name of every Vampyre appears at first blood. I heard my father talking of it with Sibilia. It is rumoured that the scroll has been taken from where it was hidden. The name of every Vampyre is on that scroll. If it ever fell into the wrong hands they could all be traced and killed.'

'But why didn't Vibica tell us if it had been stolen?' Jago asked.

'Why should she?' Henson replied as he thought quickly. 'Perhaps it would not suit her purpose. The Lodge Maleficarum was charged with protecting the scroll. If it has been stolen . . .'

'The Vampyre hunter?' Jago asked.

'None of them will be safe. They could be hunted down – simple . . .'

Henson stopped speaking. A shadow filled the doorway. Vibica de Zoete stared at them, tears running down her face.

'So you know,' she said.

'We thought you had gone for a walk,' Hugh answered.

'I came back for my coat,' Vibica answered, her voice breaking.

'Is it true? The Maleficarum, the scroll has been taken?' Henson asked.

'On the night of the Lyrid of Saturn, Friday the 13th of September. My house was robbed and the scroll was taken.'

She paused and took a deep breath. 'It had been brought to me from London so that it could be kept safe. Only two people knew where it was. I had noticed a new name appear on the scroll – Biatra Barnes. It showed that Sibilia was her blood-mother.'

'So she is a full Vampyre and not one of Strackan's thirty-day monsters?' Henson asked.

'Biatra is a Vampyre,' she answered as Jago looked to see where his cousin was. 'Don't worry Jago, Biatra is in the garden overlooking the bay. I told her I would not be long.'

'But the scroll is just names on an old parchment. They can't find her with that,' Hugh said, as his voice rose in concern.

'The Wujing Sinan was taken also,' Vibica said as she gulped her words.

'What is that?' asked Hugh Morgan.

'*That* is a compass and scrying plate used to locate a Vampyre. The Sinan is the petrified finger of Wujing, the first Vampyre hunter. It is said that if the Sinan is placed upon any name on the scroll it will then point to the direction where that Vampyre is,' Henson said.

'You know our history well,' Vibica replied. 'It is true what you say. I tried it as a parlour game. I took a scroll, chose a name and the Sinan found the person I was looking for.'

'If the assassin has this, he can find whatever Vampyre he desires?' Hugh asked.

'I am afraid he has already started,' Vibica said as again she started to cry.

5

Toran Blaine

BIATRA WAS STILL WAITING when Jago found her in the garden. They sat for a while on the seat overlooking the bay. Neither of them spoke. The wind blew in from the sea and rustled the last of the leaves that clung to the branches. He thought how different she looked. A mouthful of blood from the creature was enough for her to have been transformed. She turned and smiled at him as her long red hair trailed over her shoulders.

'Will it always be like this?' Bia asked as she touched the back of his hand that rested on the bench. 'Life like this isn't so bad.'

'Now I know there is a cure I feel so much better,' Jago answered.

'I am not sure.' She hesitated as she spoke and Jago could see the wrinkles on her brow.

'But you want to be well?' he asked.

'I am well, Jago. Just not in the way you want me to be.'

There was inevitability in her voice. It was what he had expected. Henson had explained that once bitten, a Vampyre is reluctant to return to the world as a mortal. Biatra gripped his hand and smiled at him.

'Would you stay this way?' he asked.

'If I could find a companion . . .' she said, her eyes speaking the words that she wanted to say.

'And you would watch me grow old?' he asked.

'There is an alternative,' she whispered.

'Together?' he sighed. 'Then we would need two companions. Anyway, I don't think I have the taste for blood.'

'It comes upon you. I was surprised how easy it was,' Biatra answered, remembering how she had attacked Bradick the stationmaster and thrown him on to the track. 'It's out of your control, quite simple really.'

Jago got to his feet. She was not the same girl she had been just days before. Biatra was changing in every way. Her face looked sallow, just like Sibilia Trevellas. It was as if the venom made you look like the Vampyre that took first blood.

'They want us back at the house. Vibica is worried about a Vampyre hunter – she has to catch a train.'

Biatra studied his face for a moment.

'And I am to stay here with Henson?'

'Hugh thought it would be best. Keep out of trouble.'

'I don't trust her,' Biatra said unexpectedly.

'She'll be gone in the hour and we need never see her again,' he answered.

'I don't think so,' Bia answered with a shudder as her finger crossed her lips for him to be silent. 'She is near.'

At that moment Vibica walked through the overhang of trees that formed a long avenue back to the house. She smiled and held out her hand. The hem of her long skirt trailed on the ground. She had changed and looked brighter. The tears had been wiped away and the lips were now ruby red.

'I thought I would find you here. Talking about me?' she asked.

'Jago just said you were catching the train,' Bia answered.

'Hugh had a call from the station. There will be no more trains after this morning so I have to get there early.' Vibica turned to Biatra and took her hand. 'It has been good to meet with you. I am sure you will enjoy your new life. The strangeness will soon disappear and all will be well.'

'And so it will,' Bia answered with a half-hearted smile. 'So this is goodbye?'

'A Vampyre never says that word. Life is too long and the road too twisted to say goodbye. Until our paths cross is often a better way of parting.'

By the time they had walked back to the house, the sun was covered in cloud. Hugh Morgan stood by the door of his sedan. The engine purred and twists of smoke spiralled in the air from the exhaust pipe. Jack Henson looked on and said nothing as Vibica de Zoete got into the back seat and pulled the blanket over her legs, then smoothed the red leather with her gloved hands.

'We'll be back this afternoon,' Hugh said to Henson as he nodded to Jago to get in. 'I have to collect the supplies from Goathland and some fish from the dock.'

'Can I come?' Biatra asked, already knowing the answer.

'Best if you stay here,' Henson said as he put a hand on her shoulder.

Biatra smiled; she didn't mind. 'It's getting too bright for me. I'll wait until evening,' she said, resigned to staying in Hawks Moor until the sun had touched the horizon.

Vibica burrowed in the cavernous leather purse that hung

from her arm. 'Here,' she said, holding out a small brown case through the open window of the car. 'You'll find they will help. It eventually goes away. But sunlight takes time to get used to.'

Biatra took the case and opened it. Inside was a hand-carved pair of glasses with dark lenses.

'They're beautiful,' she said as she slipped them on her face.

'To keep – for ever,' Vibica said as she closed the car window and sat back.

'We'll be back before nightfall,' Hugh said to Henson as he got into the car and drove away.

Jago looked back. Biatra and Jack Henson watched them drive off until they were out of sight. The car cut along the lane and then turned towards Whitby, its sleek, dark lines and chrome fenders pushing through the fog that brooded in the dips and hollows along the road. Soon Jago could see the gnarled fingers of the abbey ruins. They made him think of Mrs Macarty and Streonshalgh Manor, the home for orphans where he had stayed when he came to Whitby as an evacuee from London. Hugh turned the car again. Within ten minutes they were in the centre of the town and crossing the bridge that straddled the river.

'Thought we were going to Westcliffe Station?' Jago asked as the car sped along the side of the harbour.

'The line has been bombed. Everything is going from the goods yard,' Hugh answered. The car slowed to walking pace as it pressed through the throng of people.

'Does everyone walk in the road?' Vibica asked as the car got even slower.

'Only if you're a local,' Hugh laughed.

Jago saw him look at Vibica in the rear-view mirror. She reached forward and pinched his ear with her fingernails.

'Are you going to London?' he asked as the car got near to the goods yard.

'To Lyme Regis. I change trains at York and then straight through to Exeter,' she answered.

'Is it far to Lyme Regis?' he asked, having no idea how long it would take or the distance involved.

'Far enough,' she said. 'Perhaps you both would come and visit?'

'I think this is as far as I can go. There are just too many people,' Hugh said, not listening to her as he pulled the car to the side of the road.

The crowds pushed in on them. As soon as the car stopped the road ahead filled with people. It felt as if at any moment the car would be overwhelmed by the human tide.

'What are they doing?' Jago asked.

'The battalion have been recruiting and are taking the lads with them,' he answered as he tried to open the sedan door.

'But why all the people?' Vibica asked.

'They have come to see the soldiers go to war,' he answered. 'It's a tradition.'

'I remember in the Napoleonic war it was just the same,' Vibica said as the crowds began to sing.

'We can get no further. Can you take Vibica to the platform?' Hugh asked Jago as he helped her from the back seat of the car.

Together they skirted the crowd. Vibica followed on as Jago struggled with her leather case and he pushed against the mob. Soon they had got to the entrance of the goods station. It was a tall stone building with an arched glass roof that stood by the side of the harbour, its eaves laden with disgruntled pigeons.

As Vibica looked down the long platform a man in a red robe walked up the steps of an old mounting block and asked the crowds to be silent. They listened for a few moments as he spoke of the glory of war and the sweetness of dying for 'the old country'. It made Jago shiver. He looked into the eyes of a lad not much older than himself who was dressed in an ill-fitting uniform with brass buttons. Across his shoulder was slung a long rifle with bayonet already fitted. Jago felt his fear. He turned and looked at Vibica.

'Not long for this world. The Fates have him,' she said solemnly.

War had been a thing that Jago could never make sense of. When the bombing had started in London, Jago had asked his mother why there was a war. She had told him of a madman wanting to take over the world.

'Got to stop these people – stop them before they win,' she had said as she bought apples from the market in Brick Lane and made Jago carry them home. That had been the morning they had seen the opera singer on the corner of Highgate Hill. He had stood on an old wooden box and sung as people walked by. His white hair and thin face had shone in the sunlight. No one gathered around him. It was as if his words were for the angels. 'Heard he's joined the army,' she had said as she pointed at him. 'Won't be singing like that any more . . .'

Jago felt a hand touch his. Vibica de Zoete smiled.

'I will have to be going,' she said softly. 'They have called the civilians first.'

Jago didn't know how long he had been daydreaming. 'Sorry, I –' he said.

'Yes, I know. I saw it too,' she answered. 'You must miss her.'

'More than you would know,' he answered.

Vibica leant forward and kissed him on the cheek. Her lips rested upon his skin for longer than anyone had ever kissed him before.

'There is just two years between us,' she said as she whispered to him. 'Are you sure you wouldn't . . .'

Vibica stopped as if she had heard his thought. Jago gave her the bag and stepped back. She walked away as he stood and watched.

'Not yet,' he muttered when she was near to the old train that hissed and steamed and was no more than a procession of tethered wagons.

'Then there is hope,' he heard her say without moving her lips as she turned and waved goodbye.

Jago watched as she got on to the train. The black engine shuddered on the tracks. Jago could see the brass nameplate welded to the firebox. He read the name: *Leviathan*.

Then a throng of soldiers marched in line to the train. The screaming and shouting grew louder as a brass band began to play on the harbourside. A flotilla of small boats bedecked with flags and ensigns steamed up and down the estuary. It was as if the whole town had gathered to see them go. Vibica leant out of the window of the First Class carriage and waved. Jago lifted his hand, then stopped.

There, on the platform, watching her from the shadows of a ramshackle tobacconist's booth, was Rathbone. He no longer wore the uniform of the chauffeur of Ezra Morgan, but Jago knew it was him. Across his cheek was a fresh wound that looked as though it had been made by a blade.

The crowd filled the platform and jumped on to the track surrounding the train. The steam engine roared and whistled as the mob cheered and cheered. Flags were waved, bunting wafted in the breeze. Jago looked for a way of escape.

As he looked up he suddenly realised that Rathbone was now staring at him. Jago could not contain his fear. He was trapped. The engine started to pull away. The crowd surged forward, dragging Jago along the platform closer and closer to Rathbone. It was a wave that he could not swim against. Closer and closer they took him until he was an arm's reach away.

Rathbone laughed as he saw Jago struggle against the human tide. The brass band played and the steam engine whistled and smoked as the wheels spun against steel rails.

'Jago – Jago Harker. How sweet and fitting this is,' Rathbone greeted him above the noise.

Jago felt as if he were drowning. He lost his footing and slipped, only to be dragged to his feet and pushed closer to the tobacco shack.

Rathbone reached out, his fingers getting closer as the mob surged on, chasing the train along the platform. By the side of the shack, Jago could see a small stone archway. He twisted and turned as he forced his way through the huddled mass. With one hand he reached out and took hold of the brick.

'Let me through!' he screamed at a man in a butcher's coat smeared in blood. 'I need air.'

'Lad can't breathe,' the butcher shouted as he held back the mob long enough for Jago to slip through.

A hand grabbed the back of his collar and held him for a moment.

'Don't run from your friends,' Rathbone shouted. 'Ezra Morgan wants to speak with you . . .'

Jago twisted and without thinking bit Rathbone on the wrist until he bled. The man pulled back his hand. Jago fell through the arch into to an alleyway beyond.

Crowds of people spilled from both ends of the station as the train steamed along the banks of the estuary. Jago looked up as Rathbone scrambled out through the arch.

Not knowing where he was going, Jago ran. Soon the alleyway opened out into a street. It was filled with people and the brass band played. Looking back, he could see Rathbone following: his felt hat was pulled over his brow, his long coat billowing in the wind.

Jago knew Ezra Morgan would be close by – the master was never far from his servant. He looked for Hugh and the sedan but didn't recognise the road. It was a part of Whitby he had never come to before. All the streets looked the same, terrace after terrace of high houses and freshly painted shops. Jago looked up at the far cliff and in the gap between the houses could see the church and Streonshalgh Manor.

Jago ran. He chased in and out of the alleyways, down the hill and towards the river. The mob still cheered and clapped and the band still played. The music echoed through the streets in time to the clattering of his footsteps.

It was not long before he was at the bridge. He looked to where Hugh Morgan had stopped the sedan car, but it was gone. The crowd still filled the street. Old men shouted and drank from tankards of beer. A fishing boat waited in the outer harbour for the tide. 'Quicker than I thought,' Rathbone said as he grabbed Jago by the arm and pulled him into the doorway of a sweetshop with a window filled with empty glass jars. 'But still quite easy to find.'

'Let me go, Rathbone,' Jago said as the man tightened his grip.

'Keep quiet and come with me,' Rathbone answered as he dragged Jago from the doorway and into the thinning crowd.

'I'll tell them who you are,' Jago said.

'And you think they will believe you? A lad like you in a town where I have lived all my lives?' Rathbone laughed. 'Shut it and do as I say.'

He gripped Jago even tighter, his hand crushing the skin and squeezing the bone until Jago felt his arm would burst.

'Where are you taking me?' Jago asked as Rathbone dragged him on to the bridge.

'The Curio Shop,' Rathbone answered.

'How did you know I was at the station?' Jago asked.

'A piece of luck. I was there to make sure Vibica de Zoete caught the train. We are moving away and you are coming with us,' Rathbone said.

'I want to stay here,' Jago protested.

'Whitby isn't as friendly as it used to be,' Rathbone answered. 'Too many people are paying an interest in what we are doing since –'

Rathbone stopped suddenly in the midst of the crowd.

Jago could see he was staring straight ahead, his mouth wide open. It was as if Rathbone had seen a ghost.

'Toran Blaine,' he said. His hand was shaking, his face drawn and gaunt. Jago felt the grip loosen on the sleeve of his leather jacket. In an instant Rathbone had gone.

Jago grabbed the iron lamp post and held fast. He could see Rathbone running the way they had just come.

Turning slowly, Jago saw a man standing by the doorway to the Curio Shop. His long coat trailed to the floor. The cuffs were turned back and showed the white starched shirt beneath. The man reached inside the coat with his long fingers, as if he searched for something within. Then, with deliberate steps he began to walk slowly towards Jago.

'Jago! Jago, I couldn't find you!' Hugh ran from the shadows of Grape Lane. 'Where have you been?'

'Rathbone, he caught me and there was a man,' Jago said, panicking, as he looked for the man in the long coat. 'He was there – by the Curio Shop.'

[6]

Rathbone

THE MAN WAITED in the back of the Curio Shop as the street emptied. He watched Hugh Morgan and Jago walk along Grape Lane until they were out of sight. The shopkeeper struggled to breathe; his mouth was covered in black duct-tape and he was tied to a bow-backed chair.

'This is what happens when you help Vampyres,' Toran Blaine said as he taped the man's feet to the chair's legs. 'In future I would advise against it.'

The man couldn't reply. His eyes bulged as he stared at Blaine, wondering if he would be killed.

Blaine locked the door to the shop and cleared the counter with a sweep of his arm. Taking a brass plate from his pocket, he set it on the counter. Then he opened a small leather case and with great care he took out a long bone finger tightly bound in silk. The tip of the finger with its black nail stuck out from the silk.

The shopkeeper writhed in the chair. Blaine leant over and snapped the tape from his face. The man screamed as it tore his beard.

'Checking to make sure you're not a Vampyre,' Blaine said. 'Who do you work for?'

The man appeared to be reluctant to speak. He stared at Blaine as he set the bone finger on the brass plate. The Sinan balanced on the plate as if unseen hands held it in place. Slowly it began to turn around.

'I am not a Vampyre,' the man said as the Sinan pointed out of the window.

'Then who are you the companion of?' Blaine asked.

The man didn't answer. Blaine leant back against the counter and slipped his knife from the leather scabbard that hung from his shoulder under the coat. He pulled out the blade and held it towards the man.

'Rathbone,' the man answered.

'The one I saw with the lad?'

'Jago Harker,' the man answered.

'Don't think Rathbone wanted to see me,' Blaine said as he placed the knife on the counter and took an ivory parchment case from the pocket of his coat. Slowly, he pulled the vellum from within. He looked at the names inscribed on the vellum, following them with his finger. 'Theodore Rathbone, 1823?'

'The same,' the shopkeeper answered reluctantly.

'Blood-child of Ezra Morgan?' Blaine asked, reading the words from the scroll.

'Where did you get the Maleficarum?' the shopkeeper asked.

'I stole it from someone who should know better,' he said slowly, teasing the man. 'You show a great deal of interest for a companion.'

'I was to be more than that. Theodore promised that I would be like him one day,' the shopkeeper answered.

'You would have willingly given up your life to be like them?' Blaine asked as he placed the parchment on the plate and then allowed the Sinan to rest on the name.

'What will you do to him?' the shopkeeper asked.

'Isn't that obvious?' Blaine answered. 'I am hardly likely to let him live.'

'But he will be no trouble to you. He is leaving Whitby in the hour. He was going to take me with him.'

'Since when have you trusted the word of a Vampyre?' Blaine asked.

'All my life. Theodore is my father.' The shopkeeper bowed his head. It was as if he was in some way ashamed.

Blaine ignored the man and watched as the Sinan pointed to the west. He looked at the silk-covered finger and smiled before taking the Sinan from the plate and putting it in the case.

'He's not far from here. The Sinan is quite strong,' Blaine said as he rolled the parchment and slipped it back in his coat.

'Will you kill him?' asked the shopkeeper.

'Why did he want Jago Harker?' Blaine asked, ignoring the question.

'I thought you were a Vampyre hunter,' he answered as he tried to slip his hand from the binding without being seen. 'Even you must know the name of Jago Harker.'

'The one they say will bring an end to all this?'

'Unless he gives his life and becomes –'

Blaine grabbed the man by the wrist just as his hand came free. 'What would you have done – killed me?' Blaine screamed as he pushed the man back so the chair fell to the floor. Taking the duct-tape, he wrapped it around the wrist of the man and re-bound his feet. 'I will come back and deal with you later.'

Stepping outside the Curio Shop, Blaine locked the door. He looked across the bridge to the west side of the town. Holding the case in the palm of his hand, he could feel the Sinan twitch inside. It was as if it wanted to leap free and follow Rathbone. Blaine walked on, the Sinan safe in his pocket. At every corner, he stopped, took out the case and then followed where it led.

For most of the hour, Blaine walked in and out of the back streets of the town. Then, unexpectedly, he found himself outside a crescent of houses that overlooked the harbour. It was as if Rathbone had just been ahead of him all the time.

As he passed the door of Number 9 the Sinan rattled in his pocket.

'Must be the place,' Blaine muttered to himself.

He looked down the street towards the harbour below, then he walked up the steps and rapped on the door. There was no answer. He twisted the brass handle. The door opened easily. He stepped inside. The house felt eerily empty. In every room he searched he found no one. Each room was meticulously neat, as if it had been double dusted and triple swept. The floors were freshly polished and flowers were on the mantelpiece of every room. Still, the Sinan urged him to go on.

He slowly climbed the stairs, his hand on the dagger under his coat. On the first landing was a bedroom. Blaine checked under the bed and in the wardrobe. All were empty and yet he could still feel that Rathbone was close by.

In every room there was still no sign of the Vampyre. A flight of narrow stairs led to an attic room. Blaine climbed higher. He slowly opened the door and looked within. The room was empty. There was no furniture or beds. At the far end of the room some distance away he could see a small doorway to the eaves of the house. Toran Blaine smiled.

Blaine crossed the room to the door. It suddenly burst open. Rathbone leapt towards him like a dog. Sweat poured from him as if he had been waiting fearfully for what was to come. He grabbed Blaine by the leg and tipped him back. Blaine kicked out at him, pushing Rathbone back against the wall as he drew the knife.

'Why do you persecute me, Toran Blaine?' Rathbone screamed as he got to his feet.

'It has to be done,' Blaine answered. 'It is not right to live for ever.'

'And you will kill every Vampyre?' asked Rathbone as he looked for a way of escape.

'I will not rest until you are all dead,' Blaine answered, watching his every move.

Rathbone rushed towards the window and smashed through the glass. He fell to the floor below and as he did he grabbed for the rail of the balcony. With great strength, he pulled himself on to the ledge. Inside the house, Blaine ran down the stairs as Rathbone dropped to the street.

The door to the house burst open and Blaine sprinted into the road as Rathbone ran towards the harbour. He gave chase, following him through the narrow and winding streets that fell in steps towards the quayside. Through a dark arch and a labyrinth of passageways they ran until they were near the estuary. The buildings dripped with dank and fetid water; they were connected by wooden stairways and gantries that rose above the men like a hangman's scaffold.

Rathbone ran on. Every few paces he looked back. Blaine followed, always keeping the same distance, as if it was his intention to torment him. The passageways narrowed and darkened. Rathbone was being pursued through a cavern of poverty and hardship with washing lines and ragged clothes.

Leaping from a gantry, Rathbone ran towards an archway that led to the street. A group of sailors playing dice gave no attention to the man running towards the harbour. Still Blaine kept up the pursuit. Every now and then, when he lost sight of Rathbone, he would check the Sinan and then keep up the race.

Across the river and through the town they ran, Rathbone always just ahead but not far enough to escape. This was what Blaine enjoyed and he knew there would only be one outcome.

Looking up, he saw a church at the top of the steps. Rathbone pulled on the iron railing to give him more speed. Blaine followed, knowing where the Vampyre ran.

'Predictable,' Blaine shouted as Rathbone disappeared amongst the graves that surrounded the church. 'No way out from here.'

He searched amongst the graves and read the names on every stone. Rathbone had gone. Then, just as Blaine thought he had lost the chase, he saw a patch of trodden grass at the base of the wall of the church.

The stone flag that was before him on the ground was also slightly raised, as if it had been freshly laid. Blaine slid his fingers under the stone. A door in the wall opened to reveal a long flight of stairs that descended into the darkness. He hesitated, knowing it could be a trap. Like a spider entrancing a fly, the Vampyre would always give the impression it had been overcome before it struck.

Blaine entered warily. His eyes were quickly accustomed to the darkness. Far below he could make out a glimmer of light. He followed the steps deeper and deeper. The crypt below the church was filled with wooden coffins stacked in alcoves cut from the rock. A single lamp burnt on a stone table. The flame twisted as if taken by a breeze and cast long shadows over the cobwebbed room.

'Can I help you?' an old woman asked as she stepped from a small alcove behind him.

'I am looking for someone,' Blaine answered.

'No one here. Just me, Polly Peckentree,' she said as she pulled the strings on her bonnet.

Blaine looked at the woman, wondering if Rathbone had mastered transformation. He had once seen a Vampyre do this in Paris. Everything changed but the eyes. They were just the same no matter what disguise the Vampyre metamorphosed into.

'So you didn't see a man come in before me?' he asked.

'Not a man nor a mouse,' she said as she stepped closer to him. 'I am only here because the rector asked me to clean the crypt. Having a burial next week – Crispin Draigorian. Did you know him?'

'Is there another way from this place?' Blaine asked as he moved away from the woman and watched her glance to the corner of the room behind him.

'Only the stairs into the church. But that door is locked, I have the key here.' The woman jangled the key on the end of a chain she carried around her neck. 'I can let you go that way if you want?'

The woman stepped even closer. Blaine held out his hand, seeing the mole on the end of her chin twitch. She again glanced behind him as if she checked to see if something or someone was still there. Blaine paused for a moment and listened.

'Every one of these caskets contains a Draigorian?' he asked Polly Peckentree.

'Everyone from Pippen right the way through – all those years and just these to show for it.' Her eyes glanced behind him yet again.

'And in each a corpse?' he asked.

'What's left of them,' she answered suspiciously. She seemed to sense that he knew more about Pippen Draigorian than she did.

'Very strange,' he blustered. The Sinan twitched in his pocket – Rathbone was close by. 'For I would say the only Draigorian in here would be Crispin – but then again, Pippen and Crispin are the same man.'

'Are you –?' she asked Blaine with a nervous smile.

'Surely a witch like you should be able to tell that by just looking at me.'

'You're different – you don't smell like one – or even look like one. Far too well fed and healthy. But then again, something about you makes me think . . .'

Polly Peckentree sniffed the air. 'Spent most of my life making sure the likes of you didn't get out of the grave.

71

Wrapped them in holly wands, said my charms to keep them underground.'

'Surely that was just for the *meat-walkers*?' Blaine asked.

'*Meat-walkers* – never heard anything called that before.'

'The people the Vampyres killed would live on for thirty days. Then they would be left to die and rot in the grave with only their ghosts to walk the earth. The likes of Sara Clark. Didn't she die recently hereabouts?'

Polly Peckentree stuttered her words as her hand smoothed the hairs on her chin.

'Sara was a good girl and she's keeping quiet – only screams for an hour or so every night. Surprised none of them have been to dig her up and set her free.' The woman tried to smile. She could see that Blaine studied every expression of her face. 'Have you come for her?'

'She is not the one I am seeking,' Blaine answered, aware that Rathbone was listening to everything he said. 'The one I am after is a true Vampyre and he has lived in these parts since 1823.'

'A man that age would be outside in amongst the old graves by the sea wall – not in here,' she stuttered.

'Your mother's great-uncle?' Blaine asked. 'Theodore Rathbone?'

'Someone has been telling you lies. I am a Peckentree, Polly Peckentree from a long line of Peckentrees.'

'You are a witch, as was your mother and hers before that. I know your family well,' Blaine said.

'Then what are you?' she asked. Her demeanour suddenly changed, her voice sharp and gruff like an old goat.

Rathbone stepped from the shadows. 'He's a *Recanter*,

Polly. A changeling who didn't like the life he was given. Now he thinks it's his mortal duty to rid the world of the creatures that he once was.'

By his side were two boys. Each had slicked-back hair, their faces ashen as if they had not eaten or ever seen the light of day.

'*Recanter*? Uncle Theodore?' Polly asked.

'Once bitten and twice shy? Is your name still on the Maleficarum?' Rathbone asked as the wolf-like boys prowled on either side of him. 'You see, Toran, these young lads have nothing to fear from you. They are new to the life and know nothing of Recanters or Vampyre hunters – to them you are just a vessel of fresh, living blood.'

'Then they will die in ignorance,' Blaine answered as he felt for a thin metal jar in his pocket.

'So, what is it like to be a man – a Vampyre and then a man again?' Rathbone asked as he smoothed back his hair with his long fingers.

'Do you think I had a choice in the matter?' Blaine answered.

'You gave up eternal life to be a man again. You took Dust Blood,' Rathbone said. One of the boys walked slowly and quietly to the door of the stairway to block Blaine's escape.

'I will spare all your lives if you do the same. Hand yourself back to mortality, just as it is ordained for man to live,' Blaine argued, keeping an eye on the boys and Polly Peckentree.

'I would never live that life again and you cannot make me. Staxley, Griffin – finish him!' Rathbone commanded as the boys began to growl and snarl.

Blaine took a long screw-top jar from his pocket and

73

unscrewed the lid. Just as Staxley and Griffin came closer, Blaine scattered a thousand small beads on the floor. As if mesmerised, the boys instantly dived to the ground and one by one began to pick the beads from the cracks in the floor, counting each one and putting them in neat rows.

'Leave them! Get him!' Peckentree shouted in a shrill haggard voice as she jumped up and down.

'They can't resist. Some Vampyres never do get over the urge to count every bean,' Blaine answered.

Rathbone stepped back into the shadows of the crypt.

'Someone will stop you, Blaine. Someone soon,' he said as he ran to the stairs.

Blaine pushed Polly Peckentree out of the way, snatching the key from her neck as she fell over the boys who raged as she scattered their counting.

Rathbone pulled on the gate. Realising that it had been locked, he turned.

Blaine thrust the knife deep into his chest and twisted the silver blade.

'Forgive me, Theodore,' he said as blood trickled from the mouth of the Vampyre.

'Te Deum laudamus: te Dominum confitemur,' Rathbone whispered as the life ebbed from him. His words were hardly heard above the noise of Staxley and Griffin fighting over the body of Polly Peckentree as she writhed across the floor.

He was soon dead. Toran Blaine opened the iron door of the crypt. Then, locking Staxley and Griffin within, he climbed the stairs to the church. The sound of ravenous dogs followed him.

[7]

Leviathan

VIBICA DE ZOETE sat in the First Class compartment of the lumbering steam train. As it gathered speed, the train twisted and turned along the valley that led from Whitby towards the high moor. The guard had come almost as soon as the Leviathan had left the station, greeting her with a benign smile and asking for her ticket. Without hesitation she had produced the crisp green ticket and handed it to the man. Vibica thought momentarily that his hands were far too clean for a ticket collector. She had looked him up and down and noted his polished shoes and the trousers that didn't match his rough jacket. The guard had kept his smile throughout their conversation about the weather and passing countryside. He had then shut the carriage door, looked back through the glass and walked away.

She travelled alone. The carriage was empty and yet the rest of the train was crowded with soldiers. In a strange way she had looked forward to conversation and had hoped there would have been someone to keep her company. Alas, for Vibica it was not to be. The steam train rattled on, clicking on every rail. She tried to count the number of times the wheel beneath her carriage went over a join in the track.

Every rail was sixty-six feet in length, and since the train had left Whitby she had meticulously counted four hundred and eighty clicks of the track.

'Six miles,' she sighed, unable to stop the counting as she watched a lone airplane flying in circles through the clouds.

Even when the guard had held her in conversation she had still counted. It had been something she had done throughout her existence as a Vampyre. The counting she most enjoyed were the steps from Lyme Regis beach to Poulett Manor. They were never the same on the way up as on the way down. However many times she counted them from her house to the seashore, they were always a different number.

In counting she felt comfortable and in control of all that was around her. She thought that it was perhaps a way of suppressing a desire to reveal all things secret. She often had the urge to tell complete strangers on trams and the omnibus that she was a Vampyre.

Once, on an excursion to London, a small boy had sat next to her on the train from Exeter to Paddington. He had been quiet for most of the tedious journey. At one point, when his mother had left him in her care to go to the buffet, the boy had looked at her. Vibica was sure he had glimpsed one of the long teeth that could so easily betray her.

'Are you a dog?' the child had asked as he prodded her mouth with the tip of a chewed pencil, not realising the danger he was in.

'I am a Vampyre,' she had replied.

Not knowing what such a creature was, the boy had thought it would be far more impressive if she had been some type of human hound.

'I thought she was a dog – but she said she was a Vampyre,' the boy had later said when his mother returned.

Vibica had smiled and raised her brow as the mother laughed and gave her child an adoring look.

Now the Leviathan steam-train rattled through the valley girded on either side by steep heather-clad slopes. Water gushed in brown torrents down the narrow gullies to the river that ran alongside the track. Sparse clumps of wind-beaten trees sprang out of the moor and cast long shadows between brief glimpses of the sun. Soon, clouds covered the sky and the first drops of rain began to beat down. Vibica watched the drops running down the window and tried to count them as they fell. A plane circled above the train, the sound of its engine dim against the noise of the Leviathan.

It was then that the door to the carriage opened. Vibica turned and automatically smiled. The man held out a First Class ticket as if to prove his right to be there.

'It is the only First Class carriage,' he said before taking the seat by the door. 'It has taken me all this time to walk from the far end of the train.'

The man sat quietly, pulled a newspaper from his pocket, opened it and began to read.

After two miles, Vibica spoke. 'Going far?' she asked.

'London,' he said. 'And you?'

'Exeter,' she answered, hoping he would say more.

The man had no discernable thoughts or impressions. Vibica had come across this before. For some reason there had always been certain people who kept their thoughts to themselves. Usually they had been dullards who had no opinions on life or the world, people who didn't interest her.

She even suspected some people didn't have a soul and went through life concerned only with what they would eat, their eyes cast always to the ground. But this man did not look the type. He was smartly dressed, his clothes well fashioned, his shoes crisp and well cleaned. Even his socks were made of silk. Not the kind of man who had no thoughts.

'I heard the line had been bombed. Always get nervous when I see an airplane overhead,' the man said as he lowed his paper momentarily and looked at her. 'It says that all trains terminate at Grantham. But that will not effect your journey.'

Vibica felt uncomfortable. There was something about the man that disturbed her. His face was thin and his jaw pronounced. It looked as though he had not eaten for a considerable time.

'Shall you take the bus?' she asked.

'No,' he said as he rustled the paper. 'I shall stay the night there and see what the next day shall bring.'

His mind was still silent. She tried to listen to even the slightest whisper but there was nothing.

'Have you been in Whitby on business?' she asked after more than a minute of awkward silence.

'Just passing through,' he said with a melancholic drawl. 'I had been invited to a party. Sadly it was not how I expected it to be.'

Vibica noticed he had no bag or suitcase. He could hardly have spent any time there at all.

'Do you live in London?' she asked.

'Highgate, by the cemetery,' the man offered as he folded the paper neatly and slipped it back into his coat pocket.

'I can never tell what kind of airplanes are in the sky. They are things I have not got used to,' Vibica said as she watched the airplane circle lower and lower.

'It can't be a bomber – not at this time of day,' the man answered quite cheerfully.

Without speaking, he pulled the blind across the glass window and turned the bolt so the door could not be opened.

'What are you doing?' she asked knowing something was wrong.

'I don't think there is any need for pretence,' he said as he drew a long silver-bladed knife from under his coat and held it towards her. 'You are Vibica de Zoete, aren't you?'

'Why do you ask?'

'I would hate to kill the wrong woman,' he said as he briefly glimpsed under the blind and then knocked on the glass before slipping the bolt.

'So why do you want to kill me?' Vibica asked. She looked at the blade of the knife and saw that it was fashioned to kill Vampyres.

'The man I work for believes it is now time for the Lodge Maleficarum to have a new principal.'

'But I would gladly step down if someone thinks they are better suited,' she said as she got to her feet.

The door opened. Another man dressed exactly the same as the first stepped into the carriage. They were identical in every way, like the closest of brothers, except that one was rather uglier than the other. Vibica tried to think if she knew of any Vampyre who was like this. In her mind she tried to see the scroll of the Maleficarum to remember if any name could bring their faces to life.

'Who are you? I have never seen you before. You are not one of us.'

'We are not as you,' the second man said as he locked the door. 'We have come to do a job and do it quickly. In two minutes we enter a long tunnel and when the train comes out the other end you shall not be here.'

'Am I that important that you want me dead?' Vibica asked. 'How do you know me?'

'You were followed. Quite easy, really. There aren't many woman in Whitby as beautiful as you,' the man said as he stepped forward and smoothed his hand across her cheek.

'There aren't many woman in Whitby as beautiful as you,' the other man repeated to his brother, laughing. 'Shall you do it or shall I?'

'Let us toss a coin,' the uglier of the two said, taking a silver crown from his pocket. 'Heads or tails?'

'It doesn't have to be like this,' Vibica said. 'However much you have been paid I can make it more beneficial for both of you.'

She smiled and slipped off her coat as she heard the dim rumblings of the ugly brother's mind. It proved he was at least human. The man coughed as he stepped towards her. The Leviathan rattled from side to side as it sped around the long corner approaching the tunnel, and a whistle screeched as the engine roared towards the darkness. It echoed through the canyon. Then the train shook as if an earthquake had struck and suddenly the man was thrown back against the door as the lights dimmed and flickered. He looked at his brother just as the first sound of a machine gun rattled against the ground.

There was no time to cry out, no time to react in any way. Bullets ripped through the roof of the carriage. Vibica dived to the floor and huddled in the corner. Both men stood motionless. The younger brother held his stomach as blood trickled through his fingers.

Above the train, the aircraft banked steeply. Its engine groaned as it turned. The train sped on. The man held his brother, no longer caring to kill Vibica. He gripped the man close to him.

His brother tried to smile as he panted his breaths. 'Never thought it would be like this,' he said as he slumped back.

They were his last words.

The train shuddered, and then came the sound of the Leviathan exploding. Metal ripped against stone as the bomb detonated at the mouth of the tunnel. There was a brilliant flash of light and a roar of thunder. Every carriage buckled from the track and lurched to the side. The earth leapt towards them as the windows smashed. The body of the man fell towards Vibica as she gripped the seat. The brother screamed, his eyes wide with fear. Darkness overwhelmed them all, thick and black with no hope of light. The screams of the soldiers in the other carriages echoed through the valley. The Leviathan hissed and groaned like a dying creature turned on its side at the mouth of the tunnel.

'Anyone in there?' a voice screamed from above.

A chink of light broke into the carriage. Vibica looked up. A soldier with a blackened and bloody face stared down at her as she pushed the body of the man from her.

'In here,' she answered.

The soldier reached down.

'Take my hand,' he said as he lifted her from the carriage. 'We have to get out, the bomber is coming back.'

Vibica scrambled towards him as his hand held her tightly. 'There are others,' she said. 'Two men trapped here – one is dead.'

A bright torch searched the clearing darkness.

'There's just you, that's all I can see.' The man hesitated. He looked again, the torchlight searching the compartment. 'He's done for, we have to get you out.'

'But –' Vibica looked back. The other man had gone. 'How?' she asked as she was dragged through the door.

'No time, have to get you out of here quickly.'

The soldiers helped Vibica as she crawled through the corridor that had now become a tunnel of broken glass. They reached the window and then were out on to the side of the train. The air was thick with smoke and the smell of cordite. To one side of the train, several bodies floated down the river; another hung from the branches of an oak tree like a bloodied puppet.

Above them, the bomber circled like a waiting raptor. Soon Vibica had been lowered to the ground, and the soldier took off his greatcoat and wrapped it around her.

'David Shepherd. Private 23, Green Howards,' he said as he shook her hand. 'Stay here – it's coming back.'

The sound of the bomber drew closer. Vibica looked across the side of the valley where the surviving soldiers ran for cover. Clumps of heather burnt and filled the air with columns of dark smoke. The airplane swooped down faster and faster, its engines whirring as it screamed closer. Then came the sound of the bullets. They bit into the dirt and clashed against the rock and cut into those trying to escape.

In the midst of it all Vibica saw a man whose face was covered in blood and who stood in the open. In his hand he held a pistol aimed into the sky. The bullets ripped closer and closer and yet he stood his ground, waiting to fire. The shells tore the earth all around him as he stood fast and then began to calmly fire at the aircraft.

'Come back! Come back, you coward!' the officer screamed as the bomber turned out to sea. He fired another shot, emptying his pistol defiantly.

'Going far?' Shepherd asked as they sat in the shadow of the upturned train.

'Very,' she answered. 'What do we do now?'

'They'll send another train to collect us. We won't be going any further. The tunnel took a direct hit. Great target – a train full of recruits.' He sighed. 'Cold?'

It was something Vibica never felt. It was the one sensation of being human that she really missed. Occasionally, when she had been without blood for some time, she would feel a gnawing chill run through her body, but this was nothing like touching the frost that would gather on the window of her bedroom when she was a child in Dublin.

'I have to get back to Whitby. I'll walk and meet the train on the way. It's not far.'

'But it's miles,' he said.

'Seven miles, four hundred and eighty-six yards and sixty-six feet.' She laughed. 'It was kind of you to give me your coat.'

Vibica stood and slipped the coat from her shoulders and gave it to him.

'You really walking back?' Shepherd asked. 'It's a long way.'

'You've been very kind,' Vibica answered, taking care not to look at him as she walked off along the track.

The rain had stopped and the sky cleared. After an hour she had walked three miles and seen no one. As Vibica looked back, a plume of smoke reached high into the sky. It was then that she saw a man running along the track. Instinctively she knew it was Shepherd.

Vibica waited by a disused water engine on the side of the track and waited for the soldier to catch her.

'I thought I would never find you,' he said as he gasped for breath. 'The Captain has asked me to go to Whitby – a problem with communication.'

'Then we will walk together,' Vibica de Zoete answered.

'But I don't know your name,' the soldier said as he walked closely by her side.

'Perhaps that is a good thing,' she answered. She reached out with her fingers and touched his hand. 'War is never a time to find friends.'

It was late in the day when Vibica stepped on to the platform at Whitby station. The long avenue of willow trees had given way to the tall Victorian houses by the side of the line. She was alone. News of the bombing had reached the town and many people had gathered. The relief train waited in the sidings as the stoker shovelled spade after spade of black coal into the firebox. The water hissed and steamed, waiting to be set free, as billows of bright white smoke ballooned high into the still September air.

'Are you from the Leviathan?' The station-master asked

as he came towards her, his fob watch swinging across his fat stomach and tight waistcoat.

'We were bombed,' she answered, not realising that blood smeared her mouth.

'You were injured?' he asked, offering her a freshly starched handkerchief.

Instinctively she touched her mouth.

'Just a flesh wound. I am quite well,' Vibica said, trying to cover her face so he would not see that she wasn't injured.

'And you came alone?' he asked as he took her hand to help her along the platform and through the crowds of staring people.

'Quite alone, there was no one else,' Vibica said, trying to rid her mind of any thought of the soldier.

[8]

Deceit

IN THE DINING ROOM of Hawks Moor, Jack Henson finished laying the branches of holly along the oak window ledge. He had spent the afternoon clipping the berry-clad wands covered in spiked green leaves. Then he had covered each sill throughout the house so that no window was bare. Jago had followed him from room to room, dragging the wicker basket and handing him the wands. Henson had given no explanation as to why he was so meticulous in covering the sills. He had left it to Jago to discover that for himself.

For Jago, the reason was clear. He knew that holly would ward off the Vampyre more than anything else. So much so, that Biatra had difficulty being in the room with a holly wand at the window. That afternoon, she scurried around the house trying to find a place of comfort. This had been impossible. Above every door and in all the rooms, Henson had left a wand so that the night-walkers could not enter.

'What about me?' Biatra had screamed as Henson was finishing the final window in the dining room.

'It is just for the night time,' Henson had answered, trying to smile as benignly as he could. 'We will have no more trouble.'

Each branch and twig glowed ominously as if it were on fire, and their pungent sap made Biatra wretch.

'I'll take them down in the morning,' Jago said as he held her shaking hand.

'They stink like death.' Biatra slumped in the leather chair by the fire. She breathed deeply. The heat of the flames pushed back the odious aroma and at last she had found a place of ease. 'Do you think we are in danger?'

'Ezra Morgan and Strackan himself will not stop until Jago is dead. They know what it is he can do to them,' Henson said. He was twisting a sprig of green spikes around the brass handle on the door to the garden.

Jago looked at Biatra and knew her discomfort. She looked frightened and for that moment quite human. Then, in an instant, she had fallen behind the face of the Vampyre she had now become. Her eyes glistened and her lips were blood-bloated.

'If we find Sibilia we can use the Dust Blood and Biatra will be well,' Jago said, but his voice lacked true hope.

Biatra didn't reply. The idea was a fine thing, but to become human again was not what she wanted.

'Why didn't Hugh become a Vampyre?' she asked as she poked the fire with an iron rod. 'Isn't he sick because of the curse on him?'

'I didn't see the need,' Hugh Morgan said as he entered the room carrying a silver tray from the kitchen. 'There was a time when it was considered. I was hoping that medicine would find a cure for my condition.'

'But isn't it because you are not a Vampyre that you are sick?' she asked.

87

'It is a condition of the blood. A deficiency, that is all,' Henson interrupted, wanting to end the conversation.

'It is caused by the coming together of human and Vampyre blood. As I get older it will get worse,' Hugh replied. He placed the tray of bread and meat on the table.

'And that will happen to Jago?' Biatra asked.

'To a lesser extent I would expect. Jago is a quarter Vampyre and so the bloodline is not as poisonous.'

'But it will kill him like it will kill you?' she asked coldly.

Hugh shrugged his shoulders, as if this would soften his words. He took the silver teapot in his hands and poured the first cup. With precise fingers, he took a single lump of sugar with the tongs and slowly dissolved it in the tea. He watched the grains vanish and be absorbed as if he was watching the end of his own life.

'We all die, Biatra,' Hugh said. 'It is just a question of when and how. I do not think our life is measured by its length. I hope that it is the quality of the days we live that is more important.'

'But what of the pain and suffering you will endure, does that make it all worth it?' she asked. She fidgeted in the chair as the flames singed the hem of her trousers.

'They are never strangers and are to be expected in life,' Henson said.

'Vibica de Zoete didn't seem to think that. It's not what she told me in the garden,' Biatra said.

Jago looked somewhat confused. It had always been in the back of his mind that the curse that plagued Hugh Morgan would be within him. Now her words had cut his heart and made him think of his fate. As he looked at Biatra he was aware of the deepening gulf between them. She was every-thing to him, a priceless gift that came unexpectedly and someone he now loved. But with each day that the venom changed Biatra, her heart ran cold and she thought of no one but herself.

'If you were to become a Vampyre, would the disease be beaten?' Jago asked as Hugh handed him a cup of tea.

'Like everything, it would be changed. A Vampyre can taste death but little more,' Henson said before Hugh Morgan could speak. 'Hugh has decided that it would be better for him to let the curse run its course.'

'How stupid,' Biatra answered. 'He will –'

Jago dropped the cup. The fine-bone china smashed on the wooden floor. Small rivulets of milky tea trickled into the cracks.

'I don't know what happened,' he protested. 'I saw some-thing in my mind, something terrible, coming to the house.'

'It's nothing,' Hugh said warmly, seeing the fear in his mind.

'To be expected, after all you have been through,' Henson echoed, knowing the truth.

Without warning, the old bell that hung above the outer door rattled and chimed. Hugh Morgan looked to Henson, his eyes wide, as if the coming of a visitor had just been pre-dicted.

'Who could it be at this time?' he asked as he looked at the old mantel clock that ticked away beneath the portrait of his mother.

Henson was already walking towards the door, his hand on the grip of the pistol he now carried in his coat pocket.

'Let us be wary of anyone who comes here, especially after all that has happened,' he said. He turned to glance at them before he went into the hallway.

They heard his heavy footsteps cross the stone flags. The lock turned as the key grated against the iron latch.

'*You?*' he said as the door opened and a chill of night seeped across the floor like an ebb tide. 'What business do you have here?'

'Hugh Morgan – I need to see him,' a voice said. 'And the boy. Are they here?'

Slowly, the door to the dining room opened. Jack Henson stepped inside and looked at Hugh. He gave a simple nod as if the guest had been expected.

'Toran Blaine,' Henson said, announcing the return of someone he had never wished to see again.

The man stepped into the room and looked around him. It was as if he inspected them all for a sign of weakness. His glare alighted upon Biatra as she sat by the fire.

'You must be Biatra?' he asked in words that were like a song. 'And you have encountered Sibilia Trevellas.'

'She is my ward, Toran,' Hugh answered. 'Biatra was rescued from Sibilia.'

'First blood?' Blaine asked as he took off his hat and coat and casually slipped them over the back of a chair. Hugh nodded, as if he didn't want them to understand what he had asked. 'And you – you must be Jago Harker?'

'Yes,' Jago answered. He wedged his hands into his pocket to stop them from shaking.

'Is Toran Blaine so frightening that I make you shake?' Blaine asked cheerfully, his brow creasing above his gaunt face.

'I saw you in Whitby, when Rathbone tried to kidnap me,' Jago answered, his voice shivering.

'He wasn't going to kidnap you – he was going to kill you, that's what Vampyres do,' Blaine answered. He looked at Biatra. 'Isn't that right, girl?'

Biatra cowered back in the chair. She sensed that Toran Blaine knew exactly what she felt. He glared at her like a red leopard, the locks of long hair drooping over his face.

'She is under my protection,' Hugh Morgan said as he stepped between them. 'It has been an ordeal for Biatra and we are trying to find a way of solving her problem.'

'Death or blood, either way will be hard.' Blaine didn't take his eyes from her. 'What do you want from this?'

Biatra could not reply. She was frozen to the chair as if she felt he would strike at any time. Just his presence in the room made her feel sick – her fear of him added to the pungent smell of the holly.

'I don't know,' she said meekly, hoping he wouldn't ask her anything else.

'You need to decide, and quickly. The longer you leave it, the harder it will be. It is the victim who has to take the blood from the sire and no one else. Could you do that, Biatra?'

Biatra looked at the flames and took a deep breath.

'I would be with her. We could find Sibilia and –' Jago said.

'Take her on your own?' Blaine asked. 'Have you met this woman before? She is a monster from hell.'

'Jago has encountered her and did very well. If it had not been for him then life in this world would be very different indeed,' Henson answered for Jago as he reached out and put a hand on the boy's shoulder. 'This lad is a Vampyre hunter through and through.'

'Have you killed any?' Blaine taunted. 'Been up close, have you?'

'I have seen it with my own eyes,' Henson interrupted.

'Got a taste for it, have you?' he asked as he looked closely at Jago. 'I found that once you have killed one then you want to kill them all.'

'And Rathbone?' Hugh asked. 'I take it you were the one who rescued Jago?'

'I wouldn't say that, Hugh. I was in pursuit of Rathbone – unfinished business – and young Jago was in the way.'

'So that is what you do, hunt Vampyres?' Jago asked.

'Hunting makes it sound like I am a fair man who gives them a sporting chance. In reality, Jago, I track them down and kill them mercilessly.'

'And you would help us?' Hugh asked.

'If it means tracking down Sibilia Trevellas, then I would be glad to. But I give you a warning. When you have the Dust Blood I will kill her. There are no second chances.' Blaine pulled out a chair from the table, slid it across the wooden floor and sat by the fire.

Biatra shuffled uncomfortably. Blaine watched her every move.

'What do we need to do?' Henson asked him.

'Do you *really* want to be human again?' Blaine asked her as he reached out and softly touched her face. 'I need to know. I want to help you.'

'What would happen if we didn't get the blood?" Jago asked before she could reply.

'Then your friend would remain a Vampyre,' Blaine answered.

'It is something I could live with,' Biatra moaned under her breath.

'Then . . . I would have to kill you as well.' Blaine smiled as he reached toward the fire and, taking the iron rod, smashed its tip into the embers of wood. 'There would be no choice, Biatra.'

'You can't kill every Vampyre,' Jago said.

'But I can try, Jago, I can try,' Blaine answered. He leant back in the chair and stretched out his long legs. Then he looked about the room and sighed. 'I know what you are going through. I too was once like you. It was Dust Blood that saved me. It was a reluctant decision, Biatra, but one I knew would be for the good.'

'But how long did you have the venom for?' Henson asked.

'One hundred and one years, my dear Mr Henson. It took me a long time to decide.'

'So you were a true Vampyre?' Henson asked, bewildered that the Dust Blood would work so well.

'I was attacked on a journey through Romania. The life of a Vampyre suited me and I even fell in love. We lived in every city in the world and life was good. In all we did we harmed no one. The blood was always bought at a price. Then one day she was gone and I never saw her again. I returned to Romania to a small village in the forest and found the Vampyre and took my blood. I killed him and burnt the body.' Blaine smiled. 'That was many years ago. Since then I have hunted these creatures down and will not rest until they are all dead.'

The room fell silent, except for the crackling in the fire-grate. Blaine stood by the flames and rummaged in the pockets of his jacket.

'So will you die?' Jago asked. 'You were a Vampyre for so long.'

'I expect to live out my life. I already feel the aches of life and know I have limited time for my task.' Blaine held a small pearl in his fingertips. 'This is for you, Biatra. I took it from the girl I loved. It is a pearl of great price.'

Gently, Blaine dropped the pearl into the palm of her hand; it rested softly on the skin and shone in the candlelight.

'It's beautiful,' she said, admiring the gem.

'More than you would ever know,' he answered, as if it were the keeper of a great secret. 'It was finding the stone on the morning she left that convinced me I should change. The night before she disappeared she told me of Dust Blood. She was telling me to give up my life . . . and now I tell you the same.'

Blaine spoke kindly, his voice gentle.

'Who was she?' Jago asked. 'Do you still love her?'

'Jago –' Hugh Morgan protested, as if he had gone too far.

'It's right for the lad to ask,' Blaine said. 'I will never tell her name and until I see her again I will not know if I love her or not. When she left I knew I could not live an eternal life without her. Perhaps that is love.'

Toran Blaine spoke for almost the hour. He told them of Dust Blood and the lives he had lived in a thousand places. Jago sat by the window and listened. The Vampyre hunter was outlined by the blaze of the fire. Hugh Morgan sat rigidly on the other side of the room. Jago noticed he looked tired, his eyes surrounded by dark hollows. In the time Jago had known him, his new-found father had lost weight. His crisp white shirt was baggy against his neck. A slight fold of skin creased the side of his face.

Meanwhile Blaine spoke without ceasing and the room seemed to fill with the fragrance of holly. In the chair by the fire, Biatra slept peacefully. It was as if she had returned to the girl she once was. In her slumber, there was no sign of the transformation that had taken place.

As the last candle flickered to a tiny stub in the silver candlestick, Toran Blaine looked up at the clock on the wall.

'So you will help us find Sibilia?' asked Hugh.

'I think it is best done quickly,' Blaine said. He looked at Biatra, her fist clenched around the pearl of great price. 'Winter past and guilt forgiven,' Blaine whispered, as if it were a prayer.

'So,' Jack Henson said as he rubbed his hands together, 'the chase begins? How will we find her?'

'A Vampyre like Sibilia will not be hard to track down. I developed an *understanding* with the man at the Curio Shop by the bridge. It took quite some encouragement for him to help me, but help he did. I hear there is a Conventorium near to the town?' Blaine asked.

'What did you do to Rathbone?' Hugh asked. 'He was a servant here for a long time.'

'He was a Vampyre like your father. He rests in the crypt along with an old witch.' Blaine was hoping they would ask about the death, but any such conversation was stilled by the doorbell ringing again. Hugh Morgan looked at Henson, who got to his feet.

Soon the door opened. Henson stepped inside and looked at Hugh.

'There has been an accident, the train to York has been bombed and –'

'I am sorry Hugh,' Vibica de Zoete said as she stepped into the room and Biatra woke from her sleep. 'There was nowhere else –'

She stopped speaking when she saw the man by the fire. Her eyes searched his every feature, scarcely believing what they saw. From her face, Jago could tell instantly that she knew the man. Her thoughts raced and shouted in her mind.

'This is a friend of mine,' Hugh said immediately to Toran Blaine as the killer got to his feet. 'Miss Vibica de Zoete.'

Blaine held out a hand in welcome and smiled.

'It is a pleasure to meet you, Miss Vibica,' he said as he gave a gentle bow.

'I am sure that I feel the same,' she answered cautiously.

[9]

Blood Wolves

THE CONVERSATION WENT ON into the dark hours, long after Biatra and Jago were banished to their room. Midnight chimes rang out around Hawks Moor from a succession of clocks that each told a different time. It was obvious to Jago that the presence in the house of both Toran Blaine and Vibica de Zoete was not a coincidence. For an hour he heard them arguing. Doors slammed and Jack Henson pleaded for peace as the dark hand of deceit gripped them all.

Jago watched the clock above the mantelpiece turn slowly. The hands chased one another around the dappled cherubim and seraphim painted on the ivory face. He listened to Biatra snoring. She slept peacefully yet again and it was only when the clock struck the fourth hour that she opened her eyes and looked at him.

'When did they stop arguing?' she asked, her face drawn and gaunt.

'A little while ago,' he answered as he got from the bed and walked to the window.

'She knows Blaine. I could hear it in her head. She was shocked to see him,' Biatra said. She wrapped a thick dressing gown around her shoulders and tiptoed across the floor. 'I don't like him – I think he wants to kill me.'

'But we need to find Sibilia and take her blood,' Jago answered.

'I am not sure if I want to,' Biatra replied. 'I like the way I feel, can you understand that?'

Jago opened the shuttered window and looked down into the garden. The wind-blown trees cast strange shadows across the salt scorched grass.

'If you don't take Dust Blood then he will kill you,' Jago answered. 'It's your only chance.'

'We could still run away, you have the money. We could go to your old flat in London. With Julius Cresco dead it would be safe.'

Biatra put a hand on Jago's shoulder and twisted his hair in her fingers. Jago thought of the life he had left behind but it was hard to recall the rubble-strewn streets and broken market stalls of Brick Lane – somehow these all seemed so far away, a lost country in another life.

'I need to stay near my father. I have only just found him.'

'He'll be dead soon and then we can go. I heard him talking to Henson. He said he is not well, that the porphyria has returned. Hugh didn't want you to know.'

'When?' Jago asked. 'When did you hear that?'

'It was when you got back from Whitby. They were in the kitchen. Henson said that he would try and find an old cure. Hugh told him that everything had been tried and it was just a matter of time.' Biatra stepped closer. 'I'm sure if he became a Vampyre then it would not kill him.'

'He would never do that. I know it.' Jago walked away from the window and without speaking he got dressed. His shirt felt cold against his skin.

'What are you doing?' she asked as she slipped the gown from her shoulder and let her hair fall.

Jago didn't look up.

'I am going to the beach. I want to see the sunrise,' he answered as he tied the laces on his boots and pulled the buckle tight around his waist. 'Sometimes I feel as if a curse is in this house.'

'Then let us leave and go away together,' she said, seizing upon his discontent.

'I am staying,' he snarled.

Jago finished dressing and left the room. The house was quiet and candles burnt on the mantel of the hall fireplace where embers glowed in the darkness. Jago crept across the floor so as to wake no one and pushed open the drawing-room door, expecting to see Vibica de Zoete. The room was empty. Opening the front door he was soon in the garden, looking out across the moonlit sea. The breeze blew the remnants of the summer leaves into crisp piles against the fence. Jago heard the door latch and turned.

'I had to come with you,' Biatra said apologetically. 'I am sorry, you were right. We should stay here and help Hugh. I forgot what you can feel for your father.'

Jago smiled and held out his hand.

'Perhaps there is a way,' he answered.

'I am sure of it,' she said. 'I just don't want to lose you as well. Henson said that you had the same curse as your father and you would be ill too. I don't want that, Jago.'

'And you think that if I become –'

'Yes,' she said before he could finish speaking. 'I really do.'

Biatra smiled at him. Her skin looked faded blue in the light of the moon. The shadows changed her face. Jago thought how beautiful she looked.

'There is a beach below the house,' he said as he took her hand. 'Come with me.'

They walked through the paths that led from the house through the gardens clinging to the cliff. They were strewn with dead fish and the remains of broken boats that had been washed ashore by the gigantic wave on the night of the Lyrid of Saturn. The sand paths twisted and turned as they followed the contours of the steeply falling land.

Jago held her hand. It felt cool in his grasp. He felt a stranger in such an open place. He had grown used to the high walls of the buildings in London. Wherever he now looked there was sky and sea that went on for miles and miles. Far to the south were the red embers of a burning city, casting an eerie glow on the fleeting clouds. The sound of war was far away. Here, in the bay below Hawks Moor, near to the small weathered rock island, all was still.

He jumped from the path to the beach. The fine sand crunched beneath his feet. Biatra was soon with him. Instinctively they ran like children towards the crashing waves that rolled like the manes of white horses running in the surf.

'I came here before, with my mother. We walked below the cliffs from Whitby. There is a cave just over there.' Biatra pointed back to the cliff and a dark hole just above the sand. It looked like a gaping black mouth in the blood-red cliffs of alum shale. 'It was full of driftwood.'

Jago looked back to the house high on the cliff top. He could just see the high chimneys above the tall trees. They shone silver in the moonlight and cast long shadows. A large black bird, early for the dawn, spiralled above the house.

'It's the one thing I have always wanted to do,' he said.

'What?' she asked.

'Flying. I have always wanted to fly.'

'My mother told me that is what Vampyres did. They changed and flew in through your window. Now I know that isn't true.'

She looked at Jago. He knew what she wanted to say. Biatra moved closer to him. They embraced as the edges of the sea swirled around their feet.

'I do love you,' Jago found himself saying in a whisper. 'I wish all this could change.'

From the woods came the shrill cry of a dog. It echoed through the trees and across the sand. Biatra shuddered. Jago could feel her fingers grip through his coat.

'What was that?' she asked, not wanting to turn her face as the howl came again.

'It's a dog, lost in the woods,' he said, not believing his own words.

Staring from the undergrowth were two red eyes. They pierced the darkness and moved through the trees as the creature walked towards the edge of the cliff. Jago followed them, knowing this was not an ordinary creature. 'I think we should go from here,' he said slowly.

Together they ran, and as they ran the creature stalked them from the woods. Its shadow could be seen weaving in and out of the trees where the mud had slid to the beach.

'The cave,' Biatra said. 'We could hide in the cave.'

She ran quickly, a yard ahead of Jago who struggled to keep pace.

Then whatever was in the wood had vanished. The howling was no more. A breeze rattled the trees and shook the branches of the old oak that hung over the edge of the cliff as if it were about to fall.

'Biatra,' Jago shouted, wanting her to stop running. 'I was right, it was just a dog. It's gone.'

She stopped and scanned the cliff. She could see nothing.

'Just a dog,' she echoed. 'I thought –'

'That it was another . . . poltergeist?'

'We should go, get back to the house,' Biatra said.

'It will soon be light. Do you want to wait here?'

'I want to go. I feel as if I am being watched.' Biatra shuddered as she looked towards the cliff. She was convinced that someone was looking at them from far away.

'Could be Blaine keeping an eye on us,' Jago laughed.

She sniffed the air. 'Doesn't feel like Blaine. That's the thing – since the transformation I get to know who is near me. You can sense them close by. That's not Blaine.'

Jago looked at the path from the beach. It rose steeply and twisted into the wood and disappeared under the cover of the trees. He didn't want to go back in the darkness. There were too many hiding places, too many for him to feel safe.

'We could stay in the cave. I have matches, we could light a fire and wait until morning,' Jago said as he began to walk towards the cliff.

'You know it is still there,' she said as she grabbed him by the shoulder. 'That's why you won't go back.'

'It will be better,' he argued. 'There is plenty of wood on the beach. And I have a candle stub.' He pulled a small wad of wax from his leather jacket and held it before her like a small trophy.

She looked at the tree line, in her heart knowing that something or someone was still there. 'Perhaps it would be better if we went back?'

He walked away towards the cave and didn't look back.

'Coming?' he asked stubbornly.

The woods were silent and the moonlight ebbed back and forth through the branches of the trees. It was a perfect night. Far to the east the sky brightened with a dim glow. Biatra knew in her heart that the night had passed. She breathed deeply and watched Jago walking away, kicking the sand in his frustration.

She gathered wood from above the tide line, broken boxes and dried branches. Biatra dragged them to the mouth of the cave where she could see that Jago had already lit a small fire.

'Nothing to eat,' he shouted from the darkness. 'But it is warm.'

The flames lit the darkness and danced on the roof of the cave. It went back deep into the cliff. Biatra carried two fruit boxes inside and broke them into pieces. She stacked the wood on the fire and watched the embers blow in fire-streaks towards the back of the cave.

'It's like a chimney,' she said as she watched the smoke being sucked from the fire. 'Wouldn't be surprised if it went into the cliff.'

Jago wasn't listening. He stared at the flames as if he relived a memory that he never wanted to forget. The fire burnt brightly and fragranced the cave with the scent of oranges.

'Christmas . . .' he said. 'Just like Christmas.'

'Oranges, coal and a wooden duck,' she answered, and then saw the look of wonder on his face. 'In my stocking – the first Christmas I can remember.'

'Cake and marzipan, with chocolate and hot chocolate,' he answered, smiling. 'And my mother always trying to put the decorations on the tree.'

Biatra looked at the fire and watched the flames begin to fade. Darkness was pressing in and taking the light.

'I'll get some more wood,' she said. She left the cave and looked back at Jago sat on a large rock staring at the flames.

'Warm in there?' a familiar voice asked, and a figure stepped from the shadows.

'Griffin?' Biatra asked, hoping Jago would hear her.

'And Staxley.' Griffin shuddered, his words cold and sharp. 'Unfinished business with Jago.'

'He's not here. I'm alone,' Biatra lied, hoping Jago would stay in the dark of the cave.

'How does it feel to be a blood Vampyre?' Staxley asked as he came from his hiding place.

Biatra looked at him. He was different, older, and his back was twisted. Staxley spoke as if he was sick.

'What's wrong with you?' she asked as Staxley staggered towards her, his body bent.

'Keep changing . . . don't know why,' he whispered in a dog-like voice. 'Not everyone can look like you.'

Staxley reached out to touch her. His arm was bent and twisted as if the bones spiralled within the flesh.

'Is Jago going to come out and see us?' Griffin asked, his face contorted by the large teeth that protruded from his lips.

'Not here. I'm alone,' Biatra insisted.

'Then we'll kill you and get him later,' Griffin answered. He looked at Staxley, waiting for the command.

'Just tell him to come out of the cave and it'll be over quick,' Staxley growled as spit fell from his mouth.

'No,' she insisted. 'You won't kill him.'

Griffin bristled with excitement. He scratched his face with long claw-like fingers.

'Strackan wants him dead. He wants us to do it,' Griffin said. 'Gonna boil him for stew, that's what he said – boil him for stew. We're gonna take his body back with us and eat yours.'

The blow came quickly – Staxley staggered backwards as Jago appeared from the shadows clutching an oak staff. The boy clutched his head as he sank to his knees and then fell face forward into the sand.

'Take him back to Strackan,' Jago shouted. 'Tell that old monster if he wants to kill me then he will have to do it himself.'

'Why do they want to kill Jago?' Biatra asked as Griffin edged back.

'Just said that's how it was to be. The woman was talking about a potion made from his bones. Better than blood, she said. Something has gone wrong with the blooding. Just look at Stax, he's like a monster.'

Griffin bowed his head pathetically. The knuckles of his swollen hands seemed to burst through the bloodless skin.

105

'And you?' Jago asked as Staxley groaned, unable to stand.

'Have a thirst. Can't quench it. Ate a sparrow this morning, snatched it from a tree.'

Biatra thought she could see a tear roll down his cheek. She remembered just how he was at Streonshalgh Manor. When the others had bullied and reviled her, it had been Griffin who had come to her. He had been the one who gave her hope for life in the orphanage. Now he stared at Biatra like a possessed dog, all charity bleached from his heart.

'There is a man at Hawks Moor, he could help you,' Jago said as he lowered the staff.

'Toran Blaine?' Griffin hissed as he panted his vile breath. 'Strackan knows where he is. Keeps an eye on him at all times. Don't trust him, Jago. You did me a favour back then at the Manor. Can't forget that. Don't trust him.'

Griffin convulsed as if in pain as Staxley lay on the sand, his body still. Jago looked at Biatra, who eyed Griffin like a raptor.

'We are going to leave you here,' Jago said. 'Don't follow us – understand?' Griffin nodded as if he accepted. 'If you follow us, I will kill you.'

Taking Biatra by the hand he led her into the cave, always keeping Griffin in sight until he could be seen no more.

'Where are we going?' Biatra whispered when the light of the fire had faded.

'I found a tunnel. There is a door and a torch. I think it is the way the Gladlings were brought to the house,' Jago said as he ducked low.

Biatra could see what she thought was a wardrobe wedged

against the rock face. Inside the door was a dim light that shone through the cracks in the wood. She listened to hear if they were being followed.

'Is this the place?' she asked.

Jago pulled open the door and took hold of the torchlight. 'This is the way. It's much bigger than I thought. I could see the smoke was being drawn within. It's the entrance to the tunnel.' He seemed excited. 'We better be quick,' he went on. 'They will come after us, I know it.'

'What will you do?' she asked as she looked back for one last time before the door to the wardrobe was closed behind her.

'If they come for us we will have to fight,' Jago said as he held the torch above his head.

The roof of the cave had been chiselled from the rock. A thousand pick-axes had gouged the vaulted ceiling and chipped back the walls. Spouts of water fell all around them as it drained through the stone. The rock was different here. It was white and green, so unlike the red shale of the cliff.

'How far?' she asked, as the steps grew steeper and twisted in and out of columns of rock cut by hand. 'It must have taken years to make this place.'

Her voice echoed even though it was a whisper.

'JAGO! JAGO HARKER!' came a voice from the entrance to the cave.

'Staxley,' Jago said as he pushed her to run. 'Keep going until we reach the house.'

'How do you know?' she asked.

'Trust me.'

The torchlight flickered as they ran through the cave.

Higher and higher they chased until they came to a doorway. The bolt was slid across, but Jago fumbled and pushed it back and kicked at the door until the wood splintered. It burst open as it fell from the hinges.

'The cellar,' Biatra shouted as they ran on. 'Below the house . . .'

Suddenly a scream came from behind them. Jago looked back. There, fully transformed, was Staxley. His face was blistered where the skin around his mouth had torn as the teeth of a bear had pushed through. He gripped his swollen fingers and looked into the gloom with red eyes.

'You can't get away,' he growled. 'Not from me . . .'

'Look at him,' Biatra shouted as Staxley came towards them, blood dripping from his mouth.

'The stairs, get to the stairs,' Jago screamed as he beat the flaming torch back and forth through the air to keep Staxley at bay.

'Drop it, Jago,' Staxley said as Griffin burst through the doorway and into the cellar. 'Two against you – no chance.'

Jago stood his ground and when he was sure that Biatra had got to the staircase he began to walk back.

'I gave you the chance to go. Now face the consequences,' Jago said as he held out the torch.

'We're not frightened of fire. This isn't a fairytale,' Griffin said as he prowled to the side.

It was Staxley who attacked first. Like a wolf he leapt from several yards away. Smashing the torch from Jago's hand, he knocked him to the floor. Jago got to his feet, back to the wall, fists clenched.

'No more magic?' Staxley taunted as he stepped back and

forth, eyeing where to take the first bite. 'Nothing hidden? No potion or spell?'

The torch burnt on the ground just out of reach from where Jago stood. Griffin blocked the door to the stairs that led from the cellar to the room with the painting.

'I don't need anything against you,' Jago said as he looked for a way of escape.

'Strackan will cut you up for soup and boil your bones,' Griffin slathered angrily, as if being in the presence of Staxley turned his mind.

'Then take your chance. But your real enemy is behind that door,' Jago said, pointing to the stairs.

'You can't trick me again,' Staxley said.

Jago ran to the door, pushing Griffin out of the way. The boy fell back against the burning torch.

Running as if each step would be his last, Jago took to the steps. Just as he reached the hidden room, a hand grabbed his shoulder. It crushed the bone as it pulled him back.

'DIE!' the creature said as it threw him against the wall.

Jago felt teeth rip into his leather coat. He reached out and pulled the lever that opened the doorway. The beast took hold of him by the scruff of the neck and with great strength threw him across the room. The door burst open. Jago fell into the hall and spun across the cold stone floor. He lay on his back unable to move. In the doorway he could see Griffin. The boy looked down on him. His teeth were bared, his eyes blood red like a wolf.

'It shouldn't be like this,' Griffin said as he unfurled a hand of claw-like fingers. 'DIE!' The word echoed through the house. Griffin leapt towards Jago.

Then came a sound of grating steel, as if a sword were being drawn from a rusted scabbard, and Griffin howled in agony as the blade cut through his heart. 'JAGO!'

It was his last word.

Toran Blaine stood with Vibica de Zoete at his side. In his hand was a short sword and dangling around his shoulder was a metal scabbard. Griffin lay in a pool of blood; his hand gripped the stone slab. His face was softer in death, just as Biatra remembered him on the day they had first met.

'So young,' Vibica said. 'Such a waste.'

'Looks like I am in the right place,' Blaine said as he wiped the blade on Griffin's shirt. 'You and I will get on well, Jago Harker.'

10

Funeral

HENSON WORKED most of the morning and into the late afternoon to block the tunnel beneath the house. He used the last of the gunpowder that had been hidden for centuries in the cellar, and the dull thud woke Jago from his sleep. He rolled over on the bed and looked at the wall. Staring at the intricate pattern on the wood panel, he cursed the light and the morning. In his dreaming he had forgotten who he was. It was a slumberous respite from the pain in his shoulder that now reminded him of what had happened.

Jago sat bolt upright and looked to the other bed. Biatra slept peacefully, undisturbed by the rumbling far below. Pushing back his hair, he got up from the bed and went to the window. The day was bright; the sun filled a cloudless autumn sky. Looking down, he saw Vibica and his father. They stood close to each other and his father was laughing as she spoke. The way in which she reached out and touched his hand said more than any words. She looked up as if she knew what he was thinking. Perhaps Biatra was right in saying that Vampyres knew when someone was nearby.

Vibica waved and said something in a whisper to Hugh. He put a hand on her shoulder and laughed yet again.

111

It was then that the long black limousine came around the side of the house. It was obviously American. The long hood and chrome running boards were like nothing Jago had ever seen before. As it parked under the trees, Jago could make out the letters on the trunk: *Duesenberg SJ*.

A tall man in a frock coat got out and opened the passenger door. He greeted Vibica like an old friend. Vibica looked up once more and then got in and slid across the back seat of the car. She lowered the window and held out her hand. Jago watched as Hugh kissed the ornate diamond ring on her finger. Then Vibica looked up at Jago for a last time and the car drove away, its sleek black paintwork reflecting the house as it turned the corner and followed the line of trees to the road.

As he gazed out Jago noticed a pile of earth under the oak tree and a deep hole by its side. Henson appeared from the house and walked across the drive to Hugh Morgan. He carried a bundle of holly wands that trailed behind him.

'All is done,' he said to Hugh as he dropped the bundle on the floor. 'Are you sure we just want to bury the lad here and not in Whitby?'

'There would be too many questions,' Hugh answered. 'It is best we do it this way. We can keep an eye on things.'

'We'll have Mrs Macarty asking all kinds of questions,' Henson said as he looked up and saw Jago looking down. 'We have to protect the boy, can't have him being attacked again. I don't think he's up for it.'

'It is out of our hands,' Hugh replied. 'Vibica has said that she is asking the Lodge Maleficarum to meet again. They want to speak to Jago face to face.'

'A trial, that's all it will be. And for what? What has the boy done?'

'He killed a Vampyre,' Hugh said.

'And so has Toran Blaine, but they don't want to speak to him.'

'Blaine is different. He is a Recanter. Jago is more than that. They want to meet him. I feel I must allow them,' Hugh said.

'And where will this meeting be?' Henson asked as he took the spade from behind the oak tree and began to clean the dirt from the edges of the grave.

'Hackness. At the old tower,' Hugh answered plainly.

'That is a wicked place. What has gone on there cannot be spoken of,' Henson said.

'They want to meet him. I will be there and you can come too. He will be safe.'

'Lamb to the slaughter, if you ask me. Jago amongst all those ghouls. Who's to say they don't try to take him? He's worth more dead than alive.'

'Vibica has promised him safe passage. It will just be the council of elders. I know them. They would visit my father when I was a boy.'

Hugh tried to smile. He could understand Henson's concern.

'When will this take place?' Henson asked.

'Tomorrow night. Vibica has gone to Peak House to arrange everything.'

Henson held the spade with one hand and propped himself against it. He looked at Hugh Morgan long and hard.

'Vibica . . . Rolls off the tongue easily, that name. Pretty girl, very pretty. The kind of girl you fall in love with.' Henson smiled as if he already knew what was in Hugh's heart. 'Never forget that she is a Vampyre.'

'I never will,' he answered, and he walked slowly back to the house.

It was dark when Henson dragged the cart across the driveway towards the hole in the ground. Upon the barrow was Griffin's body. It was wrapped in a double tarpaulin and bound with holly wands and an iron chain. Henson hoped that this would keep him in the grave until the fire could take hold and there would be nothing of the boy left.

Biatra had insisted that she walk with him to the graveside. The bier rolled on. Henson gripped the handle, his knuckles white, his fingers clenched around the wood bar.

'Doesn't look like Griffin,' Biatra said as Henson dumped the body into the grave and then piled the firewood upon it. 'Does he have to be wrapped in holly wands?' She looked at him in a way that seemed to ask why the body had to be burnt.

'Have to stop him coming back, Biatra. You never know if they are truly dead. Except if you cut off their heads, and then they have a habit of talking to you.' He poured the last of the petrol over the wood and stood back. 'You sure you want to see this?' he asked.

'Yes.' She nodded, and her long strands of red hair fell over her shoulders in ringlets.

Henson lit the bundle of rags wrapped around a long staff. They burnt brightly, lighting the ground around them. Then Henson threw the spear of fire into the grave, where it exploded in flames. They billowed high into the air like a thou-

114

sand faces looking down. A surge of black, acrid smoke went high into the sky. In the grave the fire crackled and spat as the wood quickly cindered.

'Jago didn't have the stomach for it,' Henson said. 'I asked him but he said he would stay inside. You're different. I knew you would want to come.'

'Just had to make sure,' she answered as the fire burnt brightly. 'I can't understand what's happening.'

Henson walked away from the fire. The dark clouds surged upwards and cloaked the branches of the oak tree so they looked as if a thousand black crows inhabited them.

'I have been waiting for this for a long time. It is as if everything I have ever wanted has come at once.' Henson spoke softly as he watched the fire burn. 'Since Jago came to Whitby I knew it was the end of all their scheming. You better beware, Biatra. The longer you stay the way you are, the harder it will be to change.'

'Hugh told us that we are going to meet the Lodge Maleficarum,' Biatra answered as she walked back to the house, convinced there was now nothing left of Griffin. 'At the old tower. My mother told me about that place.'

'Don't like the idea of it. Vibica de Zoete beguiles him. One smile from a lass like that and all sense has gone from him.'

'She is very beautiful. It would be quite understandable.'

He glanced at her, knowing that she wished to provoke him. 'Vibica de Zoete is a Vampyre,' he said, 'and Vampyres should keep to their own.'

'Do you sometimes think you're going mad?' she asked honestly. 'A few weeks ago I would have said there was no such thing as God, Vampyres and ghosts.'

'*There are more things in heaven and earth, Horatio, than are dreamt of in your philosophy*. That's what a famous man once said and I tend to believe him.'

'It's one thing believing and another to have them trying to kill you,' she answered as they got to the door of the house.

Henson looked back at the flames. 'Won't be long before we can fill in the grave and have done with him once and for all,' he said as he watched the fire burn.

'Did you see where Staxley went?' she asked.

'Back to the beach. I think he sent Griffin first, knowing there was a chance that Blaine would kill him. Can imagine him telling Strackan about how he nearly killed Jago until Toran Blaine stepped in.'

'Will he kill me?' she asked.

'Toran Blaine wants to kill every Vampyre under the sun and I know he won't rest until he has or until they kill him,' Henson answered. He took hold of the handle to the door and twisted the iron head by the ring in its teeth. 'Some say he has a house with the heads of every Vampyre he has killed on poles around the room. Best if we get the Dust Blood for you. That is what the Lodge Maleficarum will decide.'

'Where has Blaine gone? Is he coming back tonight?' Biatra asked.

'Hugh didn't think it was a good thing he stayed. Said it would be too much of a temptation for him with Vibica in the district,' Henson answered.

'They were lovers, I could tell,' she said as the door opened.

'They were many things if all the legends are true,' Henson said. He stepped across the threshold and into Hawks Moor,

116

taking a last look of the fire before he closed the door. Flames swirled from the mouth of the hole as if hell had exploded. 'Sleep well, lad,' he whispered.

Jago sat by the fire in the drawing room and sipped cocoa from a china cup. On the sofa under the window, Hugh Morgan slept. Since Vibica had left he had become quiet and had said very little. Biatra could see that his ailment progressed through him. His eyes burnt red, his lips were sore.

'Done,' she said as she stood by the door and looked into the room. 'Built the fire and there will be nothing left by morning.'

Jago didn't look up from the cup, his eyes fixed on the rising steam. 'Say farewell?' he asked.

'Made sure he was gone,' she answered.

There was a sudden and sharp knock on the front door of the house. Henson looked out of the shuttered window as he held back the worn drape.

'No car . . . Can't see a thing,' he said as Hugh woke from his sleep. 'Best you all stay here. I'll see what is to be done.'

Henson went to the door. It creaked as it opened. Before him was a small man in a long overcoat. A pork-pie hat was firmly wedged on his bald head. The man glared at him over the rim of a pair of gold spectacles.

'Saw the fire from the road,' the man said. 'Came to see if you were safe.'

'Very safe, and thank you,' Henson answered as he wondered how the man had got to the house.

'Parked up the lane,' the man answered without being asked. 'Inspector Kaine, Civil Police.' The Inspector peered inside the house. 'Funny thing, was on my way here anyway.

There's been a . . .' He paused and tried to sound suitably sombre. It was difficult, and his voice whined with every breath. 'There's been a murder. I was wondering if I could speak with Mr Hugh Morgan?' The man reached into his pocket and held out his identity card. 'I am who I am. You can ring the station and check if you like. But I assure you they will confirm I am a genuine police officer.'

The man spoke with concern, giving the impression that many had doubted his identity before.

Henson stepped aside as Kaine slipped his card back into his jacket.

'Hugh Morgan is resting. I will see if he is free,'

'He is free at the moment.' Kaine laughed as he stood by the fireplace and unbuttoned his shabby and threadbare overcoat. It was far too big for him and trailed on the floor. Slithers of slug-silver covered the sleeve cuffs.

'I hear that you want to see me?' Hugh said as he stepped from the drawing room.

The Inspector eyed him warily. 'A body was found in Hagg Woods. Do you know the place by the railway line?' Hugh nodded. 'It would seem that whoever was responsible for the death had connections with this house.'

'How?' Henson asked.

The Inspector looked at him doubtfully as he rummaged in his pocket. 'I take it this belongs to you?' he said. He showed them a large silver ring with the Morgan crest upon it.

'A napkin holder?' Henson asked.

'It was taken some years ago,' Hugh said abruptly. 'I remember it. My mother reported it to the police. Taken by a disgruntled maid, we think.'

'And your mother is here?' Kaine asked warily.

'She died some time ago,' Hugh answered.

'I'm sorry. I am new to these parts. The Metropolitan Police sent me here only last week. I can't think what I am being punished for, coming this far north and so far away from civilisation.'

'It is quite magnificent when you get used to it,' Henson muttered.

'The other thing . . .' The Inspector chortled, obviously quite excited by what he was about to say next. 'A woman was seen coming from the platform and asking for a taxi to Hawks Moor. She fits the description of the last person to see the man before he was killed.'

'There are other houses near to here. I don't know of any woman who came to the house,' Henson said as he looked at Hugh with eyes that told him to be quiet. 'What was this woman like?'

'Well dressed and spoke in a southern accent. That's all I know. I have spoken to the taxi driver and he is adamant he brought the woman here.' The Inspector's ears twitched on the side of his stout bald head.

'There is no one here like that. You are free to search the house,' Hugh answered as he tried to smile.

'I don't think so,' the Inspector replied. 'I will take your word for it.'

'How did the man die?' Henson asked.

'Not a pleasant way to be murdered, having your throat torn out. Coroner suspects it was a dog. But then again, dogs don't drop napkin rings.'

Inspector Kaine turned to go. His shoes squeaked as he

119

crossed the room. Henson opened the door and let in the night. The fire in the pit still burnt brightly. The flames cast long shadows across the driveway.

'Far to walk?' he asked the Inspector as the man reached into his pockets and pulled out a pair of leather gloves.

'Just along the driveway. Didn't want to disturb you with the engine.' Kaine walked down the steps. 'What is in the fire?' he asked.

'A dog,' Henson answered without a flicker of emotion, his face still and sombre. 'It was worrying the lambs so it was killed. Thought it best to burn it. Could be moon-mad and we can't have that spreading.'

'Exactly,' the Inspector answered as he slipped the gloves over his stubby fingers. 'Far too many cases of moon-madness in Whitby. Burning is the best way to stamp it out.' The man raised an eyebrow under the rim of his trilby hat. Nodding to Henson, he strolled like an automaton along the drive to the open gates of Hawks Moor. 'One more thing,' he said, turning to Henson a few paces behind. 'If you do any more burning, make sure it is done in daytime. That way it can't be seen.'

Inspector Kaine strolled into the night. He was soon consumed by the shadows of the trees. Henson waited until he heard the sound of a car engine. The gears crunched as it turned, its dim lights casting a feeble glow along the road.

'Is he . . .?' Henson asked as Blaine stepped from the gloomy cover of a rhododendron.

'Not him, but someone in the car he is driving,' Blaine answered.

'You have the Sinan?'

'The Vampyre compass?' Blaine asked as he held out his hand to reveal the silk-covered bone finger resting in his palm. 'Look how the Sinan writhes as the Vampyre speeds away.'

'So does Inspector Kaine work for Ezra Morgan?' Henson asked as he watched the Sinan point to where the lights of the car shone against the hillside.

'Possibly.'

'So it was you who stole the Maleficarum and the Sinan from Vibica de Zoete?'

'You could say that.' Blaine laughed as he wrapped the numinous finger and hid it in the box.

'And was she the one who –' Henson stopped short.

'I loved her, Jack. She was a beautiful woman. I gave myself readily. When she knew how unhappy I had become she told me of the secret of Dust Blood. I hadn't seen her for many years until yesterday.'

'So how did you know she had the Maleficarum?'

'I killed a Vampyre in Prague. Before he died I forced him to tell me everything. He mentioned a beautiful woman who owned a house in Lyme Regis. I had lived with her at Poulett Manor. If you know Vibica, you will understand she is a creature of habit. The Sinan and the scroll were not hard to find.'

11

Lodge Maleficarum

JAGO SPENT THE DAY pacing the boards of the corridor in the attic of Hawks Moor. It was a quiet place, dark and warm. The slit windows at each end lighted the narrow passageway. It made him think he was inside a tall castle, safe from the enemy outside. It was also the only place to be away from Biatra.

She had spent the morning telling him how well she felt, but Jago knew she was trying to convince him. Since Henson had returned to the house the night before, after the visit of Inspector Kaine, she had been on edge. Hugh had told them that they would travel to Hackness and the circle of stones surround by small trees on the high ridge. There they would again see Vibica de Zoete. Now, as night approached and the time for leaving Hawks Moor drew closer, he could hear the sound of gulls as they scraped on the roof. It reminded him of the sound the pigeons made as they pecked against the window of his apartment in London. Jago would watch them as they strutted back and forth along the narrow ledge outside his room, tapping at the glass.

'Jago,' Hugh Morgan shouted. 'It's time to go.'

The words echoed up from the landing below. Jago gripped the wool hook that stuck out from the wall and looked down the spiral staircase.

'Will be there,' he shouted back, hoping that the minutes would drag and fearing what was to come.

As he got to the hallway, Biatra was standing by the fireplace. Her face was blushed, her cheeks ruby red with excitement.

'Henson has the car ready,' she said as she held her hands together and twisted on her heels. 'It will take an hour, Henson said. Hackness is quite a way. I saw the signpost once when I took the bus to Scarborough.'

Jago looked at her and smiled. Her long red hair was tied back into a tight knot at the back of her head, and she looked like a boy in her tweed pants and tight coat. He could see a trace of lipstick. It had become more evident since she had met Vibica. It reminded him of the woman who would stand on the corner of Mile End in laddered stockings and a fur coat.

'You going?' Jago asked, not knowing what else to say.

'Hugh said that I should. He didn't want to leave me here alone.'

The door opened. Henson looked in.

'All ready,' he said. He nodded his head as if to ask them to follow quickly.

The tall clock in the corner stuck the quarter hour. It rang out like a shrill bird calling out to an empty world.

As they left the house, Hugh Morgan locked the door and slipped the large iron key into his pocket. Jago watched him from the car as he checked the door again. Hugh walked slowly, his leg dragging with each step. His face looked as though he was in pain.

'Right,' Hugh said as he sat in the front seat next to Henson. 'You know the way?'

Henson half-coughed, half-laughed. 'Hackness? Should be able to find it.'

The road to the south crept back and forth up the hill from the bay to the top of the moor. In the gathering darkness, the sedan went slowly. Looking back, Jago could see the full moon rising from the sea. For a few moments it sat on the water like a blood-red orb. It looked as big as the world, and then as it climbed in the sky grew smaller with every minute.

Soon, they were crossing the moor and travelling south. Every now and then, the stumps of broken-down road signs stuck from the verges. They had been chopped down at the outbreak of war to confuse an invading army.

Jago counted them as they passed by. Biatra sat next to him on the wide leather seat. Her eyes were tightly shut, a soft smile on her face. She never spoke and yet her hands twitched as she tapped her fingers against the seat.

The long shadows of the distant hills soon came into view. They were outlined by the silver streaks of moonlight breaking through the clouds that had blown in quickly from the barren western moors. Henson turned the car towards the hills and followed a long narrow track deeper into the woods. The night grew darker until Jago could no longer see the moon. A canopy of tall trees covered the road, shading it from the night. Henson slowed as if looking for a sign.

'There,' Hugh said as he pointed to the carcass of a sheep lying at a crossroads. 'Turn left here.'

Henson turned the car on to a narrower road. The trees grew thicker, the crown of branches lower than before.

'Are you sure we are doing the right thing?' Henson asked

as he leant across the steering wheel to peer through the windshield. 'They could double-cross us both and then what would we do?'

'Vibica promised,' Hugh replied. 'She will keep her word.'

'Strange that they want to see Jago,' Henson said as he slowed the car until it crawled along the road.

'Over there, by the Rolls-Royce,' Hugh replied.

Just ahead, under the cover of the trees was a gleaming black car. A grey-suited driver sat in the front. Two men were close by. They covered their eyes to shield them from the light as Henson stopped the car.

'Bodyguards – so *he* is here?' Henson asked.

'Vibica said he would be,' Hugh answered. 'Drove from London.'

'Then it would appear to be true,' Henson said.

'He visited Hawks Moor when I was younger. He would sing for my mother. After a while he never came to the house again.'

'Who is here?' Jago asked as Henson opened the car door.

'Kinross,' Henson said as he got out of the car. 'The Prime Minister.'

'Singing Kinross?' Biatra asked. 'My mother had all his records.'

'From crooner to politician,' Henson sneered as he slammed the door.

'And he is a Vampyre?' Biatra asked as she slid from the car.

'Be careful, Jago. Kinross is a dangerous man,' Hugh said as he turned and looked at him.

Jago slipped from the car. Henson had gone ahead along a narrow grove of trees lit with candles that hung in tin cans. They walked in a line along the narrow path, Hugh far behind. The path turned and led up a small hill with steps cut from the earth. Jago stopped and waited for Hugh Morgan.

'You okay?' he asked as his father turned the path.

'Just slow tonight.' Hugh squeezed his shoulder.

'Porphyria?'

'It sometimes gets like this. I will be fine,' he answered.

Jago could tell that his father was lying. Dark purple rings burnt deep around his eyes and the skin stretched over the bones of his face. Far away he heard music. It danced through the trees as if each note was a bird in flight. At first it was hard to hear what tune was being played but then, as they walked closer, Jago could hear the words of a song. The recorded voice of Kinross barked from the speaker of a gramophone as the thick needle ploughed the shellac grooves.

'Likes the sound of his own voice,' Henson muttered. 'Face on every poster in every town, and come to the middle of nowhere you still can't get away from him.'

A tall man stepped from the trees and barred their way.

'Hugh Morgan?' he asked, his accent foreign.

'No – that is Hugh Morgan,' Henson said as he pointed behind. 'I'm Henson.'

'Then, Mr Henson, you will have to wait here. No one else is allowed into the grove other than Hugh Morgan and the children.'

Biatra did not like to be called a child. Henson bristled for a moment and then realised that it would be futile to argue. The bulge in the man's jacket was obviously the butt of a pistol.

'As long as you keep me company,' Henson laughed.

The man shrugged.

'Follow the path along the ridge and through the stone pillars. Wait and they will soon be with you.'

He pointed along a dark path with little but the moon to light the way. There was a frost on the grass all around. The leaves were crisp beneath their feet, each vein outlined with a white thread. Strangely, it was colder in this place than in any other part of the wood. Jago looked back. Henson waved.

'Don't worry,' he said with a flourish of his hand. 'I will still be here.'

Jago didn't want to go on without him. Henson was wise and different from any other man he had met, other than Julius Cresco.

'We'll see them soon,' Biatra whispered as she led on, a pace to the front of them. 'I never thought Noel Kinross was –' Biatra stopped, her voice hushed. The thought of the Prime Minster suddenly ripped from her mind. Just as she turned the corner ahead of them she was rooted to the ground. 'Look!'

Jago stared at the avenue of trees that led from the wood across an open patch of moorland. At the far end, a hundred feet away, was a small mound surrounded by trees. Each tree was laden with silver light. The moon shone on the autumn frost and glistened in silver diamonds. The purple flowers of the heather were shrouded in a low mist that made the mound appear to rise out of the clouds. Within the thick mass of trees, Jago could see the flickering of small candles. At the end of the avenue were the two stone pillars.

'Shall I go first?' Hugh asked, stepping ahead of them.

He walked boldly, his leg suddenly stronger.

Jago looked back. He couldn't see Henson.

'Beautiful,' Biatra said over and over as if a prayer.

'What do we say?' Jago asked.

'Wait for them to ask you the questions,' Hugh replied as they reached the stone sentinels that had stood there longer than Strackan had walked the earth.

Several turf steps were cut into the mound. The trees pressed in around them so that they could not see far ahead. Suddenly the path opened up beneath a canopy of branches like the vaulted heights of a vast cathedral. In the centre of the grove were the standing stones, seven tall megaliths reaching from the ground defiantly. Each gigantic rock cut by a thousand hands looked as though it were a sleeping beast. Around the base of every stone was wrapped a girdle of profuse ivy, growing from the earth and clinging to the stones as if to stop them from rising up. The ivy's twisted and gnarled thongs were like the wizened fingers of dead men.

In front of each stone was a large wooden chair that looked as if it too had grown from the earth. Jago could see three cowl-clad figures. They sat motionless in their thrones. Each had a hood covering their head and their hands were wrapped inside their cloaks.

Hugh Morgan walked to the centre of the grove. Biatra and Jago stood at his side. Around them the seven stone pillars formed a perfect circle.

'It was good of you to come,' an old man said as he pulled back his hood and revealed his face. 'My name is Aquinas. I am the keeper of the scroll.'

128

Hugh Morgan bowed his head. 'My father mentioned you and all your great work,' he said as he held out his hand as if to introduce Jago.

'Jago Harker,' Aquinas said as he looked closely at him. 'There is a look of a Morgan about you.' The two other figures removed their hoods. Jago looked at them one by one. 'Pardon my manners, Jago. On my right is Medea and on my left is Frankell. We are waiting for Vibica and Noel Kinross. They should not be long.'

Medea smiled at Jago. She looked as young as Vibica. Her hair was long and raven black. It framed a porcelain face starved of blood and like Vibica's; her lips were covered in rouge.

'I thought you would be much smaller,' she said with a wry smile. 'Just not how Vibica had described you.'

Jago looked away to avoid the cold stare of her ancient eyes.

'We would like to know exactly why we are here,' Hugh asked.

'That, my dear Hugh, will now be answered,' a tall man said as he walked from the trees into the grove and the stone circle, followed by Vibica de Zoete. 'Now we are all here, the gathering can begin its business.'

Jago knew the face well. It was on every war poster in the country. In person Kinross looked much younger than he did on the faded poster on the billboard outside Jago's apartment. He was also taller, thinner and with more hair, though his thin features and high forehead were beginning to line. The voice was just the same as he had heard on the radio at the outbreak of war. A long cloak covered a hand-made suit the same colour as the hint of make-up that tinted his eyes.

'So why are we here? Vibica was quite vague,' Hugh said.

'We have to be certain. There are rumours about the boy. Our kind is in crisis. As you know, the scroll of the Malefi-carum has been stolen and one man is killing Vampyres. If all had gone to plan at the Lyrid of Saturn then we would not be in this place.'

'What do you suggest?' Hugh asked.

'We need an answer,' Aquinas butted in. 'We have to know his intentions.'

Medea watched as Jago stared at the empty thrones.

'He wants to know who is missing. He has an enquiring mind,' she laughed.

'He should know very well who is missing,' Kinross hissed. 'After all, Toran Blaine killed Verzenzi and Jago killed Drai-gorian.'

'Draigorian asked me to. He was killing himself by not drinking blood and he'd had enough of eternal life,' Jago snarled. 'He wanted to die. It was the right thing.'

'So you took a silver knife and killed him?' Medea asked as she smiled at him.

'He gave me the knife,' Jago answered.

'And you plunged it in Strackan's neck?' Kinross asked.

'He was going to kill me. I was doing what was right.'

'Jago doesn't understand the things of your world,' Hugh argued.

'*Our* world, Hugh,' Vibica snapped. 'Are you forgetting you are half a Vampyre?'

It was the first time that Jago had heard her speak like that.

She threw back the hood of her cowl to reveal her face.

'And what of the girl? Who will take care of her?' Aquinas asked churlishly.

'I will,' Jago answered as he stepped forward. 'She will always be with me.'

'But she needs to know our ways. A mortal cannot teach her that,' Frankell muttered as he rubbed his beard.

'Dust Blood,' Jago shouted.

The circle was silent. The mist rolled in from the wood and filled the earth between the standing stones. Kinross folded his arms and stared at Jago.

'She is of the bloodline of Sibilia Trevellas. She is a woman who shuns the Lodge Maleficarum. She will not give you her blood easily, boy,' Kinross bickered.

'I don't intend to ask her permission. I will kill her if I have to,' Jago answered as he stood his ground.

Medea looked at him, her eyes searching his soul. 'Jago Harker is an enemy, with a heart that will never change,' she whispered.

'Is that what you are?' Kinross asked. 'I am a powerful man and can have your life stopped at a moment's notice.'

'Noel, please,' Hugh urged him. 'Jago and Biatra are in my care. What has happened has been a trauma to them both. Give us time, please.'

Kinross looked at the two empty thrones.

'I have very few real friends,' he said slowly, the mist swirling about him. 'I loved both Draigorian and Verzenzi as brothers. When this war was over I would have disappeared and started my life again. Verzenzi was to be with me and now he is dead.'

131

'Jago didn't kill him,' Hugh said as he put his arm around his son. 'This is my child. He is not your enemy.'

Hugh stared at Vibica, hoping she would know his heart. She looked at him for the while as Kinross regained his breath.

'I will vouch for them all,' Vibica said. 'Let me be with them and stay at Hawks Moor. They must have safe passage.'

'How can we protect them from Strackan and Sibilia Trevellas?' Aquinas asked.

'We can't, but I will be there to help them,' Vibica answered.

'I will go with you,' Medea said as she smiled at Jago and stepped towards him.

'It would not be safe,' Frankell replied as he held the hand of the girl. 'Toran Blaine knows who you are.'

'Toran Blaine knows us all and he has the Maleficarum and the Sinan. He would surely kill you,' Kinross said.

'Then why won't he kill *her*?' Medea growled at Vibica de Zoete.

'Love will not kill itself,' Aquinas said. He stood from his serpent-entwined chair and pulled the cowl upon his head. 'Love protects her from death. Perhaps when he has killed us all then she may be in danger. But Toran Blaine would rather lock her in a gilded cage like an old canary and give her *his* blood than end her life.'

'You may have safe passage from this place, Jago Harker,' Kinross said. 'On the condition that by the next full moon we meet again and you must decide if you will become one with us. A house divided cannot stand, Jago. A house divided.'

'But I won't give my son to be a Vampyre,' Hugh said as he held him close.

'It is what he was born for and you have no say in this,' Aquinas answered as he walked towards him. 'In that month, we charge you with finding the Maleficarum and the Sinan and bringing them here. The balance has to be maintained.'

'Do this for us and we will save your friend. I will get the blood you need and she will be free,' Kinross said as he walked away from the grove.

'But I don't want that from you,' Biatra shouted as he disappeared into the trees.

'Then stay as you are, child,' Aquinas said. 'Age will not weary you. Look at Medea. A girl of nineteen and yet she has lived longer than us all.'

'We will talk of all this at Hawks Moor. The moon has passed across the sky and we must go,' Vibica said taking Biatra by the hand.

Medea grabbed Jago's arm before he could walk away. He could feel her cold breath on his face. Her eyes stared at him as if they would never let him leave.

'If you change your mind and want to become one with us, it would be an honour . . .' she whispered as she licked her finger and rubbed it across his skin.

'This is not the place Medea,' Vibica snarled.

'You can't have everyone, Vibica,' Medea answered as she sensed jealousy on her tongue. 'Surely Toran Blaine is enough for you?'

[12]

Porphyria

JACK HENSON LIT THE CANDLES on the long table and then wiped the dust from the mantel of the fire. He could tell that the room had not been used for many years. The drapes that covered the window were threadbare and moth-eaten. He dare not even touch them for fear they would crumble. Hugh had told him that the last time the room had been used was the night before his mother had been killed. Since then it had been locked tight, the door bolted so that no one could enter.

After Vibica de Zoete had driven back with them from Hackness the night before, everything in the house had begun to change. The upper dining room that looked out from the galleried windows of the first floor had been opened, the table dusted and floor swept. Hugh Morgan had called in several old women from the village to clean and sweep as Vibica marched around the house giving them orders. He had even employed a cook from Whitby to live in and prepare all the food. Suddenly, Hawks Moor had come alive. It was like a beast that had woken from a long and troublesome sleep.

Vibica had brought with her much joy. It had started as

the car left the wood in Hackness. She had held hands with Biatra and sang songs until the girl had fallen asleep. Then she had recounted her travels around the world, telling of moguls and kings and of picking fossils from the beach below her house in Lyme Regis. But the greatest change was to Hugh Morgan. He smiled constantly, with eyes that followed Vibica's every move. She could change his heart and rid him of the stubborn black-dog moods that would often come upon him. In just those few hours, Henson could see that Hugh was a different man. He had watched as Vibica, Hugh and Jago had stood on the upper landing looking down to the hallway and had thought how much they looked like a family.

'Just the plates and then we can eat,' Vibica said as she came into the dining room carrying a long silver dish. 'I am so glad that you are here, Jack. I take great comfort from that.'

'Perhaps it is a good thing that we are both here,' Henson replied as he snuffed out the candle lighter. 'These are dangerous times.'

'Hugh told me that you don't like my kind,' she said as she reached across the table and straightened the knives and forks.

'It goes back a long way,' he said, knowing she could understand whatever he thought.

'Your wife and child?' she asked. 'It must be so hard.'

'It's what you do, isn't it? Kill people?' Henson answered.

'Yes,' she said without remorse.

'We had an Inspector Kaine here the other night asking about you. He said a body had been found on the railway with its throat torn out. Didn't Hugh tell you that?'

'It must have escaped his mind. Why did the Inspector want to see me?' she said nervously.

'Told us that a woman had been seen coming from the track and got a taxi here from Whitby. Later they had found a body. Was it you that killed the soldier?' Henson asked.

'Yes.' Vibica spoke softly as she rolled the napkins. 'It was an unfortunate mistake. I couldn't help myself.'

'Then promise me that you will try not to make any more *unfortunate mistakes* whilst you are living here,' Henson said.

'Did you tell the Inspector who I was?' she asked.

'No. Hugh lied for you,' Henson answered. 'He had another of your kind in the car with him. I suspect he works for Ezra Morgan.'

'More food,' Biatra said as she walked into the room. 'This is amazing,' she went on as she looked at the vaulted wooden ceiling with its brightly painted panels of animal heads. 'Why did they keep this place locked up?'

'Sometimes it is easier to lock away a thing that hurts you until the time is right to visit it again,' Vibica answered. 'It had too many memories of the death of Hugh's mother.'

Biatra sighed – so much food and no appetite to eat.

'I have forgotten what my mother looked like. I just don't have those memories any more.'

'But you will have new ones. I was just the same. It was as if my old life had never existed,' Vibica said.

'Old life?' Hugh asked as he and Jago carried in the final dishes. 'We have a life together, Biatra. All will be well.'

Jago looked at his father and wondered how four words could be so far from the truth. Though his mood had grown lighter the dark rings under Hugh's bloodshot eyes had grown

136

deeper. He had taken step after breathless step along the passageway, trying not to let Jago see he was in so much pain.

Vibica looked at Jago. He could feel her concern for his father. It was as if the porphyria had no power if it was not spoken of, and to give it a name was to give it life.

'Then we shall eat,' Vibica said as she lifted the glass in front of her. 'To a new life.'

They all drank and then took their seats. The fire burnt brightly in the grate as they talked. Hugh Morgan laughed and as the embers faded he reached out and touched the hand of Vibica de Zoete. He had not meant to, but in that moment it had happened and he would not have changed it. Vibica seemed distracted, as if she was listening to another conversation far away.

'And what will you do, Jago?' Henson asked. 'You have a moon to decide and it affects us all.'

'I haven't thought,' he answered honestly.

'It is too much for Jago to think about at this time,' Vibica said as she pulled her hand away from Hugh. 'I will speak to Noel Kinross and see if we can come to an arrangement.'

It was then that four loud footsteps clattered across the floor in the room above. Hugh looked at Jack Henson with questioning eyes. Biatra sat bolt upright and shivered as if she had heard the walking of a ghost.

'Visitors?' Vibica asked. 'Are you expecting anyone?

Henson got to his feet and went to the door. Hugh tried to follow.

'Stay here, Hugh,' Henson said. 'I think it best if I go alone.'

'I will come with you,' Jago said as he leapt to his feet.

Before they could leave the room, the footsteps continued. They seemed to walk from the room above through the wall of the dining room. It sounded as if someone was climbing down a ladder hidden with the wall. Jago followed their path with his eyes and watched small particles of dust fall from the ceiling. Biatra clung to the chair as the candles flickered. The room was still as they all waited.

'What is it?' she whispered fearfully.

'We will soon find out,' Hugh murmured as Vibica de Zoete got up from her chair and waited.

There was a sudden click of the hidden latch of the oak panel in the wall. A small door opened. A hand crept around the edge as a dark figure stepped from within.

'Toran Blaine,' Vibica sighed. 'The Vampyre hunter himself.'

'Not a very safe house, Hugh,' Blaine answered. 'I climbed the wisteria and then on to the roof. I soon found the passageway from the attic rooms and lo and behold I am here.'

'Most people use the door,' Henson scoffed as Blaine sat in his chair at the table.

'Too traditional for me. Anyway, I wanted to make sure there was no one else in the house but us,' he answered as he rummaged in his pocket.

From within a silk handkerchief, Blaine took the brass plate and the Sinan and placed them on the table. Vibica shuddered.

'Is that the Vampyre compass?' Jago asked.

'It truly is the Sinan,' Blaine answered as he pushed it towards Jago. 'Take a look, lad. It is an incredible device.'

Jago looked at the brass plate with its intricate designs and

138

strange markings. The silk-clad finger rested upon it in its lacquered box.

'How does it work?' he asked.

'You take the Sinan out of the box and place it on the plate. You either say the name of the Vampyre you seek or place the finger on the Maleficarum. That way you can find a Vampyre you seek or discover if there are any near to you,' Vibica answered. 'It was stolen from me.'

'I didn't realise you could just say the name of the Vampyre that you seek, very interesting,' Blaine said as he took the Sinan from the box and placed it on the brass plate.

'You should have asked when you broke into my house,' she answered, her words snakelike and venomous.

'I hear that Noel Kinross has asked you to deliver them to him in time for the next full moon,' Blaine said to Jago, ignoring everyone else gathered around the table.

'How do you know that?' Vibica asked. 'That has not been spoken of outside this house.'

'Walls have ears and Vampyres lose their heads,' he said as he pushed back his chair from the table and crossed his legs. 'Oliver Frankell couldn't wait to tell me. We met on the road in the early hours of the morning.'

Vibica at once saw his rapid thoughts and perceived what had happened. In her mind she saw a car pull in to the lay-by on the deserted moor road. Blaine lay on the ground as if dead. Frankell rushed from the driver's seat across the wet road and turned the body over. Blaine struck quickly, wounding the Vampyre with his knife and then walking him back to the car. It had been there that he had questioned Frankell, offering him his freedom for the information about the meeting with Kinross. Frankell had pleaded for his life. He told Blaine about the moon-pledge. In return, Blaine had taped his hands to the steering wheel and told him to travel on and not to mention ever seeing him. As the car had driven slowly away, Blaine had dropped a grenade into the open window of the car and then counted the seconds. He turned his back as he heard Frankell's helpless screams.

The explosion was the last thing Blaine allowed her to see. Vibica sat back in her chair and cried.

'What is it, Vibica?' Hugh asked.

'He murdered him. Murdered him,' she said again and again. 'I saw it in his mind.'

'Is this true?' Hugh asked angrily as he coughed back blood from his lungs.

'Of course it is, that is what I do,' Blaine said in a matter-of-fact way.

'Then you will have to leave this place. I cannot have you here with Biatra and Vibica – what will you do to them?'

'Nothing,' Blaine answered. 'I will help you find the Dust Blood and help rid them of this curse. That is why I am here. You can have the Sinan and the scroll and take it to Noel Kinross. I will give it to you on the day before the full moon when you next meet with him at Hackness.'

'Kinross will find the blood for us and all we have to do is give him the Sinan,' Hugh answered. 'Why can't we have it now?'

'I have to settle one last score and then it will be yours,' he said as he pulled the plate towards him and set the Sinan in motion. 'Sibilia Trevellas . . .'

The ancient finger trembled momentarily. It hovered above

the plate. The candlelight shimmered on the brass and made each symbol dance. Slowly it turned, seeking the direction of the Vampyre. Then it stopped. Nothing held it in place but the desire to find the creature. The long fingernail pointed to the north.

'So where is that old hag?' Henson asked.

'She is in the Conventorium to the north of Whitby. Ezra Morgan is with her.'

'And do you plan to kill my father?' Hugh asked.

'I will do whatever is needed to fulfil my task,' he said as he took the Sinan and placed it back in the box and slipped it into his pocket.

'But surely you can decide who must die and who can live?' Hugh asked. The pain in his chest grew worse and blood trickled down his chin.

'Stop this,' Vibica shouted. 'Hugh is unwell. All this talk of death is no good for him.'

As she spoke, Hugh looked up. His face was bloodless. Then, with a soft groan he fell forward, hit the table and then crashed to the floor.

'Father!' Jago shouted as Henson ran to him.

'He is still alive,' Henson said as he cradled him in his arms. 'I will take him to his room. Vibica, help me.'

'Let me,' Jago said.

'No . . . I will go with him,' Vibica replied as she helped Henson pull Hugh Morgan to his feet.

'Let her go,' Blaine said as he held Jago by the hand in a tight grip and stared into his eyes. 'She has a way of healing people from things like this.'

Vibica caught the thought as she walked with Henson.

Hugh staggered from the room, his face covered in blood and his breathing laboured.

'Will he live?' Jago asked as tears rolled down his face.

'He'll be fine,' Biatra said knowing how Vibica would heal him. 'It is the only way.'

'I have to be with him,' Jago protested as he tried to free himself from Blaine's grip.

'Stay here. It is not for you to be near your father when he is sick,' Blaine said. 'It is just the porphyria. It will not kill him.'

'How can you be sure?' Jago asked as the candles flickered to the end of their lives and the room grew dimmer.

'I have seen every disease known to mankind. Porphyria is the sickness of kings and the kin of Vampyres. He will not die.' Blaine stared at Jago. 'You have to believe me.'

'But I need to be with him,' Jago shouted.

'Biatra. Go and see Vibica. She will tell you if Hugh needs his son.'

She left the room, and Blaine turned back to Jago.

'Now, Jago, I need to talk to you.' Toran Blaine gripped Jago tightly and walked him from the room and down the stairs to the hallway below. The house seemed soundless and empty. Blaine opened the front door and took Jago outside.

'Why are we here?' Jago asked as they stood near to the grave where Henson had burnt the body of Griffin.

'That house has been the place of Vampyres for hundreds of years and it soon will be again. Don't you know why she is here?' Blaine said.

'Are you still in love with her?' Jago asked.

'What a stupid question,' Blaine shouted. 'Why ask that?'

'Because Aquinas said that you loved her and that she would always be safe because of that. Even if she was the last Vampyre in the entire world you would never kill her.'

'That is true, but it doesn't stop me hating who she is,' he said as he brushed a hair from his face. 'I chose to hunt down every Vampyre I could. There are people who know of their existence and they pay me well. That is why I need you.'

'Why?' Jago asked.

'We have to kill Sibilia Trevellas and take her blood. We can save Biatra and Vibica as well. Sibilia was the one who took first blood from each of them. It is now her time to pay.'

'But what if Vibica doesn't want to recant?' he asked, unsure that Blaine was telling the truth.

'Then we will make her. She has to do this,' he said.

'So you can be with her again?' Jago said.

'You are a wise lad, Jago Harker. Remember one thing. Never trust a Vampyre, not even Biatra. They are never the same as they were before. Understand?'

'They took my mother and used her. I know what they are like,' Jago said.

'We must leave tonight. I have rented a house near to the Conventorium. We can go there.'

'But what about my father?' Jago asked, unsure that he could leave him and still not trusting Blaine.

'We have to do this together. I am not strong enough on my own. You will tap into Sibilia's weakness. She will not know what to do.' Blaine put his hand on Jago's shoulder. 'I will bring you back to Hawks Moor by the end of three days.'

143

'But what shall I say to them?' Jago asked.

'I told Henson the night before you went to Hackness. He will tell your father. Vibica cannot know. She could contact Sibilia and warn her of what we are to do.' Blaine smiled at Jago. 'It is the right thing – a good and honourable crusade.'

His long leather coat flapped in the breeze and tapped against his boots. The night was clear and dark. In the cold and still air Jago remembered London and his journey to Whitby. In his mind he could hear the bomber before it killed his mother.

'How can I trust you?' Jago asked. 'I have been lied to since the day I was born.'

'That is a chance you will have to take, Jago. But at least you and I are human.'

'And we hunt down Sibilia?' Jago asked. He studied the outline of Blaine's rugged face and wondered why it was so familiar.

'We hunt her down and we get rid of her. It's as simple as that,' Blaine answered as he patted Jago on the back. 'I have a scroll in my pocket that gives us the name of every Vampyre alive today. We have four weeks to track as many down as we can – and kill them.'

[13]

The Smoke House

JAGO HAD NEVER TRAVELLED this way before. The old motorcycle was laden with bags that hung off the back wheel and its peeling khaki paint made it look older than it was. It swerved and weaved as Blaine steered to avoid the holes in the road. Jago held on hard, feeling as if he was on a wild horse that rushed through the countryside. The motorcycle revved as it went up the hill towards Whitby and then turned a steep corner. In the darkness, Jago could see nothing ahead. He peered over Blaine's shoulder as the wind pushed back his hair, trying to drag him from the seat and throw him to the ground.

Blaine rode on, his leather coat flapping around his legs, his hands gripping the bars and twisting the throttle. They were soon outside an old fisherman's cottage on the edge of the cliff. Its stone walls and slate roof were only feet from where the cliff had fallen into the sea. To one side was a small fish hut with a tin chimney that steamed black smoke and scented the land with the smell of oak. Jago could see the railway line that snaked its way to the north and the small village of Sandsend. From there, it took the tunnels through the cliff and disappeared.

'This is my place,' Blaine said as he pulled up his goggles, took off his leather aviator cap and ruffled his hair in the wind. 'Love the bike, best way to travel. Beats flying.'

'Never done that,' Jago answered, not sure if he ever wanted to.

'There's the Conventorium,' Blaine said as he pointed to the shadowy outline of a cathedral-like building two miles away. 'That's why I chose this place. I knew that Trevellas would hide there. They have used it for centuries.'

'But I thought –'

'Thought that the likes of them would never seek sanctuary in a place like that?' Blaine asked before Jago could finish his words. 'So did I, a long time ago. Now I know that Vampyres will do anything to keep their life a secret. Some people will help them regardless of the cost.'

'How do we get in?' Jago asked, having never broken in to a place in his life.

'That's the easy bit. We just have to make sure we don't get caught,' Blaine whispered as he pushed the motorcycle into the shadow of the old hut where fish were smoked. 'Whatever you do, don't go in there. It's a smoke house and the fumes could kill you.'

'For smoking fish and making kippers?' he asked as Blaine took a key from the chain around his neck and opened the door.

'That's how I got this place so cheap. Part of it fell into the sea last winter and no one would live here. I use the smoke hut for anything I catch. Keeps them fresh and stops the rot.'

'Fish?' Jago asked.

Blaine laughed. He pushed open the door and stepped inside, ignoring what Jago had said. 'We'll stay here until the dark hours. The trouble with Sibilia is that she doesn't sleep. Even when I was a Vampyre I had to sleep. It took my mind away from who I was.'

'Did you dream?' Jago asked as Blaine offered him a chair by a peat fire that smouldered in an iron grate.

'That was the thing. I never had a single dream all the time. Don't think they dream. They don't have to.'

'Why did you want to recant?' Jago said.

Blaine poked the fire and fresh flames leapt from within to warm the dark room. He looked about the shabby room with its cluttered table and worn armchair as if he was listening to an old memory.

'I was an adventurer, a traveller. In my years I travelled long and far. Then I met the Vampyre. There had been many stories about him and the house in which he lived. It was as if my fate and his were entwined and I couldn't escape. Then I met Vibica. She is a very persuasive woman and yet not even love could keep me from wanting to be human again.'

'What happened when you took Dust Blood?' Jago asked.

'It took me several days, but whatever takes over your body when you become a Vampyre was pulled from me. Every muscle and sinew burnt like the fires of hell were inside me. Then it was over.' Blaine stood up from the chair and locked the door. 'Trouble is, Jago . . . The trouble is that I have not aged in all this time. My face is still the same as the day I gave myself to the Vampyre.'

'Would you go back?' he asked.

'There is no reason to. I now have a task in hand that has

to be completed and you will help me.' Blaine looked at Jago as if he had just made a decision. 'I have something to show you.'

Blaine unlocked the door and stepped outside, gesturing for Jago to follow. They crossed the small yard to the smoking house. Blaine flicked a light switch and then opened the hatch on the roof that let out the smoke. It billowed from the shed, spiralling into the night sky.

'What's inside?' Jago asked nervously.

'This is what I do and who I am, Jago. It is what you will become if we are to rid the world of these creatures,' Blaine said as he turned the key in the lock. The door opened on its own. More smoke spilled out into the night. Jago stood back as he waited for the oak-smog to clear.

'Smells like roast pig,' he whispered as the scent from inside the smoking hut filled the air.

Blaine laughed as he stepped inside the shed.

'Better see for yourself, Jago,' he said as he bid him enter.

Jago followed. As the smoke cleared he gasped. In the crude and stark electric light that cast glaring shadows he saw, staring back at him through yellowed eyes, the heads of four Vampyres. They were mounted around the room on metal stakes, in amongst the racks of herring. Each had been meticulously cut from the body. Their hair had been brushed and make-up applied to their faces. Their mouths were fixed in forced smiles.

At first, Jago was not sure if they were not just mannequins. They had the appearance of the statues covered in gaudy clothes in Derry & Toms department store in London. He would pass it every day and look at the figures staring into the dimly lit street as they held a manufactured pose with stiff hands. But then he saw the head of Frankell, torn and burnt from the explosion but still recognisable.

'What are they?' he asked Blaine as the man twisted one of the metal spikes so the smiling head faced the door.

'Their names are not important. Each of them marks a death. I collect them to show my employer,' he answered. 'It is proof that I have done my job.'

'Employer?' Jago asked him as he stepped back from the room and tried to breath the cold night air.

'I would not do this alone. That would make me a murderer. If you take life in the name of something great then it is not murder.' Blaine stroked the face of the only woman Vampyre. He saw Jago staring at him. 'Do you think I am mad?'

'No . . .' Jago lied, feeling the man was quite mad to be able to do this.

'I only wish I could have claimed responsibility for killing Draigorian or even Julius Cresco. It would have been a good thing to take the life of at least one of the Vampyre Quartet.'

'I had to,' Jago answered. 'How did you find them?'

'These are just a few of my accomplishments. I have a house in Scotland. My collection there is quite magnificent. Before I had the Maleficarum I would track them down by word of mouth and rumour. Now it is far more simple.'

'Who employs you?' Jago asked.

'I am sworn to secrecy. That is one thing I can never tell you. Only be comforted that we act on the highest authority,' he answered.

149

It was not the answer that Jago wanted. He looked at Blaine as he stood by the fire and wondered how he knew his face.

'Why me? Why do you want me to be with you?'

'I actually don't believe you know of your importance, do you, Jago?' Blaine switched off the light and walked back to the house, leaving the smokery door open as the fumes spilled across the cold yard.

'I only just found out the truth about my life,' he said as he followed Blaine inside the cottage, ducking under the low door. 'Did you ever live in London?'

'Playing games?' Blaine asked.

'I think I know you,' he answered.

'Then your memory is good. I met you only once before, when you were five years old. I had heard that there was a child born of a woman and a descendant of Ezra Morgan. It was on a cold morning when I found your mother in a park. You were playing on the swings.'

'You wore a black hat and had a red beard?' Jago asked.

'That was me. I spoke with your mother. I asked her to contact me when you were to be returned to Whitby.' Blaine reached into the pocket of his leather coat. Carefully, he handed Jago a postcard.

'From my mother,' Jago said.

'Martha kept her word,' Blaine replied.

Jago read the handwritten card as if the words were spoken by his mother. 'You knew I was coming?' he asked.

'You, Jago Harker, are the reason why I am here. In the world of the Vampyres, you are a Messiah. All their hopes had been placed in you becoming one with them. The progeny of Ezra Morgan.'

'Ezra Morgan?' Jago said. 'What do you mean?'

'So you believe that Hugh Morgan is your father?' Blaine asked.

'Of course, he has to be,' Jago answered as his mind raced.

'That would not be enough to satisfy Strackan and the Vampyre Quartet. The child has to be a direct heir to the Vampyre. I asked your mother and she told me the truth. Ezra Morgan is your father and Hugh is your brother.'

'No! It can't be,' Jago said. 'He is my father.'

'That is what they have you believe. It is all lies and confusion. That is the way they live. It is only the truth that can set you free, Jago.' Blaine looked stern as his red hair fell across his face. 'I know these are words you do not want to hear, but they are the truth.'

'My mother would never have,' he answered.

'She had no choice,' Blaine said. 'The Vampyre Quartet made sure of that.'

Jago could feel his lungs about to burst. He breathed hard and clenched his fists.

'Then why say that I was the child of Hugh Morgan?'

'Hugh believes he is your father. He need never know.' Blaine pushed the blackened kettle on to the fire.

'So why tell me?' Jago asked.

'Because it is the truth. I think that Henson suspects. The only way for sure is to ask Ezra Morgan.'

'Then you will kill him?' Jago asked as he walked to the narrow window on the far wall, pulled back the dirty linen drape and looked out.

'No. You will,' Blaine answered. 'I will help you. I think it

151

only right that all the Vampyre Quartet die at your hand. You were meant to bring new life. It is sweet and fitting that you will bring death.'

Jago stared into the darkness. Far away he could see the outline of the Conventorium. It broke from the line of the hill and was edged against the trees. The moon cast its light across a silvered roof that shone as if it were the sea.

'Then we do it tonight. I can wait no more,' Jago said as he turned to Blaine.

Without another word, Blaine crossed the room and slid a leather case from under the sideboard. He pulled it in front of the fire and moved the candle so it cast more light. Flicking the brass hinges, he lifted the shabby lid and lay it open.

A black silk scarf lay over the outline of what looked like a hand flanked by two strips of steel. Blaine slowly took the silk and folded it neatly. To his surprise, Jago could now see that the case contained a severed hand covered in old wax. It lay before him with its palm outstretched and candle wicks pinned to each dried finger. Beside the hand were two long daggers with white ivory handles.

'The Glory Hand,' Blaine said as he lifted it from the box. 'The hand of a hanged man. When the fingers are lit, everyone in the house who is asleep will stay asleep.'

'But that is magic. I don't believe in magic,' Jago answered.

'Up until only a short time ago you didn't believe in Vampyres. There is more to this world than you could ever know, Jago.' Blaine laid the hand on the chair and lifted one of the daggers from its resting place. 'This is for you. It's Chinese. They belonged to Wujing. He was the first Vampyre hunter. It is made from the finest silver.'

'And it will kill a Vampyre just like the knife Draigorian gave me?' Jago asked.

'Far more powerful than any other. Hold it against their throat and they will tell you everything they know,' Blaine said excitedly. 'They cannot refuse to answer you a question.'

'And it works?' he asked.

'Before I recanted, I had it used against me. I could not help but tell everything I was asked. We will get the truth from Ezra Morgan,' Blaine answered with a whisper.

'Then how did you get them and why aren't you dead?' Jago said quickly as he plucked the knife from his hand and felt the blade balance in his fingers.

'The one who came for me was another Vampyre. François Dupec. He used the knife to try to cut off my ear. It was what he always did as a sign. That is why I have this scar.'

Blaine pulled back the strands of hair and showed Jago the scar above his ear. The wound had been deep; it sliced across his head in a long arc.

'You killed him?'

'Of course I did. Paris, 1936.'

Jago held the handle of the knife; it warmed quickly in his hand. He looked at the writing that led the eye along the blade and tried to read the words etched in the metal.

'What do they mean?' he asked Blaine.

'They are curses. Curses to bring an end to all this. It is said that Wujing wrote them himself and with every Vampyre he killed he inscribed another line.'

'What happened to him?'

'He was murdered in Byzantium. Three Vampyres lured him to a small village and killed him with poison.'

'Why didn't they just bite him?' asked Jago as he pointed the tip of the knife into the air.

'It would have been too easy. It is said that they were the last Vampyres in the whole world. Legend has it that Wu-jing had killed every one that ever lived but them.' Blaine laughed to himself. 'It is strange to conceive that neither of us would be here today if he had succeeded. It makes me think of what future lives I am destroying by fighting this crusade.'

'Cresco said we could never know the future and that here and now was all we would ever know,' Jago replied as he tested the sharpness of the blade on the skin on his finger.

'He taught you well,' Blaine said. He placed the Glory Hand back in the box. 'If we wait until the moon sets beyond the hills we can go to the Conventorium. I know a secret way inside and we will never be detected.'

'What if we are caught?' asked Jago as he handed the knife to Blaine.

'Then I will kill you before they have their way. I cannot see their wishes fulfilled.'

Jago swallowed hard as Blaine stared at him, his wolf-like eyes rimmed with silver.

'And if we find Sibilia and Ezra Morgan, what do we do then?'

'We ask them for the truth and find where Stracken is in hiding. If he is dead then we will all be safe,' Blaine said, looking to the door as if he thought someone was outside.

'Are we alone?' Jago asked as Blaine stood and crept to the door, knife in hand.

Blaine put his finger to his lips, telling Jago to be silent. In

154

two steps he was at the door, the key in his hand, waiting to turn the lock.

Jago stepped into the shadows of the room and took the other knife from the box. As he looked at the door, Jago could see a bright white eye staring through the spigot-hole. It wasn't a human eye or similar to anything Jago had seen before. It stared through the hole as if it were looking for someone it knew.

'Mr Blaine?' a voice outside said harshly. 'Mr Toran Blaine?'

14

Ozymandias

IN THE LIGHT of the turf fire, the man looked considerably smaller than he had done when he was at the door. Blaine sat in the armchair and studied him earnestly whilst Jago leant against the wall by the window. The man himself stood in his long gabardine coat and clutched an over-sized floppy hat with his grubby and bitten nails. Jago noticed that his hands trembled slightly as he stared at the fire wondering if he should speak.

'I hope I find you well, Mr Blaine. My name is Larkin. We have never met but I do know something of your work. I have taken a great risk coming here,' the man said nervously.

'How did you find me?' Blaine asked.

'I was given this address and asked to bring you a letter.' Larkin held out a crumpled envelope. 'I do hope you take the contents seriously and give me your reply.'

'You read it,' he said, aware the envelope could be poisoned.

'Very well,' Larkin said as he opened the envelope. Then, taking a pair of glasses from the pocket of his jacket hidden beneath the gabardine, he began to read. 'Blaine . . . I hope I find you well and that you have not killed Larkin before he could deliver this to you.' Larkin coughed uncomfortably.

With that, Blaine snatched the letter from him and read what was left. Then as he finished the last word he tore up the paper and threw the pieces on the fire.

'You are a brave man to come here with news like that, Mr Larkin,' Blaine said as he watched the letter burn.

'Don't you want to keep it to remind you of what it said?' Larkin whimpered, realising what his own fate might be.

'I have read enough and what was asked is quite impossible,' he said as he looked at Jago.

Larkin's eyes turned with him. They were cold and sharp and Jago felt frightened by their glare.

'Is *this* the lad?' Larkin asked as if he were already privy to the contents of the letter.

'This is Jago Harker. And he will be staying with me. Your master has no chance of ever getting the lad from me,' Blaine said. He got to his feet and locked the door of the cottage.

'Then I can tell my master it is no?' Larkin asked as he placed the felt hat on his head and pulled the drawstring tighter around the waist of his coat.

'You will tell your master nothing,' Blaine answered with a mock laugh.

'But I am expected to return. He would like the answer by morning,' Larkin replied nervously as he saw Blaine take the rope that hung on the door.

Jago saw the man shuffle on his tiny feet as he looked for a way of escape.

'I think you should stay here until the morning. It is far too dangerous at night for you to be abroad,' Blaine said as he stepped towards him.

'I saw your collection, Mr Blaine. If someone was to go to the police, Inspector Kaine would be very interested indeed.'

'If someone were to go to the police, they would find *their* head on a pole, Mr Larkin. That would not be a wise thing to do.'

Larkin began to warble quietly as if he were a small captured bird.

'I wasn't suggesting for a moment . . .' Larkin fumbled with the buttons on his coat and unclipped his belt. 'It was just a manner of speech. I found the heads fascinating, to say the least.'

'Then you won't mind staying until the morning and then you can take the message to your master,' Blaine said, watching him closely.

'Not possible,' Larkin replied. His demeanour was suddenly transformed. 'You can't expect me to do as you say Blaine.'

With a twist of his hand, Larkin removed the gabardine from his back and threw it at Blaine. In one long step he had leapt to the table and taken hold of Jago, with one hand around the throat.

'Who are you?' Blaine shouted.

'I want the boy,' Larkin screeched as he held a thin stiletto-like blade to his back. 'It is what I came for and I will not leave without him.'

Jago stood motionless. He could feel the sharp point pressing against his spine. It burnt the flesh like a scalding iron.

'You have the Trajithian?' Blaine asked as Larkin held Jago closer to him.

'You have seen the stiletto before?' Larkin said, gripping Jago by the throat. 'A blood knife – made to take the blood of Companions. It slips beneath the skin painlessly and leaves no trace. I have heard it said that it is the same as the teeth of a Vampyre.'

'But you are human. Why do you do their work for them?' Blaine asked.

'It is the most profitable thing in this time to do,' he answered. 'I will take Jago Harker with me and you will not come after me – understand?'

'Impossible,' Blaine answered as Jago stood silently, gripped by Larkin, the knife pressed into his skin. 'The lad stays here.'

'Then he stays here dead,' Larkin said as he gripped him tighter. 'Are you sure you won't change your mind?'

Jago could feel sweat trickle across his face. Larkin's hand burnt blood-hot against his skin. The knife burrowed under his flesh. He could feel his legs tremble.

'Let me go with him,' Jago said to Blaine. 'I will be fine.'

'See – the lad talks sense. Let him come with me. All will be well.' Larkin sniggered as he rubbed his stubbled face against Jago's skin.

'It would be for the good,' Jago went on, trying to beg for time as he looked at Blaine and then to the knife in his hand.

Blaine stepped back from the door and placed Wujing's knife on the sideboard. He turned and walked to the fireplace and sat in the armchair as if resigned to what would happen.

'Tell your master that if he harms Jago, I will cut off his head,' Blaine said as he folded his arms and shrugged.

'I don't think he will care about that, Mr Blaine. Jago Harker is to be ransomed to the highest bidder. There are many in his world who would like his blood. I thought you would have known that.' Larkin grunted the words like a pig.

'What does he mean?' Jago asked.

'Hugh should have told you, Jago. The blood from the child of a Vampyre is highly prized.' Blaine yawned as he spoke. 'It has the power to transform far quicker than any other. In fact it is regarded as the elixir of life.'

'My master isn't going to kill you, Jago. He will sell you and then your blood will be taken from you bit by bit,' Larkin said as he pushed him towards the door. Jago stumbled suddenly. Larkin pulled him to his feet. 'Don't go fainting on me now, we have far to go.'

'Just loosen your grip. I can't breathe,' Jago said.

It was what he had waited for. As soon as he felt the fingers move, Jago pushed Larkin back against the door, slammed the man against the wall and grabbed the kife from the sideboard. There was a soft groan. Larkin's eyes widened as he gasped for breath. His hands fell to his side. Jago pushed the knife deeper and then stepped away.

Larkin tried to pull the blade from the wall. It pinned his arm to the wood, buried to the hilt.

'As you were saying?' Blaine said as he walked towards him.

Jago trembled. His hands shook.

'Who is he?' Jago demanded.

'Larkin is the emissary of a Vampyre called Ozymandias. He is a trader in human flesh. He wanted me to sell you to him. The knife that Larkin carries is used to drain human

160

blood. The more refined Vampyres do not like to kill but still need to have their thirsts quenched. The Trajithian is a very fine blade. It is sharper than any knife known to man. It can cut you through without causing any pain. Some say it can even cut the veil between life and death.'

'And they would have done that to me?' Jago asked.

'Of course we would. News travels fast.' Larkin spat at him, unable to pull the blade from his impaled arm. 'I was sent to watch you at Hawks Moor and saw Toran Blaine take you away. I waited and then followed. Ask Blaine. He arranged it all.'

Jago seethed as he looked at Blaine, wanting an explanation. 'Is it true?' he asked.

'Of course it's true,' Larkin shouted, his mouth full of spit. 'You can tell by his silence. He told Ozymandias he would have you by tonight. That is why I came here. It was all a matter of arranging a fee.'

'You trapped me, Blaine!' Jago said.

'It was not that simple. I used you as bait, but never intended to let them keep you. I had thought of handing you over to them and following to see where you went. The blood auction would have been a spectacular event. I would have been there and could have captured Trevellas.'

'So the Conventorium?' Jago asked.

'There is no one there. It is all a lie,' Blaine answered.

'That's all he is good at, lying. It's all he does,' Larkin said as he twisted the handle of the knife. 'It wasn't to trick me that he brought you here. It was to sell you to Ozymandias. And he will – don't trust him.'

Jago hesitated, not knowing whom to trust.

Blaine calmly stood by the door and turned the lock. 'If you don't trust me, just go. It's a long walk to Hawks Moor but you'll be there by morning.' Blaine pushed the door open and gestured for Jago to leave.

'But you were going to sell me to him,' Jago said.

'It had to be that way, Jago. If you had gone knowingly it would never have worked. Ozymandias would have known you were in on the deal. He can read the thoughts of the mind and you could never have deceived him.'

Jago stepped towards the door and nodded to Larkin.

'I can trust you more than him,' Jago said to Larkin as he stepped outside the house. 'I'll walk back to Hawks Moor. At least they don't want to sell me for my blood.'

Jago looked around the yard. The moon cast silver shadows across the ground. By the cliff edge the smoke-house door swung back and forth and the electric light flickered.

'Are you sure you know what you're doing?' Blaine shouted from the cottage.

Jago didn't answer, but turned the corner to walk towards the road. Then, without warning, a hand grabbed him from the darkness and gagged his mouth with a stinking rag. There was a rush as if a bird had taken flight. Then he felt rope around him as gloved hands slipped a hessian sack over his head. It happened in an instant. He was caught unawares. His feet were kicked from him and he could see nothing. He was captured and hog-tied. A noose was slipped around his hands, another around his feet. Jago could smell the mud and the wet grass that soaked through like a cold wet knife.

'Didn't think you were going to get away that easily, did

you?' a voice asked as he was dragged towards the road. 'Ozymandias has not paid good money to have you walk away.'

Jago couldn't speak as he was pulled roughly by his feet. He heard the boot of a car being opened and leather shoes scrunch on the gravel. Then, without a sound, he was tipped into the boot and the lid slammed shut.

Inside the cottage, Larkin twisted the knife from his arm.

'He could have killed me with your tomfoolery,' Larkin protested as he wrapped the wound with a drying cloth.

'I didn't think he would do it.' Blaine laughed as he closed the door, went to the fire and warmed the room with more pieces of dried peat. 'It took me all my time to convince him that we were going to find Sibilia Trevellas.'

'And he never suspected that you work for Ozymandias?' Larkin asked as he held the cloth to his wound.

'He would not know who he is,' Blaine said. 'He thinks I am an assassin. A random killer of any Vampyre that crosses my path.'

'Will you be at the blood auction? I think you are expected.'

Three faint knocks rapped at the door, and Larkin kicked the door with the heel of his worn boot. It opened slowly. Blaine stepped back from the fire and, taking the knife from Larkin, wiped the blade and put it back in the box.

A tall man with a thin and much-lined face stepped inside. He took off his fedora hat and placed it carefully on the sideboard.

'Exactly how much do I owe you?' the man asked, taking a thick wallet from the pocket of his tweed coat.

'A thousand pounds is what we agreed, Ozymandias,' Blaine said without looking at him.

'I should charge you for wounding my servant,' he answered, looking at Larkin.

'Just don't let the lad near the Trajithian,' Blaine said coldly. 'He may take from you whatever blood you have left.'

'The only time he will see it again is when we auction him. Those gathered will want to taste the goods before buying. I take it you will be there in disguise?' Ozymandias straightened his silk tie and smoothed the collar of his shirt.

'I wouldn't miss it for the world,' Blaine replied, thinking how the Vampyre had aged since they had last met. 'There is also the matter of the other work I have done for you.'

'Four?' Ozymandias asked. 'The four I wanted?'

'Every one.' Blaine looked without compassion towards the smoke house. 'Five hundred pounds per head. I took the liberty of preserving them just as you asked.'

'Always the professional,' Ozymandias whispered as he began to count out the crisp white five-pound notes into a large pile on the table.

'Professional?' Larkin grumbled murderously. 'He could have killed me and neither of you care. He even told the boy all that was going to happen.'

'Can't have him not knowing,' Blaine said. 'That is all the fun of it. I might even bid for him myself. Could be a profitable venture to sell his blood at a pound a drop. How many pathetic creatures would pay for the best blood ever created?'

'You are a cunning villain, Toran Blaine,' Ozymandias laughed. 'And an old and loyal friend. I still remember when we met in Byzantium and killed that fool Wujing.'

Blaine turned and reached across to the man, placing his longest finger on the cold lip of Ozymandias. As he did he looked back and forth, wanting no one to hear him.

'That must always be our secret. I have never told a living soul how old I really am. I wish that part of my life would be forgotten.' He spoke in a voice just above a breath.

'Then I will tell no one how you washed your hands over the execution of the Man of Sorrows and sent him to his death,' said Ozymandias wickedly.

'A mistake I will never forget and one I will never repeat.'

'What is life if it is not for making mistakes and what is death if not for forgetting them?' Ozymandias finished counting the money and placed a silver coin of soul money on the top.

'That was a mistake that not even death can absolve me from,' Blaine said as he picked the money from the table and pushed it in his pocket.

'Are you still persisting with the lie that you are a Recanter?' Ozymandias asked.

Blaine looked at Larkin and then at the man.

'Sometimes it is good for people to think you are really human,' he said as he closed the lid of the box and slipped the catch.

'In all these years I don't think I have ever asked if you actually did try Dust Blood,' Ozymandias said. He put the wallet back in his pocket and looked around the cluttered room.

'It never worked,' Blaine said, his voice tired. 'When is the blood auction?'

'Tomorrow night,' Larkin said before his master could speak.

165

'A masked ball?'

'Of course. No Vampyre would ever want the world to know they had the boy. He will make me a lot of money.' Ozymandias wiped his gloved hand along a layer of dust that covered the sideboard. 'I can never understand how *they* could live like this. And to think they call us beasts ...'

'My name is Ozymandias – I am king of kings ...' Blaine laughed.

'Ah, Shelley. To think, he made the world believe that he drowned. I hear he is living as a baker in Wandsworth.' Then the man opened the door and walked out of the cottage to the car, with Larkin following on like an obedient dog.

15

Blood Auction

THE ROPE BLISTERED HIS HANDS and cut deep into the skin as the old sedan car wound its way along the narrow roads. Jago tried to count the twists and turns, hoping they would help him find his way back, if he could escape. He could hear Larkin mumbling and moaning as he drove the car. The other man laughed every now and then, cackling under his breath.

It was not long before the sound of the road changed. The crunch of gravel bit beneath the tyres as they slipped the corner. Jago slid from one side of the boot to the other. The hessian sack covered his face and burnt the skin. It stank of oil and creosote and with every breath it burnt his lungs. With one last sharp turn, the car stopped suddenly. Jago heard the car doors open. Feet moved quickly on gravel. The boot handle was turned.

'Do nothing stupid,' Larkin insisted as he took hold of Jago by the scruff of the neck and dragged him from the car. 'Ozymandias wouldn't like it.'

'I don't care,' Jago snarled as he tried to shake the hessian sack from his head. 'If I get free from this.'

Larkin sliced the cords that bound Jago's feet.

'You will be free just as soon as we get you inside the house,' Ozymandias said graciously as he turned the large brass key in the lock. Then his words became suddenly cold: 'Until then, be silent.' They reminded Jago of Mr Metuchen, the headmaster of Mile End School, a man who in one sentence could sound both exultant and odious.

'Fight me face to face,' Jago shouted, his words muffled by the sack.

'I shall do nothing of the sort,' Ozymandias insisted. 'Larkin will keep you tethered if you do not calm down. You are a valued cargo and shall not be damaged.'

'Cargo?' Jago asked as Larkin pushed him towards the open door. 'Let me see who you are.'

'I am Ozymandias, king of kings,' the man replied, laughing as he spoke the words.

'You're a fool,' Jago answered, not caring what would be done to him. 'If my father finds you –'

'Your father will not care,' Ozymandias replied. 'I know him well and he has more interest in your blood than I do.'

'It's a lie. Toran Blaine knows nothing.'

'It is the truth, for it was I who told Blaine as soon as I knew,' Ozymandias answered as Larkin pulled Jago up three steps and into the house.

Jago could sense the space around him. Through the weave of the sack he could make out the shapes of the two men. Candles flickered on tall stands. He could sense he was in a vast room with a marble floor. It echoed as he walked.

'Where shall he go?' Larkin asked.

'In the usual place,' Ozymandias answered. Then he pulled the sack from Jago and stared at him in the candlelight.

'Who are you?' Jago asked as he looked at the man towering above him.

'He is Ozymandias,' Larkin said as he pulled the cords tighter around his wrists.

Jago could see that the man was a Vampyre. His face was lined, the skin mottled as if dead. A sweet smell of orchid flowers pervaded the room, pungent and thick as if it oozed from within the creature.

'You're a Vampyre,' Jago said as he stared around the ornate hallway lit by a gold chandelier and lined with gold-framed portraits of the same man. 'Can always tell your sort.'

'Why do you hate us so much?' Ozymandias asked.

'You should all be dead,' Jago said, wondering if he would ever be free from this place. 'What are you going to do to me?'

'Blood auction,' Larkin said, and then realised he should not have spoken.

'That is a crude way to put it.' Ozymandias led Jago up the wide stairs to the galleried landing above. 'There will be a gathering of like-minded people who will bid to keep you.'

'So why don't you just bite me and have done with it?' Jago asked.

'It would spoil the blood,' Larkin answered as he twitched his rat-like nose. 'Once you are a full Vampyre the blood changes. No good to anyone then. Have to keep you as human as you now are.'

'My assistant is correct,' Ozymandias scoffed. 'As the product of human and Vampyre flesh your blood is especially precious. Why should should we wish to change that?'

'And if Strackan finds me?'

'I shall not really care. You shall be given to the one who pays me the most money,' Ozymandias answered grimly. 'If Strackan wants to have you then he shall pay for your blood like anyone else.'

'Can't he just come and take me?' Jago asked. 'Isn't he the lord of you all?'

'Lord?' Ozymandias sneered. 'Strackan is not my lord. I have lived far longer than him. Since before the world . . .'

'We don't fear Strackan.' Larkin echoed the words of his master. 'Care nothing for what he thinks – has to pay like the rest.'

'You really know little of the world, don't you, Jago Harker?' Ozymandias said as he placed a hand on his shoulder and turned him to walk along the long dark passageway lit only by a single candle. 'Some Vampyres would have you believe they were the rulers of this world. They huff and puff about their power when in reality they have very little.'

'Then who are you?' Jago asked. 'Why did Toran Blaine betray me?'

'Money and obedience,' Larkin said as he went along the narrow passageway. 'Why does anyone fall from grace? It's always money or power.'

Larkin fumbled with the handle and opened a high wooden door set into the wall. There was a rush of cold.

'There is food for you and blankets. I advise you to rest and please . . .' Ozymandias looked him in the eyes. 'Please do not try to escape. It is quite impossible. Many have tried and failed.' Jago felt the cords fall from his wrists but saw no knife. For a moment he thought of running, but Ozymandias stared at him as if he knew his thoughts. 'I would say you would get no further than the hallway. Then I would have to kill you, and that would be very expensive and a lot of people would be disappointed.'

Jago stood by the doorway. He could see the room quite clearly. In the corner by the curtains was a neat bed. A looming shadow of a wardrobe filled one wall.

'Very well,' he said, resigned to his fate.

Larkin pushed him inside the room and slammed the door shut. Jago sat in the darkness, the moonlight streaking in through cracks in the long drapes that covered the windows. By the bed, on a small table, was a silver upturned dish and next to the dish an enamelled flask. Jago opened the top and sniffed the liquid.

'Tea,' he whispered as he sipped.

It tasted bitter, but that was quite usual. His mother had once said that tea wasn't real tea like it used to be. The war had seen to that.

Jago drank from the flask and felt the warmth trickle down his throat. It was different from anything he had ever tasted before. Soon, he could feel his eyelids begin to close and could do nothing to stop them. He struggled, not wanting to sleep. In his waking dream he could see Biatra. She crouched by the fire of Hawks Moor with Vibica de Zoete. Dark shadows pressed around them like long fingers that stained the walls.

Though he fought for breath, Jago slipped deeper into sleep. It was as if he were drowning. The night closed in quickly, numbing his bones and freezing the tips of his fingers. The flask dropped from his hand as he slumped to the floor. The narcotic flooded through his veins; his mind emptied of every thought and feeling and even life itself hung by a spider thread.

The door opened. Larkin stared in.

'Works every time,' he whispered.

One day later, it was the burning pain in his left wrist that woke Jago from his sleep. He looked at his hand, his vision blurred. In the light from a small candle that flickered on a table nearby he could see a bandage on his arm. It was wrapped tightly but still could not stem the trickle of blood.

Jago looked up. He could make out the bars of a golden cage arching above him. The room was different. There were no windows. In the shadows were racks of wine and discarded furniture. Out of his reach, a solitary rat twitched its long tail.

Pulling back the bandage, Jago could see that his arm had been neatly cut open.

'The Trajithian,' he whispered, knowing that his blood had been taken for the auction. 'Poisoned . . .'

His head thumped with the pain of the elixir that had caused him to sleep. Jago got to his knees and gripped the side of the cage. His fingers held on to the bars as above him he could hear the sound of dancing.

Suddenly the cage jolted from side to side as if a gigantic hand were lifting it high into the air. Above him, the ceiling opened. A chain whirred and the cage was pulled higher. Jago was thrown to the floor as the cage moved swiftly upwards to the sound of loud applause.

The cage went higher and higher until it dangled from the roof of a great hall. The room glistened with a thousand candles whilst all around masked figures stared at Jago and clapped and clapped.

Ozymandias stood on a small stage with Larkin at his side. A small orchestra of powder-wigged children played violins and cellos. On a long table next to them was a rack of tiny silver thimbles. The people began to cheer as the music softened and then stilled.

'My dear friends,' Ozymandias said, his voice filled with hubris. 'Now is the time we have all waited for and above us for you all to see is Jago Harker.'

There was a respectful silence as every eye in the room stared at him. Jago looked back at the masked faces and tried to hold back the tears. In all his life he had never felt so alone as now.

'What are you staring at?' he shouted. 'I won't give you my blood.'

'As you can see, he is a spirited boy and if the legend is true then he is the product of human and Vampyre flesh,' Ozymandias said as he clutched the brass gavel in his hand.

'How do we know it is Jago Harker?' a man in a pig mask asked with a raised finger.

Jago looked at the crowd that filled the room.

'Because he was taken from Hawks Moor last night. He is the child of Morgan and a girl from Whitby. What better blood can you ask for?' Ozymandias demanded as he smashed the gavel against the table. 'Some of you may have already tasted and know of its power. Be in no doubt, drink of this blood and you will never thirst again.'

Jago looked around the vast hall with its golden chandelier that hung from the high ceiling above him. He was being displayed for all to see. He gripped the bars of the slowly turning cage and looked down at the jostling mob that filled the room.

'Very well,' Ozymandias gloated. 'Who will give me two hundred pounds?'

A voice shouted in agreement, then another and another as the price grew. Ozymandias pointed from one masked figure to another as each offered more and more.

'One thousand pounds,' shouted a tall man in a long velvet coat and the mask of a bird.

'One thousand three hundred,' quickly echoed another close by.

The orchestra of children giggled with each bid. They stared at Jago with cherubic, bloodless smiles like all the other Vampyres in the room. He wondered who could take the life of one so young.

Then the door of the auction suddenly burst open.

'Three thousand pounds,' a woman shouted as she stood beneath the gilded arch and slowly untied the mask from her face. 'Who dares to bid more than me?'

Jago knew the arrogant voice of Sibilia Trevellas.

Ozymandias looked around the room. The crowd was silent, not daring to to speak. He stared at Jago and then Sibilia.

'Is there no one who will give me more than that?' he asked hopefully.

'Three thousand five hundred,' a man in a mask of a clown shouted from directly below the swinging cage. 'And with every bid she makes, I will give you a sovereign more.'

Jago knew instantly it was Toran Blaine.

'Does madam have another bid?' Ozymandias asked. 'And do you have enough money, my dear friend?'

'I have more than enough,' Blaine answered.

'Ten thousand pounds,' Sibilia answered. 'Is that enough for the boy?'

'It would never be enough for such fine blood,' Blaine answered as he slid his hand beneath his cloak. 'I will give fifteen thousand.'

'Very well,' Sibilia said as her eyes scanned the room, sensing something was wrong. 'Let me see him and I will decide.'

Ozymandias nodded as Larkin slipped a handle. The cage was lowered to the floor. The orchestra of children played as it gently dropped inch by inch.

'Will no one else bid for the blood victim?' Ozymandias asked hopefully.

Sibilia Trevellas stepped from the doorway and pushed her way through the crowd.

'He is mine. It was for me he was brought into this world,' she shouted as Blaine stepped to one side and touched the cage.

'Do as I say and when I say it,' he whispered to Jago as Sibilia walked towards him. 'Run for the door and I will cause a diversion.'

'But you tricked me,' Jago said.

'It was necessary,' Blaine murmured, turning away.

'Getting to know him already?' Sibilia asked. 'Don't for one minute think I don't know who you are.'

'Then you have me at a disadvantage,' Blaine replied as he took hold of her gloved hand and kissed the back.

'I have heard of Toran Blaine and whilst others may be fooled I am not. You are a murderer of your own kind,' Sibilia answered sharply.

'And you are very beautiful,' Blaine answered, not wanting to let go of her.

'Fool,' she scoffed. 'Show me your money and let us not continue in this charade.'

Ozymandias sidled towards them through the gathered crowd.

'This is an auction, not a place for the settling of old scores. Are you serious, Toran?' he asked.

'Blaine is never serious. He wants the boy for his own good and will cheat you out of every penny. He is a murderer,' Sibilia bickered.

The Vampyres were silent. They stood and watched like sombre sentinels.

'Murderer? I regard myself as more than that, Sibilia,' Blaine said.

'Please,' Ozymandias argued as he took the Trajithian and screwed the glass vial into the handle. 'Let us taste his blood and then decide who shall have him for the best price.'

Ozymandias turned the lock on the side of the cage. Jago stood back from the door and gripped the bars.

'Leave me,' he shouted as those that pressed in around him laughed and growled, touching his skin with their cold hands.

'It is painless, I assure you,' Ozymandias said as he opened the door.

'Let me,' Blaine said as he snatched the knife from his hand. 'It is something I have always wanted to do.'

176

Blaine stepped into the cage and dragged Jago from within. The lad squealed in pain as the grip tightened around his neck. Sibilia shuddered with an anticipation that filled her with great joy.

'And you thought I would never see this day, Jago Harker,' she said, her voice dark and husky.

Blaine thrust Jago forward until he was pressed close to Sibilia. The crowd was gathered around them. Masked faces stared at the boy. The orchestra played. Violins shrilled like ghostly voices and the soft echo of children singing sounded around them.

'We should do it now,' Blaine said. He took the knife and then the vial was filled with blood and Blaine laughed as Sibilia took hold of his arm, unable to breathe. 'It will soon be over, madam.'

The woman fell to the floor, a stain of purple blood smearing her white petticoat for all to see.

'He's killed her!' a woman screamed as she tore the mask from Blaine's face.

'Run, Jago,' Blaine whispered as Jago stood with the Trajithian in his own hand.

The screaming crowd parted like an ancient sea of faces.

Jago hesitated, wondering if this were yet another elaborate trap.

'Leave him, he is dangerous,' Blaine shouted as Jago ran to the gilded doors, holding the blade ready to strike.

Ozymandias looked and then turned to the orchestra of half-masked children.

'Get Jago Harker!' he said as Jago fled from the room.

16

Valkyrie

THE DOORS OF THE HALL slammed behind him and Jago slid the bolt deep within its keeper. As he ran on he could still hear the screams from the ballroom where the auction had taken place. One thing he knew for certain: it was Toran Blaine who had stabbed Sibilia with the knife that Jago now clutched in his hand. He glanced quickly at the vial of her blood and realised in that instant that he had all he needed to heal Biatra.

'Dust Blood,' he whispered as he ran across the marbled floor. 'If I can get from here . . .'

Jago looked up and saw a small child standing on the circular staircase that ran upwards around the wall. The boy was dressed in a gold frock coat and white hose; black shoes with silver buckles tipped his feet. Jago had seen him before – he had played the violin in the orchestra.

'The knife,' the boy said as he held out his small hand, slowly licking his ruby-red lips. 'Ozymandias wants the knife,' he insisted.

Jago looked around. They were alone. No one else had followed. He edged slowly towards a door and carefully placed the Trajithian into his pocket.

'Go and tell him he can't have it,' he answered.

'You have to go back,' the boy-child said, speaking like a ghost from behind the half-masked face.

'I am leaving,' Jago answered defiantly as he took the door handle and turned it slowly.

The boy walked towards him one step at a time. His eyes burnt blood red beneath the mask as he smiled. 'Very well,' he answered. 'If that is what you want . . .'

Jago pulled on the door until it opened. The cold night air flooded in. He turned. There on the doorstep were three more children, each dressed just as the first. Tiny masks covered their cherubic faces. All were smiling and holding out their right hands.

'Out of my way,' Jago said as he stepped towards them.

They didn't move.

'Stop him,' shouted the child on the staircase.

In an instant each child pulled a sharp silver spike from within its frock coat. They stood with smiling faces like silent puppets waiting to strike.

'Please come with us,' they said together as if with one voice.

Jago ran to the staircase just as the child there pulled a spike from his coat. He pushed the boy to one side and ran up to the landing. Footsteps followed him, the four children running after him as fast as they could, holding their spikes before them. Blindly Jago ran on, not knowing where the long corridor of the vast baronial house would lead. In ten paces it turned to the right and then to the left.

Ahead, a staircase led upwards. It was dark and narrow, with the smell of horse liniment. As Jago looked behind, he caught sight of one of the children running faster than the others. He guessed from the long blonde locks that fell over the mask that it was a girl.

Jago turned at the top of the staircase just as the hand of the girl gripped the hem of his trousers. He stopped and turned. Then, with the silver spike, she stabbed him in the leg. Jago screamed as the child pulled the spike out and stabbed him again. He kicked out. The child fell back, her mask falling from her face. She grabbed for the banister as she slipped down the stairs.

'Get back! Leave me alone!' Jago shouted as he ran on.

The others helped the child to her feet as they gave chase.

Running along the landing, Jago saw a window. Tendrils of old ivy pushed against the outside of the sash. He took hold of the frame and tried to slide it open, but the wood was stuck fast. Without hesitation, Jago kicked at the frame. Glass and wood splintered as the window shattered into long shards.

Pulling the remains of the window away, Jago saw the children behind him. They stood silently, each one holding a silver spike.

'Please come back,' the girl said in her half-dead voice. 'Ozymandias wants you . . .'

He waited for a moment, knowing that the children were ready to attack. He could see their eyes as they stared from within their masks, their lips frozen in dumb smiles.

'Please come back,' another said, stepping forward to within an arm's length.

Jago slipped back to the ledge of the window and made ready. Just as he turned, the child lunged towards him. Defiantly, Jago grabbed the boy by the lapels of his gold coat and with a turn of the wrist threw him from the window.

The screams echoed in the night as he crashed to the gravel driveway.

Like a pack of animals the other children lurched forward, stabbing at Jago with their spikes. Jago pushed them back and then jumped through the window. With one hand he gripped a gnarled branch of the ancient ivy, then slammed against the wall of the house and dangled high above the ground. Two of the Vampyre orchestra leant out, held by the others. They stabbed and stabbed at Jago's hands. One spiked pierced the sleeve of his leather coat and pinned him to the ivy branch. He twisted as he tried to climb down and the branch was slowly pulled away from the wall of the house.

Another child stepped through the window and leapt towards him. She fell through the air and grabbed him by the throat. Her tiny fingers dug into his skin and she attempted to bite his face again and again.

'Get away!' Jago shouted as the ivy branch snapped and they started to fall.

He looked up just as the branch pulled away from the side of the house. The child lost her grip and fell. As Jago slipped from the branch a cold wind blew in his face and the tree branches rattled. Jago slammed to the ground. The body of the girl broke his fall. She groaned. Jago lifted her from the wet stones.

With a sudden jolt she stabbed him in the shoulder, but the spike jammed in the thick leather sleeve. Jago threw her to the ground. As he looked up, he could see the other children climbing down the ivy branches that gripped the wall of the house. He stepped out to run but the girl kicked him and Jago fell to the ground. She leapt upon him and tried to gouge out his eyes. He twisted and turned as he gripped her hands and fought her off.

From the far side of the house he could hear shouting. The voice of Ozymandias and a hundred other Vampyres echoed around the turrets and spires.

Jago broke free from the girl's grip and pushed her back. She lunged at him again as she tried to grab the spike stuck in his shoulder.

Taking the handle, he pulled the spike from his jacket and with a flash of his hand stabbed the girl. She shuddered and with a trembling hand reached out to Jago.

'Thank you,' she whispered as she fell back, her arms outstretched.

'That's him!' came a shout from the shadows of the house.

Larkin was striding towards him, an army pistol in his hand. A mob followed in his wake. Jago began to run faster than he had ever done in his life. He could feel the darkness press in around him as he sprinted across the dew-covered lawn towards a low wall and the fields beyond.

At first, those who followed hesitated. Then others came with burning torches and they gave chase.

Then Jago was on a road – he heard the sound of car engines and their bright headlights lit the night around him. His feet were soon sodden with the dew from the grass and far behind he could hear the mob following his trail. A car sped down the road as if to cut off his escape. Jago turned towards a copse of trees on a small mound.

In a matter of yards, the ground beneath him had changed.

Grass gave way to sprigs of heather and stone outcrops, and the moon picked out a long path. Larkin and the Vampyres still followed and Jago could see they were gaining ground. He knew there would be no escape.

Slowly, he climbed the mound. The wound to his leg would not stop bleeding. Jago walked quickly through the pine trees and boulders. He could see the land fall away to the coast, where the high cliffs of Ravenscar cut down into the sea that was covered by a pall of cloud.

A tall figure stepped from the shadow of a tree. 'What took you so long?' a voice asked. 'Won't be long before they catch you.'

'Blaine?' Jago said.

'Who else would be out here waiting for you?'

'But how did you know?'

'You too are a Vampyre hunter and we all think alike.' Blaine was shadowed in darkness. 'I knew you would escape, and if you didn't I would admire the moon and wonder how to explain your death to Hugh Morgan.'

'But what about Larkin and Ozymandias?' Jago asked, knowing they were getting closer.

'I know a way of escape that not even Ozymandias can follow.'

'Why should I trust you? You betrayed me.' Jago felt the wound in his leg throbbing.

'It was the only way to entice Sibilia to come out into the open. It was the only way to get her blood.'

'I was bait in the trap?' Jago asked as he began to walk away. The vial of Sibilia's blood was still safe, deep within his jacket.

'You wanted her blood and it was the only way to get her,' Blaine answered, following. 'If you want to live you will have to come with me.'

'Where?' Jago was unsure if he should ever believe Blaine again.

Before he could answer, a creature ran from the cover of the heather. Like a large dog, it leapt at Blaine and knocked him to the ground, and then before Jago could escape another beast took hold of him by the arm. He looked down at the face of a child. It bit and gnawed at the sleeve of his leather coat.

'Jago!' Blaine shouted as he tried to get the boy from him. 'The blade!'

Jago saw the hilt of a knife sticking from Blaine's belt. He kicked the boy and lashed out, knocking the child to the floor. Then, reaching out he grabbed the hilt and pulled out the knife just as the Vampyre child attacked again.

Seeing the blade, the child stepped back and held up both of its hands.

'You wouldn't kill me? I am just a child,' it said feebly.

Jago hesitated.

'Kill it!' Blaine shouted.

The boy leapt at Jago and grabbed him by the throat. Blaine struggled to be free from the other Vampyre child that had wrapped itself around his head and was pulling out strands of his hair.

Jago thrust the knife. The boy fell to the ground and cowered by a large stone. Its mask fell from its face, and Jago realised he knew the child.

'Boris Gladling?' Jago said, knowing the child to be the

youngest of the brothers from Streonshalgh Manor, the first place where he had stayed in Whitby after being evacuated from London.

'Jago?' the boy asked in a defenceless voice.

'Jago, now!' Blaine screamed as the other Vampyre tore at his face.

Jago lashed out with the knife, and the child screamed and fell from Blaine. Its dead body cracked over a large stone at the base of a tree.

'Gladling?' Jago asked.

'Don't be fooled by them. They would kill you in an instant,' Blaine said as he wiped the blood from his face. 'Come on – we have to get away from here.'

Blaine ran down the mound to the path below. Before Jago could find him, he heard the sound of the old motorbike. Blaine rode on to the path and stopped.

'Where are we going?' Jago asked, his hand trembling as he clutched the knife.

'Far away. I have much to tell you.'

As Jago jumped on to the motorbike, Larkin and the others appeared at the mound.

'Stop them!' Larkin shouted as he took aim and fired the pistol.

The bullets hit the hard ground and spun through the air. Blaine turned the throttle and the front wheel of the Triumph motorbike lifted from the earth. Larkin fired repeatedly as Blaine drove into the darkness.

The path fell quickly towards the coast. Far behind, Jago could see burning torches and the outline of the mound covered in trees. He knew they could not follow on the track across the moor. Something inside him, an inner voice he was tempted to trust, made him want to run from Blaine. Death came easily to this man, and as they rode across the moor all Jago could see in his mind's eye was the Gladling child looking at him.

After an hour they were far from Ozymandias and the blood auction, and on the far horizon Jago could see the high chimneys of Hawks Moor set against the light of the moon.

'It's over there!' he shouted to Blaine.

'Not going back – not yet,' Blaine answered. 'A secret place where no one will find us.'

'I thought that before. When you betrayed me,' Jago moaned.

Blaine turned the Triumph across the main road to Whitby. Lit only by the moon, they crossed the fields and rode through the woods until Jago could smell the sea. The path grew narrower, winding its way through deserted alum mines. Red shale littered the hillside as if it were freshly hewn from the rocks. Soon they turned and dropped steeply on a path to the sea that was shaded by a canopy of trees.

Blaine stopped the engine. 'As far as we go,' he said, and he pushed the bike into a hiding place amongst the bushes. 'We walk from here.'

Jago followed him through the trees and soon they were on a narrow beach with high shale cliffs at either side. A small brook fell to the beach in a long fall of water, and half hidden behind it was the entrance to a cave.

'Is this it?' Jago asked. 'What if they find us?'

'There are plenty of ways to escape,' Blaine answered with a grin, pushing back his long strands of red hair. 'Wait here.'

'For how long?' Jago asked.

Jago sat on the beach and waited. He checked that he still had the Trajithian and the vial of Sibilia's blood. As the minutes passed he listened to the breaking waves and thought of what he had become. Taking a handful of sand, he tried to rub the blood from his hands, but it was as if it had stained the skin deep red and would be there always as a reminder of that night. He kept thinking of the Gladling child who had tried to kill him.

'It's ready,' Blaine said as he returned with a lantern in his hand. 'We'll stay here tonight and tomorrow I will talk with Hugh Morgan.'

Entering the cave, Jago ducked his head and twisted through a narrow door-like opening. The cave was warm. A fire burnt in an iron stove. Coffee steamed and meat sizzled in a frying pan.

'Who lives here?' Jago asked as he sat on a wicker chair by the fire and looked around.

'Smugglers did a long time ago. I was once one of them. But had a different name then.'

'Is it something you always do?' he asked Blaine.

'Can't stay too long in one place. I am surprised the Morgans lasted so long at Hawks Moor.'

'Are you a Vampyre?' Jago asked as Blaine handed him a tin cup filled with rich black liquid.

'Would it make any difference?' Blaine said with a raised brow.

'It would make me wonder why you are so ready to kill your own kind,' Jago said. 'I had believed you were a Recanter.'

'That which was once – is now – and shall be forever . . .' Blaine laughed. 'The truth is –'

'Truth?' Jago asked before Blaine could say another word.

'You asked if I was a Vampyre or a Recanter. In truth I have been both. I didn't like the mortal life and chose to become a Vampyre again. That is what I am,' Blaine said as he chewed on the meat.

'Then why do you kill your own kind?' Jago asked.

'I would like to say it was because I wanted to rid the world of those that are dangerous and out of control. You have seen for yourself what the power of living for ever can do to some of my kind.' Blaine stopped speaking and picked his teeth with the tip of a silver spike. 'The trouble is, Jago, I actually enjoy what I do. It is an art and has now become a way of life. Like a Valkyrie, I choose who lives or dies.'

'Murder? A way of life?' Jago said as he shook his head in disbelief. 'You lie and kill and show no remorse.'

'A liar I most certainly am. And as for a murderer – look at your own hands, Jago. They are stained with blood and you are but a lad.'

17

Inspector Kaine

IT WAS THE THOUGHT of seeing Jago again that forced Hugh Morgan from his bed and down the stairs to the breakfast room. He sat in the cold grey light that streamed in through the leaded panes and looked out across the moor. As Hugh lifted the china cup from the saucer, he noticed that his hand trembled. Sharp pains jabbed through his fingers and into his chest.

Vibica de Zoete sat in the opposite chair and watched his movements with her cat-like glare. She could see his breath was laboured as she tried to listen to his thoughts. It was something that as a Vampyre she couldn't stop herself from doing; it was part of her life and she enjoyed knowing what was really in his heart. There was something about Hugh Morgan that Vibica adored. He was so unlike his father and yet in some ways was exactly the same.

'Are you enjoying watching me?' Hugh asked her as he tried to pour another cup of tea from the chipped teapot.

'I didn't think you had noticed,' she answered coyly as she dabbed the edges of her lips with the napkin. 'You seemed to be so far away.'

'And you read my mind?' he asked.

189

'I try not to read the thoughts of people that I like,' Vibica said, knowing he was worrying about Jago and could not understand why the boy had disappeared. 'He will come back. If he can, he will come back.'

'He left without a word. I fear he was taken.' Hugh sat back in his chair and rubbed his eyes.

'If your father had him then we would know by now. He was a man who always liked to gloat over his victories,' Vibica answered.

'How well do you know him?' Hugh asked, his voice weak.

'There was a time when we were good friends. Long before he met your mother, in Paris at the time of Napoleon.'

'Don't you get sick of living for so long?'

'A life without sickness, the mild discomfort of taking blood, these things you get used to.' Vibica looked at his drawn face and lips tinged with purple. 'I take it that the porphyria is no better?'

'It is the worry over Jago. I can't sleep, not knowing where he is. The pain grows with every day.' Hugh slumped the cup back on to the saucer and gave a sigh that said more than a thousand words. He looked at Vibica, his eyes tired, unable to think of the words he wished to say.

'Will this disease kill you?' she asked, already knowing the answer.

'Of course,' he said as if he spoke of the price of bread. 'I will be dead within the month. There is no cure.'

'And you will let that happen? Jago will be alone and you shall sleep in the grave and he shall have no one to care for him.' As she spoke she dug her knife into the side of a red

190

apple and watched the juice trickle across the blade. 'Is that something you are prepared to do?'

'It is something that I cannot stop. How else can I avoid death?' he asked.

'I take it you have already thought of what I am about to ask you?' Vibica said, hoping he would allow her to speak the words.

Hugh nodded. It was a slight and frail move of the head, as if he was resigned to what was to come. 'I have thought of it and repented of that thought many times,' he answered. 'In my father I saw everything I never wanted to be and to take his creed is not what I desire.'

'But you would live and Jago would have a father,' Vibica said.

'In life, we often cannot have what we want.'

His words were bleak and without emotion. Vibica tried to listen deeply but there was nothing but the sighing of his soul.

'In life we can have everything,' she whispered to herself as she watched a man walking along the gravel drive towards the house. 'Inspector Kaine,' she said, standing up from the table.

'Jack will answer the door. Go to the secret room in the hall and wait there,' Hugh answered as he struggled to get from his chair.

Before Hugh Morgan could get from the table, the door-bell rang. It echoed through the house. He heard Henson's long strides as he strode across the hallway. It was too late for Vibica to hide.

'What if he finds me?' she whispered.

'Stay here . . .'

'I am investigating a murder,' Kaine said abruptly as Henson opened the door. 'I believe the suspect resides here.'

'Didn't I tell you before that she is not here?' Henson asked.

'This is a different murder and one to which we have a reliable witness.' Kaine stuttered nervously as he fumbled with his trilby hat and tried to adjust the tight belt of his gabardine. 'Mr Larkin informs us that the boy in question lives here – Jago Harker.'

'Who has Jago murdered?' Henson insisted, not letting Kaine cross the threshold of Hawks Moor.

'A child in the care of Mr Larkin at Wear Head Manor. A boy by the name of Gladling.'

'Impossible. The Gladling boys drowned when the wave struck the coast and haven't been seen since,' Henson said as he stepped forward and stared down at the Inspector.

'Since the night of the great wave they have been in the care of Larkin. He was full of admiration for the lad and now the child is dead. He has sworn on oath that it was Jago Harker who killed him with a knife. I have seen the body and confirm all he has said.'

'Jago is not here,' Henson answered. 'Gone to London two nights ago. It couldn't have been him.'

'Then you have no objection to me searching the house?' Kaine asked.

'If you have a warrant.'

Henson folded his arms and leant against the door and smiled. Kaine fumbled for a moment and then looked back to the car parked by the gate.

'Will you make me go back to the car or will you take my word?' he asked.

Henson studied him, not knowing what to do.

'I think it will be quite appropriate for Inspector Kaine to search the whole of Hawks Moor if he so requires,' Hugh Morgan said, stepping from the breakfast room and walking slowly to the doorway with his walking stick. 'If your officers want to start on the ground floor that will be fine.'

'I work alone, Mr Morgan. It's the only way. Too many cooks . . . And conscription, of course.'

Kaine wiped strands of white spittle from his lips with the cuff of his sleeve as he eyed the inside of Hawks Moor. Rubbing the dirty soles of his creased leather shoes on the doormat he stepped inside, squeezing by Henson who refused to move. 'I am so glad that you have seen sense. If the boy is here, give him to me now and we can forget your complicity in the murder.'

'What you have already forgotten, Inspector, is that Jago is not here,' Hugh answered.

Kaine ignored what he had just said and placed his grubby trilby hat on the mantelpiece. 'If I were to believe that every time I went for a suspect, I would not be where I am today,' he answered as he looked up the stairs.

'And where exactly is that?' asked Vibica de Zoete as she stepped from the room behind him.

Kaine turned and looked at the woman. Henson noticed his hands tremble as he looked at her and then at Hugh Morgan.

'Miss de Zoete?' Kaine asked, his voice on the verge of a squeal. 'I didn't realise . . .'

'Wasn't the last time we met in London?' she asked him as he stood slack-jawed, staring at her.

'Perhaps. Perhaps it was,' he answered cautiously.

'I thought I remembered clearly that you and I were at the same ball?' Vibica replied nonchalantly.

'The Groucho Ball, at the Coliseum in 1934. See, my memory isn't as faded as you thought.' Kaine seemed to be disturbed by her asking. He fidgeted with his fingers as he thought of what to say. 'If I may commence with the rooms upstairs?' he asked.

'Are you sure you don't want to talk further with Miss de Zoete?' Henson asked, closing the large oak door and turning the lock. 'Wasn't it her you were seeking in connection with a murder of a soldier in Hagg Woods?'

Vibica looked surprised that Henson should mention such a thing. She stared at him coldly.

'It was decided the man was attacked by a wild beast. The police have no further interest,' Kaine answered nervously. He paused and then licked his lips. 'I am not sure if a search will be necessary after all. I think I should be going back.'

Vibica looked at Henson.

'Isn't it the custom for a police inspector to take tea when they call in these parts?' she asked. 'I am even sure there is breakfast left over for you to eat.'

Kaine shrugged his shoulders, the sleeve of the oversized raincoat falling to cover his hands.

'Not necessary, not necessary,' he said quite agitated. 'Thank you and I shall be on my way.'

The Inspector stepped towards the door. Henson leant against it as Vibica paced toward the fire.

'We would regard it as an insult if you left,' Henson answered him as he slid the bolt.

Inspector Kaine thought for a moment and then turned to Hugh Morgan. As he did so he undid the buttons on his gabardine and slipped his hand inside.

'I take it you know who I am?' he asked.

'You are Inspector Kaine of the Metropolitan Police,' Hugh said.

'I think we can do away with all the pretence. Inspector Kaine is the companion of the Prime Minister,' Vibica said.

'Noel Kinross . . . I have been with him for many years.'

'And that is why you were at the Groucho Ball when I saw you last,' she said.

'Indeed.' In the uncomfortable silence, they all stood and looked at each other. 'I take it that I am not allowed to leave?' he asked.

Morgan looked at Henson as if he should decide.

'If he works for Kinross why is he a danger to us?' Henson asked.

The reason for Kaine's nervousness suddenly became clear.

'Our friend serves two masters,' Vibica said in reply as she undid the top button of her high-necked shirt. 'Kinross felt betrayed and that is why Inspector Kaine was sent here.'

'Is that true?' Hugh asked the Inspector.

'It could possibly be seen that way, but there is still the matter of a murder,' he said as he pulled a small pistol from his coat and pointed it at Henson. 'Therefore stand away from the door and allow me to leave.'

Without warning, Vibica de Zoete leapt from the fireplace and grabbed Kaine by the hand. In one swift movement she spun him on his heels. Kaine fired his gun as Hugh Morgan rushed to her. The Inspector was pushed to the floor and Henson bound his hands with the cord from the drape that covered the doorway.

'Take him to the cellar and we'll keep him there,' Hugh said.

'They know I am here, I told them. Others will come for me and not just the police,' Kaine warned as Henson lifted him from the floor by the scruff of his neck.

'Who will come for you – who do you work for?' Hugh asked.

'Strackan,' Vibica said, baring her teeth. 'That is why Kinross could no longer trust him.'

'A far better employer than the Prime Minister and one with better prospects,' Kaine said as he spat in her face. 'The Lodge Maleficarum is finished – all of you are finished – don't you see that?'

'Take him, Jack. Take him before I rip out his throat,' Vibica snarled.

'You can't do that,' Kaine argued as Henson dragged him to the secret door in the panelled wall. 'If I don't return they will look for me.'

Hugh Morgan looked at Henson.

'What if he is right?' Hugh asked, his face etched with pain.

'I know a place on the road where there have been many accidents. I will make sure his car goes over the cliff and report it as a tragic accident,' Henson said as he pressed the wall and opened the door with the tips of his fingers. 'That should keep them off his scent.'

'Strackan will find me, be sure of that,' Kaine argued as he was thrown through the door. 'He will come for me.'

'Perhaps that is just what we want,' Henson said as he closed the door behind him.

'Do you think Strackan will look for him?' Hugh asked Vibica.

'He has no concern for his companions. Madame Trevellas is all he cares for and I think you already know that.' She tried to smile, but could see he was in pain. 'But you are unwell . . .'

'More than I have ever been,' Hugh said as he covered his mouth with his hand. 'I need to be in my room.'

Vibica walked with him up the staircase and along the landing until they got to the door of his room. Opening the door she helped him to the unmade bed and then crossed the room and closed the curtains. Several orbs of light fluttered around the posts of the bed and danced under the crinoline canopy. Vibica had noticed before that on every shelf and table were pictures of the same woman.

'Your mother?' she asked.

'Taken just before she was murdered,' he said as he slumped to the bed.

'She was beautiful,' Vibica answered as she took a bowl of water from the nightstand, dipped the cloth and wiped his forehead.

'Just like you,' he said as he looked at the contours of her shadowed face. 'You are most kind.'

'Kind? Only to those I like,' she replied as she stroked his face and ran her long nail along his chin. 'I just wish you would allow me to heal you.'

197

'If that should be the way . . .' He looked at her, knowing that sleep would soon overwhelm him.

In the silence of the room, as Hugh Morgan slept peacefully, Vibica leant towards him. The blue-green orbs danced around her as though they came from within. Vibica looked back to the door as if she could hear someone outside. She waited, held her breath and then bowed even closer. She could feel Morgan's warm and laboured breath on her face. Her hair fell and draped over his neck. Hidden from the world, in the tranquillity of the darkened room, she slowly bit his neck.

Like a cat she lapped the first drops of blood that seeped from the two minute puncture wounds. With a dull murmur of her voice she bit again, allowing venom to mix with his blood. Hugh woke for a moment, struggled to break free and then slumped back against the embroidered pillows. His blood tasted of salt. It was more bitter than she expected. Vibica purred to herself in contentment, rubbing her fingers through his hair and smoothing them across his face. He was beautiful, she thought as she held him close.

Vibica lay with him, pressing her head against his chest and counting the beats of his faltering heart. With each beat it became weaker and weaker. Then, with a sigh, it stopped. Hugh Morgan dropped his hand from the bed, the arm hanging loose, fingers touching the fine thread of the rug. Vibica stayed close to him and waited. She looked at his face and watched the colour drain from within. His lips turned the darkest shade of purple and the lids of each eye changed to almost black. She held him close as if she would never let him go. Her head was pushed against his ribs as she listened to the silence. Then Vibica began to smile as she heard a familiar sound.

Slowly as if it were reborn, the heart began to beat again. She pressed her hand on the wounds of his neck and spoke in words that even she did not understand. Hugh coughed as his body shuddered. As if waking from sleep for the very first time, he opened his eyes.

'It is finished,' she said as she kissed his lips. 'The sickness has gone.'

Unable to speak, he squeezed her hand and smiled.

The door opened. Biatra stood in the shadow like a dark statue, her face unseen.

'Is he one with us?' she asked, her voice hushed.

'Indeed,' Vibica answered.

18

Aldus Flood

THE FIRE BURNT BRIGHTLY in the cave. Toran Blaine sat in the wicker chair and watched Jago as he slept. In his hand was the creased Maleficarum scroll. His eyes scanned the final name that had appeared during the night. In thick black ink, edged in purple, was a name he never thought he would ever see. Jago turned and rolled on the low bed that was pushed against the wall of the cave. As if he had heard Blaine thinking, Jago opened his eyes and looked across the candlelit room.

'Is it morning?' Jago asked, unsure how long he had slept.

'It is the afternoon, I can smell the tide,' Blaine answered.

'When can I go back to Hawks Moor?' he asked.

Blaine looked flustered, his face reddened. 'That could be more difficult than I ever thought,' he answered eventually. 'Things have changed whilst you slept. I am not sure if it will be safe.'

'Safe?' Jago asked. 'Safe for who?'

Blaine held out the scroll for Jago to see and pointed to the last name that had appeared.

'Hugh Morgan is now a Vampyre and I do not know the circumstances in which this came about.'

'It can't be, he would never . . .' Jago got to his feet and searched the room for his leather coat. 'Who took his blood?'

'The name on the scroll is Vibica de Zoete – look for yourself,' Blaine said.

Jago looked again. In fine purple was the name. He read the words slowly.

'Vibica de Zoete,' he said as he looked up from the scroll and stared at Blaine. 'Why would she?'

'That I need to find out. If he gave himself willingly then things have changed. I would never have thought that *he* would ever become a Vampyre,' Blaine answered as he looked at Jago and then to the entrance of the cave. 'I will go alone and then come for you.'

'And I will stay here?' Jago asked, not wanting to be left alone.

'You will be safe. No one knows this place. It is a secret.' Blaine folded the scroll and placed it in the pocket of his long coat. 'This makes it difficult. I will have to see what is to be done.'

Jago found his coat and looked for the knife and the vial of blood. He held it in his hand and then turned to Blaine.

'If I give this to Biatra, will it work?' he asked.

'If the blood is prepared well. I will do that for you – don't worry.' Blaine reached out and touched Jago on the shoulder.

'But will it work?' Jago looked around the cave. It was more like the inside of a fine house. Though the walls were of rock and sand was scattered across the floor, everything else was of the finest quality. The love of beauty was the one thing that he realised all Vampyres shared. 'It has to work.'

Blaine stepped towards the entrance. 'I promise, if I can save the girl I will. Not everyone is meant to be a Vampyre. That is the reason why I live.'

'Who do you work for?' Jago asked, still wondering why Blaine could kill his own kind.

'It is best that you do not know. Not yet, anyway,' he answered.

And then Blaine was gone.

'When will you be back?' Jago shouted.

'Later . . .' echoed the cold reply from far away.

Jago was alone. He put the knife and vial on the small oak table and then slumped on the bed and looked around the cave. As the fire dimmed, he pulled the drapes across the entrance to the small alcove where the mahogany bedstead had been placed. He laid his head on the pillow and wondered what had happened to Hugh Morgan.

It was only later, when a breeze rattled the long jet beads that hung across the doorway, that Jago knew he was not alone. Inside the cave he could hear breathing. Each breath was laboured and harsh, snatched from the air, the stolen breaths of a beast beyond time. He listened intently and he tried not to move. Books had been cast aside; furniture was tumbled out of the way as if a poltergeist had been in the room. He lay still and held his breath. Whatever was in the cave was now close to the bed.

Jago took his finger and slowly pulled the drape to one side so he could peek through the crack. In the dim light of the candle he saw a gigantic bearded figure wearing a long coat that trailed on the ground and swept the sand. Fingerless leather gloves covered his thickset hands.

'Who's there?' a hoarse voice snapped as the figure turned and looked at the drapes. 'Who is it?'

Jago did not move. He could clearly see the man through the narrow crack. A single staring eye looked at him; the other eye was nothing more than a jagged scar that ran across his face. 'I can tell when I am being watched,' the man said. 'Can smell you – know you are human . . .'

Jago felt in the pocket of his coat for the Trajithian. He sighed, realising he had left it on the table next to the man.

'I have a gun,' Jago said, hoping the man would heed his bluff.

'So do I,' the man answered. 'Found it in a car that had gone over the cliff just south of Whitby. Think it's a Luger.' Jago heard the click of the hammer as it was pulled back. 'From your voice I would say that you are not more than sixteen and come from London. Probably lived most of your life within a mile of Brick Lane.' The man paused and drew his breath. 'What's a lad like that doing here?'

Jago heard the wicker chair strain under the weight of the man as he sat down.

'I'll fire,' Jago answered.

'I would be surprised if you knew how – get yourself out here and let me see who you are.' The man laughed, his voice warm.

Jago folded the pillow over his hand, making it look as if it covered a gun, then slowly pulled the curtain to one side.

'What do you want? This isn't your cave,' Jago said.

'Neither does it belong to the man I saw leave here two hours ago,' the man answered as he pointed the Luger pistol at Jago. 'You his son?'

'Why?' Jago asked.

'Wouldn't want him coming after me if I killed you. He looked dangerous. Looked like a madman. Is he a spy? I heard there were spies all along the coast hiding out in caves and woods.'

'He's no spy. What are you doing here?'

The man looked at him and then to the folded pillow on his hand. He thought and then clicked the hammer on his gun and placed it on the table.

'Let's not do anything stupid. Put down your gun and we can talk. I was here just to see what I could take. That's what I do. I don't want any trouble from your dad.'

Jago slowly put his hand on the table and covered the Luger with the pillow.

'There – we are even,' he said as he stepped back and leant against the wall.

'Fine place you got here. Looks like you have been here for some time. You a smuggler?' the man said as he gleefully eyed the room.

'Who is asking?' Jago asked. 'He'll be back soon and I wouldn't want to be you when he does.'

'Flood, that's who I am. Professor Aldus Flood,' he said. 'You're not his son. I can tell by the eyes and the way you hold yourself. He walked like a cat, but you're different.'

'You a professor? You look like a tramp,' Jago said rudely as he looked at the man warily and wondered if he could outrun him.

'Such an easy observation. You will have seen many people like me in your time living where you did,' the man said as he folded his long arms and put his rough boots on the table.

204

'Life can change our fortunes in the twinkling of an eye. I was a professor of linguistics at Oxford University and then this happened.' He pointed to the scar on his face where his eye once sat. 'Strange how lives can quickly change.'

'Why should that stop you working?' Jago asked.

'It was all part of a wager. I had a duel – with a sabre. And I lost. It was as simple as that.' Flood stared at the floor. 'It was a stupid thing that at the time seemed important.'

'You fought a duel?'

'I was once a different man from the one that sits before you today. Half the size and twice as proud. It never crossed my mind that I would ever scavenge the shores of this country looking for things to sell to earn a living and sleep under the sky winter and summer.'

'So why did you fight?' Jago asked, wondering if the man was lying.

'It was over a duck. A duck that was released to fly around my lecture hall. The lad who did it should have known better. Jack Lewis – I remember him well. He was a suave blighter, full of his own importance. He thought of himself as a master of the sword and we fought. He won . . . I was a victim of my own pride. I had agreed that should I lose, then I would resign my Chair.'

'So how did you know I was from London?'

'Quite simple. I have studied accents all of my life and yours was so easy to recognise.'

Jago looked at him warily. He was a large man wrapped in a long coat that covered at least two other coats, a waistcoat and a shirt. What lay beneath that was a matter for the imagination.

'So why come here?'

'Be you not as the horse, or as the mule, which have no un-derstanding: whose mouth must be held in with bit and bridle. Isn't that what the Book says? For that is my life. I go where the tide and storm takes me. I heard that a huge wave had broken on the shore and I thought I might find something of interest and instead I have discovered you.' Flood laughed, his mouth opening so wide it seemed he would swallow himself.

Jago slowly moved towards the entrance and reached for the firewood stacked against the wall. When he turned, Flood was on his feet and standing over the stove.

'Are you – are you a Vampyre?' Jago asked warily as he clutched an oak log.

'Vampyre?' Flood asked. 'I do not have the teeth to be such a creature – if they ever were to exist. Is that what is foremost in the imagination of a lad from Brick Lane?'

'You're different.'

'A one-legged dog is different, but it is not a Vampyre. Do you have a name?' Flood asked.

'Jago. Jago Harker.'

'Well, Jago Harker – why are you in a place like this?'

Jago sat on the woodpile and told Flood about London and the death of his mother. It was easier than he ever thought. The man listened, not wanting to interrupt. Jago talked for an hour but never mentioned Hawks Moor or the Vampyres.

'And then I came to this place. I met the man by the road and he said I would be safe. He's gone for food,' Jago said, letting his hands fall to his side as he lied about Blaine.

'He has a motorbike hidden in the wood. I heard it start up

206

and roar off. Not your usual kind of man to be living on the beach,' Flood answered. He yawned and tugged at the long strands of his black beard. 'Do you have room for the likes of me in your home from home, Jago?'

'You want to stay?' Jago asked.

'I could sleep by the fire in the wicker chair and that would do me,' he said, already assuming that this would be the place he would lay his head. 'Anyway, I don't think your friend will be back for some time.'

Jago nodded and tried to look welcoming as Flood stoked the fire with more wood and tidied the chair before sitting down and propping his legs against the stove.

'What shall you say to the man when he gets back?' Jago asked.

'I will tell him who I am. I don't expect any trouble,' Flood answered. 'This is the first fire I have seen for a long time. It is strange how cold your bones can become.'

'Then stay by the fire as long as you want,' Jago said as he sat on the edge of his bed and watched the man unfurl like an opening flower. Before he could leave he would have to wait until the man was asleep.

Flood pulled the collar of his coat around his ears and slipped deeper into the layers of coats and undergarments. In a matter of a few minutes he had begun to snore. Jago slowly slipped his hand under the pillow on the table, took the Luger and put it in his pocket. He looked at the man once more before he slipped quietly from the entranceway and along the passage to the beach.

'You'll need more than a pistol to kill those who are after you, Jago Harker,' Flood muttered, but Jago couldn't hear him. *'Many sorrows shall be to the wicked: but he that trusts shall be surrounded by mercy.'*

Outside, the night was cold. On the beach the waves crashed against the stones and rattled them like bones. A strong wind blew through the trees above the cliff and pushed against the falling water that fell from above.

Striding out, he was soon in the wood. The path was marked well and as the moon rose from the sea he began to walk north. For two hours he twisted up and down as the path took him onward. Every so often he stopped, waiting to see if he was being followed. He clutched the pistol in his hand, its metal warm against his skin. Later he followed the railway through the quarry that skirted the village before Hawks Moor. Where it ran along the cliff top and the road crossed the railway, Jago could see the broken path of the car that had driven over the cliff. Looking down he could see the debris of the car as it lay on its roof in the shallow water, its doors open.

Climbing the hill, Jago was soon overlooking Hawks Moor. Night had fallen thick and dark. The roof of the house was lined with silver, and moonlight reflected from the glass in every window that faced the sea. All was still, nothing stirred. On the gravel drive at the front of Hawks Moor, just by the door, was the motorbike propped on its stand. Jago waited, suspecting he could not trust Toran Blaine no matter how much he had wanted to. He knew that the scroll of the Maleficarum wouldn't lie and that Hugh Morgan was a Vampyre. All had changed: he wasn't even sure that Hugh was in fact his father; he felt like an outsider. As he hid in the hedge by the gateway, Jago thought he should run. The cold night air soon began to chill him through his leather coat. He pulled it tightly around him and squatted in the grass, not knowing what to do.

It was then that he saw the door open. A sudden shaft of light eased into the night and cast a shadow across the gravel. Toran Blaine stepped outside, followed by Vibica de Zoete. She held his hand and when he turned to leave she put her arms around his neck and, pulling him towards her, she kissed him.

'I'll always love you,' Jago heard her say as she walked with him to the Triumph, her long velvet dress trailing on the gravel.

'I know,' he answered, 'and when all this is finished we will be together.'

'How was Ozymandias?' Vibica asked as she held him close.

'As he has always been for the last thousand years,' he answered glibly.

'When I have lived that long I will know what you mean,' Vibica said as she tenderly scratched his face with her fingernail.

'I got the blood from Sibilia,' he said.

'The girl doesn't want it. She told me she wishes to stay as a Vampyre. It's only her love for the boy that makes her talk as if she would recant.'

'If she looks at you then why would any woman want to be mortal again?' Blaine said as he touched her lips with the tip of his finger.

'What about the boy?' she asked.

'He's safe with me in the cave. I'll keep him for a couple

of days and then bring him back. Can't have Hugh worrying about him, can we?' Blaine answered as he sat astride the motorbike and kick-started the engine.

Jago heard no more. The sound of the engine drowned out their words. Blaine turned the machine and with a wave of his hand rode off. Vibica de Zoete stood and watched as Blaine disappeared along the road that twisted up the hillside and towards the wood. She waited by the door until he was completely out of sight. Then, just before she went into the house, she looked along the line of trees towards the gate. It was as if she was aware that she was being watched. Jago hid in the long grass and the shadow of the branches of a holly bush and waited until she went back inside.

Clouds blew in from the ocean. In the room in the high tower, he could see Biatra looking down. She twisted her ringlets of red hair in her fingers, then tapped her nails against the leaded glass as if she were beating out the tune to a song. Jago reached inside his coat and felt for the knife – but the pocket was empty. He realised he had left the Trajithian on the table in the cave with Aldus Flood. In anger, he snapped a holly branch and held the splinter tightly in his hand.

[19]

Bitter-Spike

THE KITCHEN DOOR OPENED with ease, moving silently on its well-oiled hinges. Jago waited before he stepped into the house. The atmosphere was different from before; it seemed to be tainted in some way, as if harsh words had taken away all happiness. Slowly he walked through the kitchen and taking the back stairs made his way higher. He was soon outside the door to his room. In the silence he could hear the sound of Biatra still tapping on the window with her fingernails. Opening the door slowly he looked inside.

'I saw you hiding,' Biatra said without turning. 'Why did you run away?'

'I didn't. Blaine took me and handed me over to a Vampyre called Ozymandias. They were going to sell my blood.' Jago closed the door and walked towards her.

'Your blood is the most precious they know,' she said.

'My blood has cost too many lives,' he answered, thinking about young Gladling.

'You killed him?' Biatra answered, as if she had seen his thought.

'I didn't know it was him,' he said. He reached out to touch her.

211

'And you would do the same to me,' she answered. She moved away from him.

'Is it true about Hugh?' he asked.

'He was dying. There was nothing more that could be done. Hugh was worried about you. We didn't know where you had gone. Then a man came to the house and they fought.' Biatra turned from the window and looked at him. Her eyes took in everything about him. 'He has been healed. It is as if he had never been ill. The change is wonderful,' she said.

'He has become a Vampyre. It is something he said would never happen,' Jago answered.

'That's what Jack Henson said before he went back to Whitby. He said there was no place for him amongst a house full of blood-monsters.' Biatra smiled as if she found the words funny. 'Henson said that if you knew what was good for you, then it would be best that you never came back here. He told me that before he left. Then Blaine came to see Hugh.'

Jago looked about the room as he thought. A candle flickered on the fireplace and the moon shone in through the leaded glass, casting criss-cross shadows on the floor.

'Do you remember the first time we were here?' he asked.

'I find it hard to remember anything before I was *changed*.' She tried to smile at him and then realised he was more of a stranger than a friend. 'With every day of my new life I feel as if we grow apart.'

'I could end all this for you. I have the blood from Sibilia. Toran Blaine took it from her,' Jago said.

Biatra swallowed hard, as if recalling a memory from her

212

past life. Her eyes widened and then, like a snuffed-out flame, her smile vanished. The sallow, pained looked returned as her eyes dimmed through want of blood.

'Keep it,' she replied. 'I am happy with who I am now. Vibica said it would be like this at the beginning. I am sure it will pass.' Biatra held her breath as if about to say more. 'Vibica has changed my life.'

'Is she all you can think about?' he asked. 'I heard her telling Blaine how much she loved him. Don't you understand why she is here? It is more than coincidence.'

'Her train was hit by a bomb, that's all. This is a safe place for her,' Biatra answered, her voice raised.

'And she poisoned my father – took his blood and changed him into a Vampyre. I saw his name on the scroll. That is why Blaine came here, to see if it was true. Jack Henson was right. This house is full of blood-monsters.'

'Then what will you do?' Biatra asked.

'What I should have done all along,' he answered as he felt the holly splinter in his pocket. 'Blaine was right. Killing Vampyres isn't such a bad thing after all.'

'Stay, Jago, stay . . .'

Jago walked from the room and made his way down the stairs to the landing below. The night was still in the house; the air was thick as if a fog filled the hallway and clung to his face like frosted web. Coming from under the door of the master bedroom was a faint light. Jago looked at the door handle, took hold of it in his grasp and then turned it slowly.

Looking around the door, Jago could see the four-poster bed. Its curtains were open, and a fire burnt in the grate. Hugh Morgan lay asleep, his face lit by the soft glow of the burning embers. Jago gripped the splinter of holly like a knife. He looked at Hugh Morgan and then stepped towards the bed, trying to stop his mind from thinking of what he was going to do.

'NO!' A scream from far away echoed through the house. 'NO – JAGO!'

Vibica ran along the landing from her room. It was as if the house had come alive. Every door slammed open and then shut. The house shook as if it were within an earthquake and a wind blew through the corridors, lifting the rugs from the floors and pushing over the furniture.

Jago took the holly and raised it above his head. Hugh slept deeply, unable to move. Holding the splinter tightly, Jago looked at his father.

Hugh Morgan opened his eyes just as a hand grabbed Jago by the wrist.

'Jago?' Hugh whispered, unable to believe what he saw.

Jago stood as if frozen. He tried to twist free as Vibica gripped him and then turned him to her in one swift move.

'No, Jago,' she said again as she tried to shake the holly from his hand.

Jago held tight as Vibica growled like a panther, spitting venom in his face. With his free hand, Jago took hold of the water jug on the bedside table and smashed it on her head. Vibica stepped back, took her breath and then lunged towards him. Jago dived out of her way as she fell to the bed.

'Why did you do it? Why did you do it to him?' Jago shouted as she turned.

'Because he was going to die,' she answered. 'I love him.'

214

'That's what you said to Toran Blaine – I heard you when you said goodbye. You are lovers,' Jago screamed as Biatra ran into the room.

'That is not true. He is a Vampyre hunter. I have known him for many years,' Vibica said as she looked at Hugh Morgan.

'He is a Vampyre. He took me from here and gave me to Ozymandias. They were going to sell me for my blood. That is what they are really like,' Jago said to Hugh Morgan. 'Blaine said you were not my father. That you were only my brother.'

'It's not true, he has lied to you,' Vibica said. 'Even I knew of your birth and how you came to be. Listen to me – Toran Blaine is lying.'

Jago looked at Hugh and then at Vibica. Biatra stood close by, her hand clutching the handle of the door as if she would stop his escape.

'You are my brother – that's what he said. Ezra Morgan is my father – that is why they needed me. I am a half-blood like you.'

Before Hugh could speak, Jago ran the five paces o the bed and leapt towards him. He closed his eyes and thrust the holly dagger as hard as he could, hoping it would pierce the heart, but it was Vibica de Zoete who cried out in pain.

'Leave her,' Biatra screamed as she dragged Jago away.

'You stopped me,' Jago shouted.

'I had to. You can't kill him. He is your flesh and blood,' Vibica said as her blood dripped to the floor.

'That died when you took him,' he snarled, looking for a chance to strike her again.

Like a wounded cat, Vibica leapt towards him and pushed

215

him through the door. Jago fell back on to the landing as she tried to push him over the banister. He kicked her legs and pushed her to one side as he ran for the stairs.

'Quickly,' she shouted to Biatra, 'go the other way.'

Jago saw her run to stop his escape. He leapt from the balcony to the landing below, pushing Biatra out of the way. Vibica dropped to the floor below and then came running towards him as if she would tear out his throat. In his heart he knew she would kill him. Jago turned and ran along the passageway to the back stairs.

He plunged into the darkness, chased by the ever-nearing footsteps that shook the boards of the staircase.

'Vibica! Vibica!' he heard Biatra shouting, her cries echoing around the walls of the house.

'This way,' Vibica answered.

Jago knew she was close behind. He ran down the steps and through the kitchen. The door to the hallway was open; he could see the fire burning brightly. In four strides he had crossed the room. Vibica de Zoete was nowhere to be seen. He ran into the hallway towards the front door.

It was then she struck, grabbing Jago by the hair and throwing him to the stone floor. He looked up as she leapt upon him and began to bite at his neck. Jago tried to move his hand from under her, twisting and rolling as she pressed down. With a final push he broke free. Then, with all of his strength, he plunged the holly splinter into her back.

Vibica arched and curled as she screamed. Her hands lashed at the dagger that stuck in her back.

'What have you done?' Biatra screamed as she ran down the staircase, followed by Hugh Morgan.

216

'She was going to kill me,' he shouted.

'Are you not surprised after all you have done?' Hugh answered angrily.

Vibica de Zoete turned and rolled. The holly wand pushed deep within her until it was submerged in her back. She sighed and groaned, unable to move, as it slowly poisoned her. Finally she became silent.

'You have killed her,' Biatra shouted as she ran to the body.

'Holly cannot kill a Vampyre. It just holds them as if in death until it is removed,' Jago said as he walked to the door, not even stopping to look at his father. 'Blaine will remove it from her. After all, they are in love.'

Jago looked back at Hugh Morgan as he opened the door and let in the cold of the night.

'We could have all been together in this place,' Hugh said as he held out his hand.

Jago wiped blood from his face with the cuff of his coat. 'A happy family of blood-drinkers?' he asked.

'It could have been different. I have been cured,' Hugh answered. 'Life would be good.'

'I would not want to spend my time hiding from the world, wondering if someone were hunting me down.'

'What will you do?' Hugh asked.

'Return to London and never come back. There is a war that is destroying this world – or hadn't you realised, in your ivory tower?' Jago stepped from Hawks Moor and slammed the door without looking back.

'What about Vibica? Shall I go for Toran Blaine?' Biatra asked.

'There isn't time. Help me turn her over.'

Together they turned Vibica and rolled her on to the rug by the fireside. Hugh dug his fingers into the wound until he could feel the tip of the holly. Slowly and carefully he began to pull the sprig of wood from within her. As the tip of the holly left the wound, Vibica began to breath. She lashed out with her hand as if she was being woken from a nightmare.

'Where is he?' she demanded. Her eyes flickered around the great hall, shining brightly in the light of the fire. 'We have to stop him – he is thinking of killing us all.'

'He is my son,' Hugh said. 'There must be another way.'

'I could find him,' Biatra said. 'Talk to him, make him see sense . . .'

'She is right,' Vibica insisted as she squeezed his hand. 'Biatra could be the one to save us all.'

Hugh thought for a moment before he answered. The wind shook the chimneys of the house and hail beat against the roof.

'Where has he gone?' he asked. 'How do we find him?'

'I think I know where he could be,' Biatra said as she helped Vibica sit before the fire.

'You must sleep, Hugh,' Vibica said. 'Burn the holly stake in the fire and then sleep. Biatra will care for me.'

Biatra looked at Hugh for his agreement. He reached out and touched her hair. Then, taking the bitter spike he threw it on the fire. It burnt quickly as the blood and sap sizzled in the flames.

'I should stay with you,' he said as he looked at Vibica.

'You are still weak from the transformation. It will be many days before you are fully well again,' she said.

218

Together, they watched Hugh Morgan walk up the stairs to his room. They listened for the closing of the door, as if each knew in their minds what the other was thinking. When all was quiet Vibica slowly got to her feet.

'I need blood,' she said as she wiped her mouth with the back of her hand. 'The holly spike has to be healed with blood.'

'I know a house nearby – we could . . .' Biatra stopped speaking as she saw Vibica look to the secret door and smile. 'Inspector Kaine?' she asked.

'We can't let him leave this place – he works for Strackan. But there is a way he could become useful to us.'

Vibica laughed as she opened the panel wide enough to step through.

'But what about Hugh?' Bia asked.

'He will understand, soon he will feel the same need. That is our life.' Vibica's voice was tinged with excitement. 'I will teach you the best way.'

As they walked through the long corridor of the cellar, Biatra could smell the sea far below. When they reached the door, Vibica handed her the key. Turning it in the lock, she opened the door to the cell and looked inside. Chained to the wall was Inspector Kaine. He looked up and nodded.

'Brought any food?' he asked cantankerously. 'I would expect to be fed.'

Biatra didn't speak. She took two paces into the cell and then stopped again. Taking a small key from her pocket she held out her hand to the man.

'I have come to set you free,' she said softly, her eyes meeting his momentarily.

'Free?' the man asked as he looked around the cell for his hat and coat that hung on the rusted hook above the slop bucket. 'Are you joking?'

'You work for Strackan,' she answered, still holding out the key.

He looked at her suspiciously. 'What if I do – why should you set me free?'

'It's better that way,' Biatra said, knowing Vibica was hiding behind the door.

Kaine got to his feet. He looked awkward and wary, his eyes never leaving the girl.

'How do I get out of the house?' he asked as he reached forward with his wrists that were fastened by manacles.

'Henson has gone and Hugh Morgan is asleep,' she answered as she undid each lock and let the manacles drop clumsily to the floor. The metal chains slid across the cold stone and formed into a clustered snake of iron.

'And you will just let me go – just like that?' he said nervously as he tried to look beyond the door.

Biatra nodded in agreement. A thrill of excitement rushed through her as she tried to stop herself from gulping. Her heart raced as she waited for the moment, trying to remember everything that Vibica had told her.

'How old are you?' she asked softly.

'Forty-two – why?' he answered, pulling on his long shabby overcoat.

'Have you enjoyed your life?'

'An odd –'

He had no time to finish what he was about to say. Biatra did just as she had been told. The strike was instant, quick and fatal. Inspector Kaine fell to the floor. He made no sound. Blood trickled from the wound in his neck.

The door to the cell opened.

'See,' Vibica said as she looked at the man laid on the cold stone, his arms outstretched so that he formed a perfect cross. 'I told you it would be quick – so what was there to fear?'

'Nothing,' Biatra answered in a mutter as she looked at what she had done.

She stood back, unsure what would happen next.

'Best drink whilst the blood is still warm – do you think you could?' Vibica asked, seeing the anxious look on the girl's face.

'I will just imagine it is someone else and not some old grubby man,' she answered as she knelt beside the body of Inspector Kaine as if she were about to pray.

'I know who you are thinking of – perhaps one day that will happen,' Vibica replied. She scooped some blood into the palm of her hand and sipped it like a cat.

[20]

The Apothecary

IT WAS MORNING when Jago reached Whitby. The
night had cast down its dark showers and thunder had
broken the sky as he walked from Hawks Moor along the
edge of the cliff. By the time he came to the pinnacles of
rock that were the remnants of the ruined abbey his leather
coat dripped with rainwater, hanging upon him like a sodden carcass. Each step brought into his mind another painful
thought. All that he had known he had to leave behind, and
as he looked over the high cliff he seemed to stare into an
abyss of emptiness. He kicked the clumps of grass that edged
the cliff top as he walked alone in the beating rain.

He could soon see the towering chimneys of Streonshalgh
Manor. The house looked cold and empty. The windows
were shuttered and there was no sign of Mrs Macarty or any
of the children. He walked on and turned into the churchyard, where rain had washed the mud from the mounds of
fresh earth of the new graves. A solitary figure knelt by an old
marker stone. She covered herself from the rain with a black
umbrella as she placed a garland of dried flowers against the
stone. In a brief glance their eyes met. The woman smiled.

Jago walked on, not realising that the woman had begun

to follow him. The rain pounded on the flattened gravestones that formed the pathway. She kept pace and with an extra stride grew nearer. As he trod the first of the one hundred and ninety-nine steps to the town below he felt a touch on his shoulder.

'You should get something done to the cuts on your face,' the woman said, taking hold of Jago by the arm.

He turned; the drips from the black umbrella fell on his head as from a spitting drainage pipe. The cloud above them was so thick that it remained as night, the morning sun unable to break through.

'I didn't realise,' he said touching his face and then looking at the thin red stain on his fingers.

'Was it a dog that did that to you?' she asked as she tipped back his chin with her long fingers to examine the wound. 'You can see the teeth marks.'

'Last night,' he answered, unsure what to say.

'Do you live around here? You look familiar.'

'Going to see a friend of mine, Jack Henson. My name is Jago,' he answered.

'Jack has friends? I have never seen the man smile in all my life and he has never said more than a goodbye to me in all of my thirty-nine years. I sometimes think that when he looks at you he is eyeing you up to see how big a hole to dig for your grave.'

Jago laughed. The woman looked kind. Her eyes were wide and hopeful as they peeped from under the brim of her black hat.

'I thought that when I first met him,' Jago said. 'He's a nice man when you get to know him.'

'I'm Stella. Before you go to see him, let me clean up your wounds. You can't be going to see Henson bleeding all over the place, can you?' The woman seemed sure that Jago would not disagree. 'I live at the bottom of the steps. I have a shop down there. It's early in the morning still and the kettle should be boiling by now.'

Jago nodded. The woman linked arms with him and covered them both in the lee of the umbrella. As they took the last step and turned on to the street, Jago saw the sign of the shop. It hung above the doorway and swung gently in the breeze:

Miss Stella Corey, Apothecary

'What's an apothecary?' Jago asked. He had seen the shop several times before when he was at Streonshalgh Manor but had never looked through the window.

'I heal people,' she said in a whisper.

'A doctor?' he asked expectantly as she took a brass key and opened the door of the shop. She waved the now folded umbrella to rid it of every raindrop.

'More like a witch, according to some people around here.' She laughed. 'I use herbs and old ways. Medicines that I can pick from the wood or on the cliff.'

'Why do they think you're a witch?' he asked, thinking she looked the most unlikely witch he could ever imagine.

'Could be because I use a pot to boil up the mash,' she laughed. 'Or it could be because that's what I am . . .'

The woman turned and led him into the shop, locking the door behind her. It was tiny, a single room cluttered with sprigs of dried herbs that hung from the beamed roof. On every wall were jars of spices and pots of cream. Wooden buckets of lavender soap were stacked against the wall. An old brass-fronted till with the last sale still in the glass was on the counter. Most peculiarly, on one shelf was a glass jar that contained the pickled remains of what looked to Jago to be a dead cat. As Jago took off his coat and slipped it on the chair the creature appeared to be staring at him through a bloated eye pressed against the glass.

'What's that?' he asked, pointing to the jar.

'Rupert,' she said quietly as she rooted in and out of a stack of drawers, looking for the things needed to tend his wounds. 'I had him for so long that I didn't want to get rid of him.'

'So you put him in a jar?'

'It was either that or bury him on the beach and have the seagulls dig him up. I couldn't find anyone to stuff him so I had him pickled. Quite fitting really.' She turned to him holding a wad of sheep wool and a bottle of green liquid clearly marked *POISON*. Stella saw Jago reading the warning on the bottle. 'Don't worry, it won't kill you. It'll sting like bozo – but that's all. You ready?'

Jago shrugged, not knowing what to expect.

'How did he die?' he asked, trying to take his mind from the burning liquid that now coated the wounds to his face and throat.

'Fell off the roof. He was drunk at the time. That was his habit, always lapping the last of the beer at the back of the pub.' Stella wiped away the blood. 'This isn't a dog bite,' she said as she stepped away and looked at him. 'What did this to you?'

Jago looked down to the lino floor and found himself

trying to work out the pattern of the maze design. 'I had a fight,' he said quietly.

'What with?' she asked.

Jago shrugged again. It was obvious that he didn't want to answer.

'I only saw something like this when . . .' She looked at him closely. 'I found a body when I was a girl. The marks on the neck were just like that. Henson said it was a Vampyre that did it.'

He looked at the door and thought of running. The door was locked. There was no escape.

'You wouldn't believe me. Ask Jack Henson,' Jago said as the liquid burnt against the wound.

'Wait here,' Stella said. 'I'll call him and I'll get something for that. If it's a Vampyre bite then I have something for it.' Stella took off her pug-like black hat with its stiff brim and lace top. Thick curls of blonde hair fell from within. She went to the counter and picked up the receiver of a large black Bakelite telephone and waited until the operator answered. She asked for Henson by name. 'He's here,' she said quietly without saying the name. 'Just seeing to him now.'

'You knew who I was all along,' Jago said when she put down the telephone and brought him a cup of tea.

'Strange times are these, Jago,' Stella answered. 'Jack asked me to keep an eye out for you. He left Hawks Moor and came back here. Told me what had happened. I saw you talking to him from my window on the night you first met. Always knew there was something different about you.'

'Is he coming here?' he asked as he sipped the hot tea.

'Soon,' she said as she rummaged in the back of the shop

226

and brought out a small pellucid jar of ointment. 'When he does, I will try this. Never thought I would ever have to use it.'

'What does it do?'

'Henbane can make you fly.' She laughed as she always did after every sentence.

'But I don't want –'

'That is a joke. You are such a serious boy. Henbane is a powerful herb. Good for getting rid of Vampyre venom.'

The small brass bell on the shop door rattled as a tall shadow covered the opaque glass. Stella took the key from her pocket and opened the lock and then the door.

'Jago,' Jack Henson said as if greeting a prodigal child. 'You never came back and things had changed so much at Hawks Moor.'

'I know,' Jago answered. 'She did this to me.' He showed Henson the marks on his neck.

'Things are different now. I take it you know about Hugh Morgan?' Henson tried to speak in such a way that Stella would not understand.

'Everything has changed,' Jago answered.

'Stella, I will take him to Abbey Cottage. Not a word to anyone about him being here. They will come looking for him. I am sure of that.'

'Then I shall bring him a change of clothes. Can't have Jago going around like that,' she said as she wrinkled her nose, curls of hair falling in thick spirals over her face.

The rain beat down as they walked from the shop through the ginnels and up the cliff to the cottage. Stella Corey followed them to the corner of the street and then turned towards Market Place. Henson looked back constantly and then went ahead to make sure no one was watching the door to the cottage.

'Can't be too careful,' Henson said as he sat Jago on the chair by the fire and brought him a towel to dry his hair. 'There is anarchy in the heavens since Blaine has been in these parts.'

'He's a Vampyre,' Jago said. 'Sold me to Ozymandias and then he rescued me.' Jago told Henson all that had happened.

'Playing games with us all,' Henson answered. 'What will you do now?'

'I have money,' Jago said, not knowing what the future would bring for him. 'I could go back to London.'

'They will follow you even there, Jago. Until this matter is ended, they will try to track you down.'

He thought for a moment before answering. He had to tell Henson what Blaine had said. It broke his heart even to think of it.

'Hugh Morgan is not my father,' Jago said solemnly. 'Blaine told me that it is Ezra Morgan who was with my mother. That is why they want my blood.'

'And why Sibilia Trevellas wants you dead,' Henson said as he peeked from the small window by the door to see if all was still clear. 'Before I left Hawks Moor, I heard Vibica talking with Ezra Morgan on the telephone. She told him what had happened to his son. All the man really wanted to know was what had happened to you. Vibica knew that you had gone with Toran Blaine. That is why Sibilia was there to bid for you.' Henson tried to look calm. His eyes stared into the bright flames of the fire as if he were about to bring bad news.

'What is it?' Jago asked.

'The reason I left Hawks Moor was because they turned against me. I said we should find Strackan and Ezra and finish what should have been done years ago. Vibica silenced me. She believes that the Lodge Maleficarum is the only authority that can do those things. They also believe it is time for you to join with them. I heard Hugh and the woman talking of preparing you for what was to come. They think it is the only way to stop Sibilia trying to kill you.' Henson took his gaze from the fire and looked at Jago. 'Blaine told me about Ezra Morgan. I am sorry, Jago, but I think he spoke the truth. Hugh is your brother.'

'But he loved my mother,' Jago said. Tears ran down his cheeks and his hands shook with rage.

'Some Vampyres have the power to transform themselves into the presence of another. Ezra Morgan could have easily done that. Your mother was cheated and then lied to, as was Hugh. All along the Vampyre Quartet knew that you were Ezra's child.'

'And I was promised to Strackan?' he asked.

'Indeed.' Henson looked to the flames as if they would purge his mind of the thoughts that danced on his tongue as he spoke. 'Blaine also told me that the Lodge Maleficarum and Strackan were at war. That the world of the Vampyres had split into a civil war. You, Jago . . . You are at the centre of a battle between powers and principalities and I cannot see a guardian angel in sight.'

'A war?' Jago asked. 'Between Vampyres?'

'It is all a question of vanity and power. Sadly for you, the name of Jago Harker is on everyone's lips.'

'What must I do to be saved from this?' Jago asked.

'We have to stop Strackan. You are the only one who can do this. That is why they are so frightened of you,' Henson answered.

'Then I have to kill Sibilia and Ezra Morgan,' Jago said, knowing this meant he would have to kill his father. 'How can it be done?'

'Since my family were murdered by Sibilia, I have made a collection of artefacts that will help in our task. I will not leave you alone in this. But I cannot kill Strackan.' Henson nodded to the panel in the wall. Jago knew it led to the chamber under the churchyard.

'But how do we find them?' he asked.

A gentle tap beat against the door to the cottage. Henson went to the door and looked out of the window before he slipped the latch.

'Better come,' Stella said quietly to Jack Henson. 'They have found the body of the copper, Inspector Kaine. He was on the cliff top – his neck ripped out.' Stella cast an accusatory glance at Jago. 'It was not far from where I met Jago.'

'Did you see any one on the path from Hawks Moor?' Henson asked.

'I was alone,' Jago said. 'And I'm not a Vampyre.'

'I know, lad,' Henson answered. 'Strange that Inspector Kaine was alive when I saw him at Hawks Moor. Better be going to see for myself. You stay here and answer the door to no one.'

Jago was left alone. The fire burnt in the grate and outside the rain eased its beating against the window. Several shadows and hurried footsteps passed by the door in the narrow alley outside. He knew they were making their way to the cliff top to see the body of Inspector Kaine.

Looking into the fire, Jago felt helpless. He bit his lip and rubbed his hands as his leather coat steamed in the heat of the embers.

'Stiff as old boards,' he said as he got up from the chair, curious to see again the chamber concealed at the back of Henson's cottage. He pressed the panel in the wall and it clicked open. He could feel the draught blowing from within. 'I could just look,' he said to himself, and he opened the door and climbed inside.

The passageway was narrower than he remembered. In twenty strides he was in the chamber. Six candles lit the room and yet it was still cold and gloomy. Jago looked at the old wooden box on the table. Opening the lid he could see it was empty.

'Thought I would find you in here,' a voice said from the shadows of the passageway beyond.

'Staxley?' Jago asked.

'Been watching you. Followed you across the moor from the house.'

'How did you get in the chamber?' he asked.

'Seen Henson do it hundreds of times. Stupid old fool is losing his touch. Shame what happened to Griffin. Got a score to settle there,' Staxley answered in a mocking voice.

'You could be healed from all this,' Jago said. He stared into the shadows but could see nothing more than a dim outline. 'It doesn't have to be this way.'

231

'But it does,' Staxley answered, panting like a dog. 'From the moment I saw you it had to end this way and no other. Thing is, Jago, we are too much alike. When I let that old hag take my blood I thought it would be different. They promised me the world and all I have become is sicker and sicker.'

Staxley walked slowly into the light. His face was bloated. Two long fangs broke through his lips. His eyes bulged frog-like from his head.

'What did they do to you?' Jago asked.

'Bad blood,' he said as he gripped the table with a hand that was twice the size of the other. 'Went wrong. They both wanted some – the woman and Strackan. Venom mixed and caused this. Good job Griffin was killed. He could never have taken the pain.'

'What do you want of me?' Jago asked as Staxley came nearer.

'Only right that you die as well,' he said. 'Every day I am transformed. Hunger and grief are all I know.' He stopped speaking and looked at Jago. 'Then I see you. Jago Harker – the charming man with a charmed life. A sleuth, a jumped-up pantry boy who never knew his place.' Staxley coughed the words as his bulging eyes stared about the room. 'Trouble is, Jago Harker . . . I don't think I have the strength to kill you.'

Staxley slumped to the carved chair by the table and carried the weight of his deformed face in his hands.

'Let me help you,' Jago insisted.

'I'm not alone, Jago. Ezra Morgan knows you are here.'

[21]

The Monozein

THE DULL CHIME of the church clock heralded the first hour of the afternoon. It had rained most of the morning and now clouds crowded the sun and brought darkness to the town. The door to Abbey Cottage clicked open. Jack Henson peered inside. He felt a sadness filling the room.

'Jago? Jago, are you there?' he asked as he opened the door wider.

'In here,' Jago answered from the room off the passageway where Henson kept his bed.

Henson followed the words. He looked in to the room and gasped.

'Is that – is that Staxley?' he said, unable to believe how the boy had changed.

'It is,' Staxley moaned, unable to lift his head from the pillow.

'He's dying, Jack. There was something in the venom that is killing him,' Jago said as he put another compress on Staxley's brow.

'I will telephone Stella. He needs more than we can give him,' Henson said hurriedly, a worried expression on his face as he went to the telephone.

He soon returned.

'What can we do?' Jago asked. Staxley was gasping his breath and squeezing Jago by the hand so as not to be alone.

'Stella will find a way of easing the pain. But without Dust Blood there is nothing we can do,' Henson said, knowing in his heart that Staxley would soon die.

'We have to find Sibilia. She did this to him and through her it can be stopped,' Jago answered.

'We don't know where she is,' Henson said. A frantic knocking rattled the door of the cottage.

'She is with Ezra Morgan – they are hiding in the Conventorium. There is a room in the far tower, that is where she rests,' Staxley whispered.

'So Blaine did not lie,' Henson muttered as he looked at Jago. 'The Conventorium is not far from here.'

'I saw it from the cottage that Blaine had rented. I know the way,' Jago said.

'Know the way? You can't think of going,' Henson argued.

'There is a vial of Sibilia's blood in a cave near Ravenscar. I cannot go back there and that is what we need – blood,' Jago answered.

'Just let me die. Take away the pain and let me die,' Staxley moaned as tears filled his eyes.

'I will try to save you, Stax, promise.'

The beating came again. Henson left the room.

'Is he here?' Stella said as she ran into the bedroom and then stopped suddenly when she saw Staxley. 'You poor child – what have they done?'

'Jago –' Henson said with a look that he knew meant he should leave Staxley.

'Don't go, Jago, please,' Staxley begged as he held out his hand.

'You're not going to die,' Jago said as Henson pulled him from the room. 'I'll get the stuff for you, Stax.'

'Stella will look after him. Please, Jago,' Henson insisted.

'I am going to find her,' Jago answered. 'I'll find her and kill her.'

'You can't go there. It is too dangerous.' Henson led Jago into the passageway to the chamber. 'The *whisperers* have been talking about you. All they say is that it will end in death.'

'I don't care what ghosts in a churchyard say to you, Jack. I don't care if I am killed. She took the life of Biatra and now Staxley is dying like a poisoned dog,' Jago replied as Henson lit more candles in the vaulted room. 'I have to get the blood of Sibilia Trevellas.' Jago looked the man in the eyes and stood his ground.

'Your life depends on the death of Strackan, not Sibilia. It would be futile to rush an attack for the sake of that boy. These things take time to prepare. One day you will face her – but please, Jago, this is not the day.'

'That boy is dying. Before he was made a Vampyre, Staxley was my sworn enemy. But now he needs help in his suffering. I cannot let him die without trying to help him,' Jago answered. 'I thought you would want her dead after what she did to your wife and child?'

'I want nothing more than that, Jago. In fact I help you out of complete selfishness. Very well,' Henson said reluctantly. 'If this is the way it is to be. I have what you need.'

Henson went to the fireplace and, reaching inside, pulled a small lever hidden in the wall. Above the mantel a small door sprang open. 'This is what you will need,' he said as he slid a long thin box from the hiding place. 'It is as old as Ezra Morgan and once belonged to him.'

Henson unclipped the box and opened the lid. Inside was what Jago thought looked like an old flag wrapped around a cross.

'Is that a knife?' he asked as Henson unravelled the crumbling material.

'It is the dagger that Ezra Morgan used on the night he went to kill Strackan when Sibilia betrayed him. It is forged from the cross that stood on the altar of the abbey. There is nothing as powerful as this blade.'

Henson gave the dagger to Jago. It fitted his hand perfectly, a long silver blade with a gold hilt that glinted in the candle-light.

'And it will kill her?' Jago asked.

'Instantly,' he answered. 'But they will know when you are near to them. The dagger will sing of its presence to any Vampyre and it cannot be silenced. Take it and kill her if you can. And take this sash,' Henson said as he gave Jago the long strand of material that had been wrapped around the blade. 'Soak up her blood with this and all will be well.'

'And if I fail?' Jago asked.

'I will make sure that Staxley does not suffer.'

'And Biatra?' he asked.

'I know what to do,' Henson answered solemnly.

'If I am not back by the morning . . .' Jago said slowly, but was unable to finish his words.

'I will pray that you are returned to us,' Henson answered. 'Take the knife and do what is to be done.'

Jago stepped from the door of the cottage and into the narrow lane that led to the town. He heard the sea beating against the harbour wall and crashing on Tate Hill Sands. Though it was only late afternoon, the sky was as dark as night.

Walking the silent alleyways, he made his way to the town and then across the bridge. By the time he had followed the cliff path and left the final houses perched on the edge of the cliff, he could see the Conventorium. Its walls of neatly cut stone broke from the damp earth. The high gabled roof and stone ramparts cast the shadow of a castle on the rough grass. It was surrounded by a high stone wall broken only by an arched gateway.

Far away, Jago could hear rooks tearing at the treetops and cawing in the approaching darkness. He walked the edges of the fields until he found the road that led towards the gate. As he walked, he checked the pockets of his now dry leather coat. He had pushed the dagger through the lining so that it was held in place but could not be seen. In one pocket was the old sash and in the other the Luger he had taken from Aldus Flood. Jago ran his fingers over the serrated grip of the gun and wondered if a Vampyre could be shot dead. Something told him that it would not be possible, but he could at least try. A myriad of thoughts swirled around in his mind. Jago often found himself arguing with with his own thoughts; sometimes he would shout out and beg the thoughts to stop. Words would leap from his mouth unexpectedly as his anxiety mounted.

Fighting to keep calm, he followed the wall of the Conventorium until he reached the gate. Peering in through the slatted bars, he could see a long driveway to the steps of the castle. On the wall by the gate, Jago read the golden words on the black sign:

The Order of Catharatium - Keep Out

The building seemed deserted. A small gatehouse that formed part of the wall was empty. Strands of ancient ivy had sealed the entrance years before and held the door shut, but reaching through the bars Jago slipped the bolt. The gate opened just far enough for him to squeeze inside. Once again, he checked the knife in his pocket, feeling the soft, velvet handle and gold hilt. Cutting through the trees that lined the drive, he soon stood at the bottom of the main steps. The oak door looked as if it had never opened. He looked up. The tower that Staxley had spoken of was to his right. It was the highest part of the Conventorium. The tall ramparts looked like the upturned teeth of a dragon frozen in stone.

A small door stood ajar as if it had been purposefully left for him to find. All was still; Jago could see no one.

Once inside, Jago followed the corridor. In the distance he could hear the singing of cherubic voices. Suddenly, lights shimmered on the stone as a procession made its way towards him. The singers walked in time along the granite floor, all covered in hooded black robes. The dim outlines of their faces were visible beneath the cowls. Around the waist, each robe was tied with a red cord. Jago hid in the portico of the passageway and watched them pass by. The thirteen hooded figures chanted as they walked by in file, their soft, angel-like words filling the air with sweet and mournful praise and echoing through the long corridors.

Jago waited until they had gone. Then, striding out, he

walked to the door at the end of the passageway. Turning right he took the staircase. Soon he found himself in a small room with a door to another corridor. There, hanging from a brass hook, were three black cowls. Jago slipped the largest of the robes over his head and pulled the cord around his waist, making sure he could still feel the knife in his pocket.

Taking the stairs, Jago turned the landing. Before him was a small oak door with a crack of light shining from underneath. Jago listened. The crackling of a gramophone that played Wagner's *Parsifal* opera seeped under the door. He lifted the latch and pressed against the door, which opened slightly. A log fire burnt brightly in the room, its flames reflected on the shimmering silk of a tall Japanese screen.

'Who is it?' asked Sibilia Trevellas as the draught from the door swirled across the wooden floor and lifted the dust in spirals. Jago did not answer. He stepped into the room and closed the door behind him.

'Who is –' Sibilia stopped speaking. Jago saw the bathrobe slip from the top of the screen where it rested. 'I never thought I would ever feel that presence again. Is it Jago Harker and do you have the dagger?'

Sibilia walked slowly from behind the screen as the music played. She stood before him, dressed in the thin bathrobe that trailed to the floor, a pool of water around her feet. Brushing her cheek with her fingers she tried to smooth away the smudged make-up from her eyes.

'Staxley is dying,' Jago said. 'I need your blood.'

'I thought you got enough from me the other night?' she asked.

'I was betrayed by Toran Blaine,' he said.

'I could have told you that all along. Toran Blaine is a mercenary who kills for the highest price.' Sibilia looked at him. 'I take it you have the dagger. I can feel that it is near. Strange, really, that something so deathly can make you feel so . . . excited.'

Jago could see that Sibilia was looking for a way of escape. Her eyes glanced to the window and then the door. He flipped back the hood from his head and turned the volume higher on the gramophone.

'Fitting, really. I never really liked music like this. Wasn't Kinross a singer in a past life?' Jago asked as he slipped the knife from his coat.

'There are other ways that we can sort this matter out, Jago. It doesn't have to be like this,' Sibilia said, her voice made fearful by the presence of the dagger. 'We could come to some sort of arrangement. You are almost a man – there must be something that you want from me?'

'Tell me who is my father?' he asked as he pointed the blade towards her.

'Don't believe anything you are told about that. All they seek to do is confuse you,' she said as the gown slipped from one shoulder to reveal the tattoo of a snake.

'Who do you think my father is?' he asked again.

'You don't have to kill me to get what you want,' Sibilia said as she moved towards him. 'You are such a handsome boy.'

Jago looked at her. In the light of the fire and the flickering candles she looked human and beautiful. His hand lowered to his side as she reached forward and touched his face. 'See . . .' she said softly. 'Things could be made well between us.'

Jago could not take his stare from her eyes and her face. She moved closer towards him until he could feel her breath on his face. 'Give me the dagger, Jago. It is far too powerful a device for you to have.'

All his strength ebbed from him. His fingers could hardly keep hold of the velvet handle. Slowly and gently it began to slip from his grasp.

'Will you give me your blood to save his life?' Jago asked as the music played and swirled in his mind.

'His is an ugly life. In so many ways it is best to rid the world of horrid people. Don't you think so, Jago?' Sibilia asked as she slipped her arms around him and pulled him close.

'But he will die,' Jago whispered as the scent of blossom and myrrh was all around him.

'They all die eventually. Is it such a bad thing for people like that?'

Sibilia held him close to her. He could feel her body beneath the robe.

'And what of me?' he asked.

'I think it is time,' she said as she licked his neck. 'Just relax, I have done this –'

Jago twisted the knife deep into her side. Sibilia gasped for breath as if she were drowning. She fell back as he pulled the blade from her.

'It *is* time,' he said as he took the sash from his pocket and wiped the blade.

Sibilia reached out, unable to speak, and then slumped to her knees. Her whole body trembled as her eyes closed. Jago took the knife and cut the back of her hand, binding it in the sash. Then he stood back and watched as she slumped to the floor. When she breathed no more he took the sash from her. The wound had gone. Sibilia Trevellas was dead.

Dumping her body in the bath, Jago hurried from the room. The music stopped, the needle stuck in the final groove of the disc, clicking the beating of a woodpecker. As he walked down the stairs and then along the corridor, Jago folded the blood-soaked sash and slipped it into his pocket.

Footsteps echoed from the passage below. Jago stopped and hid in the shadows of a doorway as the choir of cowled figures made their way back from whence they had come. He felt the handle of the Luger pistol, and as he did so he heard a slow and rhythmic organ music that spilled from the doorway of the chapel. It reprised the opera that Sibilia had on the gramophone. A brusque voice sung the same words of the Mittag over and over: *The hour has come. My lord, permit your servant to guide you . . .*

Jago knew it was Ezra Morgan. He took the Luger from his pocket and walked in the shadows until he was near the doorway of the chapel. Looking inside, he could see Morgan at the seat of a pipe organ. A large vaulted apse towered above him as he played, the music ringing out in time with his voice. The altar candles shimmered with each note that he struck, and the air around him vibrated violently. Jago slipped inside the chapel and waited. The radiant light of the innumerable of candles cast stark shadows of the stone pillars that lined the chapel.

Taking aim, Jago held the pistol towards the Vampyre, his hand shaking. He flicked the safety catch and rested his finger on the trigger. The music was piercing, the rhythm faster, hypnotising as Morgan sang louder. Jago felt the music beating inside his chest and shaking his bones. He lowered the gun, wanting to be sick where he stood. His head spun and his eyes could no longer focus as wave after wave of sound beat against him.

Without warning, the music stopped. Ezra Morgan got to his feet and wiped the sweat from his brow with a crisp white handkerchief. Jago slid into the shadow of one of the large stone arches. He looked on as Morgan turned and gazed around the chapel.

'I can feel the presence of the dagger. If you are there please make yourself visible,' Morgan said. 'I think it is time that we clear up all of the lies that have been said in this sordid game we play.'

Jago stepped from the shadows, the pistol gripped in his white fingers.

'Sibilia is dead,' Jago said as he walked towards the door.

'I expect she is and I am thankful for what you have done. After hundreds of years she was becoming quite tiresome.' Morgan laughed. 'And one by one you come for us, take our lives and end our eternity.' He turned slightly and looked up into the air above him. 'I can still hear the words of that song. They talk about a quest just like yours. Are you a knight in search of that which cannot be found? The hour has come, Jago. It is your time.'

'Is it true?' Jago asked.

'Is what true?' Morgan answered. 'That you are really asleep and will wake up and find all this a tragic dream?'

'Are you my father?'

Morgan clapped his hands together three times. The door

to the chapel slammed shut and Jago heard the bolts slide into place.

'Now we are alone. We will not be disturbed,' Morgan said without emotion, tapping out the rhythm of the words on the keys of the organ.

[22]

Lestrigon

THE CHATTER OF A THOUSAND hidden voices filled the air of the chapel. Jago could see no one and yet it was as if the room was full of people. Morgan stood by the altar and stared at him, looking for some fault or weakness. Jago held the Luger in his hand and wondered if he should just raise the gun and shoot him dead. He was not sure that a bullet would kill a Vampyre, but he knew that it would certainly have some effect. As he began to aim the gun, he could only think that he was about to kill his own father.

'You never answered my question – are you my father?' Jago asked.

Morgan raised one eyebrow slightly as if he wanted Jago to understand the point of what he was about to say. 'It matters not how you came into this world, Jago,' Morgan said as he stepped away from the oak panel inlaid with the ivory keys of the organ. 'What is more important is who you are and what you want to be.'

As Jago held the Luger towards Morgan the chatter of voices dulled to a whisper.

· 'I have to know,' he answered. 'It is important to me. Are you my father?'

'I doubt you would want someone like me as your father, Jago. I have cheated, lied and killed most of my life. It is strange the way of the blood has changed my heart. I was once a man who would do as you are now. In fact if I had not gone to the woods that day in search of Strackan then I would be at peace in the grave.'

Morgan sat on the altar rail and flicked back his head as if he no longer cared. Jago could see he had no concern for the gun aimed at him. The man sat quite casually, looking around the chapel as if he were admiring the architecture for the first time.

'Can you remember how you felt that day?' Jago asked as he leant against the stone pillar. 'What was it like to go after the monster?'

Morgan smiled as if the memory was still quite close to him. 'I was a fool. Tricked by my wife and walked into hell. We chased Strackan through the woods. I carried that dagger,' he said, pointing to the hidden knife in Jago's jacket. 'It had been forged out of the tip of a silver spear carried by the centurion Longinus. It had a power beyond the imagination, but I did not expect what was to come.'

'You were tricked?' Jago asked.

'I led my friends into a trap that had been prepared for us by someone I loved,' he answered coldly. 'And you have killed her.'

'Why not use the dagger on yourself when you knew what had been done to you?'

'When I stepped into the hermit's cottage, the beast attacked. Strackan left us as if we were dead. Three days later we awoke. The dagger was gone, as was my sash.' Morgan stopped and looked at him quizzically. 'It was then that Sibilia told us of our fate. We were to be a quartet of Vampyres tied to life and each other, and the gateway to Strackan. We were his servants.'

'And you never thought of killing him?' he asked as Morgan walked towards the altar and ran his finger across the pattern engraved in a candlestick.

'Your mind changes . . . life changes. Blood does that to you,' Morgan answered. 'We got on with our life and he made few demands. Then he wanted blood and I think you know it all from there.'

'But what of my mother?' Jago asked.

'That is a question I dare not answer,' he said as he looked at Jago, wondering if the boy would ever put down the gun. 'Are you going to put the Luger down or shall I wait to be shot?'

Jago thought for a moment and then lowered the gun. 'I came here to kill you,' he said, 'and to take her blood. Staxley is dying and it is what will help him.'

'He will need more than Dust Blood. Strackan as well as Sibilia bit him. It will be hard to free him from the poison.' Morgan looked concerned. All around the whispering grew louder. 'You can hear that?'

'The voices?' Jago answered.

'They are the Lestrigon. Since you stabbed Strackan he has been in hiding.'

'And what are they?'

'Strackan now lives his life through these creatures. The Lestrigon are joined with him. They are those people that he has killed. Each is just an empty vessel that Strackan can live through – see through and control as if it were his own body. When they are not doing his work they sing and dance around the stone on which he is laid.'

'Then Strackan is here?' Jago asked.

'Beneath our feet in a vault that cannot be entered. You are so close and yet so far away.' Morgan tapped the toe of his shoe on the stone floor. 'That is why we can hear their whispering and why you should leave this place and try to save your friend.'

As Jago looked at Morgan the whispering hushed and then the soft singing started again.

'And you would let me go?' Jago said, his voice hesitant.

'I am not a monster. I know you will not kill me because in your heart you still want a father. I hear that my son Hugh has become like me?'

'Vibica de Zoete. Hugh was dying.'

'I never pressed the matter. Like all religions, it is best for your children to make up their own minds – don't you think, Jago?' Morgan smiled and then clapped his hand. Like before, the bolts slid and the door slowly opened. 'Go from here. This is not the time or place for more death.'

Jago looked at the open door, wondering if it were a trap. He felt the grip of the pistol and knew he could not kill Morgan. His hand shook as he slipped the gun back into his pocket.

'And I can just leave this place?' he asked as he searched Morgan's face for the truth.

'I will not harm you. Go and try to heal your friend. But beware there are others who seek you. Your blood is a precious thing and many more desire it than Strackan.'

'So why didn't you?'

'I have grown weary with all this. I should never have come back to this country. My friends are dead and I find the other Vampyres quite boring. When once it was rather select, now we even have tradesmen who are blood-bibbers. In truth I have lived too long.'

Jago walked towards the door, afraid to turn his back on Morgan for fear he would strike. 'I will see you again,' he said as he stepped into the shadows of the porticoed corridor.

'Be gone, Jago. This is not a place for you,' Morgan said as he heard the running footsteps of the lad as he sped along the passageway.

'You were supposed to kill him,' a voice said as the stone door at the side of the altar slowly opened.

'I couldn't – he had the knife. It was enough just to stand in its presence,' Morgan answered as a tall dark man with a lifeless face stepped from the hidden room. The eyes of the man flickered as if someone else gazed through them. He hesitated in the bright candlelight and sniffed the air like a dog.

'This is not what I wanted,' the man said, his mouth not moving, the words of Strackan coming from within. 'I need his blood and you let him go.'

'I am sorry,' Morgan said as he bowed his head. 'He looked so much like Hugh. It would have been impossible for me to do so.'

'Now Jago Harker leaves this place having killed Sibilia and you do nothing to stop him?' the man said, his face motionless.

'There will be other opportunities,' Morgan tried to argue as the voice of Strackan growled from within the walking corpse of the Lestrigon.

'I have the world turning against me and my last companion does nothing for me. If I was not so sure I would say that you worked for Kinross and not for me,' Strackan answered.

'My loyalty cannot be questioned,' he said.

'The Lestrigon will find him and bring him to me,' Strackan said.

The obedient Lestrigon, the corpse through which Strackan now lived, pushed Morgan out of the way and jumped the altar rail and ran from the chapel. Morgan did not answer; he knew that Strackan could no longer hear him.

Like a hunting dog, the Lestrigon followed Jago's scent along the corridor, out of the small door into the night. Outside, it looked at the ground, its eyes following the footsteps that led across the sward field in a luminous trail. It was as if each step Jago took had burnt the impression into the ground. The Lestrigon rubbed the hygroma that covered its forehead; the growth pushed against the skull, forcing out one eye that sat on the Lestrigon's cheek like a small bird. The creature pulled the collar of its thick tweed coat around its neck and then began to follow the trail.

Jago ran on, unaware that he was being followed. Anger blinded him. He chided himself for not killing Morgan whilst he had the chance – it would have been so easy, all he would have had to do was shoot him or stab him with the knife. Yet something inside had made him afraid. Whether Ezra Morgan was his true father or not, it seemed he did not want to kill anyone who knew his mother.

The path followed the muddy cliff down to the beach. Along the shore was an entanglement of barbed wire put there against an invasion. There were no soldiers or look-outs. The cliff was steep and ran underneath the houses that looked out to sea. The moon shone on the wet sand as the tide retreated and exposed the rocks. He walked quickly, the sand making each stride cumbersome. It was as if he were walking in a dream.

As his legs began to tire Jago saw the dim outline of the abbey far ahead of him, sticking out of the cliff top like the black teeth of a beggar. But he did not notice the tall man skirting the edge of the cliff and gaining ground on him.

Jago stopped, out of breath, as the clock on the church struck the eleventh hour. He wondered how he could get through the town now that the curfew was about to begin. There would be soldiers on the bridge that went over the narrow estuary. Jago thought of stealing a boat and rowing to the other side and then taking the donkey path to Abbey Cottage.

Jago instinctively looked back. Just for a moment he saw the movement of a shadow, a movement that looked out of place and was too slow to be that of a bird. He walked on, gathering pace with each step, and some distance away he could see the jetty that led from the beach to the pier where the old orna-mental gun was mounted. It glimmered in the moonlight. The long brass barrel pointed impotently out to sea as the sand below stretched out like a freshly washed canvas.

It was then that his spine shivered and he knew he had to run. A fearful urge spurred him on. Jago fought against the sand with each step as he ran. Looking back he saw a figure chasing him, a figure that ran as if it did not touch the sand and whose glowing red eyes darted back and forth as it sprinted towards him.

Jago fell in the sand. His face smashed against a stone and he felt blood trickle from his mouth.

'Thought you could get away, did you, Jago?'

He heard Strackan's words and shuddered with fear. Lifting his head from the sand he looked at the man.

The Lestrigon smiled. He did not have the teeth of a Vampyre. On his neck were the cuts of the bloodletting. They were surrounded with the marks of the plague, as fresh as the day the man had died long before.

'Strackan?' Jago asked as the man cowered over him, his deep bloodshot eyes staring at Jago.

'And to think Morgan was afraid of you.'

Instinctively, Jago felt for the knife in his coat. 'I won't let you take me,' he shouted. 'I would rather die.'

'Don't wish for something that could happen. I want your blood and care not if you are dead when I take it,' Strackan said through the Lestrigon that was his unwilling vessel.

Jago slowly pulled the dagger from his pocket. He gripped the handle tightly in his hand and shielded it from the Lestrigon with his coat.

'Then kill me now,' he said, waiting to strike.

They eyes of the creature followed each minute movement as if it were a hawk.

'Does it not frighten you that I speak through this creature?' Strackan asked.

'Why should I be frightened?' Jago asked. 'You have dipped your finger in every part of my life and for that I hate you.'

The Lestrigon bent towards him, its stinking breath pouring over Jago like a dank mist. Long fingers reached out. The skin was broken from the bone and open to the night air. The hand touched him on the shoulder, gripping the collar of his coat and slowly lifting him from the beach.

Jago struck quickly. The dagger went deep into the arm of the Lestrigon. It flung back its long strands of matted hair and screamed through bloated lips as Jago twisted the blade. But suddenly the creature stepped back, threw off its coat and heaved Jago on to the sand. Before Jago could move it pounced on him like a dog biting at his neck. He gripped the creature's jaw as it tried to rip out his throat and then, slipping from its grasp, he got to his feet and ran three paces. The Lestrigon caught him by the ankle and pulled him to the sand. It raised up, hands outstretched as if to strangle him. Jago closed his eyes, knowing what was to come.

Then the air cracked as if it thundered. There was a pain in his stomach as he lay winded, and all he could think was that the creature had cleaved him open.

Reaching down, Jago tried to find the wound. His hand touched the face of the creature. With eyes still closed he felt the shape of the head with his fingertips. Then, looking down, he saw the body of the Lestrigon lying on the sand.

'Didn't think I would see you again, but I did think you would come back this way,' said Aldus Flood as he sat on a large rock like an oversized homunculus and slipped the shaft of an axe back into his shabby overcoat. 'I have not seen a Lestrigon in many years. They are most dangerous, most dangerous indeed.'

'I thought you were a professor?' Jago answered as he

tipped the severed head of the creature from his lap and watched it roll in the sand.

'Hah!' He threw back his head and laughed out loud. 'If only that were so.' Then Flood looked suddenly very serious, all sense of mirth gone from his face. 'You are causing lots of problems, Jago, and something has to be done.'

'Problems? What have I done that you know of?' he asked as Flood walked across the sand and lifted Jago to his feet.

Flood looked about him as if they were being overheard.

'You have not realised who you really are, have you?' he asked as he put a hand on Jago's shoulder. 'I am here to make sure that all of this is sorted out very quickly.'

'What are you?' Jago asked. 'I knew there was something strange about you when you were at the cave.'

'What I may or may not be is of no consequence. All I have been instructed to do is to take you to see Kinross. The Prime Minister is insistent that he will talk with you.'

'But I met him, at the Lodge Maleficarum,' Jago said as Flood ushered him along the sand, leaving the body of the Lestrigon to the incoming tide. 'What is all this about?'

'It is about your future, which is something that will affect us all,' Flood answered as they walked up the slipway and on to the pier.

'I have to take something to a friend, they need what I have,' Jago said.

'Jack Henson, I take it?' Flood asked as they walked through the empty streets, the long tails of his coat dragging along the road. 'I will make sure it is taken to him immediately.'

'I thought you were a tramp?' Jago asked as they came closer to the swing bridge that crossed the estuary.

'The disguise has its uses,' Flood replied. 'I work for Mr Kinross and have done for many years.'

Jago could see that the bridge-keeper was not in his hut. The soldiers on the corner by the bank had also gone. The streets were strangely empty.

'What have you done?' Jago asked, as they got closer to the crossing.

'It is a matter of security,' Flood answered. 'No one must see that I am taking you to Kinross.'

'The Prime Minister is here?' Jago asked as they crossed the bridge.

'There is a table just for you.'

'Did you know I had gone to the Conventorium?' asked Jago as they turned the corner and walked into a dark street.

Aldus Flood stopped and looked about him, checking they were not being followed. Jago leant against the wall that overlooked the harbour. 'That was a risk we had to take. Mr Kinross is staying here. We knew that your friend Staxley was in need of help and that you had gone for the blood. I take it you have the sash? I will get it to Henson for you.'

'Who told you?' Jago insisted as he handed Flood the bloodstained sash.

'That is a matter of national security,' Flood replied as he opened the door of the Griffin Hotel and stepped into the entrance.

Jago stood back, aghast at who was there waiting for him.

'I'm sorry, Jago. You will think this is all a terrible conspiracy,' Stella said as she stood in the light of the door lantern and smiled.

23

The Labyrinth

SHE HAD TRIED TO SLEEP and still her mind from the confusions of life but the bed on which she rested had become like brambles. In the middle darkness Vibica de Zoete went downstairs. She opened the door of the secret room where the portrait of the Vampyre Quartet was kept. Taking a seat on the oak bench opposite she stared in disbelief at what she saw: there before her, above pale hands clutching an apple, was the face of Sibilia Trevellas. She knew that it could mean only one thing – the Vampyre was dead. Strangely, she felt as if her own mother had died. It had been Sibilia who had brought her into the world in 1742.

The Dublin night long ago flitted like a minatory bird through her mind. Vibica shuddered as she remembered the two years she had been imprisoned in that one room on Eden Quay overlooking the dark and turgid waters of the River Liffey. On the eve of St Walpurgis Sibilia had come to her with a last request and Vibica had given herself willingly. Together they had fled Dublin on the day of the witch riots, when the townsfolk looked for the creatures that had stolen their children night after night.

On a high-rigged bark to London they had sailed for several nights until a storm had wrecked the ship. They had been washed ashore on Lyme Regis sands and had started their new life together. Within the year, Sibilia had lost all interest in her companion and had fled to London leaving only a note, the keys to the house and a banker's draft for more money than Vibica could ever spend. Now, the woman she had loved was dead. Her portrait was complete and she stood side by side with Draigorian and Julius Cresco.

'I couldn't sleep and thought you would be here,' Hugh Morgan said as he opened the door to the room.

'She is dead,' Vibica answered as he placed a cold hand on her shoulder.

'Then Jago is alive,' he said as he looked at the portrait that hung on the wall. 'There is only my father alive and then it will be complete . . . See how the colours get brighter with each death. It is as if the painting is taking their life.'

'When Ezra Morgan is dead then Strackan will be vulnerable,' she said as she got to her feet and looked closely at the painting.

'Isn't that what we want? Morgan asked. 'Hasn't he tried to control your world for an eternity?'

'It is our world now, Hugh. In time you will forget what it is like to be human. You will look back on your life now as if it were a dream.' Vibica sighed as she ran her finger down the painted face of Trevellas. 'I can remember so much about her and yet it is as if she is a stranger to me.'

'But we are not strangers – not any more,' Hugh said as he touched her face. 'I am so glad you have come into my life.'

'Do you regret what I did to you?' Vibica asked.

'Never,' Hugh answered as he kissed her cheek. 'I wish it had happened sooner.'

'You must drink soon,' she said. 'It will be good for you.'

Hugh Morgan hesitated.

'I thought I would wait until I had to,' he said. 'It is one thing I can't bring myself —'

Vibica covered his lips with her fingers to stop him speaking. 'I thought you would feel that way. I took the liberty . . .' She opened the door of a small cabinet under the table and lifted a covered chalice. She slipped the silk cover from the cup.

Morgan could see that it was half filled with blood.

'Where is this from?' he asked.

'Inspector Kaine. Biatra and I —'

'You killed him?' Hugh asked.

'It was Biatra. I did try to explain that it need not be that way but . . .' She left the words hanging in the air. Morgan looked at the cup, took it from her and put it to his lips.

'Drink,' Vibica insisted. 'It will clear your mind.'

Hugh Morgan sipped the thick liquid and then in one swallow tipped back the chalice and filled his mouth with cold, gelatinous blood. Wiping his face he looked back at the portrait.

'I will not be concerned if I see my father's face appear,' he said stoically as he felt his stomach twist. 'Some things are meant to be.'

'Surely he should be kept alive to protect the Order,' Vibica answered, taking the chalice from him and licking the rim.

'What has become of Inspector Kaine?' Hugh asked with

a shudder as the blood digested and he felt surges of energy run through his veins.

'Like any stone you stumble upon, it has been thrown into the sea,' she answered with a wry smile. She twisted a lock of his hair in her fingers. 'I am so glad I have found you. I have waited so long for someone like you.'

'Then we will be together?' he said as the clock struck the fourth hour of the night.

'Of course,' she answered dismissively, and she walked from the room and stood in the hallway. 'I would like some air – perhaps it would help me sleep.'

'I will come with you,' Hugh said, holding out a hand.

'No, please . . .' Vibica answered as she thought of what to say next. 'If I could just be alone – the news of the death of Sibilia has not gone well with me.'

She half-smiled, knowing that Hugh would agree.

'Don't be long away,' he said like a lost boy.

Vibica left Hawks Moor and, closing the door behind her, made sure she was not being followed. A cold wind beat leaves across the gravel drive and rattled the bushes. It blew in from the high moor, bringing the last of the heather scent. Looking around, Vibica walked to the entrance of the Labyrinth. The once tall walls of the intricate maze had been broken by the tidal wave that had crashed against the cliffs but it still stood defiantly, broken in places, dying in others. The pathways were encrusted in salt and seaweed.

Walking quickly, Vibica was soon in its shadow. She followed the path of the old hedges as it twisted and turned until she was at the very centre. Resting on the fine shingle made from the shells of a million dead creatures was a stone slab. It was broken, cleaved in half by the sea. Toran Blaine leant against it, looking to the sky.

'What took you?' he asked, his voice in melancholy.

'Hugh Morgan is in love with me,' she said churlishly as she took his hand and brought it to her lips.

'Aren't we all? Isn't that what you do to all men, my dear spider?' he said. He held her close to him as if he would never let her go.

'It wasn't supposed to happen – well, not yet,' Vibica said. 'Sibilia is dead. I saw her face in the painting of the Quartet.'

'Jago Harker, I presume?' he asked as he let go of the embrace. 'Will he become a problem to us?'

'Not if we become a problem to him. He will only inherit what is meant to be his if he becomes a Vampyre.'

'And the master?' Blaine asked as the hedge rattled and shook its dead leaves.

'I thought you would have news of him,' she said, looking around as if she sensed she was being watched.

'I left word that I was meeting you here,' Blaine said. 'This would have been the place where Jago Harker should have ended it all. If he had become a follower, then this mess would never have come upon us.'

Vibica laughed. 'You have been killing your kind since I first met you, Toran. This is what you enjoy the most,' she said mockingly.

'But I would never kill you,' he answered.

'Not even for the right price?'

'There is never enough money to take the life of one you truly love.'

Vibica looked him in the eyes, wanting to believe his words and searching his broken thoughts to see if he spoke the truth.

'The silken tongue of a killer. I remember Paris and Madrid. What was her name?'

'Sara Giardina,' he replied.

'You used her as bait, someone you said you loved and yet you allowed her to become the piece of meat in a trap for a Vampyre,' Vibica scolded him.

'It was the only way – how else was I to find him? I knew his weakness.'

'Dangled like a maggot on a hook to catch him and even then Vincenzo Verzenzi got away.'

'I caught him eventually,' he argued.

'You tracked him down with the compass – the compass that I gave you.'

'And I am grateful. It was for *you* that I did it. One by one they have to die. Then you shall be the Master of the Lodge Maleficarum. Isn't that what you want?'

'And what the world can never know,' she muttered as she looked away.

From the shadows of the trees that overhung the cliff, a solitary figure pulled itself from the undergrowth. Walking purposefully in its tattered grave-clothes, it entered the Labyrinth and followed the path until it found Toran Blaine.

Expecting the figure's arrival, Blaine stood as it approached and looked at the tight-skinned face that clung to the bones and sallow eyes that bulged from its head.

'We have been expecting you – but not like this,' Blaine said as the man tried to smile.

'Not how I would expect to be seen,' the voice of Strackan said through the creature. 'A Lestrigon comes in useful – but they have their limitations. The last body I used had to be discarded very quickly.'

'But you are safe?' Vibica asked.

'For the time being,' Strackan answered through the mouth of the Lestrigon that spoke his words. 'I need the boy.'

'If I'd known that was your desire I could have helped you,' Blaine answered.

'Sibilia told me that you tried to sell him at a blood-auction. Will your loyalty ever be as strong as your need for money? I sometimes wonder whom you serve.'

'I serve myself and whoever pays me well, Strackan. There is no loyalty in that.'

'Do you not see the chaos that is happening to our world?' Strackan grunted through the creature.

'At least you know I will serve you – for the right price,' Blaine answered. He took hold of Vibica's hand and pulled her closer to him. 'The world has changed and chaos has brought new order. Perhaps you are getting old.'

'Old?' Strackan grunted. 'You show me no respect. I could crush you, Blaine.'

'From your hiding place – through the body of one of your victims? I think not,' he said arrogantly. 'You now live your life through the sinews of a Lestrigon – a puppet under your command. You need us for what you want.'

The Lestrigon shook with anger. Blaine laughed.

'If I were not so sick I would kill you, Blaine,' Strackan said through the beast. 'Get me the boy and you will be well paid.'

262

'The price has changed. It will cost you one thousand pounds.'

'But that is a ransom,' Strackan replied.

'It is more than a ransom – it is the cost of your life.'

'Don't treat me as a fool,' Strackan said as the hand of the Lestrigon grabbed Blaine by the throat. 'I will not be messed with.'

Blaine slipped a knife from his pocket and placed the tip of the blade on the creature's hand. 'And don't treat me as a skivvy,' he said. 'I will cut off this hand and come and find you, Strackan. I am not afraid of your vacant threats. How many empty bodies do you have left? You cannot always hide and live your life through the feeble eyes of a Lestrigon.'

The creature let go of him and stepped back. It appeared to have given in. The voice of the Lestrigon changed; it was calmer, softer and without malice.

'So you will work for me at the right price?' Strackan sighed.

'I always have and always will. I am your assassin.'

'Find Jago Harker and bring me his blood. Do it tonight.'

'But he was to become one of us – wasn't that the plan?' Vibica asked.

'The plan has been changed. There are others interested in the boy. You are too young to remember the Wars of Mithras. Long before your time – as now, some of our kind plotted to take control of the whole world. There was a great battle in the deserts of Persia and it was settled. Some who were alive at the time would like to see that happen again.' Strackan sighed and the Lestrigon shuddered, unable to control its convulsions. 'Our world and even the Maleficarum is under threat. Since I failed to get his blood at the Lyrid of Saturn there are those who see me as being weak. They want my power.'

'Who would wish for such a thing?' Vibica asked.

'Today a creature I was using was killed. The last vision I had through its eyes was a man with an axe. That man was Aldus Flood.'

'Flood?' Vibica asked. 'I thought he was dead.'

'So did I,' Strackan replied. 'That was supposed to be his fate, but I saw him. I saw him with Jago Harker.'

'And they were together?' Vibica said.

'On the beach by the pier in Whitby. Flood has him and for what purpose I do not know. With Sibilia dead, I have only Morgan as a companion. He is the last of the Vampyre Quartet. When he is dead, my own life will be in the balance. I will give you half of everything I own, Blaine – half of everything . . .'

Blaine smiled. He loved to see weakness in others and share in their discontent. 'And how much would that be?' he asked inquisitively.

'A fortune of a king – more than a king,' Strackan answered.

'When would you like his blood?' Blaine asked.

'Quickly,' he replied as the Lestrigon turned to walk away. 'I will find Aldus Flood and meet you at midnight in the Market Square. Don't be late . . .'

The creature slipped through the broken hedge of the Labyrinth and disappeared towards the cliff. The sound of cracking branches faded, leaving them alone in the night.

Vibica looked at Blaine and tried to smile. 'I still feel frightened in his presence, even when he speaks through a Lestrigon,' she said.

'He is not to be feared. It is *you* that matters. If Strackan were dead, the world would be a different place,' Blaine said as he held her face in his hands.

'I could not think such a thought – Strackan has always lived. A world without him?' Vibica replied, as if she feared her words alone were enough to betray him.

'Think of it. A new order of Vampyres with you as our leader. No more conflict, no more death – a world of peace.' Blaine spoke softly, his words kind to her heart.

'And what of Jago?' she asked, wondering if he would kill the boy.

'He is the heir to all of this and his blood is worth a fortune,' Blaine answered.

'So you would kill him?' she asked.

'I think that it would be best if he stayed human until such a time as we could *dispose* of him,' Blaine said, thinking of the money every drop of the boy's blood would bring.

'There was once a time when I thought we would never be together,' Vibica said as she held his hand.

'I have waited for this moment,' he answered.

'Then it is not just my dream?'

'It is mine, Vibica. But everything must be in place. All our foes must be defeated and everything that could stop us brought down.' Blaine kissed her forehead.

'What do you mean?' she asked, unsure of his words.

'I saw the way you looked at Hugh Morgan. It cut my heart,' Blaine replied. 'What do you feel for him?'

'It is nothing like what I feel for you,' she said, breathing faster.

'I was jealous of what I saw. I couldn't live knowing he was in the world and wanting a piece of your heart.' Blaine looked over her shoulder and smiled, knowing she would do whatever he asked.

'Then I will rid myself of him – *if* we can be together. I will move from this place and stay with Ozymandias.'

'But I would still suspect that you could be with Hugh Morgan. He would surely come after you, Vibica,' Blaine whispered.

'Then we could go away together, forget all this intrigue and live far away.'

'It could never be far enough, for one in love with you would surely find you.'

'Then what can I do?' she pleaded.

'You could always kill him,' he said quietly. 'Then I would never fear him stealing you again.'

'But . . . But Hugh would never . . .' She was amazed he could ask such a thing of her.

'It has to be you, and that has to be the way of my un-conditional love.' He whispered his words as if they were a prayer.

'Very well, Toran. So mote it be . . .' As Vibica answered an unseen tear trickled down her cheek.

They kissed, unaware of the eyes that watched from the thick murk of the hedge. Biatra stared out of the darkness, trying to hold her breath and not cry out.

24

The Griffin

CIGAR SMOKE HUNG IN THE AIR of the the long, dark room like a thick blue cloud and coated everyone with the scent of Havana. Tendrils of smoke from a log fire danced across the beamed ceiling like the hands of ghosts. All around, men sat at tables and sipped their drinks in silence as they watched Jago being led through the bar of the hotel.

Aldus Flood went ahead. His long coat trailed on the floor and he gripped the trilby hat in his fingers. Stella followed behind, keeping Jago between them. She appeared to be different, more confident and no longer a shopkeeper. Her china-white skin was caked with make up; her cheeks were covered with rouge and her lips were bright red. They glistened in the light of the oil lamps that hung from the low ceiling.

'Does Jack Henson know who you are?' Jago asked, feeling as if the woman had betrayed him.

Stella adjusted her hat and pushed in the long strands of hair so that they hung like garlands around the rim. 'He has no reason to know. I work for the government. That is all that matters, Jago.' Stella's voice was as sharp as her eyes. 'This meeting could change your life.'

'I want to go back to London,' he answered.

His world had fallen in around him and he could no longer understand what was happening. He remembered how it had felt to be trapped under the rubble back in London when the bomb had exploded and killed his mother. Now he felt the same. The walls of the room pressed in against him, he could hardly breathe and all he wanted to do was run. He looked at the men at the tables; in the shadows of the room it was hard to tell if any of them were human. Jago tried to remember how many Vampyres were alive. He was sure he had been told that there were only two thousand. He felt that over the last few days he had met every one of them.

They went up a long flight of rickety wooden stairs to a room above. The three waited outside as a bodyguard in a pinstriped suit looked them up and down and then rubbed the stubble on his chin. Flood muttered something to him and the guard stood aside, turning the brass handle of the door.

Stella pushed Jago in front of them as the door opened. The room was in darkness, lit only by the flames of a small fire that brunt in the grate. A long table set for dinner stretched from the door to the window. There, Jago could see the shadowy figure of Noel Kinross. He sat, a white napkin folded neatly over his arm, picking the shells from a plate of prawns.

'So soon,' he said in his soft voice. 'It is always a pleasure to meet someone as charming as you again.' Kinross's lined face broke into a smile. 'You found him,' he said to Flood.

'Just as we thought, coming back from the Conventorium. He had a Lestrigon behind him. Strackan spoke through the creature,' Flood answered with a nod of his head.

'Then he is weaker than we thought,' Kinross answered and turned to Stella. 'I suggest you keep the Conventorium under observation. Take some of our kind and report back to Flood.'

'But first take this to Jack Henson. You know what to do with it,' Flood said as he handed her the bloodstained sash he had taken from Jago.

Stella didn't answer. She turned on her heels and left the room, closing the door behind her.

'Why did you bring me here?' Jago asked as he stood by the fire.

'Are you frightened by all that has happened to you in these last weeks, Jago?' Kinross asked as Flood pulled up a chair for Jago to sit.

He waited before he spoke, not knowing if he should tell the truth.

'Yes,' he said softly with his head bowed, his eyes counting the forks on the table. 'Wouldn't you be?'

'I am sure I would. Thankfully I was more than twice your age before I had to come to terms with all of this.' Kinross picked a prawn from the plate and tore off its shell. He looked at it for a moment, then snapped it in half with his teeth. 'If I had not had Aldus to help me on the journey then I am not sure what would have happened to me.'

Kinross looked at Jago intently. He knew that the Prime Minister was trying to glimpse his thoughts. Jago filled his head with memories of London, fishing in the canal and mudlarking in the Thames. Kinross laughed. 'I am so sorry to try and pry into your mind – and you now know how not to let a Vampyre within. That shows true talent, Jago.'

'It's rude to go digging where you don't belong. Is nothing private?' he snapped.

'That's something they all do,' Flood muttered. 'I remember it well. I gave up talking to him in the end and just let him find out for himself.'

'And he would often think things that were not true just to put me off and make a fool of me. That is the kind of man Aldus Flood really is . . . But I would never be without him.' Kinross smiled at Flood as he poured two glasses of wine and handed one to Jago. 'We have much to celebrate, Jago.'

'Why am I here?' he asked as he sipped the drink and tried not to show his disgust.

'It is because of your birth and who you are. There is something very special about you and there is nothing you can do to change that. I take it that you have killed Sibilia? I didn't think she would have given her blood so easily.'

'She had to die,' he said softly.

'We all agree with that. She had become quite troublesome and very greedy. Sibilia began to enjoy what she did and that sort of thing attracts attention.' Kinross finished the last of the prawns and, taking a piece of bread, wiped the juices from the plate. 'Stella will heal your friend if she can. I feel the presence of Ezra's knife.'

'I also have the knife you left behind at the cave when you took the Luger,' Flood said as he held out his hand to take the gun and the knife Jago had hidden in his coat.

Jago reached into the pocket of his coat and gave the man the gun. Flood smiled as he pushed the lever and the magazine slid from within the handle. Jago then handed him the knife.

'I wouldn't have used it,' Jago said.

'It would have been a fine thing to be assassinated by someone I am trying to help,' Kinross whispered. He stood up, pulled the curtains across the window and then warmed his hands on the fire. 'What do you know of the Lodge Maleficarum?'

'You control the world of Vampyres,' Jago said as Kinross came closer and put his hands on the boy's shoulders.

'We used to do that,' he said, 'but over the last hundred years one man has tried to take more and more control.'

'He's even paid for some of the Lodge to be murdered,' Flood interrupted angrily.

'One by one he is trying to kill us all and take what is ours,' Kinross said. 'Do you know who that could be?'

'Strackan?' Jago answered.

'With the help of Vibica de Zoete and a renegade called Toran Blaine,' Kinross replied.

'I know them both well,' Jago answered, wondering why Kinross was telling him all this.

'They have killed many of my friends and betrayed me. Vibica gave herself to the love of a demented fool. I gave her chance after chance but inside I knew she was lost.'

'How can I be of help to you in that? I'm not a Vampyre,' Jago answered.

'You are the son of a Vampyre. A famous and once proud man whom I regarded as a friend. Ezra Morgan, as he is now known, was a good man. He would try to resist the wiles of his master. You are of true and noble blood. Many would follow you,' Kinross said.

'The thing is, Jago,' whispered Aldus Flood benignly, 'you

would have to be a Vampyre before they would follow.' He let the words hang in the air as he patted Jago knowingly on the back. Then he tipped salt into the palm of his hand and threw it over his shoulder. 'But that can be arranged.'

'It would then mean that you would be worthless as a giver of your blood as it would no longer be human. That would mean Strackan would not benefit from drinking it,' Kinross said as he licked prawn juice from his lips.

'But he would still want me dead.'

'Possibly,' Kinross answered. 'But if he was already destroyed then the world would be a safer place.'

'We are at war, Jago,' Flood muttered in a succession of grunts. 'At war with our own kind.'

'They would see us dead, the Lodge destroyed and a new order take control. Like the war we fight upon the land, there is another taking place around us that we cannot see. The powers behind it want to see this country defeated and their rule imposed on us all,' said Kinross as he went to the curtains and looked out on the night. 'There are those of our kind who have given allegiance to foreign powers.'

'And they would see us all dead, Jago – especially you. It wasn't an accident that your mother –'

Flood stopped short as if he had given too much away.

'You knew of my mother?' Jago asked, his voice hopeful.

'The Lodge could not intervene. It was not the right time,' Kinross insisted. 'I wish it could have been different.'

Jago sipped the wine. It warmed his heart, and the room swam about him as his face reddened.

'Did you know she would die?' he asked as he pushed the glass away.

'Strackan wanted them both dead – Martha and her sister. There was nothing we could do,' Flood added as he pushed the glass back towards Jago. 'It was Strackan or someone working for him.'

Jago swigged from the glass, taking as much as he could in one gulp. The wine burnt his throat and slid into his stomach like burning coals. He breathed the vapours as his mind swirled. The heat from the fire grew more intense and scalded the back of his neck. He wasn't sure, but Jago thought he could see something coming from within the glass. A small, swirling, green hand held the rim, looking as if it was made from a thousand strands of jade silk. As he stared, the night dimmed, the faces of Kinross and Flood distorted, and their voices changed to the growling and grunting of pigs. Jago started to laugh uncontrollably. His stomach heaved in pain as he held his chest and the hysterical laughter echoed around the room.

'He has drunk too much,' Kinross said angrily. 'I only wanted him to sleep.'

'He is a half-blood. The wine is for Vampyres,' Flood answered as Jago slid to the floor and rolled under the table.

Jago looked up. Flood looked like a gigantic pig with a curled nose and a clown's feet. Then, as the night darkened further and the light from the fire dimmed as if the embers died, Jago could see no more. His laughter turned to gentle sobbing as he closed his eyes and curled himself into the pattern of a sleeping infant.

'Is he dead?' Kinross asked as Flood dragged him from under the table, his body flopping like a rag doll.

'I can still hear his heart beating,' he answered as he held

273

the boy close to him and listened to his chest. 'It is as strong as ever.'

'And Medea?' Kinross asked.

'All is ready,' Flood answered as he cradled Jago like a small child.

Soon a black sedan car left Whitby with an army outrider, the motorcycle speeding ahead through the empty country roads as they travelled south to Hackness. Leaving the main road they cut across moorland tracks until the valley fell steeply away. In the lee of the hill was a small house. It was more like a hunting lodge built from the moor and roofed with heather so it could not be seen. Its windows reflected the light of the moon.

The car stopped outside. Flood carried Jago into the house. Kinross followed, his steps urgent as he looked around to see if they had been followed. His feet crunching on the stone-flagged lobby, Flood took the steps to the cellar. A servant closed the door as the outrider stood guard in the porchway.

'Is she here?' Kinross asked. 'It will have to be done before he wakes.'

'You worry too much,' a voice said, and he turned to see Medea close behind him. 'I have been waiting so long for this moment.' She giggled as she pushed back her long raven-black hair from her face.

'Be careful, Medea. It is dangerous blood. We do not know what it will do to you,' Flood said as he laid Jago on a small stone slab raised from the dirt floor.

Medea stopped, looked about the small cellar and smiled. 'I remember this place when it was a Roman temple for the Ninth Legion. You chose wisely,' she said.

'And I remember what you did to them in the darkness of the forest, night after night until they were all dead,' Kinross answered.

'Happy memories,' Medea said, her sharp eyes watching the dust fall from the floorboards above them. 'I will be careful with him and teach Jago Harker everything I know.'

'And now?' Flood asked.

'Alone – it must be done alone . . .'

'We have to be sure that you don't kill him,' Kinross snapped.

'Trust me, I would never do such a thing to one as sweet as him. To think that Vibica thought that she would be the one to take the boy's blood.'

Aldus Flood tied Jago's wrist to the iron rings that were embedded in the floor. Then, with more twine, he secured his feet.

'Can't have him running away.' He laughed as he stepped back and looked at Jago. His words echoed around the room until they slowly faded. Kinross sighed as he walked to the stairway.

'Be sure not to kill him, Medea,' he insisted.

Medea waited until she was alone. She took a small knife from the pocket of her tweed suit. One by one, she cut the buttons from the neck of Jago's shirt and pulled back the collar with the tip of the blade. With one hand she pressed against his flesh until she could see the vein. It pulsed beneath her fingers with his pulsing life. Jago groaned, half asleep and thinking this was but a dream.

Then, pulling his head to one side, she examined his neck, trailing the blade across his skin, and sniffed his flesh. 'This will be very painful,' Medea whispered as she opened her mouth.

Like a striking wolf, the woman fell upon him. Jago stiffened, his body in spasm. His arms jerked as he woke from sleep.

'No!' he screamed, trying to break free from the binding that held him fast.

Medea gasped and stood back as blood trickled down her mouth. Jago opened his eyes. His body began to tremble as he saw her staring at him with cold and ancient eyes.

'It will soon be over, Jago – just one more bite.'

Again Medea struck. Jago could feel the teeth sink into his skin. The pain burnt like a fire of molten lead that trickled through his veins. He pulled at the binding until his wrists began to bleed.

As the venom seared through him, he felt his lungs would burst. His heart pounded in his chest, his body shook.

'Leave me!' he screamed as Medea continued to drink from him.

Jago gulped his breath as his heart beat faster, then slumped back, unable to move.

'Enough,' Flood shouted as he burst in and pulled the woman from him. 'He will die.'

'Jealous, are we, Aldus Flood?' Medea asked as she got to her feet, blood dripping from her fanged teeth. 'Did you want him for yourself?'

Without warning he slapped her bloodied face. She spun back, falling against the foundations of the ancient temple.

'This was almost until death – that was not what we had planned.'

Medea looked to the floor to avoid his eyes. 'Taste the blood for yourself. It is not human. He is a freak,' she bickered.

Flood wiped his finger across Jago's bleeding neck and slowly tasted it.

'We should tell Kinross,' Flood said as his face twisted with the taste of the blood.

'You said he was the son of Ezra Morgan. That is a lie,' Medea said as she spat the blood on the ground as if to rid herself of a poison.

'I can't understand,' Flood answered, reaching out to Jago and tasting the blood that had formed in a pool in the hollow of his clavicle. 'It has to be different.'

'We have been cheated. It is not what it seems.' Medea screamed in agony as her face burnt with the acid-like blood that smeared her face. 'It is poison.'

Hearing the disturbance, Kinross ran into the room. 'What is it, Aldus?' he asked.

'We have been cheated,' his companion answered. 'The blood is defiled.'

Kinross remained calm. He looked at the sleeping body of Jago, then stooped over and licked the blood from his neck. In horror he stood back from the body and spat the remnants of blood from his mouth.

'What is it?' Medea asked, seeing the disdain on his face.

'I cannot understand . . . This has the taste of death.'

25

Gammel Dansk

THE SCENT OF FRYING EGGS wafted through the rooms of Hawks Moor. In the dark kitchen the wireless chirped dance music while Vibica de Zoete stood over the wood-burning stove and pushed the crisp bacon to one side and cracked yet another egg. A cloud of grey smoke hissed from the frying pan.

She sensed Biatra enter the room and stand by the door looking at her. She felt the anxiety of the girl and waited for her to make conversation. The eggs crackled as they fried quickly, gorged in butter.

'We cook but don't eat. Sit at table and just look at the food,' Biatra said as she folded her arms and watched Vibica cooking.

'I love doing this. Whenever I get the chance I try to do all that I would have done if I was fully human. I couldn't imagine a day without routine.' Vibica smiled and washed the fat from side to side in the pan.

'I just feel sick at the smell unless I have had blood. I don't want to eat.'

'Understandable with all you have been through. You will find that it gets easier and food can be sometimes quite enjoyable.' Vibica lifted the pan from the cooker and served the food onto a china plate. 'Still,' she quipped, 'Hugh likes to eat and that makes me happy.'

Biatra stiffened as she watched Vibica neatly fold the napkin over her arm and take the plate from the table.

'Can I join you?' Biatra asked, not knowing if she wanted to be alone with him.

'Bring the teapot and some hot water,' she answered casually. 'Hugh still likes to drink in the morning.'

Biatra followed dutifully, carrying the silver try through the hall to the morning room. The gilded high ceilings glistened in the sunlight. The long room was spacious and warm with damask sofas in front of the fireplace. Hugh Morgan was at the window table folding the crumpled pages of a newspaper that was several weeks old. She thought how different he looked now that the sickness had gone from him.

'It smells strange,' Biatra said as the fumes from the pot filled her nostrils. 'I have never smelt tea like that before.'

'Gammel Dansk,' Vibica said, quickly trying to divert the conversation away from the scent of the tea. 'It is a tradition where I once lived. A mixture of herbs and spices to give it taste.'

'Then it will be most welcome,' Hugh answered. He touched Vibica's hand as she laid the plate before him. 'Will you be eating with me?'

'I will sit and watch. Now is not a good time for me,' Vibica said as she poured the tea into a small cup and slid it towards him. 'Could you bring me the milk, Biatra?'

Biatra didn't want to leave the room. All the words of the night before – when from her hiding place she had seen

Vibica and Toran Blaine kiss, and had heard what they had said about Hugh Morgan – spilled through her mind in a constant turmoil. She left the room and ran to the kitchen. Just before she returned she noticed three small pieces of diced leaf. She picked the largest piece from the stone flag and examined it. The leaf blistered the tips of her fingers. It had the same odour as the tea.

'She lied,' Biatra whispered, now knowing the tea was poisoned.

'Pardon?' Vibica asked suddenly from the doorway.

'Sorry . . . I thought . . .'

'Hugh needs the milk – take it to him and I will be with you soon,' Vibica said as she eyed the girl warily.

Taking the silver jug, Biatra walked as fast as she could. Entering the room, she closed the door behind her and turned the key in the lock.

'What are you doing?' Hugh asked. 'Where is Vibica?'

'She wants to kill you. I heard her last night. I couldn't sleep. She was in the Labyrinth with Toran Blaine. They are lovers,' Biatra said as she looked to the door, listening for footsteps.

'You must be wrong. Impossible – we are to be . . .' Hugh stuttered.

'The tea is poisoned. Dip your finger into it and see.'

'That is just stupid,' Hugh answered.

'Do it now. I am not lying,' Biatra insisted as she took the teapot and made him hold out his hand.

'Why are you doing this? Vibica is in love with me,' Hugh said adamantly.

'Look . . .'

Biatra tipped three smouldering drops of tea into the palm of his hand. It burst on the skin like fat in the pan, scorching the flesh.

'I can feel it,' Hugh said as Biatra twisted the key in the lock at the sound of approaching footsteps.

'Don't drink it, please,' she said, trying to appear calm as she opened the door.

'Now we can have breakfast,' Vibica said cheerfully as she walked in carrying some toasted bread. 'Nothing will ever be rationed in this house.'

There was an uneasy silence. Biatra looked at Hugh, her stare telling him not to be wary.

'I am not hungry,' he answered. 'I think it could be what I had last night.'

'At least drink. You must have something,' Vibica protested meekly as she tilted her head to one side and gazed at him like a wounded sparrow.

Hugh Morgan pushed his chair from the table and shrugged his shoulders. 'I think I will go for a walk. We have to decide what will be done for Jago.'

'Drink your tea, Hugh, and then we can talk,' Vibica answered as she lifted the cup from the thin white saucer and handed it to him.

Hugh held it in his long fingers. It looked out of place, as if he were a giant and it the drinking vessel of a creature far too small. Watching her closely, he smelt the liquid and held the cup to his lips. Vibica gulped with excitement.

'NO!' Biatra screamed. 'It will kill you.'

'What?' Vibica asked. 'What are you talking about?'

'I heard you – in the Labyrinth, last night . . .'

'Impossible. I was never there,' Vibica answered. She stepped back and looked to the open door. 'I would have seen you, heard you . . .'

'When you left me last night you said you couldn't sleep,' Hugh said as he stood up.

'True, yes . . .' Vibica stalled as she edged away.

'And who were you with?' he asked.

'It was best you did not know. Toran Blaine came to tell me what he knew of Jago. It was the business of the Lodge and didn't concern you.' She flustered as she took minute steps away from him.

'Blaine asked her to kill you,' Biatra shouted. 'He said the only way for them to be together was if you were dead. He is jealous.'

'I would never have done such a thing to you. I couldn't, I love you.' Vibica held out her hand, knowing the gesture was out of reach.

'She would have you dead and steal Hawks Moor from you. That is what they would do.'

'Be quiet, girl,' Vibica screamed, her face changing as she hissed through her teeth.

'Why?' Hugh asked as his hand trembled.

Vibica looked around the room and wondered what they would do.

'You would have fallen asleep. The henbane would have burnt your throat and that would have been it. The linctus works in seconds, I have used it many times. Don't you see, Hugh, that you are on borrowed time.'

'So you would have killed him?' Biatra asked.

'In time you will understand. A bite of a Vampyre can bring

life or death. I thought that it could be different between us, Hugh. Toran Blaine has never before told me we would share eternity. Now I think we will. He is jealous of you. He knows what my heart feels.'

Vibica spoke slowly, tapping her finger on the table in time with each word.

'Then you must leave this place,' Hugh said as he began to walk from the room.

Suddenly Vibica leapt on to the table, grabbing Hugh around the neck and pulling him to the floor. In one long and continuous movement, like the last notes of a ballet, she grabbed at his throat. Hugh threw her off and pushed Biatra out of the way. Vibica screamed as loud as she could.

'TORAN! TORAN!'

Her voice went beyond the house. Without warning the window of the morning room burst in. Glass shattered on the floor as twisted pieces of lead fell all around them. Toran Blaine landed by the fire and for a moment crouched like a wolf.

'Leave her, Morgan,' he growled as he bared his teeth. 'It is time for you to die.'

Hugh tried to back away from her, knowing that together they would easily kill him. Biatra stood by the table, half hidden by the long chintz drapes. She looked on as both Blaine and Vibica prowled closer to Hugh Morgan.

'Take her if you want her,' Hugh shouted, knowing that Blaine was about to strike. 'Just leave me and the girl – that's all I ask.'

'Too late for all that,' Blaine answered. 'I have been told to kill you both. As of last night, Jago Harker became a

Vampyre. Medea the Witch saw to that. It is written on the scroll.' Blaine took the Vampyre compass and the scroll from his pocket and, stabbing the bone finger through the vellum, pinned it to the wall. 'See for yourself and know that after I have killed you, he will be next.'

'Why do this? What have we ever done to you?' Hugh asked.

'It is what you will do in the future that is important,' Vibica said as she slipped a knife from the ruffle of her skirts.

'I will do this,' Blaine said to her. He looked Hugh Morgan up and down. 'I have been waiting such a long time to tear the smile from his smug face. Go build up the fire in the hall and we shall burn what is left of him.'

Vibica left the room. Biatra could see the look of fear on Hugh's face. He was not a man of violence. Murder would not come easily to him, even as a Vampyre. Blaine laughed as he stepped closer, sensing the fear.

'It doesn't have to be this way,' Hugh pleaded, looking for a way of escape.

'Then let me kill you and have done with it. I am sure you will be welcomed in the next life with open arms . . .'

With the words fresh on his lips, Blaine leapt across the back of the sofa. Hugh Morgan grabbed the fire-iron from the hearth, holding it awkwardly before him. With one swift movement, Blaine kicked it from his hand. Hugh jumped out of the way and, just as he leapt towards the broken window, Blaine caught hold of his ankle.

'No!' Biatra screamed. She grabbed the teapot from the table, took three long strides and threw the liquid in his face.

Blaine screamed as his skin burnt.

'The door!' Hugh shouted as he kicked free.

Biatra reached the door just as Vibica de Zoete ran across the hallway. She slammed it in her face and turned the lock.

'Let me in!' Vibica screamed as she beat against the wood with her fists.

'Get out of the window,' Hugh said to Biatra.

Blaine staggered about the room holding his blistering face. 'What did you do to me?' he asked, one eye blinded by the henbane linctus.

'Vibica was going to poison Hugh. I thought you would like it,' Biatra answered as she picked up the fire-iron from the carpet and crossed the room.

'I cannot see,' he answered, both hands covering his face as if to stop the light from blinding him.

'That is a good thing,' Biatra said.

Blaine slumped to the floor, falling on to the Persian rug in front of the fire with a dull thud. As he groaned a pool of dark claret spilled from the cut on his head.

'My goodness,' Hugh said, open-mouthed and frozen in his place. 'What have you done?'

'Saved our lives,' Biatra answered. She snatched the Sinan and the scroll from the wall, took Hugh's hand and dragged him to the broken window. 'If it's true we must find Jago.'

As they jumped from the window to the garden below, the front door of Hawks Moor opened. Vibica ran from the house, her hands gripping a small sword she had taken from the wall.

'You will not leave,' she shouted as she ran towards them.

Biatra pushed Hugh Morgan out of the way. 'Your lover

is dying and you come after us?' she asked, standing her ground.

'What have you done to him?'

Blaine appeared at the window above them. The skin on one side of his face hung in shards of flesh. He held it back with his fingers.

'KILL THEM!' he screamed still unable to see.

Vibica raised the sword above her head and jumped for Biatra like a gazelle leaping.

Biatra sidestepped out of Vibica's way, stabbing the Sinan into her back. Vibica screamed in pain as the blow pierced the skin like a hot knife. She twisted through the air, landing roughly.

'You are too good at this,' Vibica said as she looked at the girl and made ready to strike.

'And you are too old,' Biatra answered.

'But you will not live as long as me,' Vibica said as she lashed out with the sword, cutting the air.

Biatra slipped under the blade, blocked it with her arm and then kicked Vibica's feet away. The woman fell to the ground, dropping the sword. Biatra took the blade in both hands and lifted it above her head ready to strike.

'Biatra,' Hugh said. 'Please, no . . .'

'But she would kill us,' Biatra answered as Vibica lay at her feet.

'It's not the way,' he answered.

Biatra ignored him. Looking Vibica in the eyes she smashed the sword down as hard as she could. The blade pinned Vibica's arm to the ground so she could not move.

'Stay away from us – both of you. There will be no more

286

chances. I have the Sinan and the scroll and will know where you are. Stay away.'

Biatra walked away. As she looked up she could see Blaine at the window. He was sobbing and holding his face as the henbane still burnt through his skin. Vibica lay on the ground looking towards the brightening sky.

'How did you do that?' Hugh asked pulling the collar of his jacket.

'I was at the Mission School by the harbour. I fought every day from the age of five. Vibica is just another spoilt brat who deserves a good hiding.' Biatra smiled and squeezed Hugh's hand. 'With the scroll we can find Jago. I have much to say sorry for.'

'They will come for us and we will have to fight them yet again,' he said, his voice anxious.

'It was your choice when you became like me,' Biatra answered as they made for Blaine's motorcycle propped against the gate. 'This is the real world, Hugh. There's his bike – we can take that.'

'But –' he protested.

'You've never ridden one before?' she asked. Hugh nodded. 'Don't worry.' Biatra stepped on to the bike, taking the balance easily. She kicked over the pedal and the engine started. 'Get on,' she shouted above the growl.

'How did you know?' he asked.

'My father had one. He taught me how to ride before he went to war. I would take his bike for rides around the town. No one knew it was me.'

Morgan looked back to the house. Blaine had vanished. Vibica lay pinned to the earth, screaming to be set free.

'I can't leave her like that,' he said as he hesitated.

'She was going to kill us both and wouldn't have cared. That is what Vampyres are really like – can't you see?

'Is it what we will become?' Hugh asked.

'There has to be another way of living this life. We must find Jago.'

Biatra steered the machine along the driveway and through the small valley before turning up the hill towards Whitby, Hugh Morgan gripping on tightly. She leant into each corner as if she had ridden this way a hundred times before. The wind blew through her hair as they passed the old church on the hill before cresting the top of the road. There before them was the abbey ruin. The empty road dipped away as it cut through the fields.

'We should find Jack Henson,' Hugh shouted, his words snatched from his mouth by the wind.

[26]

The Brood

THE BLACK SEDAN CAR left the streets of Whitby far behind as it sped along the country road towards Hawks Moor. The driver gave little attention to the girl and her father as they rode an old army motorcycle towards them. Both vehicles slowed and the pillion passenger on the motorbike waved in thanks as the car crept by.

'Never seen that before,' the driver said to Aldus Flood, who gripped the door handle as the car drove on. 'How far to Hawks Moor?'

'Once we are at the top of the hill we should see the place. I haven't been there for many years,' Flood answered as he checked the pocket of his coat.

'And they don't know we are coming?' the driver asked as he pressed the accelerator and the car charged faster.

'We will be an unwelcome surprise.' Flood glared out of the window. 'I don't think they will cause much trouble.'

'And if they do?' he asked.

Aldus Flood tapped his pocket and laughed. The driver smiled; he needed no words to understand what was meant.

Soon they had breached the hill and were turning on to the track toward the house. It snaked in and out of the trees, making its way closer to the ivy-clad ramparts of Hawks Moor, where the driver stopped the car under the trees.

Flood looked at the smashed window of the morning room and the broken front door. 'I smell blood,' he said as they both stepped from the car and walked across the gravel.

'Look,' said the driver pointing to a trail of blood that led inside the house. 'I think someone is injured.'

They pushed open the broken door and stepped into the house. The burly driver pulled the belt of his leather coat tighter, as if making ready to fight. They looked around the hallway, then followed the trail of blood to the kitchen. There, at either end of the long wooden table, were Vibica de Zoete and Toran Blaine.

'I take it you are both alive?' Flood said.

'Aldus Flood, the grand protector,' Vibica answered. The bleeding in her arm had finally stopped and the flesh was beginning to heal. 'I take it you are here for us?'

'There will be no dispute in that. I have *it* with me and it would be pointless to resist.'

'But you would die as well,' Blaine said as he held the wound on his face. 'Would it be worth it?'

'With what is happening in our world and the chaos all around it would be a blessed relief,' Flood answered. 'May I ask who caused this to you?'

'It was the girl – Biatra. Hugh Morgan was frozen with fear, but the girl fights like a mad dog,' Blaine protested. He was still unable to see.

'Long red hair, scarred lip and riding a motorcycle?' the driver asked as he turned back the cuff of his sleeve.

'That is her,' Vibica replied. 'Pinned me to the ground with a sword. If Morgan hadn't pleaded for my life she would have killed me.'

'Then he still loves you. I take it you were going to kill them both?' Flood asked Blaine.

'If she hadn't thrown henbane in my face. Look at what she has done,' Blaine growled, showing the wound beneath his fingers. 'This is why we can't have human garbage as our kind.'

'Words of a man who has been killing *our kind* one by one for very large sums of money. You, Toran Blaine, are a mercenary,' Flood said.

'And you are here to take us to the Lodge Maleficarum?' Vibica asked.

'Treason. It has been decided that Kinross will deal with you both. Your war is now over.' Flood took two lengths of holly bark from his pocket and wound them around his fingers. 'This is just to make sure you do not decide to try to leave us on the journey.'

'Look at me, you fool. How could I do anything?' Blaine sobbed, not daring to even look at his own face. 'You will not want me now, Vibica.'

'It is not what you look like that makes me love you, Toran. I don't care,' she answered.

'See, nothing to worry about – all will be well,' Flood said sarcastically as he smoothed back his hair. 'If you wouldn't just mind . . .' Without waiting for an answer he strapped the holly around their wrists and they were both led to the car. 'I suppose you thought all this would be yours, Vibica?'

'If the girl had not got in the way,' she seethed.

'Perhaps all is not lost,' Flood muttered as he double-locked the car door.

There was silence as the car drove across the moor. By late morning it turned on to the drive of the house of Ozymandias. Parked outside, in the shade of the tall colonnade and the rattling branches of the spruce trees, was the car of the Prime Minister. Two guards stood by the door and watched the car as it approached.

'So what will you do to us here?' asked Blaine, whose face was now covered by a cloth.

'Kinross will decide that,' Flood replied. They walked towards the vast doors that looked as though they kept guard over the dead in an ancient mausoleum. 'I take it you do not mind being kept in the dark?'

The guards laughed as the doors opened. Vibica was bundled through a small opening and down a flight of narrow steps. The cold seeped from the earth around them as they went deeper and deeper. The long corridors that led under the house were lit with meagre candles inside old cans. Ahead, one of the guards opened a small door. Blaine and Vibica were pushed inside. The guards led them across a low, dark room and locked them in two small cells like wicker cages.

'And what now?' Vibica asked.

'I suspect there will be a trial and then a sentence,' Flood replied warily as he looked across the room to a pile of rags locked behind the door of a similar cage. 'What is to be done with you is to be debated.'

There was a slight movement within the folds of the thick blankets. Jago Harker stared out in the half-light. He looked at Aldus Flood through blood-red eyes.

'Jago Harker?' Blaine asked as the guard locked the door of his cage. 'What is he doing here?'

'A victim of modern times,' Flood said.

'But I thought he was now with us, a Vampyre in the line of Medea?' Blaine asked.

'And so he is, so he is . . .' Flood glanced at the boy and then walked to the door. 'I am afraid the hospitality is not as good as it should be,' he mused. 'I don't know how long you will be here. That is very much down to Mr Kinross.'

The door was slammed shut as Flood left the room. The candles shuddered in their tin cans nailed to the dank walls.

'What brings you here, Jago?' Vibica asked when the room was silent and the footsteps in the passageway had gone.

'I was tricked by Kinross. Medea took my blood,' Jago answered as he tried to wake from the deep sleep that had pursued him through the long hours of the night.

'Should have stayed with me – we could have been a great team,' Blaine said, his voice weak with pain. 'We know what it is like to be betrayed. That brother of yours and the girl, Biatra – they sold us to Kinross. Perhaps they did the same to you?'

'It's true, Jago,' Vibica said, echoing his words. 'I heard them talking about you. They said they would give you to Kinross in exchange for a place in the Lodge. It looks as if that is what they have done.'

Jago tried to stir from the blankets. His body ached; the blood from his neck parched the skin. 'They wouldn't have done that,' he tried to argue. 'Not Biatra.'

'Look at what she did to me,' Blaine said, taking the cloth from his face so Jago could see. 'Attacked me whilst having breakfast at Hawks Moor. Threw acid in my face and then she stabbed my Vibica.'

293

His voice sobbed pathetically. Jago raised his head and looked at his face. He could see the scar that cut deep into his skin, covering the left eye with seared flesh. Blaine hung his head and sighed.

'Can you see what they did to him, Jago?' Vibica asked. 'They'll do the same to you. Kinross will see to that.'

Jago reached to the bars of the cage and lifted himself from the floor. He stood against the metal rods, his legs weak.

'You are one with us,' Blaine said. 'No matter what, we are in this together.'

'If we get the chance we have to escape,' Vibica said as she rattled the gate of the cage. 'Just seize a chance, anything . . .'

Jago couldn't speak. He slid down the bars and slumped to the ground.

Not sure how much time had passed, Jago opened his eyes as the door to the cellar opened. He looked up into the face of Aldus Flood, who had been staring at him for some time.

'Not thinking of dying, are we, Jago?' he asked. He poked him with his stubby fingers through the bars of the cage. 'Can't be having that – we haven't decided what we will do with you.'

'You won't let him go,' Blaine snarled from across the dark room.

'Nothing is decided,' Flood replied as he turned the key and opened the cell door. 'Better be looking at that wound. Medea got carried away with herself, she did . . .' He pressed his hand against the wound in Jago's neck and smoothed away the dried blood. 'Still taking in the poison. There's enough to kill most people. I can't see that it has done much to you.'

'I feel sick,' Jago said as he tried to stand.

'Understandable under the circumstances,' Flood answered. 'I do hope you don't die. I was wanting to get to know something about the boy who will change the world.'

'Destroy it, more like,' Kinross said. His shadow filled the doorway. 'I wish to talk with Toran Blaine. Please bring him to me.'

'Just finishing . . .' Flood muttered.

'Now,' Kinross said before turning to leave.

Flood turned the lock on Jago's cage. Before he walked away, Jago dipped his hand into the pocket of Flood's coat.

'Better do what Kinross wants,' Vibica sneered as Flood took Blaine from his cell.

'Don't worry, Vibica. I will bring him back,' Flood answered as he left the cellar with Blaine and the guards.

'I take it you dipped his pocket and got the key?' she asked.

Jago got up from the blanket and showed her two door keys.

'Did it all the time in London,' he said as he tried one key in the door lock and turned it quickly. 'I have to go.'

'And what about me?' she pleaded. 'Are you going to leave me here?'

Jago thought for a moment. He was still weak. The poison ebbed and flowed through his veins and pounded in his head. It was hard to think.

'I can make that better for you,' Vibica insisted. 'You don't have to be in so much pain. I can take the poison from you.'

'How?' Jago asked as he stepped from the cage, his legs weak.

'Let me see the wound. I will help you,'

Jago walked towards her, not knowing what she would do. She smiled at him and reached out her hand. Without thinking, he took the key from his pocket and turned the lock. The door clicked open. They stood before each other. Vibica took his hand.

'Why is all this happening?' Jago asked nervously.

'It will all make sense, one day,' Vibica answered as she pulled him closer. 'I meant what I said to you that day. There are not many years between us, Jago.'

'But what about Blaine?' he asked as he looked at her face, thinking how beautiful she was.

'You saw him. He is different. I know a place we could go to. There is a man who would help us.'

'Why me?' Jago asked.

'Because you are different than any other. You are our redeemer.' Vibica smiled.

'People have said that before – what do they mean?' Jago asked.

'You are more than just a young lad who is now a Vampyre. It is said that you are as strong as Strackan. He was once the most powerful of all our kind. You could be even greater than him,' Vibica said as she held his hand close to her.

'They said I was a Vampyre hunter.'

'That was just old Henson wanting to get you on his side. Kinross knows you are a threat to him, to his power. He doesn't trust you. I have to get you from this place. We will leave Blaine here.'

'And then what?' he asked.

'You and I could . . .' She pulled Jago towards her as she spoke. They stood together as she tightened the embrace.

With one hand she smoothed away the shirt from the scars on his neck. 'There is too much poison,' she whispered. Jago could feel the bite; it pierced the skin quickly. The pain in his neck subsided. Vibica felt warm against him. He entwined his fingers in her hair as he felt the blood run down his neck. 'Enough,' she said as she wiped her mouth with the back of her hand. 'You will be well.'

Jago looked into her eyes. For a brief, transient moment he glimpsed the trail of her thoughts. Suddenly all was very clear. He tried not to let it show on his face. In his mind was a portrait of Strackan. Vibica was next to him and their arms were entwined.

'This is a deceit,' he said, not knowing where the words had come from.

'What?' Vibica asked. 'What do you mean?'

'I saw him. I saw him in your mind. He was different from in life but I know who it was,' Jago answered as the impression of Strackan grew stronger.

Her face changed, all fondness departed as it set in stone.

'He is the only one who can save you, Jago,' Vibica said coldly as she stepped away from him.

'I thought he would have me dead?' Jago asked trying to see inside her mind.

'If we went to him, spoke with him, I am sure he . . .'

'And all this with Blaine is just to make sure he does what Strackan wants?' he asked.

'There is only one thing that Blaine wants from me and one thing that controls his thoughts. He is a man and like any other man, he is shallow in his thoughts. Full belly, warm bed – that's all he needs.' Vibica's voice was taut and strained.

'And Strackan?'

'There is something about power that is so attractive. I never knew it in human life but as a Vampyre you can feel it when you are in the presence of someone powerful. I feel it when I am near you, Jago,' Vibica said almost breathlessly.

Jago could no longer feel the poison in his neck. He looked at Vibica de Zoete and then to the door. In that one second he had made his decision. His eyes flickered, giving away his thought. Vibica stiffened, as if the hackles of her neck burst through the collar of her jacket.

'It's not to be,' Jago whispered.

Vibica struck first. She grabbed him by the throat. Jago pushed her back inside the cell. He took hold of the cage door and, holding her arm against the metal, slammed it shut. Vibica screamed as her grip loosened. Jago locked the door and stood back, panting.

'You will not get far,' Vibica said as she held her wounded arm close to her. 'They will all betray you. That is the way of Vampyres. We are not to be trusted. Too long for this world – we lie and play games just for the fun of it.' Vibica held on to the bars as she spoke, her long white fingers wrapped around each metal pole. 'Now you are of the line of Medea, she will follow you until the ends of the earth. There will be no escape from her.'

'There is always Dust Blood,' he answered.

'Dust Blood is a half-life and no life at all. Once you have lived like us then you will never return. Look at Blaine. He tried the cure and then was soon back in our land, begging to be taken in and have someone bite him. You will not go back to your old ways. One moon and we have you for eternity.'

Jago dropped the key to her cell on the stone floor.

'It's there if you can get it,' he said as he walked to the door. 'I don't want your world.'

'You have no choice, Jago Harker. It will be this way unto death . . .'

The Termagant

JAGO WALKED IN THE SHADOWS along a high corridor of the house of Ozymandias. After locking the cellar door, it had been his intention to make his way to the back door of the house, but this he had found impossible. A small woman who was clearly some kind of Vampyre guarded the way. So, unnoticed by the woman, he had made his way above stairs.

The circuitous route had taken him through the empty kitchen and up the servants' stairs to the long galleried landing lined with paintings of Ozymandias in various stages of his long life. In each painting the eyes were portrayed in the same way, and instantly Jago knew the artist. Every brush stroke showed the hand of Julius Cresco. As he hid in the darkened doorway and regained his breath, Jago remembered the night when Cresco had taught him how to draw.

It had been the day that Jago had found a dead mouse under the cooker of his kitchen. He had placed the creature in the pocket of his school coat and taken it to show his neighbour, Mr Cresco. Instead of being alarmed at what Jago had found, Cresco had taken the frail creature and pinned it to a wooden board and tilted its head. The mouse looked as if it were alive, caught in a moment of forgetfulness. Then, over the next few hours, Cresco had instructed Jago in the way of drawing. Every line of black lead the man scratched on the surface of the paper had brought the creature to life. Soon it stared back at Jago from the paper as if it would leap from the vellum at any moment.

He sensed the presence of Julius Cresco all around him, and recalled bitterly how the man had betrayed him. As he stared at the paintings of Ozymandias each line of thick paint, every brushstroke and mark, reminded him of the man he had thought was his friend. He felt no remorse now for killing Cresco.

From far away, Jago could hear voices. The words spiralled upwards and danced off the vaulted ceiling of the hallway. Creeping like a fox, Jago was soon on the balustrade that looked down to the room below. He remembered this place from the night of the blood-auction. The gold ceiling was decorated with fine, porcelain-like paintings of angels, each with a sweet face and a half-smile. From the centre of the ceiling hung a large chandelier fitted with electric lights.

Below, Jago could see a gathering around the fireplace. Only one man was standing; the others were seated on two long sofas separated by a long coffee table. He recognised them instantly. Kinross stood by the fire. Blaine perched on the edge of one of the sofas holding his freshly scarred face and next to him was Aldus Flood. He appeared quite different than before. Jago realised that he had shaved off his long beard. This made him look younger, and in that moment Jago knew that Flood was also a Vampyre just like the others. The only person he did not know was the man

301

sitting opposite. He was smaller than the others, of diminutive stature, with a long and crooked nose. In his lap was a thick vellum book with pages that had torn edges. The man grasped a pen in his gnarled fingers and held it expectantly above the pages.

'I don't think that would be unreasonable under the circumstances,' the man said, nodding his head to agree with something that had just been said.

'Then we should make him sign?' Kinross asked.

'Only if he agrees,' Flood added.

'Then it shall be done,' Kinross replied, clapping his hands as if to end the conversation. 'There is only one thing and that is why I have summoned Blaine to be with us. Hugh Morgan and the girl Biatra need to be eliminated if our plan is to succeed.'

'Can they not be brought before the Maleficarum?' the man with the quill asked.

'Impossible,' Kinross replied, tapping his fingers on the mantle. 'It would be out of the question. I have decided that the only way in which we can have true power is if we limit the number of people with our *gift* . . .'

'You'll be talking of killing Vibica as well?' Flood asked, not really expecting an answer.

'I think it is time to have a fresh start, my dear Aldus. When this war is over there will be many new opportunities. I have my scientists developing a bomb that will kill off a whole city with one blast. Imagine that – the whole world would be in our control. They will think they are being governed by politicians when instead it will be us.' Kinross gloated as he spoke, his hands moving excitedly.

'And what about Harker?' Blaine asked, as if he wanted to settle an old score.

'That is a difficult decision,' Aldus answered before Kinross could speak. 'It would appear that the boy is not who he seems to be.'

'He is the son of Ezra Morgan,' the man with the quill pen chirped, as if he spoke the name of a king.

'I am afraid not,' Kinross replied, his face perplexed as he tugged the cord of his silk housecoat. 'It cannot be so. The blood was defiled. Medea has been taken ill with its effects. It is quite poisonous to Vampyres.'

Jago thought of Vibica de Zoete. She had taken the poison from him, but he knew that she had also drunk some of his blood.

'Then who is he?' the man asked. His pen was poised, waiting to inscribe the answer in his book.

Aldus Flood got to his feet. 'What we are going to do is kill him quietly. I will explain to Strackan what has happened and you, Blaine, will bring your master here as we have agreed on the night of the equinox.'

'The old Vampyre Ball?' Blaine asked in a half-laugh.

'It is our tradition and one not to be discarded,' Kinross said.

'We live in a modern world with modern things. Do we have to go back to the dark ages?' Blaine asked.

'I was alive in the dark ages. I survived the plague. It was not a nice time,' the man with the book said as he pointed his pen at Blaine. 'The Vampyre Ball is an act of unity.'

'It is what we need at this time. It could stop the war between us,' Flood said. He took the man by the hand and

303

stilled the wafting quill. 'Strackan and his followers will be invited, Blaine will see to that.'

'And in return?' Blaine asked.

'I will forgive you for all you have done and give you more money than you could ever spend in a thousand life-times,' Kinross said. 'I believe you said that you would be meeting Strackan at midnight tonight in the Market Place in Whitby?'

'It will be a Lestrigon,' Blaine answered.

'A Lestrigon?' the man said as he wrote the word in his book. 'A skin-reaper. How exciting, I have not seen one of those for many years. Do they still eat children?'

The others ignored him.

'You must bring Strackan to the Ball in person. I do not speak to puppets,' Kinross demanded.

'And what of Vibica?' Blaine asked.

'Do you really love her?' Flood answered.

Blaine did not reply. He looked to the pattern of the mo-saic beneath his feet and traced its outline with the tip of his boot.

'These are not questions for this place,' Kinross answered as he turned to Blaine. 'You have betrayed me, Toran, so many times. Now is the chance for you to redeem yourself. If you do as we have asked then all will be forgotten.'

'Very well,' Blaine muttered. 'I will find Hugh Morgan and the girl and do what I have to do.'

'Make it look like an accident,' Flood insisted.

'I have been informed that they are at the house of Jack Henson by the ruined abbey. He should not be too difficult to find,' Kinross said as he took Blaine by the hand and began to walk him to the door. 'I will have a car take you to Whitby. You will be met by one of my agents. She can be trusted.'

Jago instantly knew it would be Stella from the apothecary's shop. He wondered how she could have lied to Henson about who she really was. Now it all made sense why she was waiting in the graveyard. It was as if an invisible force was following his every move. He shrugged his shoulders and brushed the dust from his jacket as if he were removing invisible strings.

Jago heard the door close and listened to the footsteps clatter back across the parquet floor.

'Do you think he will do what we ask?' Flood asked Kinross.

'If we get Strackan to the Vampyre Ball then all will be well. I have had my scientists prepare a little experimental bomb.'

'A Doomsday weapon?' Flood asked.

'It will be delivered tomorrow in time for the ball. It will explode at midnight. There will be nothing left of this house or even the valley.' Kinross laughed as he spoke. 'Strackan will not be able to survive. He will be toasted where he stands along with all his followers.'

'But what about us?' the old man asked, his pen quivering in his hand.

'I will make sure we are long gone. I have ordered a train to take us to York. By the time of the explosion we will be far away,' Kinross said smugly as he took a cigar from the pocket of his coat and lit it from the embers of the fire. 'It is a masked ball so no one will know we have vanished. I will tell the press that it was an attempt on my life by enemy bombers.'

'Three hundred of our kind will die,' the old man said nervously. 'Most of those are loyal to us.'

'In war there will always be losses. It cannot be avoided. Blaine and Strackan and his cohorts will all be incredibly and deliciously dead . . .'

They all laughed. Jago crawled from his hiding place along the landing. All he knew was that he had to be in Whitby before midnight and warn Jack Henson. But it would be impossible for him to be there before Toran Blaine even if he were to escape from this house.

As he crawled along the passageway, Jago thought he could hear the sound of a child crying. The memory of the Gladling brothers persisted in his mind. As Jago got nearer to a tall wooden door, the sound grew louder and louder. Pressing his ear against the wooden panel, Jago listened to the sobbing voice. It sang in a bitter lament.

'Tend my heart, I sleep no more. All alone in darkness now, shall I cry for you . . .'

The words seemed fragmented, spoken rather than sung. The hushed voice breathed each word hopefully.

Jago opened the door and looked inside. The room was shuttered, dark and foreboding. Chinks of daylight broke through cracks in the window shutter and fell upon the back of a child. He was dressed in a miniature frock coat with a ruff collar. On his legs were tight white stockings that were tucked into black ankle boots. The boy clutched the reins of a large dappled rocking horse and moved slowly back and forth in time with his lament.

As Jago entered the room, the boy swayed on and on as if the rocking horse were the whole of his world. Jago had to know if the boy was one of the Gladling children. He stepped closer, reached out his hand and touched the boy on the shoulder.

The wooden horse stopped suddenly. Its mane fell over its face. The child gripped the bridle between its ghostly white fingers.

'Have you come for me?' he asked in a hush, not wanting to turn his head.

'Why have they kept you here?' Jago asked.

'The man took my mother – told me to stay here, she will be coming back,' he answered shyly.

'I'll get you from here. Take you away, somewhere safe,' Jago answered as he took hold of the boy as if to lift him from the horse.

'He said I can't leave, not now, not never. The man said he would catch me if I tried,' the child answered as he gripped the horse even tighter.

'What man?' Jago asked. 'You are here all alone.'

'The man in the cupboard, he stands in there day and night to make sure I don't leave.'

Jago looked to the tall cupboard in the corner of the room. The door hung slightly open so he could see the empty darkness inside.

'There is no one there. If you come now we can get away from this place,' he said to the boy as he tried to lift him from the toy horse.

'Leave me here,' the boy squealed. 'He will catch you and not let my mother return.' Jago pulled the boy from the horse. 'He'll come from the cupboard, I've seen him before.'

'Look, I'll show you. The cupboard is empty.' Jago took

one stride towards the door and pulled the handle. The door opened fully with a shrill creak. 'Empty, completely empty.'

Jago turned back to the boy, hoping to see a smile on his cherubic face. The boy stared back at him fearfully; his lip began to gently quiver as if he were about to cry.

'Can't you see him?' the child asked. 'He looks angry with you . . .'

Jago reached out to take the boy's hand. 'There is no one there,' he answered. But then his eyes caught the reflection in the mirror on the opposite wall. It held Jago fast. He was rooted to the boards as he looked at the two glowing red eyes that stared from the dark recess of the cupboard.

'He says he'll kill you,' the boy chirped. 'You shouldn't have come to this house. It's a bad place.'

Jago dived towards the door of the room but the door slammed shut and plunged the room into dark shadows. The Lestrigon stepped from the cupboard and moved towards him. Jago fought to open the door and pulled it from the frame just far enough for him to slip in the cap of his boot. The child ran towards him, arms outstretched. Jago pulled and pulled against the handle. The child ran the last few tiny paces and sank its teeth into his leg. Jago screamed just as the Lestrigon grabbed hold of his coat and threw him across the room. He crashed into the horse and fell to the floor.

Getting to his feet, Jago tore a leg from the rocking horse and beat it against the boarded window. The shutters fell open and light streamed into the room. He stared at the child, its face gaunt and dead like a ghost's. The Lestrigon cowered momentarily, shielding its eyes from the sun. Jago slipped the window catch and pushed back the wood just as the creature ran towards him. Instinctively he struck out as hard as he could and the creature fell to the floor stunned, its hand twitching.

'I won't let you leave my room. Not now, not never,' the child said as he came towards him. 'I asked for someone to play with and they sent you.'

'Don't make me do this,' Jago argued as the Lestrigon reached towards him with twisted fingers.

The child came closer, crossing the long room with tiny, precise steps as if it were the start of a dance. Then he slipped his hand into the pocket of his coat and began to smile and mouth the words of the song he had sung before. As the boy pulled his hand from the pocket Jago saw what was on each finger.

There, shining with a silvery gleam, was a strange device. Like a metal glove that attached over the hand and around the wrist was a set of razor-knives. The boy flexed each finger one at a time so that Jago could see the glinting blades.

'Are you sure you wish to try?' the child asked as he flicked the fingers of his hand. 'The blades are silver, the only thing that will kill a Vampyre.'

Jago felt the fingers of the Lestrigon pull the laces of his boot. He stepped back to the window and looked down. It was too far to jump – he was trapped.

'I don't want to hurt you,' Jago said just as the Lestrigon grabbed his ankle.

He lashed out with the leg of the rocking horse. The creature slumped back to the floor. The child dived towards him, punching at his face with the knifed fingers. Jago parried with the wooden club. The blades embedded deeply in the wood.

In one swift and seamless motion Jago twisted the child from his feet, spun him around and pushed him back into the cupboard.

Taking the remnants of the broken horse, he barricaded the door as the child beat against the wood from the inside. The silver blades pushed through the door panel as he tried to break free. He screamed in his pathetic voice to be released as Jago slipped from the room and into the corridor outside.

The Lestrigon watched his every move as he made his escape. In the tower room overlooking the house, Ozymandias lay on an ornate red chaise longue. His fingers twitched as if he had felt every blow that Jago had beaten down upon the creature.

'Jago Harker plays games with us all,' he said to his companion as he woke from his communion with the creature. 'Best not tell Kinross just now. We can save his escape for later. Follow him . . .'

28

Whitby

JAGO SLIPPED SECRETLY from the house and was soon crossing the field to the large wood. He could sense the way north and wondered how long it would take him to walk to Whitby. Once he was through the wood, the road cut across his path. It was quiet and still. The rationing of petrol had stopped most of the traffic and it was far too early for the steam bus to be making its way across the moor. He knew he could walk safely and if approached would plead that he was an orphan on his way to Streonshalgh Manor.

His only fear was that the slight changes to the bones of his face would be noticed. Already he craved food and as he sniffed the air he thought of the taste of blood. Biatra had been right in what she had said. There was nothing he could do to stop the hunger until it was quenched. This he did not want to do – taking blood would make what had happened so final.

What had changed the most was that he now saw the world differently. Colours and sounds were far more heightened than they had ever been. The sky shimmered bright blue and the smell of the last flowers of the year was carried on the wind. He could hear birds in flight and creatures hiding in the long grass. Every muscle in his bruised body was alive as if it were the first day of their life. Jago could hardly breathe with the excitement that pulsed through him.

Before long he had become bored with the journey. He had calculated the miles from the house and the point where he now stood on the hill overlooking the bay had been five miles. Now he looked out to sea. Far below he could see the tall chimneys of Hawks Moor and to the north the rocky fingers of the ruined abbey. It was only when he heard the distant engine of a car that Jago looked back along the road.

In the distance he saw the green roof of a small parcel van. It came slowly, struggling to climb the hill. Instinctively Jago stood back from the road into the shadow of an old yew tree by the entrance to a field. It towered above him, its shape gnarled by summer gales and bowed down by winter snow. He knew if he waited the van would soon go by and he could walk on unseen. The railway line was just below the road and it would take him straight to the town.

As the van came closer Jago stepped deeper into the shadows of the tree. He listened to the churning of the gears as the engine slowed and slowed.

To his surprise the van stopped by the gate. Jago looked at the fine gold writing and the advert for tea on the side of the van. Inside, a woman took the long strands of her blonde hair, rolled them in her fingers and then pinned them tightly to the back of her head. When she had finished she turned her face towards him and smiled.

'I wondered where you had gone, I saw you when I was on the other hill,' she shouted through the open window. 'Are you going far?'

Jago shrugged uncomfortably and tried to smile without showing the teeth that he knew had grown in his mouth. The woman looked like a movie actress, even in her blue overall and white shirt.

'Whitby?' he said in a question.

'Me too. There is rain coming. Want a lift?' She smiled again as she opened the door.

'Perfect,' he mumbled, keeping his head down.

Jago got into the van. The woman prattled on and he understood that she was on her way to Whitby to deliver packages of tea. Listening to the thoughts of others was not as easy as he first believed. The thoughts came as pictures and impressions, brief glimpses into the working of the mind. They were never complete and often too vague to be pieced together. Like a fairground seer, Jago tried to understand what the woman was thinking.

'You look like you have been in the wars,' she said, taking his mind from what he was thinking.

'A fall,' he said.

'Better get your face seen to. It looks quite bruised and I can see your leg has been bleeding,' the woman replied as she started the engine and drove off. 'Have I seen you before, your face looks familiar?'

'I was at Streonshalgh Manor, an evacuee from the bombing,' Jago answered slowly as he unconsciously rubbed his bite wound and looked at the veins in the back of her hands.

'I can take you to the bottom of the steps if you want. I have a delivery to a shop near there,' she said. 'Don't get a chance to meet many people on the road these days. Not since the coming of the war.'

'You could forget we are at war in this part of the world,' he answered.

'Heard there was a bombing in Hull the other night. Place took it quite bad. I was told not to talk about it. Careless thoughts cost lives,' she answered.

Jago thought he had misheard her. 'Careless thoughts?' he asked.

'Did I say that?' she laughed. 'Whatever am I thinking, Jago? Carless *talk* – isn't that what the Prime Minister says on those posters?'

He swallowed hard; he had not told the woman his name and yet she knew. She smiled at him as she drove on. The car speeded up for the next hill along the road, rolling from side to side as the tyres clunked into the potholes. Jago edged nearer to the door and wondered if he could survive jumping from the car. The woman appeared to sense what he was doing. 'Fine place, Whitby. Perhaps a bit remote and not as busy as Scarborough.'

'Never been there,' he answered. 'Perhaps one day.'

The next five miles were spent in silence as Jago closed his eyes and allowed the buffeting of the car to rock him into a disturbed sleep. Suddenly the car turned sharply and bumped as it dropped down a track. He was woken from sleep as the car speeded up.

'This isn't the way to Whitby,' Jago said, knowing he was travelling east.

'Main road is blocked – have to go around. There was a sign. You were asleep,' the woman answered.

'But this road goes to Hawks Moor,' Jago said.

'Perhaps that is where you should really be going?' the

woman asked, and as she turned to him Jago noticed the two small marks in her neck and the tell-tale drops of blood on the collar of her white shirt. He tried not to look surprised as he slowly reached for the door handle.

'I have no reason to go there,' he answered, feeling panic rise in his chest.

'It's where I was told to take you. Ozymandias needs to talk,' she said slowly as she tightly gripped the steering wheel. 'You will be safe.'

'Who are you?' he asked.

'I am a companion. But then again, you already know that.' She paused and smiled. 'I saw you looking at my neck.'

'What does Ozymandias want?' Jago asked cautiously.

'He would like to offer you a way out of all your problems – especially now you are a Vampyre,' the woman said as the light shimmered on her ruby lips.

'Ozymandias tried to sell my blood,' Jago answered.

'That was then. Now things have changed. He will be following on very soon, when it is safe to do so,' she said as she reached across to Jago and nipped his chin with her long painted fingernails. Jago pulled back his head.

'Will he tell Kinross where I am?' Jago asked. 'After all, I was held prisoner in his house.'

'That is part of the problem. Kinross and Ozymandias are not good friends. Ozymandias is bonded to him as a slave to his master.'

The woman turned the car at the next left and dropped into a small lane shaded by oak trees. She drove faster, the branches slicing the sunlight above them.

'I don't want to see him,' Jago said after a while.

'There is no choice,' she replied, her voice now deeper as if Ozymandias spoke through her. Jago grabbed the door handle. It was locked shut. 'Can't have you getting away again,' she said as she stared at him through narrowed eyes.

'I want to go to Whitby,' he insisted.

'After you have seen Ozymandias,' the woman answered sternly. '*He* will decide.'

'NO!' Jago shouted, and he pushed the steering wheel away from him.

The van veered across the track, hitting the embankment and bouncing back into the road. Jago pushed the wheel hard as the woman fought against him.

'Let go!' she screamed as it again struck the side of the road. 'You'll kill us.'

'Stop the van,' Jago shouted as with his foot he tried to push the brake pedal.

The woman lashed out, striking Jago on the side of his face with her clenched fist. He grabbed her shirt, ripping the collar as he pushed her back and forth. As they came to a corner the van lurched. It went up the side of the embankment and clipped a hedge as it turned over, crashing on to its roof. The door burst open and Jago was thrown to the road.

Looking back, he saw curls of smoke coming from the engine and spiralling like will-o'-the-wisps in the gentle sunlight. The woman lay slumped against the door, a trickle of blood rolling slowly across her lips. The wheels of the van spun above her and Jago could see she was alive. She rolled her head back and forth, trying to regain consciousness.

'Jago . . . Jago . . .' she breathed quietly as she opened her eyes.

He went to her, dragged her to the side of the road, and in the shadow of the holly tree she became his first companion.

Wiping the blood from his mouth, Jago propped the woman against a tree.

'Your master will find you here,' he said as he touched her lips with his finger. 'Tell him I am going to London and want nothing of his Vampyre war.'

'They will come for you Jago. There will be no hiding place,' she answered. 'Ozymandias needs you.'

'Then he will have to find me,' Jago said as he walked away into the dark of the wood.

He hiked north, following the railway track. By late afternoon he was nearing Whitby. As he walked through the gravestones next to the old church, he looked down on the town. The streets seemed empty. The funnels of the boats in the harbour appeared cold and dead. Jago made sure he was not being followed.

Then he heard a sound that had become familiar. Steel slipped against mud and stone as by the church wall a grave was dug deeper. He watched as mud and earth were flung with each tilt of the shovel. Jago walked to the grave. Looking down, he smiled.

'Took your time,' Henson laughed as he looked at the shadowy figure above him. Then his laughter stopped as he saw the signs that he dreaded in any man. Henson stared at Jago, hoping it was not true. As with all Vampyres, it was in the eyes that he first noticed the change. 'When did it happen?' he asked.

'It was Medea. Kinross and a man called Aldus Flood. They kidnapped me.'

'Wicked and evil. Will they ever stop?' he asked as he climbed the small wooden grave-ladder. 'Where did they take you?'

As they walked to the cottage, Jago told him of what had gone before. 'It is blessed that you are alive, Jago,' Henson said as they got to the door. 'Don't be surprised by what you will see.'

'Staxley?' Jago asked.

'More than that. Hugh and Biatra are here.'

'Here?' he asked, his face showing his concern. 'What shall I say?'

'Speak the truth wisely,' Henson answered. 'They need to see you.'

Jago was not sure if he wanted to see them. In the time that Vibica had been at Hawks Moor he felt that he and Biatra had become enemies. He swallowed hard as Henson opened the door and stepped inside. Jago followed, leaving the alleyway for the warmth of the peat fire and smell of the oil lamps.

Hugh Morgan looked up from the armchair.

'Jago?' he said in great astonishment.

'Jago . . . Jago,' Biatra repeated. Jago turned to her. What little light came into the room through the small window splashed on his face. She eyed him warily. 'Who did it to you?' she asked.

'There is no time for that now,' Henson said as he looked at her. 'We need to think of what to do.'

'Jago?' came a voice from the other room. 'Jago is back?' Staxley limped from the bedroom. His face had almost returned to normal, his hand gripped a walking stick. 'The

318

woman brought the sash and made Dust Blood. It stopped the poison from killing me.'

Jago tried to smile. He wondered if it would have been better just to let Staxley die. 'So glad you are well, Stax,' was all he could say.

In the following hour Jago told them everything that had happened to him. He spared no detail and listened in turn when they told him of Vibica and Blaine. 'She is being held captive by Kinross. Toran Blaine is arranging a meeting for the night of the Vampyre Ball. They want to kill each of us.'

Biatra sighed and twisted her hair nervously. 'Can't they just leave us alone?' she asked.

'They have to be stopped, all of them,' Henson said. 'It will not end until they are all dead.'

'There has to be another way,' Hugh Morgan argued. 'Kinross wants to kill everyone at the Ball. He wants to end the war between them.'

'Then we should let him do just that,' Henson said. 'The fewer the better, if you ask me. The girl I bury tonight was found at the bottom of the cliff. I suspect they had killed her for blood.'

'How does he want to do that?' Biatra asked.

'He has a bomb. Kinross said it was more powerful than anything known until now. It can destroy a whole city,' Jago answered.

'Then we should leave them to do what they have to.' Hugh closed the book in his lap. 'It would be best if we stayed out of their way until all this is over.'

'But they will come looking for us. That is what they said. I am to be killed and so are you. It is what Kinross demanded. I heard them,' Jago argued, his voice restless.

'I know a place that we can go to,' Hugh said. 'It is far away. No one would ever think of looking for us there. Jack can find us a car. We can be gone by the morning. When Kinross has done what he has to, then we can try to return.'

'He could have you all arrested. Tell the country that you were spies,' Henson said in a voice marked by irritation. 'He is the Prime Minister.'

'He knows we are here. I heard him tell Blaine before he sent him away. Stella works for Kinross and always has. She was watching this house. It may be too late,' Jago argued, anxious that they would do nothing.

'I will prepare things for us to get away.'

Jago could see that Henson was worried. His thin face looked haggard and forlorn. He folded a small piece of paper over and over in his fingers as he thought.

'So we let them all die?' Biatra asked.

'Why worry?' Henson asked. 'He does our job for us.'

'But they are innocent,' she snapped.

'Innocent?' he shouted. 'How can a gathering of murderous blood-drinkers be innocent?'

Henson stopped as they stared at him. He realised what his words meant.

Jago laughed and shook his head. 'That is what we are, it is what we have become,' he said as he reached out and took Biatra by the hand. 'Our lives have been changed by all of this and we will never be the same.'

'Jack is right,' Hugh said uncomfortably. 'We should go away and leave them to it. All will be well.'

'And what if Blaine is waiting for us now? How will we escape from him?' Biatra asked.

'He is meeting Strackan in the Market Place at midnight – we could take the fight to him,' Jago said, hoping they would agree.

'Now isn't the time, Jago,' Henson replied, seeing the look of despair on the face of Hugh Morgan. 'Once the funeral is out of the way tonight, then we can escape this place.' Henson paused briefly as a sudden inspiration came to him. 'We can take the hearse out of town and wait at the stables. No one would ever suspect . . . If anything happens we carry on. There is no going back if one of us is captured.'

29

The Telearch

JAGO WAITED OUT THE DAY until the darkness fell on the town. In that time, Henson had gone to the church-yard to prepare for the funeral. Before he left the dark cot-tage in the shadows of the abbey, he didn't speak any further about the girl who had been found that morning. Biatra told Jago that it was common in those parts to treat anyone dis-covered at the foot of the cliffs as a victim of the Vampyre.

'They did it all the time, even when my dad said it was just an accident,' she said as she looked out of the window into the dark night. 'That's what it is like here.'

'And I remember the day we met and you didn't believe any of it,' Jago reminded her. 'Now look at us.'

Biatra moved closer to him and encircled his waist with her arm. She cupped her long fingers under the belt of his trousers as if she would never let go.

'I am glad of it,' she said softly. 'I would not change a mo-ment for all the world.'

'So you will stay this way?' Jago asked.

'If it is possible,' Biatra replied as the clock chimed the ninth hour. 'Funny having nothing to take with us. It's like we are starting life afresh.'

'We have to be at the churchyard in fifteen minutes. That's when the funeral will be over.'

'She'll be holly-bound and fastened in with silver nails. They'll put a stone in her mouth and bury her face-down in the coffin,' Biatra said in a way that made it sound terrible. 'If anything ever happens to me, make sure they don't do that.'

'Nothing will happen,' Jago insisted. 'I know it.'

She looked at him and laughed. 'You cannot lie, Jago Harker,' she said as she moved forward and kissed him.

'We have to leave,' he answered uncomfortably. 'I will go for Staxley and Hugh.'

They were all soon walking along the narrow path towards the churchyard. The moon hung in the sky like a sliced cheese. Scant clouds crossed its face, dimming the light. Walking in silence they kept pace as Staxley beat out a slow march with his stick. Jago could see he was in pain even though by now all the swelling to his face had subsided. He looked just as he did on the day they had first met.

As Jago turned back, Staxley smiled at him. 'You didn't have to do all this for me, Jago,' he whispered as they walked together.

'I had to. I couldn't see you suffer,' Jago said, and he patted the boy on the back.

'What about all that I would have done to you?' Stax asked.

'Forgotten,' Jago answered simply. 'It doesn't seem to matter any more.'

Together they followed Biatra and Hugh Morgan. The pathway led to a steep slope embedded with stones to stop the carts slipping. Then they crossed to the small gate into the churchyard.

Waiting in the shadow of the old church, they heard the carriage grind along the lane towards them. Its wheels scraped on the cobbles as the fenders creaked and moaned. The sound of iron horse-shoes clattered on the stone as they came closer.

'They're late,' Henson said from the dark archway of the church door.

'Didn't know you were there,' Hugh answered, surprised by his sudden appearance.

'They had a bit of trouble with this one,' he said. 'They sent on to say that she would have to be staked.'

Jago knew what Henson meant. The girl would have a stake driven through her to stop her becoming a Vampyre. It suddenly felt gruesome and vile, a pinnacle of human hatred of what he now was.

'Do they think she is like us?' he whispered.

'More than that,' Henson replied. 'There have been stirrings. When night came it looked as though she was coming back to life.'

In the shadow of the church two mourners opened the tall iron gates. The carriage slipped through. The horses with their black plumes shook their heads against the cold wind that blew about the gravestones. Two small candles cast out a weak light from the silver lamps on either side of the lacquered coach. The driver huddled in his long coat as he brought them to a halt by the open grave.

'Here she is,' he shouted to Henson. 'I will be happy when she is deep under the earth. This was no accident.'

Henson nodded in agreement. 'Then let's be going. The sooner the better for me as you well know,' he answered.

The mourners opened the doors to the hearse, not bothering even to glance at the figures in the darkened church porch. The coffin, wrapped in holly wands, was carried to the graveside. It was small, no more than a casket for someone quite young. Henson stood silently, his lips moving as he prayed for the dead child. Every now and then he would stop and look around him as if others were listening to him. Jago looked on, knowing that the *whisperers* were all around them. He could feel their ghostly presence and wondered if these spirits would ever be set free.

Four tallow lanterns gave light. The mourners lifted the coffin unceremoniously to slide it into the grave.

'Not much of her,' one man said as he doffed his top hat in respect. 'Shame no one will come and say goodbye to the little mite.'

'Who'd want to think anyone could do that to a child?' the other man asked.

Jago felt a hand on his shoulder. He looked back and saw Staxley.

'Could have been me,' Staxley whispered as he squeezed Jago's shoulder. 'Won't forget that, Jago.'

Jago nodded and bowed his head. He tried to think of the future but all he could see was a black void. It seemed as if there was nothing there for any of them.

'Where are we going?' Jago asked Hugh as they waited for the burial.

'There's an island off the coast a way north of here. A place called Castle Lutyen. We will be safe there.'

'An island?' Biatra asked. 'Is it far?'

'About a day's travel. Henson has arranged for this carriage to take us from Whitby. No one will ever think of searching it. Then we have a car to take us to the castle.'

'Will Blaine come after us?' Jago asked.

'If he can find us. Sadly, Henson is right. The only way to be sure was if he is dead.'

'Then why don't we search for him now?' Jago asked.

'I don't think –' Hugh tried to answer.

'I would go with you Jago,' Biatra said. 'I have nothing to lose.'

'I won't hear of it,' Hugh insisted. 'We will get from this place and be done with it. When we are at Castle Lutyen we can think of what to do.'

'But what about all the people who will die when Kinross blows them up?' Biatra asked him in a whisper.

'So mote it be . . .' a voice behind them, and the hammer of a pistol clicked. 'I have six silver bullets, enough to kill each one of you and still have some left over.' Blaine laughed.

Hugh turned. Blaine stood in the church doorway, his long coat trailing on the ground and his hat was tilted on his head.

'Been listening for long?' Hugh asked.

'Long enough to know where you are going to hide,' Blaine answered smugly. 'Shame to think you will get no further than the church gate.'

'What are you going to do to us?' Biatra asked as she moved closer to Jago.

'It would appear that I am going to kill you all,' he boasted as he stepped closer and pushed the barrel of his pistol into

326

Staxley's back. 'I don't know if I should wait until the funeral is over.'

Staxley gripped the walking stick in his hand. He leant against it with all his weight. Jago could see the grim expression on his face and the pained look in his eyes.

'I'm sorry for what I did to you at Streonshalgh Manor, Jago – you too, Biatra. It was wrong of me,' Staxley said in a whisper. 'I should have got to know you. I have wasted too much time being angry with myself.'

Both his words and the lines on his face were those of a man far older than himself.

'Repenting for past wrongs?' Blaine asked sarcastically. 'I find that quite touching.'

'What would you know?' Biatra asked.

'Becoming quite a madam,' Blaine replied. Then he realised that the funeral had stopped and now Henson, the mourners and the carriage driver were staring at him. 'Don't let me stop you from what you are doing.'

'Won't you even give us time to do this in silence?' Henson asked Blaine.

'If silence is what it takes,' he answered. 'Which one of you has the Sinan?'

'I have,' Hugh answered.

'Good. I will take it from you when you are dead,' Blaine replied casually. 'Get on with the burial and then we can use the grave for my guests.'

Henson looked to the mourners and nodded. They held the coffin high above the grave.

'Better do as he says,' Henson grumbled. 'Never thought I would end up in here.'

'We all end up somewhere,' Blaine answered.

'You'll be dead in two days,' Jago said. 'Kinross plans to kill you all.'

'Don't be so stupid. I don't work for Kinross. What I agreed with him does not stand. Strackan still wants you, Jago, that I know.'

'How can you be sure? Don't Vampyres take great pleasure in the game of cheating?' Hugh asked.

Blaine held the gun towards him. It was then that Staxley struck out with the walking stick, smashing Blaine across the hand. The gun fell to the floor. Hugh Morgan pushed Blaine from the porch. He fell back towards the grave, pushing the two mourners and the coffin to one side. The coffin fell to the stone path and the wood spilt open. A small hand fell from within. It was bound in holly rings, its tiny white fingers open to the sky.

Staxley struck again, hitting Blaine with the stick. Blaine lashed out as Biatra leapt towards him, grabbing for his neck. The mourners ran towards the town, running in and out of the gravestones. Blaine dived out of the way as Biatra fell across the open coffin and into the grave.

'This way,' Henson shouted as he ran to the carriage, took the reins and started to turn the horses.

Jago took hold of Blaine and punched him as Staxley gripped his legs. 'Get Biatra and go,' Staxley shouted as he fought with Blaine.

Hugh Morgan pulled Biatra from the grave and dragged her towards the carriage.

'Quickly,' he shouted, as the carriage now rumbled towards the gate. 'Come on!'

Staxley looked up as he struggled with Blaine.

'Just go, please!' he shouted as Blaine beat at him with his fists.

Jago saw the girl hanging from the coffin. In her chest was the wooden stake. Frantically he pulled the holly bands from her wrists and took hold of the stake. For a moment it held fast, but then with a desperate heave he pulled it from her ribs. The girl coughed as she came to life. Her eyes opened and stared at the sky. Jago stabbed at Blaine with the stake.

'Don't be stupid, Jago,' Blaine shouted. 'We could be together, nothing would stop us.'

'Go, Jago,' Staxley shouted. 'I have him – get away.'

Jago hit Blaine a final time with the holly spike and then ran after the carriage. Desperate to escape, Blaine knocked Staxley to the floor and picked up the revolver.

'Stay where you are!' he shouted at Jago as the boy took hold of the brass rail at the back of the carriage.

'Come on, Jago!' Hugh Morgan shouted as he hauled Biatra on to the hearse.

Blaine aimed the gun and pulled back the hammer.

Just as he was about to pull the trigger, Staxley struck him again. The bullet exploded from the barrel and cracked into the ground. Blaine smashed the pistol into Staxley's face, knocking him to one side. Staxley slumped to the ground as Blaine set off to chase the carriage.

Jago heard another shot as he grasped the rail of the carriage.

Henson whipped the horses faster and faster as the coach rolled from side to side. Biatra reached down as Jago held on to the door.

'Slow down,' Morgan shouted.

'We can't, Blaine will catch us,' Henson said as he looked back and saw him running through the graveyard. 'He's trying to get to the road before us.'

The horses neighed as they ran, their heads baying at the moon as the shadows of the gnarled ruins chased them across the heath. Jago clung to the carriage with one hand as the wind beat against his face. Biatra held on to him as tightly as she could, hoping her grip would not give way.

Far away, Blaine ran through the darkness. He leapt the fallen stones as he headed for the road, the carriage racing towards him. Henson whipped the horse onwards. They galloped faster, the carriage jumping over the broken stones.

'He's gaining ground,' shouted Hugh Morgan as he watched Blaine running across the heath, pistol in hand.

'I think he shot Staxley,' Jago said as he scrambled inside the coach and looked back.

'Where are we going to hide? Blaine knows about Castle Lutyen,' said Biatra as she held on to Jago and the the carriage rattled like a bucket of bones.

'We shall still go to the castle. Blaine won't dare come for us,' Hugh shouted above the noise of the horses.

The corner came suddenly. The coach veered to one side. Blaine stood on a small outcrop of rock by the side of the road, waiting.

'He's beaten us to this place,' Henson shouted as he urged the horses on faster and faster.

'Keep going. We have to take the chance,' Hugh answered.

There was a loud gunshot. The bullet smashed through the

330

lacquered wood of the roof. The hearse lurched to one side and then to the other. Jago tumbled inside the carriage as the glass window shattered in its frame. Biatra held her side.

'I've been shot,' she bawled as she held the wound. 'It's cut the skin – that's all.'

'Keep down,' Hugh screamed as another bullet smashed through the roof of the carriage.

Without warning, the carriage tipped as it hit a rock by the side of the road and two wheels left the ground. Jago was smashed against the doorframe and the door swung open. The blow stunned him. He slipped into the mourners' seat with his eyes wide open, staring at the roof in a muddled stare.

'Jago!' Biatra screamed in panic as she was tipped from the carriage.

She fell to the road and spun several times until she stopped in the verge. Blaine jumped from the rock as he fired the pistol once more.

'Stop!' Blaine shouted as he fired a final shot. 'I will trade the girl for Jago. Think on it – I will set her free if you give me the boy. The Vampyre Ball . . .'

His words faded into the distance as the carriage rattled furiously on. Jago looked back; his eyes were blurred and the noise jarred his mind.

'Biatra,' he said helplessly, knowing she was gone.

'We'll have to go back for her,' Hugh Morgan said as he banged on the carriage roof for Henson to stop.

'He can't be trusted,' Henson answered as the carriage turned towards the sea. 'You heard what he said – the Vampyre Ball.'

'We have to stop Blaine,' Jago screamed angrily as the mist cleared from his mind. 'We have to find Biatra.'

'It could be a trap. Blaine is a liar, he'd keep you both,' Hugh answered.

'Then I will go alone. I have to find her,' Jago shouted as he tried to jump from the carriage.

Hugh Morgan grabbed him by the sleeve and pulled him back.

'I can't lose you again. Not in that way,' he said as he held Jago tightly.

'Please – I have to go to her. She's alone with that madman,' Jago pleaded.

The horses galloped onward into the night. The light of the moon faded, masked by clouds that came from the hills to the west. Jago could see the distant outline of the abbey ruins and knew that Staxley and Biatra were out there.

Then, as ghostly wisps of mist chased the funeral carriage across the moor to the north, Jago could see nothing but the outline of the hills and the cliff falling to the sea. The moon had set behind a high bank of clouds and darkness crept across the land as if it were a hand pursuing them. It chased the carriage, plunging the lad into a blackness where all light vanished and not a thing could be seen.

Mile by mile, they were being hounded by an army of chaos.

'How far?' Hugh Morgan shouted to Henson as they crossed the narrow bridge by the Ruswarp Inn.

'Not far,' he answered as he looked back and saw the chasing blackness. 'All will be well.'

30

The Philoverba

THE DULL GREY DAWN stretched out to the far horizon as the waves beat against the shingle beach. There was no sun, just a growing light that hardly penetrated the thick cloud that seemed to blanket the earth and colour the sea. Jago Harker stood on the bank of pebbles and looked down at the breaking waves. He had spent the night in the barn of the Hart Inn. Jack Henson had stabled the horses and hidden the funeral carriage. He had stayed awake, making sure that Blaine hadn't followed them.

As the darkness had faded, Jago had walked across the road to the gravel shoreline. Swirls of seabirds had spiralled in the air, squawking shrilly as they flew out to sea. The fate of Biatra consumed his thoughts. He knew he couldn't leave her alone. She was all he really had in life. Slumping down, Jago sat on the stones with his head in his hands, listening to the pounding of the sea as it rolled the shingle back and forth.

Looking back, Jago could see the car that Henson had bought to take them to Castle Lutyen. It was a green sedan with red leather seats, white-walled tyres and a silver jaguar on the bonnet. He had never seen anything like it before.

Jago didn't see the woman collecting driftwood until she

drew near. She was dressed in a long grey skirt that matched the colour of the sea. In the haze of morning she was almost invisible as she meandered slowly back and forth, picking wood and placing it carefully in a hessian sack.

She sang softly and although he couldn't make out the words, Jago turned to listen. The woman smiled. Jago tried to read her mind. He looked for the marks of a Vampyre, the sunken red eyes and engorged lips. To him she looked ordinary. Her thoughts were far away and undecided. She looked for what she could burn to stoke her fire, boil water and dye cloth. Jago could see that her hands were stained purple.

Jago reached forward and picked up a piece of wood that lay at his feet. 'More for your sack,' he said as he handed it to the woman.

She stopped and rolled up her grey sleeves. There was a tidemark of purple dye around each arm. Dumping the sack on the ground, she wiped the sweat from her face.

'Looks like you've been thinking,' she said warmly. 'I had a son that used to think all the time. Day and night he would sit out here and look at the sea. He used to say that his thoughts were a way of escaping. Nothing can stop your thoughts, he would say. My lad was right, nothing can stop your thoughts.'

'I couldn't sleep,' Jago answered. 'Lot to think about.'

'Did you like my singing? I could see you were listening,' she asked.

'Cheerful,' Jago replied, not knowing what else to say.

'Heard it called many things before but never cheerful. You planning on staying in Sandsend?' she asked. 'Not that I am prying.'

Jago shrugged and picked another slip of wood from the shingle and placed it in her sack. 'Put it this way – I won't be seeing the smoke from your fire,' he said.

'That would be a fine thing. Boiling the dye is a terrible stink. You can see what it has done to me.'

He looked at the woman intently. Her hands were purple and wrinkled. Around her face were patches of dye where she had wiped her brow. She looked old, but Jago could tell that her body had been broken by years of hard work. 'Before you ask, I am only forty-three. I know I look a lot younger,' she laughed.

'I would never ask – my mother told me –' He stopped. A sudden guard stopped his lips, as if he knew he should give nothing away.

'She's not in this world any more, is she?' the woman asked. 'I can sense things, she seems far away.' Jago nodded. 'Thought so. My lad is in the same place. He was shot down over France. Too young to fly a Spitfire, that's what I always said.'

'My mother was killed in a bombing,' he said, hoping to share her grief.

'This was his,' she replied, taking a chain of four flint pebbles from her bag. Each stone was gouged at the centre with a perfect hole and they were tied together with a leather cord. 'It's a Philoverba – a hag stone. All you do is hold it up to the wind and listen. Some say it tells you what is to come. Others say that those who are dead will talk to you. You have to listen careful. Not everyone can hear what the Philoverba is saying.'

'Why a Philoverba?' he asked as she dangled the stones before him like the spinning watch of a hypnotist.

335

'I heard it said there were once three giants who were killed by a boy with a sling. Each stone was perfectly round and had a hole cut through, eaten away by a sea-creature. When they were dead he cut the stones from the giants' foreheads and tied them together with the leather from his sling. Then again, it could just be an old story,' the woman said.

'I never believed in stories like that until I came to Whitby,' he answered.

She handed the chain to Jago. He held the smooth stones in his hand and examined the holes with the tip of his finger.

'Do you think it works?' he asked.

'All depends what you want to hear. Sometimes I try and listen. Once I thought I could hear my son. Then again, could be wishful thinking.' The woman patted Jago on the back. 'I tell you what, you keep it . . . Does me no good and it just reminds me of Harry. You have it and think of what you want it to say. Perhaps it will tell you what to do with your life.'

'I leave that to other people,' Jago said as the woman got up to walk away.

'That's what happened to my son. He listened to everyone but himself and it got him killed. I wouldn't want that to happen to you, Jago.'

The woman walked away, gathering more remnants of the wood from the shingle. Jago watched as she picked up the sack and slung it across her back. She stooped as she walked from the beach. Never looking back, she was soon out of sight.

Jago held the Philoverba in his hand and let the stones swing in the breeze. Inside he was frightened to listen. The stones swung back and forth and turned as the leather cord twisted.

The wind blew through the holes in the stones and they begin to spin faster.

'*Don't run . . .*' he heard a faint voice say. '*Don't leave the place . . .*'

'Who are you?' Jago asked.

'*We are legion for there are many of us . . .*'

He was not sure if the words were coming from the stones or from within his mind.

'Where is Biatra?' Jago asked.

'*The Vampyre Ball in the house of Ozymandias . . .*' The stones sang as they spun faster. '*She is wanting you, wanting you now . . .*'

'How do you know?' he demanded.

'*Jago . . . Jago . . . I can hear you . . .*'

Jago bolted to his feet, dropping the Philoverba to the ground. It was the voice of Biatra as if she stood before him.

'Where are you? Where are you?' he screamed at the sea.

'Who yer lost, Jago?' Henson asked as he walked towards him.

Jago purposely stood on the Philoverba so it could not be seen.

'No one,' he answered nervously. 'I was just –'

'Shouting?' Henson said. 'We are making ready to leave this place. Hugh asked me to come for you.'

'I'll . . .' he replied as he looked out to sea.

'We'll wait for you. If it helps, Jago, I understand what it is like to lose someone you love.'

Jago waited for Henson to walk back to the Hart Inn before he reached down to the shingle and picked up the Philoverba. He hid it in the pocket of his torn leather coat.

Holding the largest stone in his hand, he thought of Biatra once more.

'I hope I find you,' Jago whispered as he followed Henson across the pebbled beach.

Inside the Hart Inn the fire had been lit. The room was just higher than Jago, low and haunting with dark beams and a smell of cabbage soup. Henson sat by the hearth drinking a steaming mug of tea as Hugh Morgan mulled over the lines of a map.

'If we take the north road we can avoid the towns and be at Lutyen within five hours,' Hugh said as he looked up to see Jago. 'I was worried,' he said putting the map on the table. 'Jack said you were on the beach.'

'Do we have to go?' Jago asked directly. 'I thought we could go back for Biatra.'

'Wouldn't be wise, Jago,' Henson said. 'I think it could be a trap.'

'So we just leave her there?' he asked irksomely.

'Sometimes we do things that are difficult,' Hugh said.

'*Difficult?*' Jago asked. 'Is that what it is?'

'You don't understand, Jago. There are more things at stake.' Henson put down the cup. 'We have to protect you.'

'But not Biatra – she can die?'

Hugh Morgan looked at Henson, not knowing what to say.

'It's decided. We know what is best. You have to be kept alive,' Henson replied, pained by Jago's protestations.

'And that is it – my life over hers?' he answered. He walked from the room and into the yard, wanting to call Hugh a coward.

Hugh Morgan was soon with him. They stood uncomfortably together by the green sedan.

'It's just until Kinross has gone. If he has a bomb then we shouldn't go near the house, it would be too dangerous. There is nothing we can do for Biatra. She will have to get out of this on her own.'

'Are you afraid?' Jago asked him.

Morgan thought for a moment and looked him in the eye. 'Yes,' he said softly. 'I have no shame in telling you.'

'We cannot let her die.'

Morgan didn't say anything. His eyes looked remorseful and brimmed with guilt. He looked down at the ground and then walked through the door, leaving Jago in the yard. Jago took the Philoverba from his pocket and held it in his hand. The stones twisted and turned. 'Should I return?' he asked.

There was silence as the wind spun the stones. He could hear nothing, and then came the low whisper.

'*You would lay down your life for another. That wish may be granted . . .*'

The words were eerie and whispered in a voice that Jago had never heard before. He had hoped he would hear his mother. All he had wanted was to listen to her speak.

'Then it's decided,' Jago said as he put the stones back in his pocket.

Without saying goodbye, Jago was quickly on the railway line and walking towards Whitby. Head down, he pulled his coat tight against the rain as it beat down and soaked his boots.

Within an hour he was walking along the quayside and looking down at the boats that were moored against the harbour wall. By the bridge across the river he saw the sign for the cinema. It offered an all-day showing of *Jamaica Inn*. He looked across the river to the church clock and then rummaged in his pocket and found a well-rubbed pound note. He needed to rest and gather his strength before searching for Biatra.

Once inside he took off his coat and slipped low in the seat. The screen flickered for five hours and yet afterwards he could remember nothing of what he had seen. The images that jumped from the projector and danced on the wall were far more peaceable than those in his mind.

People came and went. Most didn't stay for long. They hid on the back row to escape the war or their wives. A woman with a red torch passed by several times. She shone the light in his face and asked if he was enjoying the movie. The woman smiled as if to be friendly, but Jago just nodded and shrugged, hoping she would soon go away.

By late in the afternoon he knew it was time to go. There would be a rush once the factory had called time. He had seen the workers running along the quayside to get to the cheap seats before anyone else. Jago didn't want to be seen. He thought that Henson and Hugh Morgan would probably have returned to look for him. They would search near enough to the house of Ozymandias without being in danger.

Leaving the cinema, Jago took the steam bus from the town towards the long valley far to the south. It called in every village, dropping off women with perambulators and old men in tattered scarves.

Eventually, Jago recognised the road that led to the house. A sudden chill slithered down his spine as he pressed the bell for the bus to stop.

'Jugger Howe?' the driver asked as Jago stood on the plate waiting to jump to the road as the bus slowed. 'What is there for a lad like you right out here?'

'The rest of my life,' Jago muttered as he stepped on to the road.

He waited for the bus to set off again in a pall of steam and black smoke. On a far hill Jago could see the house of Ozymandias. He looked along the empty road. Jago knew that as night fell the guests for the ball would arrive in their polished cars with gleaming chrome, all finely dressed with the men wearing neat bow ties. It was the way of every Vampyre; their fastidious sense of fashion was a sign that gave them away.

Jago looked down at his muddy boots, his ripped trousers and his bedraggled coat, and laughed. Then, paying no more attention to himself, he set off across the moor. The wide path led directly to a line of trees on a distant ridge. By the time the sun was falling in the sky, Jago was hiding in a copse of tall birch. In the valley below he could hear the grumbling of a steam train. Crawling through the wood he peered down to the small halt and the makeshift platform. At either end was a man carrying a rifle. He could see them walking up and down, guarding the train. High above was the house. It grew from the trees as if it had been there since the beginning of creation.

He knew it would take him an hour to get through the wood without being seen. All he could think of was finding Biatra and setting her free. Blaine would want them both and his effort might be futile, but Jago knew he had to try.

As he approached the house the first cars had begun to arrive. One by one they drew up in a long procession. Jago watched from the cover of the old ice-house as the guests walked the candlelit pathway to the ornate front door. Most of the men wore long velvet cloaks lined with crimson; the women clutched masks edged with the feathers of exotic birds and wore elaborate hair combs. Their long dresses trailed behind them as if this were Cap Ferrat on the Riviera in peacetime.

Still the cars arrived, as music played from the lawn at the side of the house. High in the eaves Jago could see the face of the ghost child pressed against the window of an upstairs room. As he crawled closer to the house, he noticed Kinross standing at the door with Ozymandias behind him like a large lapdog, greeting the guests to the Vampyre Ball one by one.

Then Jago heard the grunting of a motorcycle as it came along the road to the house. It chugged and spluttered, a plume of flames and black smoke coming from the tailpipe. Blaine sped by with Biatra tied to him, her hands wrapped in holly bracelets. A black patch covered the scar over his eye and his hair trailed back in the wind. As he pulled up outside the house Biratra cowered behind him.

Kinross looked up and smirked as if he expected Blaine's arrival. He twitched impatiently as Blaine untied Biatra and walked her to the door. Jago looked on as Kinross examined the girl as if she were a horse. He pulled back her lips and looked at her teeth and then turned her around so he could see her dress.

As Blaine took her inside the house Kinross whispered to Ozymandias, who followed them in. When he had welcomed the final guest, Kinross went inside the house. Just before he crossed the threshold, he stopped and looked out towards the ice-house, searching the darkness for an unwelcome guest.

As Jago moved from his hiding place and walked towards the house another car turned on to the drive. The dimmed headlights cut close to the gravel in a meagre glow. It roared towards him. Jago opened the back door of a parked Rolls-Royce and slid on to the seat to hide.

There was a squeal of brakes as tyres slid on the fine gravel. The car stopped and the door opened. Jago peered from his hiding place.

In the dim light Jago could see Ezra Morgan. He stood upright and dignified, wrapped in a long fur cloak. Morgan muttered to the driver of the car and then strode purposefully to the steps of the house and without ceremony opened the door and went inside.

[31]

Lost

THE LONG PASSAGEWAY from the door was lined with masked figures staring at Biatra. All she could see was their blood-red eyes and cold gaze. They stood silently, like a parting sea. Toran Blaine dragged her by the arm, ignoring those around him.

'They would rip your throat out as soon as look at you,' he said as he pushed a fat man in a plum corset to one side. 'All the madness in the world contained in one room.'

'Then let me go. Why have you brought me here?' she asked.

'It has to be done this way. There is more at stake than you would ever imagine,' Blaine answered, his voice harsh and strained.

'But why do you want Jago?' Biatra asked. 'I thought his blood was of no use to you.'

'Kinross wants him dead and Strackan wants him alive. I will give him to whoever pays me the most,' he answered.

'Hugh Morgan would pay,' she begged. 'Then Jago could be free.'

'Hugh Morgan could never pay what I require. He will come here and I expect Jago Harker too but he will not see

344

out this night. I hate that man more than I hate the name of Jago Harker.'

'And all because you are jealous of him and Vibica?' she asked.

Blaine pulled Biatra to one side and pushed her against the wall.

'How do you know?' he asked. 'Who told you?'

'I was listening when you spoke with her, I heard what you said. That is why I knew she was trying to poison Hugh,' Biatra said, the tips of her toes just touching the ground as he held her against the wall.

'You fox,' Blaine scoffed as he let her go. 'And I used to think you were just a child.'

'They won't come for me. I know that. We agreed that if one was caught the others would carry on,' Biatra told him.

'I cannot see Jago leaving you behind. His heart hankers for you like mine for Vibica. I have seen the way he looks at you. Jago Harker is in love with you.'

Blaine dragged her into the crowded ballroom of the house.

The crowd parted as Blaine swirled her in a dance to the music played by quartet of finely dressed children on a small dais in the corner of the room. As he pulled her to him and swung her around his clasp grew tighter, his fingers gripping her skin until she felt it would burst. Faster and faster they spun through the crowded room of masked figures in long black cloaks. The noise burst in her ears and she could see nothing but a haze of faces.

Then he stopped suddenly by the door of a gilt cage. With one hand he opened the lock and then pushed her inside.

'What are you doing to me?' she asked.

'We cannot have you escaping yet again. This should make sure you are safe,' Blaine answered as he waved his hand.

The cage was raised from the ground. Those gathered around him applauded politely as if they had never seen such a spectacle before. Biatra hung in the air, gripping the bars of the cage and looking down as a thousand eyes stared at her.

'What you gawping at?' she screamed from her prison. 'Never seen a Vampyre before?'

The crowd hissed and bared their teeth like a pack of wolves. Biatra laughed and rattled the cage door.

'Let her down, Blaine, and we can eat her,' the fat, corset-clad Vampyre mocked as he picked his teeth with a cocktail stick. 'I am sure that dress would fit me perfectly.'

'What would fit you perfectly is a silver bullet,' Biatra answered with a growl. 'You don't frighten me, you fat fool.'

Then a deathly silence swept suddenly through the crowd. The music stopped and the chatter of conversation died away. Biatra looked down from the cage and saw a solitary figure walking along the corridor from the hallway to the room. As he walked by each guest they stopped and bowed their heads in deep reverence. Though he looked younger than she had imagined, not much older than Hugh, when the man entered the ballroom Biatra recognised him. Ezra Morgan stopped at the threshold of the room and smiled. His hair was brushed back and his eyes sparkled. She could tell that he had just eaten.

'My lords and ladies – I never thought you would have started a Vampyre Ball without me. As you can see, I am on my own. Some of you will already know that Sibilia is *dead* . . .'

The room shuddered. A small door opened. Kinross rushed in, followed by Ozymandias.

'Let us not stop the party,' Kinross shouted above the silence. 'Ezra Morgan is our honourable guest. Let us dance and drink to all that we celebrate this night.'

Ozymandias waved nervously for the orchestra to play. A violin rasped sharply and those around him began to dance. Ezra Morgan crossed the room and looked up at the gilded cage.

'My dear Biatra,' he said happily, trying not to laugh at her predicament. 'You remind me so much of your mother.'

'What would you know of her?' she screamed as the cage swung from side to side, her plight ignored by those dancing below.

'I knew her well – very well,' he laughed. 'I suppose you will want to know what happened to her?'

'She'll come back. She's missing – just like my father,' she answered.

'Maria Barnes is just like you and always will be. I have it on the highest authority,' Ezra Morgan scolded as Biatra slumped in the cage. 'Just ask Strackan the next time you see him.'

'What do you know? What happened to her?'

Morgan turned to Kinross and laughed. 'I hate it when I am sworn to secrecy. Perhaps you could inform her later,' he said.

'You never change, do you, Ezra?' Kinross said as he patted the man on his shoulder. 'I think it would be best not to tell her anything.'

'Why is she here?' Morgan asked.

Blaine stepped forward from the swirling crowd. 'It is so that your son hands over Jago Harker,' he said.

'Ah, Toran Blaine . . . The murderer. I thought I could smell the blood on your hands,' Morgan answered.

'And you should know what blood smells like, Ezra Morgan,' Blaine answered. 'Did you know that Jago Harker is going to kill you when he gets the chance? When you sired the boy, didn't you know he would come after you?'

'There was always that possibility,' Ezra replied as he looked around the crowded room and nodded politely to those who danced by. 'I hear that you have recovered my dagger and I can feel it nearby. Can I have it?'

Kinross slipped his cloak to one side and pulled the dagger from a leather sheath. Those dancing near to him stood back warily.

'It is best kept hidden in a gathering such as this, Ezra. Its power makes even the most hardened Vampyre quite squeamish.'

'I see you have managed to bring together your friends and adversaries,' Morgan said as he slipped the dagger into his jacket. He could feel the heat of the blade against him as if it were alive. 'It is reassuring to hold it so close again. I remember the night that I took it to the wood to slay Strackan. Sadly we had all been deceived.'

'If you had killed him then we would not be in this terrible position today,' Kinross whispered as the music played. 'I would not have needed to try to bring the broken parts of the world of Vampyres back together. There would have been no feud and no factions. Strackan would not have paid for the murder of many of our friends.'

'I have lost good friends, Noel, and not at the hand of Strackan,' Kinross said, remembering Draigorian.

'We are all ready for the fireworks at midnight,' Aldus Flood interrupted with a slight bow.

'Then we have half an hour to wait for my son to come with Jago Harker,' Ezra answered. He looked at the clock on the far wall that ticked above the heads of those dancing below.

'And we have prepared a viewing gallery so that they can be seen from the house,' Flood mumbled as he pointed to the door in the side of the ballroom. 'It will be quite spectacular.'

'What about the curfew and blackout?' Morgan asked.

'Noel is the Prime Minister . . . I have told the authorities that we are to detonate a new bomb,' Flood said with a raised eyebrow.

Kinross laughed. 'Yes, my dear Ezra. I decided that we need to celebrate in these dark times and nothing would be better than lighting up the skies over Whitby. A firework display is quite wonderful – I saw one once in China many years ago,' he said, taking Morgan to one side.

'What will you do if your plan doesn't work?' Flood asked Blaine as the two stood alone.

'They will be here. Jago will come for the girl and Morgan will come for Jago,' Blaine answered.

'I have heard that Jago Harker was seen at the cinema watching *Jamaica Inn*. Hugh Morgan left Sandsend this afternoon. They had a pact that if one was captured the others would go on. That is what the landlord of the Hart Inn told me shortly before he –'

'My dear Aldus, could you get Ezra a drink and bring it to the study,' Kinross asked as he stepped from the shadows of the room. 'And please keep Ozymandias away from us – the man has taken to hovering and listening to everything I say in the most annoying manner.'

Flood nodded politely as Kinross walked away with Ezra Morgan. Blaine watched them closely.

'What game are you playing? When do I get paid for bringing the boy?' he asked.

'When he arrives,' Flood answered. 'And when you bring Strackan.'

'Strackan cannot come. He needs blood and he refuses to drink anything other than from Jago Harker,' Blaine said curtly.

'But that was the bargain. You would bring Strackan,' Flood answered.

'He sent Ezra Morgan – isn't that enough?' Blaine asked. 'From what I can see you have most of those who would oppose the Lodge Maleficarum here tonight. Wasn't that your plan – get them here and then kill them?'

'Who told you such a thing?'

'I heard it from the lips of Jago Harker – he had been listening to you before he escaped. Your surprise is that there *is* a bomb ready to explode. I presume this is the way in which you will rid the world of the faction against you?' Blaine asked.

'Tell me on which side you stand and I will answer that question,' Flood snapped as he turned to walk away. 'Whatever you decide it is too late to warn them.'

'I could shout it now and they would all hear me. I gather

350

that when the fireworks explode so will the bomb?' Blaine asked.

'That is correct, Toran. But if you so much as open your mouth then you will be shot down where you stand,' Flood said, and he pointed to the gallery above the room. There, Blaine saw a dark-clad figure, bow in hand. 'A quiver of silver tipped arrows. He has been watching you all the time with instructions to shoot you down should you make one wrong move.'

'Then his arrow guarantees my silence,' Blaine said meekly as he smiled at the bowman.

'But does it guarantee your loyalty to us?' Flood asked.

'My loyalty will always be to those by whom I am outwitted,' Blaine said as he looked around the room trying to work out how he could escape the flight of an arrow.

'Try it,' Flood answered as if he could read his thoughts. 'You will not get far. There is a guard on every door, Kinross ordered it in case you caused trouble.'

Blaine looked up. Above the gallery, on the high landing that surrounded the room, he saw a figure.

'Harker . . .' he whispered to himself with a smile.

'What did you say?' Flood asked.

'Doesn't Kinross want a drink?' Blaine reminded him. 'You can't keep the Prime Minister waiting.'

As Flood walked away, Blaine leant against the wall and looked up at the gilt cage as it slowly spun around and around.

'What are you looking at?' Biatra asked as she looked down at Blaine, her legs sticking out through the bars of the cage.

'Your hero has come for you,' he answered.

'Are you not going to catch him then?' she asked.

'If I move from here I believe I will be shot down with a silver arrow and I don't want to take that chance,' Blaine replied, trying to make his words look as though he was singing to the music.

As the ball moved around him and Vampyres danced, Blaine waited. Above, the shadowy figure moved in the candlelight and disappeared through a landing door. Then, closer, Blaine saw a face appear behind the figure of the bowman. As the music played, a hand gripped the assassin's throat and pulled him back into the darkness of the gallery.

'So where is he? Do you still play games?' Biatra asked.

Blaine watched the bowman on the gallery draw back the cord.

'Make ready Biatra – your hero awaits your freedom,' Blaine screamed as he jumped to the side.

'Biatra, jump!' Jago shouted as he let go of the arrow. It shot through the air and hit the rope, making the cage shudder. Another arrow smashed into the lock. The gate cracked open and the cage descended. 'NOW!' Jago screamed as the dancers began to flee.

A bullet cracked from a barrel and smashed into the wall above Jago's head. Across the room on a far balcony, Jago saw the shooter load the weapon again. Jago fired another arrow. The man fell just as Biatra leapt from the cage and ran to the door. '*This way!*' he screamed to her as the crowd ran from the room.

'The doors are locked,' the fat man in the plum corset shouted, unable to get from the room.

'Jago, help us!' Blaine screamed as he hauled on the rope

that had held up the cage and wound it around his arm. 'Catch this and tie it firm. Trust me or we will all be killed.'

Blaine threw him the rope. Jago tied it to the rails of the balcony.

'Biatra first,' Jago insisted as he pointed the bow at Toran Blaine.

'Very well,' Blaine answered. He helped her climb from the mass of panic, beating off the Vampyres who clawed at the rope.

Biatra pulled herself higher hand over hand until she got to the balcony. Then Blaine started to climb, but hands grabbed him and held him back. He was pulled from the rope and as people screamed to be free he was trampled underfoot. Everyone pulled and pushed at the doors that were locked and barred on the outside.

'It is a trap,' the fat dragoman screamed as he sat in the middle of the ballroom and sobbed until the rouge from his lips was smeared across his face. 'We cannot escape.'

'Keep calm, carry on!' Ozymandias shrieked as he clutched a silk handkerchief to his brow.

The clock above his head struck the quarter hour. The quartet of children continued to play as if the dance continued.

Jago looked down at the mass of people who fought each other to take hold of the rope. As soon as one had taken hold they were pulled from it and dragged away by more hands. He could no longer see Toran Blaine, who had disappeared under the mob. He took hold of Biatra and held her close, stealing a kiss from her as they embraced.

'How will we escape?' she asked as they ran from the balcony and along the narrow passageway.

'I know a way from the house, it's not far. We can climb down from there.' Jago held her hand as they ran.

'Where is Hugh – are they waiting?' she asked.

'We are alone,' Jago answered sadly. 'They would not come back. That is what we had agreed.'

'But you did,' she said. 'You wouldn't leave me.'

'I . . . I love you,' he murmured in an embarrassed whisper.

[32]

The Vexillum of Nine

THE WORDS HAD JUST LEFT his lips when Biatra
stopped running. In the opening of a doorway the ghost
child stood, one hand hanging limply at his side. Jago could
see his fingers were still encased in the silver blades. He was
dressed in a miniature frock coat with a ruff collar. On his
legs were tight white stockings tucked into black ankle boots.
Biatra didn't move.

'What is that?' she asked hesitantly and afraid.

*'My name is Ozymandias, king of kings. Look on my works,
ye mighty, and despair,'* the child sang, his voice broken and
out of tune.

'We have no time – out of our way,' Jago demanded.

'Stay with me?' the child pleaded as powder flaked from
his face and dripped to the bib of his frock coat.

'Just go back,' Biatra said, keeping her eye fixed on the boy.

'Stay with me?' he asked again as he paced forward, arms
outstretched.

'Stand back,' Jago said as the child ran towards him, the
finger knives ready to strike.

The child dived for Jago, lashing out with his blade-gloved
hand, stabbing the air. Jago froze. Biatra grabbed the boy by

355

the wrist and mercilessly threw him to the ground. As the boy thumped against the floor she grabbed him by the laces of his boots and dragged him along the corridor. He slid from side to side, lashing out with the knife-hand. Biatra lifted him by his feet and threw him through a door, then slammed it shut and turned the lock.

'I thought you would stop him?' she asked.

'I couldn't – I don't know why,' Jago answered as they again ran on.

'It will soon be midnight,' Biatra said. 'The bomb . . .'

'We can get from here. There is a room below. The window is broken and the ivy is strong. We can climb down.'

They jumped the rails of the landing to the floor below.

'Going far?' Ezra Morgan asked, with Kinross and Flood at his side blocking the passageway. 'We thought you would come this way. At least you didn't release three hundred Vampyres trying to escape.'

'They will kill you. That is what all this is about. A trap for Strackan but he hasn't come, has he?' Jago asked.

Morgan laughed. 'Did you hear that?' he said to Kinross. 'He thinks you will kill me.'

'And after all – it was your idea,' Kinross said as he put his arm around Ezra Morgan.

'The trouble with us is that our scheming is often our downfall,' Morgan said. 'Kinross has made me an offer. I am to leave Whitby and not return. Nothing will stand in my way, not even Jago Harker.'

'You cheated,' Jago said to Kinross. 'You play games with us all and change your mind as to who will live or die.'

'After tonight things will be far better than they have ever been. All those troubled and irksome people will be no more. The bomb will explode in seven minutes. It is packed with tiny fragments of silver. Every Vampyre within one mile will be evaporated as if they never existed.'

'And what of Strackan?' Biatra asked.

'You should not care for him, my dear Biatra. It was Strackan who took your mother,' Kinross said.

'Is she dead?' she asked.

'Does it matter?' Aldus Flood said softly as he looked at his watch.

'Is she dead?' she asked again.

'She is safe and very much like you. Maria always believed in Vampyres. She had a very good reason to believe. She was my companion,' Morgan said pitilessly as he looked at Kinross. 'What shall we do with the boy?'

'He is worthless to Strackan, his blood is torrid,' Flood replied as the distant screams from the ballroom grew louder.

'It is Strackan's blood and not mine.' The words were cold, chilled and heartless. 'It was an investment for the future – for a time such as this,' Morgan said as he looked at Jago. 'I am not your father and neither is my son. It was Strackan who deceived your mother and came to her in the form of Hugh. He mesmerised her. Before you came to the Conventorium he told me the truth. You are the son of Strackan. Until now he did not want me to know. He lied to me, Jago – he lied to *me* . . .'

'Liar! Liar!' Jago shouted. 'Blaine told me it was you.'

'I thought it was. Strackan tricked me into believing that was so. Your mother was his companion long before she was ever mine. We have all been cheated.'

Kinross stood back in surprise. 'And this is the truth?' he asked Morgan.

'On the oath of the Lodge,' he replied, hand on heart.

'Then he must come with us. He cannot be killed,' Kinross said urgently.

Jago shook with rage. He felt as if he were a sewer of filth.

'NO! You are all liars!' he screamed.

'Bring him with you, Aldus,' Kinross said to his companion. 'And the girl.'

Just as Flood reached out for them, Biatra jumped forward and slipped her hand within Morgan's cloak. In a single move she pulled his dagger from the belt and held it to his face.

'We go nowhere,' she growled as she held them back with the glinting tip of the silver blade.

'Don't be stupid, Biatra,' Kinross said as he moved away. 'Aldus could kill you with one hand – we wouldn't want that, would we?'

'Then let him try,' she said as she pushed Jago towards the stairs, keeping her eyes on the three men.

'We don't have time for this,' Aldus said.

'We can't just let them go,' Morgan protested. 'Not Jago Harker, not now that we know –.'

'It is five minutes to midnight. We have to leave this place,' Aldus insisted as he tugged Kinross by the cuff of his sleeve.

Biatra saw her chance. 'Run, Jago!' she shouted as she pushed him away.

Aldus grabbed for her, catching her dress and holding it tight as Morgan took hold of her wrist. The dagger fell from her hand. Jago dived, caught the dagger by the hilt and lashed out.

Ezra Morgan screamed in pain. He fell against the wall, clutching his arm.

'This way,' Jago said as Biatra broke free.

Together they began to run. The long dark corridor echoed with their footsteps.

'We have to set them free. They cannot die this way,' Biatra said as she heard the sounds of panic and fear coming from the ballroom.

'There isn't time,' he said, looking back and seeing Flood and Morgan pursuing them. 'We have to get away.'

'If I can open one door . . .' she answered as they ran down the stairs towards the ballroom.

It was then that a silver-tipped arrow shot between them and crashed into the wall. Ahead was a bowman standing in the doorway to the ballroom. Jago saw him slipping another arrow into the string as they ran towards him. The man fired again, the arrow aimed for Biatra. It flew towards her chest. Jago snatched at the air. Catching the arrow in his hand, Jago ran on and before the man could fire again Jago smashed him into the wall with all his might.

The man dropped to the floor, pierced by the tip of the arrow.

'Now!' Jago screamed as he kicked at the beam that secured the door to the room.

Biatra looked back. Flood and Morgan were gaining ground.

'Let the people out, let them out,' she said as Jago pulled and kicked at the beam.

Suddenly it gave way. The door burst open. The screaming mass pushed Ozymandias from within. Biatra grasped Jago by the hand as the mob streamed through the door, blocking Flood and Morgan.

'This way,' Jago said as they ran on. 'We have to get out before the . . .'

His words were too late. From within the ballroom came the sound of the clock striking the first chime of midnight. Ahead was the doorway to outside. Jago held Biatra's wrist tightly and in ten paces they were through. The screaming horde followed quickly. On a large veranda lit by oil lamps a single piper began a lament, and as he strained and blew the first rocket exploded in the sky.

'When it ends the bomb will explode,' Biatra said as they ran towards the woods.

'There is a train at the halt-platform in the valley,' Jago said as he slid the dagger into his belt.

Biatra didn't need to speak. She smiled at Jago and squeezed his hand.

Without warning, a dark figure stepped from the shadows and a blow struck Jago across the back. He fell face-down to the ground.

'Jago!' Biatra screamed.

'Leave him, we don't have time,' Vibica de Zoete said as she and Toran Blaine seized Biatra.

Jago could hear Biatra cry as she was dragged away. He tried to get to his feet but his legs buckled beneath him. In the sky above rockets and firecrackers exploded as if the invasion had started. All around, the Vampyres fled from the house. Ozymandias stood on the steps begging them forlornly to return as Jago crawled to the wood.

In the distance he could see Biatra being led away. Toran

Blaine held her close as if in an embrace and Vibica de Zoete ran behind as they headed for the train.

The house crackled in the changing light as rocket after rocket exploded above. Jago knew that at any moment the bomb would explode.

Getting to his feet, he staggered a few steps and then fell into the darkness. The steep bank dropped away from the house. He tumbled and twisted as he rolled down, his path stopped by a fallen tree. All around he could hear the screams of the Vampyres as they fled.

There was a final explosion in the sky and then silence. Jago buried his face in the dirt, knowing what was to come.

The ground rumbled and shook. The trees quivered and rattled their branches as the earth exploded. A flash of bright white light shot over the valley, burning the tops of the trees and smashing off the branches. There was a low groan from below as the earth wrinkled beneath him. Jago covered his ears with his hands. The explosion burst high into the air as the whole house melted in the fireball.

Jago lay face-down as the bomb turned night to day. Then the flash subsided and there came the screaming of those who had survived. They ran through the wood, not knowing which way to escape.

Jago got to his feet, his head ringing from the blast. In the valley below he could hear the engine of the train whistling steam. He stumbled down the bank as fast as he dare, the bracken snapping beneath him as he ran.

Jago was soon on the track. Ahead he could see the tail light of the train and the steam billowing onto the track.

Several dark shadows boarded the single carriage. As he

ran along the track, he saw the tall figure of Toran Blaine disappear inside the train. He knew Biatra would be with them. A whistle blew and the steel wheels slipped on the track as the train took steam and gathered pace.

Jago ran faster but with each step the train gained a yard. He reached out, his fingertips touching the guardrail. With one last grasp he took hold of the rail just as his feet were pulled from beneath him. Jago was dragged along the track. His feet scrambled to get on to the ladder. Then he kicked out, jumped on to the train and sat by the door panting.

Taking the knife from his belt he pushed on the door. It opened slowly. Jago peered inside the dark carriage. It smelt of cigars and brandy. He could see the back of a long sofa and three chairs in the gloom. He stepped inside.

A light flickered. Jago was not alone.

'You are a tenacious young man,' Kinross said as he lounged on the red sofa in his silk smoking jacket and tasselled hat.

Flood and Morgan flanked him. At their side were Blaine, Vibica and Biatra, who was gagged with duct tape. They stared at Jago.

'Happy families?' Jago snarled as he held out the knife.

'You will not escape from us this time. And now that Blaine knows your true identity he assures us that you are even more valuable than we could ever have imagined,' Kinross said as he crackled the skin of a cigar next to his ear.

'Let Biatra go and you will never see us again. That I promise,' Jago answered.

'You are too important – did you not know?' Blaine said. He dumped his dirty boots on the low table. 'We cannot let you loose in the world of men.'

362

'Then we go nowhere,' Jago answered as the train gathered speed and rattled along the tracks.

Blaine got to his feet. 'Give me the knife, Jago,' he demanded. 'You are outnumbered and will not get away from here.'

'Then I'll take as many of you with me as I can,' he snapped.

'Tell him, Biatra, tell him what he needs to do,' Blaine said as he ripped the duct tape from her mouth.

Biatra looked at Jago and smiled as the engine whistled.

Suddenly the steam engine groaned and squealed. The wheels seized against the iron rails. It slid along the track, sparks shooting from beneath to light the night. There was a violent crash and the train shook. The lights smashed and the carriage tilted. Jago grabbed Biatra by the hand and pulled her close. It was as if they were on a capsizing ship. The sofa tipped Kinross and Ezra Morgan against the window. Flood was thrown to the floor and Blaine gripped the luggage rack.

The door burst open. Jago saw his chance. Pushing Biatra through, he dived with her from the train as it buckled and twisted. The steam engine was lifted high into the air and beneath it was the battered shell of a green sedan with white-walled tyres.

Jago looked at the burning steam engine as it slumped across the road crossing.

'It crashed . . . There was a car,' he said, and suddenly realised he had seen the car before. 'Jack Henson. It was the car he got to take us to Castle Lutyen. It must have crashed with the train.'

'Are they dead?' Biatra asked.

'Jago! Jago Harker!' Jack Henson shouted as he ran along the track with a lantern in his hand. 'Hugh is at the road. We have another car. We have to go.'

Jago looked back at the burning train. No one else had escaped.

'What did you do?' he asked as they ran along the track to the road.

'It was the only way we could stop the train. We couldn't find you. Kinross had blocked all the roads with guards. We knew he was leaving by train. The Sinan told us you were nearby and that Biatra was with you. When the train set off the Vampyre compass followed you along the track and we blocked the crossing with the sedan,' Henson answered breathlessly.

'You could have killed us,' Biatra said.

'It was a chance we had to take. We would never have got you back,' Henson answered as they got to the road. 'Get in – the guards will be here soon.'

Henson slid into the small black van and opened the back doors from inside.

'Tell them nothing,' Jago whispered to Biatra. 'They haven't to know who I am.'